SIGILS OF SPRING

INHERITANCE, BOOK SEVEN

AK FAULKNER

SIGILS of SPRING

A.K. FAULKNER

Sigils of Spring © AK Faulkner 2019.
Cover design by Dominic Forbes.

First electronic publication: November 2019.

discoverinheritance.com

Sigils of Spring is set in the USA, and as such uses American English throughout.

CONTENTS

PROLOGUE

1647

"WITCHES ARE ALWAYS CONVINCED THAT THEY ARE MORE CLEVER than the common man."

It was difficult for Nicolas to engage fully with his captor's taunting. Not when he was tied naked to a chair while a flunky pricked his skin in search of that one spot which he neither possessed nor imagined any other of the witch finders' victims to have owned. He supposed that any person pricked from head to toe would eventually fail to respond to the torment — or plead guilty, desperate for it to be ended.

The pricker stuck him once more with the thick pin, and Nicolas grunted, because the moment he failed to do so would be the instant they declared they had their evidence.

"I was sorry to learn of your brother's fate," he finally managed to say. Why he wished to taunt this bastard any further was perhaps an indication that he was no longer of sound mind, but something within him urged it, and he was too weak to refuse.

The barb seemed to sting, for Thomas Hopkins' face twisted into a snarl like that of the devil himself, and his hand dropped to the dagger at his waist. "You caused his death, with your imps no doubt!"

Nicolas fought not to roll his eyes. It was always devils and imps with the Puritans. Gone were the days when men were held accountable for their own evils. "According to the parish, it was tuberculosis — would you stop that for one moment, you arrant spewbleck?" he added as the pricker stabbed him in the thigh. "If I had an imp, do you not think it would make itself busy with the unfastening of these bonds? You are the worst kind of patch!"

He thought for one moment that perhaps he *was* compelled by a devil. Why else would he be so foolish?

Had he really survived the war to die like this?

For a moment, he saw the battlefields again. The New Model Army bore down on his own regiment, their horses screaming louder than thunder.

That war was over, and King Charles was in a Scottish jail.

As a Royalist, Nicolas was a wanted man wherever he traveled, but to come this far south was lunacy and he knew it. The men who slaughtered both innocents and witches made their home here in Essex, where they used their faith as weapon and shield alike.

He refused to die like this. He would drive these accursed witch finders out of England single-handedly if he had to.

In the space between one breath and the next, his plan fell into place.

The pricker stuck the pin in him, and it took all his will to suppress any response.

It was as though the room became still.

"Again," Hopkins hissed, fervor compelling him to step closer.

The pricker jabbed downward.

Nicolas grit his teeth against the burn. It was nothing, he told himself. *Nothing.* He had fought in war! This was but the mere bite of a gnat by compare, though verily an angry and persistent gnat.

"All your witchcraft," Hopkins laughed as he came nearer still. "All your devil-borne power, and it cannot protect you from the righteous!"

Closer. Nicolas urged it silently, and he tipped his head aside as though ashamed.

Thomas Hopkins was barely a year older than Nicolas himself. That much was obvious as the self-proclaimed witch finder neared him. Nicolas had been stunned to discover, after traveling many miles south to Manningtree, that not only had his primary target already died during the weeks it had taken for Nicolas to find him, but also that the deceased Matthew had been little more than half the age he had presented himself to be. The old, wise lawyer was truly a man with no legal training and a sincere, abiding loathing of women.

But Thomas? Thomas was dangerous to more than ladies who gossiped in taverns. Nicolas had never met his like. For all Nicolas' wards and charms, all his family's ancient power which had served generations so well in battle, had been but a fiction in Thomas' presence. It was as if Nicolas had woken from an astonishing dream and into dreary reality.

His magic was gone. His power, too.

But he still had his wits.

"I confess," he whispered, pitching his voice to tantalize, to lure, to be just below the threshold of what Thomas might hear from where he stood.

"What was that?" Thomas stepped closer still.

"He confesses!" crowed the pricker.

Thomas rushed in, the glee of the madman writ across his twisted face. He gripped Nicolas by the shoulders and loomed large above him. "Do you confess, witch?" he bellowed.

Nicolas rolled his head back and eyed Thomas. "I will whisper it to you," he breathed. "And only you."

The zealot was controlled by his fervor, that much was obvious. Why else would he do as Nicolas requested?

There would be only one opportunity, and so Nicolas waited another second.

There. Hopkins was perfectly positioned now!

Nicolas rocked his head forward with every ounce of strength he could summon. He directed the solid front of his forehead into the fragile structure of Hopkins' nose so hard that he immediately felt the blood gush across his own skin.

Hopkins reeled back, clutching at his face, then fell to the ground. He writhed and kicked for a moment.

The pricker screeched.

Nicolas raised his head as though he weren't dizzy and splashed with blood. "Untie me," he barked, "or I will curse you that all your teeth will fall out and your bones will crumble. I will curse your family, your children, your entire miserable little town, and even once your bones have turned to dust inside your bodies I will curse you to live, unable to move, unable to speak, trapped forevermore and unable to ever reach your God!"

The words poured out of him, made up on the spot, in the hope that this sort of rubbish was exactly what Puritans thought witches could do, and the pricker stared at him in horror.

"Do it!" Nicolas roared.

The pricker fumbled for the dagger at Hopkins' waist and freed it, then sawed at the rope which bound Nicolas' feet, all the while begging for his mercy.

He was Nicolas d'Arcy. He was created the first Duke of Oxford barely two years ago for his loyalty in the war, and now it all hung in tatters after King Charles' arrest. If he was to build a legacy for his family, he not only needed to eradicate these witch finders, but also somehow restore Charles to the throne so that his new rank bore weight and meaning. He would *not* lose everything he had worked his whole life for just to have some idiotic peasants strip it from him.

Once the pricker freed his hands, Nicolas thanked him, and then stabbed him in the heart with Hopkins' dagger. He had no time for traitors, and he would be as merciless to them as they had been to the innocents they had destroyed.

He stabbed Hopkins too, before the witch finder could

regain his wits. It was not honorable, but nor was a single man in the Hopkins family, it seemed.

Hopkins rattled his last breath, and Nicolas summoned the rope which had bound him.

It leaped obediently to his hand, as it should. Proof, then, that Hopkins' power — whatever it had been — had died with him.

But Nicolas was familiar with the way these things ran in families. He was not so much a fool as to assume that only Thomas held this awful ability.

There were more, and Nicolas would divest his country of the parasites which beset it, for if he did not, lands and titles would not save him from their hunts.

1

QUENTIN

"This is... this is me. I am a monster."

"Bullshit."

Quentin raised his head. He searched Laurence's gaze, as if somewhere in those deep brown eyes lay the key to his own salvation, but something else tugged at his attention. He didn't need to take his eyes off Laurence's to know that it was there, because he was the one who had placed it.

Accidentally. Without intending to.

He had wiped the blood from his own face and then grabbed Laurence by the throat, and now Laurence's skin was smeared with red, and it sang sweetly to him, seductive and insistent, tapping into the evil in his heart and urging it to come forth.

Laurence's arm was cradled in his lap, and Quentin's fingers traced along it, drawn inexorably back to where they had marked him.

He didn't dare break free from Laurence's gaze, or the violence inside him would rise again. And so his fingers found their own way. Up Laurence's arm. Over his collarbone.

Around his throat.

They fit there.

They belonged there.

Laurence didn't even blink, didn't look away. His breath

quickened, his throat bobbed beneath Quentin's palm, but he didn't break eye contact for a single moment.

He knew he was Quentin's. He had to. Why else would he allow Quentin to do this? To hold him like a possession?

He knew, and he liked it.

To know that he had such power, such control, made Quentin's heart race and his body ache.

"I want you," he breathed.

He was a monster.

He jerked awake with such force that he was upright and half out of bed before he realized what was happening.

The bedroom was dark but for the green glow from the windows, which seemed more pronounced at night. Quentin fumbled at the mattress to keep himself from falling, but ended up leaning against it and panting heavily, one leg still coiled in sheets.

"Baby?" Laurence's voice was a mumble. He likely wasn't fully awake yet.

"I'm fine," Quentin rasped as he eased his leg free and stood up. "Bathroom," he whispered.

If his lie was quiet, perhaps it was less awful.

Laurence made a faint noise and sounded like he might have settled back down, so Quentin marched himself into the en suite and locked the door. He didn't turn the light on. There was true darkness in here, and he could hide in it for now.

He felt his way toward the wall and settled on the floor with his back against it, then rested his head on his knees and wrapped arms around his legs so that he could take slow, mindful breaths and focus exclusively on them.

In. Out. In. Out.

By morning he would no longer be a monster.

"Quen?"

This time, he woke sluggishly, half responding to Laurence's voice, and half fixated on why the bed was so hard.

Light trickled in beneath the door, and Quentin was almost eye level with the shadow cast by Laurence's feet.

Laurence knocked on the door. "Hon?"

"I'm coming," Quentin said. He waved a hand vaguely, and considered unlocking the door from where he sat, but decided that allowing Laurence to see him lying on the floor was not an ideal way to start the morning. "One moment."

He stood and stretched, yawning while tiny cracking sounds squeezed free from his spine.

"Is everything okay?" Laurence sounded concerned, but not panicked. Hopefully he might believe that Quentin had been using the bathroom like a normal person.

Quentin adjusted his pajamas and ran hands through his hair, then rubbed his face. Stubble scratched his palms, but it could wait. He finally unlocked the door, turning the handle with his hand and stepping back.

Laurence was there. Breathtaking, beautiful Laurence, who wore nothing but boxer shorts and an ever-growing collection of talismans to bed and still managed to look like a million dollars. His curls were lightening now that they were home in San Diego, and his tan was almost entirely restored. The hunter had returned to his natural habitat, and begun to flourish.

"Sorry, I, um." Quentin waved to the loo as though that was what had kept him, then bit his lip.

If he'd really wanted this to work, he should have flushed it before he opened the door.

"You had a bad dream," Laurence said softly, "and hid out in here for the rest of the night?"

It was almost a relief to be so precisely unmasked. The burden of his attempted lie was immediately lifted. But he wondered whether it might have been nicer to have a shield to cling to a little longer.

"I heard you sneak off." Laurence stepped in and took Quentin's hands. "Did it help?"

"I don't really know." He sighed and leaned forward until he was resting against Laurence's chest, and placed his chin on Laurence's shoulder. Their fingers remained entwined.

"Yeah." Laurence brushed lips against his jaw. "I know that feeling," he whispered. "Do you want to put things off until the weekend?"

He was about to ask what things, but as his mouth began to form the question, his brain finally clicked into place.

Birthday things.

Jesus Christ, it was his birthday.

He was getting *old*.

Quentin groaned and peeled back from Laurence. "No. I'm so sorry. You had plans?"

Laurence favored him with a soft, lop-sided smile. "I'm gonna make you have a birthday on your actual birthday, but it doesn't have to be this year if you don't feel like it."

"All right. But—" He released Laurence's hands and darted to the mirror as a matter of urgency, then leaned in to scrutinize himself. He plucked at hairs and tested the skin around his eyes, searching for any trace of grey or a single wrinkle.

So far, so good. Moisturizer and sunscreen seemed to be saving his face from the San Diego sun.

Laurence's laugh was gentle, and he joined Quentin at the mirror. "I don't think old age comes on overnight, baby. And not when you're twenty-six."

Quentin eyed Laurence's reflection, only to see him smile back at Quentin.

"Anyway, you'll always be hot. You're totally gonna have that silver fox thing going on in like thirty years. Don't sweat it." Laurence lowered his head and peeked up at Quentin's reflection through his lashes, then reached for his toothbrush. "Happy birthday."

With no idea what a silver fox was supposed to be and no

intention of sweating until he took the dogs for their run, Quentin nodded and took up his own toothbrush. "Thank you, darling."

"Tell you what. Wake up properly, walk the girls, then text me and let me know whether you want me to cancel?"

Quentin drew a deep breath and hung on to it a while, then forced his lips into a smile as he released it. "No. Don't cancel. Just promise me that it's nothing..." He waved the brush, then reached for toothpaste. "Extravagant."

The smirk Laurence gave him was absolutely no reassurance whatsoever.

"Sure," Laurence chuckled. "Nothing extravagant. No yacht parties. Cross my heart."

Quentin eyed him, then inclined his head.

"Very well."

THEY HAD FLOWN home to San Diego the moment the weather allowed them to leave New York, and in the weeks since their return, Quentin felt as though life had taken on some semblance of normality at last. Soraya had given him the cold shoulder for being gone so long, but it soon faded once he gave her a sanitized run-down of events.

Myriam's Valentine's party had been raucous, but hardly as destructive as last year's. Windsor was learning new words, some which were marginally less frightful than his first, and he was almost fully grown, with a truly astonishing wingspan to accompany his ever-increasing vocabulary.

Perhaps most disappointingly, Quentin had made an attempt at seeking therapy. Two attempts, in fact, but neither therapist had made him feel any better. He had a third already booked for next week, but the search itself was rather demoralizing.

He thought that he was prepared. The first therapist he'd met with explained patiently that Quentin might need to shop around a while until he found the right help; but Quentin was good at shopping, so how hard could this be?

Well, apparently, the answer was very. The first — a man twice his age, with a kind smile — seemed almost too soft. In three weeks, Quentin had utterly failed to make himself admit why he was even there, and had given up. The second was a woman with tight grey curls and bright teeth who talked about things like massage and sunshine and didn't really seem to listen to much of what Quentin had to say, which admittedly was very little.

Laurence was helping him select potential therapists from a website, but Laurence's time last Samhain spent watching dozens of potential futures had largely only informed him as to which therapists wouldn't breach Quentin's confidence should he lose control in their office. Laurence hadn't really nailed down which therapists might be of real psychological assistance — not through lack of effort, but because what Laurence had been searching for turned out to be vastly different from how Quentin's past had ultimately been revealed to him.

Until last night, Quentin had begun to convince himself that perhaps therapy was not required after all. His nightmares had abated after his return from Annwn, he supposed as an after-effect of the armor he had worn while there. But of course things began to head south once his birthday came.

His birthdays had brought nothing but pain for thirteen whole years. Now that February had ended, the first of March had arrived; and for the first time in his adult life, Quentin understood why he dreaded it so, why he brushed it under the rug and allowed it to rush by in a haze of whisky and bars.

This time there was no whisky, and there was no bar.

How long could he go on like this? If the nightmares returned, he couldn't possibly continue to share a bed with Laurence. The best solution he could conceive of was to turn the mansion's former bomb shelter into a rudimentary bedroom, but it would need to be soundproofed if he was to avoid waking Estelita with his screams every night. And how would he get dressed each morning? Run up the stairs in his pajamas and hope nobody saw him, in a house that was home to a gaggle of gifted teenagers?

Goodness, no.

No amount of short-term fixes would solve anything in the long run. He would have to keep pushing himself until he found a therapist he could work with, but the thought of wasting more time and money on ones who could prove ineffectual sapped energy out of him in a way that he had never before experienced.

Actually, that wasn't quite true. Not once he thought about it. No, it was rather akin to turning up to exams when he was sixteen, fully aware that he was about to fail and yet being unable to escape. Sciences had been his particular downfall, and were the exams which he dreaded as pointless actions which only served take hours of his life and exchange them for humiliation.

He didn't recall being so pessimistic, either. Was this because of his newfound knowledge, Gwyn's brutality, or just the lingering flashes of his nightmare?

Regardless, he could not wallow. He had dogs to care for and a raven to feed, as well as a group of teenagers who viewed him as some sort of father figure, even though he was barely eight years older than most of them. He had Mia, with whom he had finally been able to negotiate a salary for all her time and assistance, thanks to the influx of cash his father was depositing directly into his accounts.

And Laurence.

Laurence, who spent his days rushing between a day job, his teacher, and his lover, desperate to cram in as much of all three as he possibly could in the most deft juggling act imaginable. He now wore talismans to protect him from magical attack, Frederick's telepathy, location spells, and goodness knew what else, and all were woven onto a single leather thong which Laurence wore coiled around his left wrist. He didn't even remove it to shower, bathing around and under it, but never taking it off.

Quentin did his best to disregard the ever-present glow from the brass pentagrams. Whatever magic Laurence now knew was none of his business. Quentin wanted no part of it.

This was his life now. Incompetent surrogate parent, pet-owner, and partner. He would hold himself together, because if he did not, Laurence could not study, and it was clear that Laurence was nowhere near as competent a witch as he would need to be should Quentin's father renege on his word.

All he needed do was take it a day at a time until he found the help that he needed. Today was just another day, and he would get through it.

In. Out. In. Out.

Surely that was all it would take.

2

LAURENCE

LAURENCE'S NATURAL INCLINATION WAS TOWARD unannounced birthday parties, but he figured that might not be the best idea ever for this one. He'd missed Quentin's birthday last year while recovering from his fight with Jack, and Quentin had probably had enough nasty shocks since then to be startled in a bad way if he came home and everyone yelled *Surprise!* when he walked into the room.

Instead he'd gone for warning Quentin it was coming, then getting him to stay inside while everyone prepared the yard. His mom and Lisa made cakes. Estelita, Soraya, and Kim worked on putting snacks in bowls, and Mia took care of preparing hot food. Ethan and Aiden ran in and out of the mansion to arrange everything on the tables by the pool, and even Sebastian had managed to arrive before the party could get started.

It was the busiest Laurence had ever seen this place, and though it didn't belong to them, he was starting to feel like it was their home.

"This is the last of it, Laur," Ethan said as he put a bowl of pasta salad in a space Aiden cleared for him. "You wanna go get the guest of honor?"

He wiped his palms on his shorts, then nodded. "Yeah. Okay. Everyone hold on."

Windsor eyed Myriam's hand-made birthday cake.

"Win," Laurence chided. He could feel the bird's desire for that cake vibrate across the link they shared, and while he suspected Windsor wouldn't really dive in the way he wanted to, his familiar did have amazingly bad impulse control, so a warning couldn't hurt.

Windsor ruffled his feathers and cawed at him. *I'm only looking.*

Laurence chuckled and patted Windsor's head, then hurried toward the house.

It wasn't weird any more, which was kind of weird in its own way. He was literally a poor boy from a poor family, and now he lived in an enormous La Jolla mansion which overlooked the ocean, had its own pool, and their landlord was a sociopathic telepath whom Laurence would prefer never to meet again.

He ran his fingers over the talismans at his wrist, reassuring himself that he was safe from Freddy, even while stepping inside the house Quentin's brother owned.

How could a mansion Freddy had snapped up as part of a sprawling game of chess against his own father feel so warm and welcoming?

Laurence shook his head and headed for the lounge. Now that the renovations were complete, the house was totally different from when he'd first entered it. There was no more chintz, no horrendous '70s wallpaper. Quentin had insisted that the builders install lights in the ceilings, so all the frilly table lamps were gone. Now the interior was clean and modern, not Quentin's style at all, but not horrible either.

He walked in on Quentin at the piano, lost in whatever he was playing. Laurence could hear it softly through Quentin's headphones, but didn't recognize the music. Still, he stopped in the doorway, letting himself appreciate the moment.

Quentin was amazing. Oh, sure, he was hot, but everything

cooped up in that frail-looking body went way beyond simple stuff like his silver-grey eyes or soft, delicious lips. More than the sum of his parts, Quentin was grace and passion, kindness and smarts, and his love burned with a raw intensity that wasn't diminished by anything he'd suffered. Laurence was enchanted from the moment he saw a vision of Quentin playing the piano, and he considered himself blessed for the number of times he'd seen Quentin do what he was doing right now.

Laurence shook himself free and moved closer. He was a panther on the prowl. He was a man approaching his lover. He was a slave to his needs. He was all those things at once, and he no longer tried to separate them. Instead he stopped behind Quentin and lightly lowered hands to his shoulders, watching Quentin's slender fingers stumble in surprise and then glide to a halt.

He leaned down and softly kissed the back of Quentin's neck as Quentin tugged the headphones off, and he sprinkled kisses over that soft skin, nose brushing against the short, neat hair behind Quentin's ear. "Hey, baby," he breathed. "Everything's ready outside."

Quentin mumbled, and his head began to droop forward.

Laurence grinned and placed a few more kisses as he slid his hands down over Quentin's chest and held him close. He was so adorable like this, when he succumbed to Laurence's touch and turned to jello in his hands, but they couldn't stay here all night, so he stopped and gave Quentin a while to get his shit together.

"Must we?" Quentin finally whispered.

"No. Win's got his eye on your cake, and Felipe's already called shotgun on the enchiladas." Laurence rested his cheek against Quentin's ear and smiled lazily. "We can tell them to dive in without us, if that's what you want."

He felt the rise and fall beneath his hands, heard the lightest of breaths against his jaw, and waited.

"No." Quentin cleared his throat and finally set his

headphones on top of the piano, then closed the key cover. "I'd like to proceed."

Laurence laughed lightly and stepped away to give Quentin the space to stand, then moved in for a kiss. He watched, as always, for any sign that Quentin didn't want him so close, but none came.

"Happy birthday," he said, lips brushing Quentin's. "C'mon. Everyone's waiting. It's gonna be awesome."

Quentin gazed up at him, features inscrutable, until his lips curved into a wry smile. "It had better be."

"Right? Mom closed the shop early to be here!" He took Quentin's hand and drew him away from the piano.

If he could keep Quentin distracted from his own memories until midnight, then he'd call it a win.

Maybe it wasn't the kind of party Quentin was used to, but Laurence hoped it would grow on him. There were no rock stars, no movie actors, no producers or agents. No alcohol, no gold-diggers, and absolutely no paparazzi.

It was a beautiful evening. Tufts of cloud hung in the sky, lit from below by the sinking sun, which hovered at the horizon and turned the water golden. A group of seals played in the water not too far from the wall between garden and ocean. The food laid out across parasol-shielded tables smelled as amazing as it looked, and everyone waited until Quentin came close before they cried out "Happy Birthday!" in unison, then rushed in to hug and congratulate him in a mob.

Laurence hung back, petting Windsor, watching to make sure Quentin didn't wig out, but he needn't have worried.

After the initial rush, everyone descended on the food in a free-for-all, and then they took to sitting on the lawn to eat, drink, laugh, and tell stories to each other.

This, he thought, *is my life now.*

And it's awesome.

THE SUN HAD GONE. The kids had showered Quentin in little birthday gifts, and then it was the adults' turn. Now a table was littered with trinkets, and the teens had drifted inside to head to bed.

Laurence looped an arm around Quentin's waist and leaned against him while he sipped an alcohol free beer straight from the bottle.

"Hey, when do you think Neil's coming back to town?" Ethan asked, looking to Quentin for his answer.

"Not for another month, I think." Quentin paused to pull his phone from a pocket and peer at it; he frowned, so Laurence stole a glance at his screen.

Happy Birthday, Icky.

The sender was listed simply as *Frederick.*

He felt Quentin's faint sigh, and watched as Quentin typed out a cursory *Thank you.*

Laurence drew on his beer and looked at Ethan. "You want him to sign your ass?"

Quentin blinked, which made Aiden laugh.

"No. I want him to sign Aiden's ass," Ethan said.

"Do I get a say in this?" Aiden spluttered.

"Everyone gets a say once asses are involved." Myriam chuckled and stuck her fork into her cake.

Mia clicked her tongue. "Now I see where Laurence gets it from."

Quentin slipped his phone away. "I do not believe that Neil's interests lie with signing, ah..." He gestured a figure-eight through the air.

"Men's asses," Ethan prompted.

"Just so."

Laurence caught the faint tilt in Quentin's voice, the subtle catch that suggested he was forcing cheer, and he looked over in time to catch Quentin's manufactured smile before it was hidden behind a glass of orange juice.

They were talking about asses.

On Quentin's birthday.

Laurence put his beer down and searched for a change of subject. "The cake was amazing, Mom. Did you bake it from scratch?"

Myriam went with him readily. "Yes. Eggs, flour, butter, sugar, and just a little vanilla essence. The frosting was easy, too."

"It really is wonderful," Quentin agreed. His muscles shifted beneath Laurence's arm, relaxing slowly. "Thank you. In fact, thank you all. This has truly been…" he took a breath. "Special. I appreciate it."

There was a chorus of acceptance, of *no worries* and *any time*, but Laurence knew what was coming next, so he began to move his arm clear.

"I would like to head inside, if it's quite all right with everyone?"

Laurence said, "Hey, it's your party, hon. It's over whenever you want it to be."

"Oh, no!" Quentin's eyebrows lifted. "I don't mind if people continue without me."

"We've got work in the morning," Aiden offered.

"And we need to tidy up," Myriam added.

"And we don't wanna keep the kids awake all night," agreed Mia.

Ethan bounced to his feet, and offered Aiden his hands to help him up. "It was a great party. Thanks for having us over."

"No, no." Quentin eased off the grass and patted it off his trousers. "The gratitude is all mine, I assure you."

Laurence bounced up and laughed as he looped his arm through Quentin's. "I'm gonna take him inside, or you're all gonna be thanking each other for the next hour. C'mon, Quen."

He steered Quentin into the house, hiding his concern

with smiles all the way up the stairs, and only dropping the act once the bedroom doors were closed behind him.

Quentin sat on the edge of the bed, hands between his knees. He puffed out his cheeks for a moment, then allowed the air to escape between his lips. "Goodness, I'm exhausted," he admitted.

"Yeah, it's been a long day." Laurence shed his sneakers, then pulled his shirt off overhead and carried it with him to drop into a chair, careful not to give Quentin too much of an eyeful or give the impression that he was approaching the bed. "How do you feel? Other than tired, I mean."

"Thank you for the, ah." Quentin blinked. "The timely intervention."

"No problem. It's what I'm here for."

"Among other things."

Laurence laughed gently and dropped his hands to his waist. "Okay if I get into my PJs?"

"Oh, yes. Please do." Quentin pushed himself up and moved away to begin undressing himself, crossing around to his own side of the bed before anything got removed.

Was it good that Quentin was still willing to undress in the same room? Laurence had no idea. He shared Quentin's frustration over the lack of progress on finding the right therapist, especially since Laurence had clicked with his own the moment they shook hands. There wasn't anything to feel guilty about, but he did it anyway. He was good at it, and maybe they could work on that, but first Laurence had bigger problems to deal with.

Problems like Mikey.

It was hard, accepting that Mikey's abuse was exactly that. It made it even harder to know that Mikey seemed to have moved on, accepted what he'd done and found some way to cope with it before Laurence had even recognized how much it had fucked him up. He always felt that because he'd said yes he'd had some measure of consent, but it was just a lie he'd told himself, too deep in the grip of his addiction to think clearly.

But Quentin had never even gotten the illusion of choice.

That was why Laurence had worked so hard to make this birthday happen, and on time. If they could start a new tradition, something good, maybe one day Quentin could break the association between March the 1st and everything the duke had ever done to him.

Talking about asses probably hadn't helped.

Laurence turned away to swap his boxers for his PJ shorts, then settled on top of the sheets. If Quentin wanted him under them with him, he'd ask.

Quentin slipped beneath the sheets and wriggled up against him, tucking himself beneath Laurence's chin, and draped an arm around Laurence's waist. The sheets were an illusion, a barrier that made Quentin feel safe, and a clear indicator that they weren't going to get physical tonight. Laurence hadn't expected that they would. Not tonight, and maybe not for a while after. That was okay.

"Was it a good evening?" he murmured against Quentin's silk hair.

"The very best," Quentin replied. "I could not have wished for better."

"So you wanna do it again next year?"

Quentin let out a faint sigh. "I would like that. Thank you."

"You got it."

Quentin turned out the lights without moving from Laurence's side, and Laurence smiled faintly into the dark.

His life might not be perfect, but they were both working on it.

They'd get there.

3

QUENTIN

THERAPIST NUMBER THREE WORKED FROM AN ADDRESS NEAR Petco Park, and since that wasn't awfully far from the Jack in the Green, Quentin decided to ride with Laurence and Windsor that morning, then entertain himself in the Gaslamp Quarter until it was time for his appointment.

Laurence had shown him how to use the navigation on his phone, just in case he got lost, but thankfully San Diego was as much of a grid as New York, and Quentin was more familiar with it now that he had lived there over a year. The Gaslamp Quarter in particular was a nice, simple system, increasing from First Avenue upwards as he walked east, all while climbing alphabetically as one headed south. Tenth Avenue and J Street was, thus, easy for even him to find.

Still, he checked his phone once he arrived to ensure that he was on time and at the correct address before he entered the cool air of the lobby.

His previous two therapists had worked out of different medical centers, which gave Quentin cause for concern lest he lose control and do harm. An address in one of the area's few towers seemed almost as unwise, but he had no say in where people chose to work.

He made his way to the correct office, on the tenth floor,

and pressed the buzzer. He was already listing the reasons why this would fail when the door opened, and he blinked quickly.

The lady at the door was perhaps two or three inches shorter than him, and seemed to be around Myriam's age. Her hair was a medium reddish-brown, and her dark eyes radiated kindness.

It was, he supposed, rude to assume that this would fall apart before he had even introduced himself.

"You must be Quentin," she said, and offered her hand. "I'm Violeta. Won't you come in?"

He inclined his head as he shook her hand, then stepped over the threshold and took in his surroundings while she closed the door. "Thank you," he said absently.

The door opened directly into a lounge area, decorated in neutral tones and dotted with potted plants and photographs of sandy beaches, but thankfully she led him beyond it and into another room which had a more familiar setup. Comfortable armchairs faced each other across a low table, with a box of tissues prominently placed. Presumably some people cried at these things.

The room had a large window which filled an entire wall and provided an attractive view toward Coronado Island, with a glittering strip of the San Diego Bay visible between buildings.

He kept as neutral an expression as possible while seating himself in the armchair she guided him toward.

This room would not suffice.

Another failure.

"Can I get you anything?" she asked. "Water? Coffee?"

"No, thank you. I'm quite all right." He crossed his legs and settled his hands together in his lap, offering up a polite smile as she sat facing him.

She briefly neatened the lines of her skirt, and rested an elbow on the arm of her seat. "Then let's get started. Why don't you begin by telling me what brings you here today?"

Quentin pressed his lips together and did his best not to look out of the window. He was not a child. He could have a conversation with a stranger.

A conversation about the most intimate aspects of his life.

His gaze slid to the view. He couldn't stop it.

"Because I need to improve," he sighed.

"What makes you think that?"

"I am a danger to those I love the most, and if I cannot control myself fully I will harm them." If it sounded mechanical, it was only because he had said some variation of these words already, both to himself and others.

"You don't want to hurt them?"

He blinked and stared at her, but found her features as neutral as her tone. "Of course not!"

"What would a loss of control look like?" she asked, as though mildly curious. "Would you hurt them physically, emotionally, or both?"

"Both," he muttered. He looked at the window this time, rather than the view, his eyes fixed on the glass. "Physically, which would do emotional harm."

Assuming that I hadn't killed them.

He shifted slightly in his seat.

Good God, he had to pull himself together. He had barely been here five minutes and he was already fidgeting like a dog with fleas.

"And what things do you notice cause a loss of control?"

He felt his eye twitch.

He could do this. She was asking for his triggers, just without using that word. He had pieced them together with painstaking precision so that he could tackle them head-on, although his own cowardice frequently made him not try as hard as he should. Christ, he'd even made a snap decision about inviting Laurence to go further, and then raised a wall so that it went nowhere. Laurence might have applied the brakes for a moment, but Quentin had leaped on them and made sure they stayed there.

Then his birthday had come.

Violeta said nothing.

Quentin slowly flexed his hands as though warming them before piano practice. It gave him something to focus on other than the wall of potentially lethal weaponry that overlooked the island.

"Sex," he forced out between clenched teeth.

Magic.

How far could they go down this road before he was forced to confess that magic terrified him every bit as much as sex did? Before he had to defend that fear to someone who didn't believe magic existed?

How long before he had to out himself, either voluntarily or because he lost control?

"Tell me about yourself, Quentin." Violeta's tone had shifted from neutral to more friendly, and when he glanced her way her posture had relaxed somewhat. "Who are you? What do you do?"

He wanted to ask whether it was important, or why she needed to know, but this was simply a variation on questions previous therapists had asked. He supposed it was intended to help him relax, except telling people who and what he was in this country invariably led to the opposite.

"I'm Quentin d'Arcy," he sighed. "Earl of Banbury, although it's merely a courtesy title. Heir apparent to the Duchy of Oxford, not that I want it. No, I don't expect you to address me with the appropriate styles, let's not argue over that." He idly fussed over the crease in his trousers before he forced his hands to still themselves. "I spend my time waiting for my partner to come home from work."

She nodded faintly and offered a slight smile. "I feel like you're leaving out more than you're including. Would you agree with that assessment?"

"Of course." Quentin pursed his lips and straightened in his seat as he regarded her.

Violeta was perceptive. He would hope that to be the case,

but she was also intent on not allowing him to wriggle his way out of talking to her. She was like Laurence in that regard, except that it had taken Laurence some months to learn how to handle Quentin's evasiveness. Violeta had taken minutes.

Christ, he hadn't found the right one at last, had he?

She said nothing, waiting for him to fill the time with words. It was a tactic he himself used to great effect, but then what would be the purpose of him refusing to speak? Two hundred dollars to sit in a room with a stranger and say nothing, then return next week for more of the same?

No. Laurence had added Dr. Violeta Núñez to the list he had painstakingly worked on. Even if she was not the *right* therapist, she would not betray Quentin's trust. The ball was in his court, and she couldn't help him unless he gave her the truth.

He drew a deep breath through his nose, then let it out slowly past his lips.

"Very well. This goes no further than these walls. I am psychokinetic." He regarded her as she straightened slowly in her seat. "My gift operates of its own accord if I do not retain an even emotional keel. If I do not suppress my temper — or, indeed, my joy — I unleash a storm which I sometimes cannot contain, and anything around me becomes an immediate threat to any*one* nearby. I spend my days practicing three things: the piano, martial arts, and my gift."

Violeta blinked slowly, then cracked a wide smile. "You play the piano?"

His brain was still spinning wheels over confessing to his abilities. Her question was like a tree branch jammed in the spokes.

"Yes?" He sounded uncertain, even to himself. Goodness knew what she must think of him.

She nodded faintly and leaned forward, making eye contact as she rested her elbows on her knees and laced her fingers together. "Nothing goes any further than these walls," she said. "Anything we say here is confidential. Have you sought therapy in the past?"

Quentin nodded. "I have."

"How did it go?"

"Poorly."

"That can happen. For whatever reason, clients and therapists aren't always the best match for each other. Now, you say that you're psychokinetic? Can you explain what that means?"

It really was like talking to Laurence. She had parried his nonsense, feinted with a smile, and then reached in for the truth once he had relaxed his guard.

"It means that I have control over my surroundings," he murmured, "without exerting physical effort. I am able to apply or alleviate pressure, move or stop objects, manipulate the temperature, generate or extinguish fire..." He tailed off as he watched her response.

Violeta, to her credit, barely batted an eyelid, though she had gone quite still. "You'll understand if I ask for a demonstration?" she asked, her tone level.

She was skeptical. Anyone would be. Quentin had been, when Laurence first posited the notion to him. You had to be a fool to assume that someone might take such a claim at face value.

"Yes," he agreed.

The tissue box would make for the best prop. It was light, it belonged to Violeta, and he could pass it to her so that she was able to check it for whatever forms of trickery she could imagine. He reached for it telekinetically and raised it from the table, then offered it to her, his hands still firmly in his lap.

Violeta's composure cracked slightly, and he couldn't blame her in the slightest. Her eyes grew wide and her hands felt around the box, tugging on it against his invisible grip. "This is... pretty wild," she admitted. "How do we not know about this? I mean... the public. Why don't we know?"

"Because we are few and far between, and as such largely

seem to keep quiet about it, lest we face persecution." Quentin released the box into her hands.

Her gaze dropped to it as she drew it into her lap, and she nodded slowly. "I know exactly what you mean." She pursed her lips, then put the box back on the table and sat back in her chair to meet his eyes. "I give you my word. Above and beyond my legal obligation as your therapist, I personally promise you that I will not breathe a word of this."

He was struck by the depth of her sincerity, and raised his chin in response. "Thank you."

Perhaps he had found the right therapist after all.

THE REMAINDER of the hour was spent covering what Quentin considered absolute basics. A brief history of his mother's passing and his subsequent travels around the world. A lightly skimmed recounting of how he'd met Laurence. It felt as though he hadn't stopped talking once the dam had burst, and yet he hadn't even touched on his uncovered memories. He was too intent on trying to explain his life, telling himself that he was providing context with which Violeta could understand him better at a later date, but he suspected she was fully aware that he was skirting the issue.

It was a start. A good one, even. He had made an appointment for the following week, paid, and now he was free.

He stepped out of the building, wrapped a little cool air around himself, and slid sunglasses on as he headed for the street. To his left he could see a well-maintained park, beyond which sat the stadium, but otherwise this area was mostly offices or bars, and the street lacked the distinctive palm trees found almost ubiquitously elsewhere. Instead the trees were what he might expect to see in London or Paris. He was sure Laurence could name them, but to Quentin they looked like beeches, every bit as out of place as he was.

He continued all the way to Fifth Avenue, then turned up it. There were streets with fewer tourists to stroll along, but Fifth occasionally had street markets or open-air stages, and it didn't hurt to take a look in case there was something interesting in progress. It didn't hit him until he was halfway back to the shop that those things took place at weekends.

This was one of the issues with not working for a living. He often forgot what day of the week it was, and the weekend was an abstract concept at best. It had been a lot easier to keep track of time when he was at school, but now, by and large, a weekend meant that Laurence was home, and a weekday meant that he was not. There was no cause for finer granulation than that.

He drifted past a cluster of electric scooters and bicycles parked outside a restaurant on the corner of Market Street and turned right, then picked up the pace, but he was only just past the end of the restaurant when a door flew open and a frazzled-looking woman shot out onto the pavement as though late for something critical.

Quentin pivoted easily to avoid a collision, breezing out of the way while also reaching a hand out to catch her elbow as she stumbled. She leaned into him for a moment, then caught her breath and snapped back.

"I'm sorry," she blurted.

He removed his hand. "You have nothing to apologize for. Are you all right?"

She nodded and her cheeks flushed. "Wait, aren't you that..." She snapped her fingers quickly. "I'm so sorry, I've forgotten your name."

He inclined his head, and cast a glance to the door she'd come from. It had a small, tired blue awning overhead which proclaimed it to be the entrance to an apartment building, and it had closed again, so he looked back to her. "So long as you aren't in any trouble."

"Me? Oh! No!" She swore, then added, "But I am so late it's

not even funny. Nice meeting you, Mr. I-Don't-Know-Your-Name."

Quentin laughed softly. "You also."

She eyed him, then checked her phone and broke into a near-jog toward Fifth Avenue with one last little wave.

Quentin looked up to the building. It was four stories tall, and the ground floor was occupied by another restaurant. There didn't appear to be anything untoward about it. Fire escape ladders ran down either end, and it was well placed for anyone who worked in the area. It was, he supposed, utterly normal.

So why did he feel as though he were being watched?

He turned on his heel and glanced back toward the lady he'd nearly collided with, but she was holding her phone over the handlebars of one of the scooters and paying him no attention whatsoever.

Quentin was feeling jumpy after baring himself to a therapist, he supposed. Violeta already knew one of his most closely-guarded secrets, and if things went well she would know more of them soon enough. It was hard to accept, but he would have to if it was to work, so he shook his head and continued on his way.

By the time he reached the Jack in the Green, the feeling had disappeared.

4

LAURENCE

LAURENCE BIT INTO HIS CUCUMBER SANDWICH AND TURNED THE page, pausing only to shake a stray crumb out of the book he was reading and onto the bench, where Windsor could steal it.

He wondered whether this was what it felt like to cram for exams. He'd been too busy getting high to bother with studying in high school, so he couldn't compare directly, but a bunch of other kids had seemed frazzled back then, and he empathized with them now.

When he'd dug his dad's book of shadows out from under the floorboards at the farmhouse, he'd half expected it to be full of bad jokes and candy wrappers, but instead it contained a random assortment of interesting little spells, and as an added bonus not a single one of them was written in Latin or any other language Laurence couldn't read. They were, probably thanks to his dad being a Pagan, written in English.

Some of them were older English than others, and he'd spent time Googling to figure out how words like *mannes* and *couthe* were pronounced or what they meant, but it was still comforting that they were written in his dad's own hand, chosen as important for reasons only his dad knew.

He didn't want Rufus to find out about it, and spell books made Quentin uncomfortable, so Laurence read it in his lunch breaks at work and kept the book in his old apartment over the shop. It contained spells to make music more enchanting and food more nutritious, to encourage rain or to call a storm. They were mostly spells to help a solitary witch survive off the land, and it was humbling to realize that Eric had probably relied on most of them throughout his years of traveling with his wife and young son.

Windsor darted in to steal another crumb, then hunkered down to preen himself.

"Still reading that thing, huh?" Ethan clattered through the bead curtain and made for the fridge. He dug out a plastic tub, put it on the bench, then went to pour himself a coffee.

"It's like every time I go over it there's something new." Laurence finished his sandwich and picked up his mug of tea. "He makes little comments about magic, or life, or things his mom and dad said. Makes me wish he'd kept a diary."

Ethan just nodded as he pulled a homemade sandwich out of his lunchbox. Windsor eyed it, so Ethan eyed the bird right back and took a bite.

Laurence closed the book and drained his tea, then stood. "Okay. Time's up, I guess. Catch you later."

"Yeah, later!"

He darted up the stairs, let himself into the apartment, and tucked the book away on a shelf next to a couple of others that Rufus had loaned him for study, then locked the door as he left and hurried back down. He swept the bead curtain aside and slowed his pace so he didn't look like there was a fire out back, smiling warmly as he heard a couple of customers chatting.

Rodger looked toward the sound of the beads from where he was putting new flowers out on display, so Laurence nodded to him, and Rodger tidied away before he slipped out back for his own break.

"Hey, Mom," he said as he joined her at the counter. "Looking quiet, if you wanted to go?"

She shook her head and nodded toward the customers. "I'll wait."

"All right." Laurence went to continue Rodger's work, checking that flowers on display were in their prime and adding new ones wherever there were gaps.

It wasn't the worst way to pass the time. He appreciated his job a whole lot more now than he used to. It paid, provided structure to his days, introduced him to the widest range of people imaginable, and surrounded him with beauty. Sure, it reduced the hours he had available for learning magic or hanging out with Quentin, but it was like a break from those things, too. It gave him the space he needed to be able to go back and study more, or give Quentin his full attention.

The women in the store eventually chose some flowers and made their purchase, then left together, and Myriam sighed.

"There," she said. "I'll just take a quick break."

"No rush, Mom," Laurence said wryly. "You're allowed to sit down for more than five minutes, you know."

"When you get to my age, Bambi, you learn that the longer you sit, the harder it is to get up again." She laughed and patted his shoulder as she passed him.

"You're not exactly old," he retorted with a sniff.

"No, but you don't have to be old to start falling apart." She grinned and disappeared through the curtain.

Laurence gave a dramatic sigh, even though she probably couldn't hear it, then continued neatening up the displays.

All manner of things could make a wall of flowers look messy. Customers loved touching petals and stems, moving them and creating accidental gaps. Staff needed to take some out to create arrangements, and those spaces left behind were no less unsightly for being deliberate. Then there was the simple fact that all cut flowers were slowly dying, so now and then a leaf or petal would fall.

The bell above the shop door tinkled, accompanied by the subtle flash of lights that were dotted around the store so that

Aiden could tell if the ringing was from the bell or his own tinnitus whenever he was working the register.

Laurence wiped his hands on his apron and turned to face the woman who had entered with a friendly, customer-service smile. "Hey, welcome to the Jack in the Green. Let me know if there's anything I can help you with."

"Sure. Hey! You're Laurence Riley, right?"

Laurence paused and shifted his weight slightly. "That's right."

That wasn't creepy at all. Nope. The hot lady with the brunette waves and low-cut top knew his name, that was totally normal.

He didn't think he was doing a good job of convincing himself.

"I follow you on Twitter," she said with a sly smile. "You were on TV last year, after that party?" She looked around the store while she walked toward him. "You're like low-key famous."

"Oh." He laughed to shrug off his own discomfort, and loosely crossed his arms. "Thanks, but I'm really just a florist."

"Now we both know that's not true, don't we?" She lowered her voice as she came closer, and offered her hand. "I'm Angela Tate."

Laurence shook her hand briefly, and raised his chin. So far, nothing she said felt like a lie, but there was also a whole lot left unsaid. "Nice to meet you?" He intentionally made it a question to see if she would offer more information.

She chuckled as she released his hand. "I hope so. It's nice to finally meet you. Maybe you'd like to get together after work one day?"

Laurence went back to crossing his arms, and he couldn't keep the skepticism from his face. "I'm not interested in dating, if that's what you're asking."

"I think you are interested in a conversation, though." Angela dipped a manicured hand into her oversized purse, and she dug around a little while before she retrieved an envelope and offered it to him.

It wasn't large, nor padded. The envelope was letter sized, and bulged in one corner.

"Are you trying to serve me with papers?" Laurence asked cautiously.

"No." She turned aside and tossed the envelope onto the counter beside the register. It landed with a heavy little *thunk*. "I'm making you an offer. You're smart, I think. You seem smart online, anyway, and your television interviews were very persuasive. If you're as smart as you seem, you'll like my offer. But it won't last. I'll give you until the weekend to consider it."

Laurence glanced to the envelope, then back to Tate. "And if I don't take you up on it?"

Tate shrugged. "I can't rescue every stray," she mused. "If you don't accept, I'll move on to help someone else. I don't waste time." Then she smiled again, and her blue eyes brightened with cheer. "It really was lovely meeting you. I hope we speak again."

Laurence watched as she made her way out of the shop and along the sidewalk outside, and he heard the curtain move behind him, his mother's footsteps approach.

"That was unusual," Myriam murmured.

"Yeah," he agreed. He leaned against the counter and reached for the envelope, then glanced to his mom.

Myriam nodded.

He touched the paper but nothing happened, so he drew it into his hands and tore it open, then tipped the contents out onto the countertop.

Two things slid out, one more quietly than the other. A business card, and a pendant.

The pendant had a nearly-invisible red glow about it.

Laurence straightened up immediately and picked up the pendant to examine more closely. There was no chain or necklace attached to it, but his own talismans would make sure it couldn't hurt him, so he raised it into the light from the windows and peered at it.

It was small, half an inch across at most, and consisted of a black jewel held within a silver mount shaped like a bird's foot. The jewel's surface was scratched, minute sigils carved into the sides, and the spell seemed to delve in and out of them. He suspected that if he were able to deface one of the sigils, the spell would evaporate altogether.

"What is it?" Myriam asked.

"Magic," Laurence said softly. "No idea what it does. I don't recognize any of these sigils." They were so small they were a real test of his eyesight. He imagined that whoever had made them needed to use a magnifying glass when they did it. "But there's definitely a spell anchored here."

Myriam frowned as she reached for the business card. "Angela Tate," she mused. "I can't say that I like it. It feels off."

"Yeah," Laurence agreed. With no idea what Tate actually wanted him for, contacting her could be anything from a great idea to a terrible mistake, and he wouldn't know until he met her again.

Unless he looked into the future to find out what it was she wanted.

He clicked his tongue and dropped the pendant back into the envelope, then held it open for Myriam to add the business card.

"You're going to check?" she asked, looking up at him pensively.

"Yeah. But go finish your lunch first," he added. "It can wait."

She patted his arm, then made her way back toward the bead curtain, and Laurence lounged against the counter, idly weighing the envelope in his hand. He couldn't look now, in case his vision was horrible and a customer walked in on him, but the temptation was amazingly strong. His curiosity had been piqued, and it took most of his willpower just to stuff the envelope into the pocket of his apron. That didn't get rid of it, though. He could hear the paper crinkle when he moved, and he went back to neatening the flower displays to try and distract himself.

The bell tinkled again, and this time when Laurence looked up, it was Quentin who had entered the store and was slipping sunglasses away into a pocket. He smiled, and Laurence finally managed to put the envelope out of his thoughts for the time being.

"Hey, baby," he cooed as he crossed the shop. "Everything go okay?"

Quentin leaned in for a kiss as he eased his hands around Laurence's waist, and smiled faintly up at him. "I believe so, yes."

Laurence raised his eyebrows and settled his hands on Quentin's hips. "You think you're gonna keep this one?"

Quentin inclined his head a touch. "We shall see, but she seems promising."

Relief and joy swam together, and Laurence broke into a broad grin. All his guilt at finding a good therapist the first time he'd tried could be swept away at last, so long as things continued to go as well as this first meeting seemed to have.

"That's awesome, hon." He dipped in for another kiss, and lingered this time, letting his hands wander around to cup Quentin's ass and rest there before the kiss broke apart.

There was a spark in Quentin's eyes that had been missing for a few weeks now, and his own hands toyed with the hem of Laurence's shirt in the small of his back. "I should make my way home," he murmured. "When will you be free, do you think?"

Laurence was mesmerized. Those grey eyes were intense when Quentin wanted them to be, and he obviously wanted them that way right now, because they were drilling right through Laurence's head and straight to his cock.

"Uh," he managed to utter. "I mean, uh. Not for, uh, a while…"

"I can wait." Quentin kissed him once more, then backed away, his smile mercilessly enigmatic.

"Yeah," Laurence croaked. "Not sure I can."

Quentin slipped his shades back on with a twist of his lips and eased himself out of the door with a faint wave of his hand.

Laurence coughed into his hand and reached behind himself to tuck his shirt back in.

Goddess, he was one lucky asshole.

He forgot all about the envelope right up until the moment he had to take his apron off to leave the store for the day.

5

QUENTIN

THE HOUSE WAS RELATIVELY QUIET BY THE TIME QUENTIN returned home. Some of the older children such as Clifton and Felipe had jobs, and the younger teens like Kimberly were at school. Lisa was in the lounge with her tutor, a lady named Kayleen. The dogs greeted him at the door and followed him through to the kitchen, where he met Mia coming in through the back door.

"What you need," she said without any preamble, "is a maid."

Quentin raised an eyebrow. Everyone in the house, by and large, took care of their own chores. It was one of his earliest rules, and for the most part the children stuck to it. Obviously there would be shoes abandoned in the hallway or coats hung over the backs of chairs in the kitchen now and then, but a stern look was usually enough to make their owners tidy them away.

"Can I get you anything?" he asked as he reached for a glass and stepped up to the fridge.

"A maid," she reiterated. She crossed to the sink and washed her hands, then sighed. "You know I live here to protect the children, yes?"

He nodded as he filled the glass with water, then he turned

to face her and give her his fullest attention. "I am aware, and grateful. We could not manage without you."

She held up a hand. "But I have started vacuuming the floors, or filling the water bowls."

Quentin blinked at her. "That is not your job," he agreed.

He was fully aware of how households ran. He'd grown up in one that worked like a well-oiled machine, and every single member of staff had had their own duties. None of them were expected to do another role's tasks. The head of household did not clean things, and the footman did not prepare dinner. If Mia had taken to vacuuming the halls, she was absolutely correct in raising it with him.

"No, it isn't!" Mia crossed her arms and frowned at him like she wasn't entirely sure he was taking her seriously.

"How do you feel we should proceed?" Quentin moved to the dining table and settled into a chair. "Add these things to the children's chores?"

Mia pursed her lips, then sat facing him. "They work hard already," she sighed. "Extra tuition for the school they've missed, keeping their rooms tidy, taking care of their own laundry. As much as I don't like to suggest it, I think a maid is the right way forward." She pointed at him across the table. "But you pay them fairly, not the rock-bottom wages most people in La Jolla pay for their staff."

"Of course. And I would appreciate any input both you and Laurence can give me into what constitutes a fair wage. I apologize that you've been put in this position." He sipped his water, and then placed the glass on a coaster. "But thank you for bringing it to me."

"You could learn to use a vacuum yourself, you know," Mia snorted.

Quentin blinked at her.

Mia burst out laughing and leaned back in her chair. "The look on your face. Priceless!"

He huffed faintly and picked up his water again, finishing it slowly while she continued to chortle. Apparently, his inability to do anything remotely domestic amused her endlessly, and in the end he got up and put the glass in the dishwasher to get away from her laughter.

Then he tried to remember if he'd ever turned the dishwasher on.

Or whether he knew how to.

THE TRAIN of thought stuck with him throughout the dinner preparations, too. Oh, certainly he could slice vegetables and drop pasta into a pan, but that was about his limit. The only reason he'd made it that far was that Laurence worked most days, and it seemed unfair to expect him to be the one to make dinner on his return, too.

But could he do better than a variety of salads?

Kimberly set the table, and Soraya filled pitchers with water and fruit juice, but even now Mia was helping prepare the food, and this also wasn't her job. While she hadn't included cooking in her complaint, she would have been right to do so.

He needed to hire someone.

Where to even begin, though? Were they back home, Quentin would simply speak to the head of household and it would be taken care of, but the only people he had hired here had been Mia and Sebastian, both of whom were freelancers who took care of any paperwork. All he had to do was put money in their bank accounts.

Myriam, however, was au fait with the process. Quentin could ask her about it tomorrow.

Satisfied, he checked that the pasta was simmering nicely, then stepped away from the stove to feed the dogs. He had just let them out into the back yard when Laurence strolled into the kitchen.

"I'll get Lisa," Soraya said.

Quentin nodded to her, then smiled at Laurence, reaching for his hand as he came near. "How was work?"

"It was great," Laurence said. Windsor hopped off his shoulder and landed on the back of a chair at the table. "There was this hot guy who kissed me. It was awesome!"

Quentin chuckled and leaned in for another kiss. "You're just in time."

"Great!" Laurence squeezed his fingers, then let go and pulled a crumpled envelope out of the back pocket of his trousers. "My day was kinda weird, actually. Before you came in, some lady stopped by to give me this."

"What is it?" Quentin eyed the envelope, but there was nothing remarkable about it. It wasn't even addressed.

"Some kind of talisman." Laurence kindly didn't remove said talisman from the envelope, thank goodness. "She wants me to meet up with her before the weekend."

He crinkled his nose and frowned, turning his attention to the dogs outside. "What does she want?"

"No idea. Figured I'd look and find out. That way, if it's a trap of some kind, I can just not go." Paper rustled, then chairs were pulled away from the table. "Why don't you sit, hon? I can finish up from here."

Quentin arched an eyebrow and looked back just as kids began piling into the room and settling down at the table. "No," he murmured. "I have it under control. Why not take a seat?"

"I'll help," Laurence said dryly.

The dogs came back inside, Laurence helped drain the pasta and stir olive oil and a little balsamic into it, and then they took bowls to the table so that everyone could help themselves.

All the while, Quentin mulled over whether or not he was grateful for the help, or affronted that Laurence believed he needed it.

ONE OF THE woes of becoming proxy parents was that Quentin could not disappear off to the bedroom with Laurence whenever he wished. They had to remain accessible until bedtime, offering advice on everything from homework to social situations, playing games or supervising chores. But they were finally able to slip away, and Laurence continued upstairs to his den while Quentin went to the bedroom to brush his teeth and then read a little.

He had discovered a liking for some of Kimberly's novels, and couldn't help but wish he'd been at all interested in reading when he was her age. Not that Father would have allowed such stories under his roof. If Quentin had been allowed to read anything recreationally, it would at least have been in French or Latin to ensure that he was practicing a language at the same time, but he'd had no inclination to spend his time in books back then.

Laurence entered, without the envelope, and Quentin slid his bookmark into place before setting the book aside.

"Success?" he asked.

"Yeah." Laurence pushed curls back from his forehead and looked bemused. "She wants to teach me magic."

Quentin's nose crinkled with his distaste. "You are already learning it."

"Sure, but she doesn't know that. She heard Dad had died, and gave me the pendant to gauge whether or not I'm capable of learning." He reached over his head and pulled his t-shirt off, then tossed it to a chair. "I think I'll give her a call."

Quentin was all too readily distracted by the exposure of Laurence's skin, his sculpted frame and delicate dusting of hair. "Mmm," he agreed.

Laurence snorted at him. "Anyway, remember I told you about this hot guy? Came to the store earlier?"

"Vaguely," Quentin murmured. He couldn't take his eyes from Laurence's skin, or the way his muscles rippled lightly beneath the surface as he moved.

"Yeah. He kinda suggested we get naked together tonight." Laurence's hands moved to his own fly and began to unzip it. "And I thought that sounded great, so I was hoping he was still interested."

Briefly, Quentin's brain tried to replay their earlier conversation, to assess whether or not he had said any such thing. Then he caught up, and managed to get himself into gear. He *had* rather implied that, hadn't he? And he'd assured Laurence that he would wait.

He sucked his bottom lip, then leaned back in his chair and crossed his legs loosely, resting his hands on the arms of the seat and allowing his fingers to dangle over the edges.

"Am I the only one getting naked?" Laurence chuckled.

"Thus far." Quentin raised his head slowly. "Although you seem to have stopped."

It frustrated him that his interest in sex seemed to wax and wane in no particular pattern. He would seek it incessantly and then not want it at all, and the worst part was knowing that Laurence didn't suffer from these fluctuations in the slightest. He was always ready. Quentin had only to look at him a certain way, and Laurence would perk up and prepare to shed his clothes.

But sometimes it did not run the other way. When he had suffered a bad dream, or buckled under the weight of an unexpected memory, it could be days before he felt at all inclined toward arousal, and the time spent trying to work with different therapists had only irritated him more.

He'd lost interest on his birthday, but a week later it was back, and he wasn't about to let it go to waste.

Laurence's cheeks darkened as he pushed his jeans down over athletic thighs, but he did it slowly, showing off with a slow twist of his waist, a light tilt of his shoulders. His head drifted down, following his hands, until his face was out of sight, and his fingers bunched the denim around his ankles.

Quentin watched. He'd come to realize that it was something he particularly enjoyed. He liked the feeling of remaining fully clothed while Laurence stripped for him. He didn't know why, and didn't particularly care to find out. It did neither of them any harm, and Laurence clearly reveled in the attention, so it benefited them equally.

Laurence finally stepped out of his jeans, peeling his socks off at the same time, and gave a balletic twirl on the balls of his feet as he straightened up, drawing his hands up his legs and over his hips as he moved. One hand ran along the length of his other arm as he raised it above his own head, and then he was facing Quentin, back arched, head high. His chest rose and fell evenly with each breath.

What would he look like on his knees?

Quentin felt his cheeks tighten at the mental image. He wouldn't even undress. He could remain as he was right now, and Laurence…

He trapped the inside of his cheek between incisors and counted down from ten, all while taking in every little detail of Laurence's waiting body.

When he was ready, he beckoned Laurence closer. "Come here."

Laurence moved toward him, cock straining in his boxer shorts, eyes dark with eager lust.

Quentin uncrossed his legs and pointed to the floor between his feet. "Kneel."

The whimper Laurence released was exquisite, and he sank to the ground, gazing up at Quentin and waiting for the next order.

He reached forward and ran his fingers tenderly through Laurence's curls, sweeping fingertips across Laurence's scalp and then running his fingernails down and up the back of his neck.

Laurence's lips parted. He groaned out loud. "Let me suck your cock, sir," he breathed. "Please."

"Is that what you'd like?" he whispered.

He was fooling nobody. They both wanted it, and they

both knew it. But the way Laurence keened with desperation made everything so much sweeter.

"Yes. I want to suck you off so bad. Sir," Laurence added quickly.

"Then do it."

He leaned back, but kept hold of Laurence's hair, and soon Laurence's mouth was too full for any more words.

6

LAURENCE

"You're certain you wish to call her?"

Laurence sipped his juice while he toyed with the business card between his fingers, then looked over at Quentin. "Yeah. I mean, I think it's a good idea to have more contacts."

They sat at the dining table, breakfast arranged along it so that everyone could help themselves as they passed through on their way to work or school, but at the moment he and Quentin were alone. Well, as alone as they could consider themselves with Pepper staring hopefully up at Laurence's toast and drooling, and Windsor perched on his shoulder. Grace was more relaxed, lying down by Quentin's side, content to snooze.

"Do you think she knew Eric?" Quentin was slowly but surely forcing himself to eat a bagel. "Personally, I mean?"

Laurence shook his head. "No. She knew *of* him. There's a third party in between."

"Who?"

"I don't know."

He chewed his toast while he watched Quentin, and allowed himself to marvel at how far they'd both come. He had a theory that the vortex inside Quentin that pulled on Laurence constantly was Quentin's body reaching out to steal life from his surroundings because he didn't eat enough, and experimentation seemed to support the idea. The more Quentin could make himself consume, the less insistent that pull became, until it was little more than a soft eddy. Some days it tugged harder, and it became an instant giveaway that Quentin hadn't bothered having lunch without Laurence there to remind him to.

Quentin's vanity had veered into less adorable territory over the whole thing. He was concerned that eating more would make him gain weight, but it only seemed to counterbalance the lack of energy from less physical sources. He was still thin as a rake, and he remained satisfied so long as his tailored clothes fit perfectly, but for a while Laurence had worried that Quentin starved himself to stay slim.

Laurence's greatest relief was that his own desire to get down on his knees for this man didn't go away when the vortex stopped pulling, or when he made his talisman to protect him from mind control. It only really occurred to him that either could have been a factor after Quentin started to eat better and the talisman was made. After all, Quentin's power to control animals was a tiny fraction of his twin Freddy's gifts, but what if it influenced people to a lesser degree? What if it made them submit to his admittedly astonishing will?

But he felt exactly the same. It was like rediscovering his sexuality all over again, except this time his brain was filled with snatches of imagination and desire for acts, not people. The person was always Quentin.

His mind drifted back to the collar he'd toyed with in New York. He was having serious regrets about not buying it then and there.

Quentin cleared his throat.

"Huh?" Laurence jerked upright in his chair. There was slobber on his hand, and his toast was missing.

The *cronch cronch* from his side told him all he needed to know about where it had gone.

"Oh, gross!" Laurence grabbed a napkin and wiped his fingers, then reached for a new slice of toast with his slobber-free hand. "Guess I zoned out, huh?"

"Somewhat," Quentin chuckled. "I suppose that it could be beneficial to network, at the very least."

Laurence nodded like he knew what Quentin was talking about until his thoughts dragged themselves out of the gutter and back to the business card he'd dropped on the table. "Yeah. I mean, if I hadn't reached out when I had the chance, we wouldn't know Basil. Maybe Tate's got some other kind of magic we don't know about. If nothing else, the more information we have, the better prepared we are, right?"

Quentin inclined his head briefly. "So long as you are certain that she cannot harm you."

Laurence stretched out his left arm so that the edges of his leather bracelet poked out from under the cuff of his work shirt. "I don't know how more sure I can get, baby."

Quentin glanced to the talismans as he finished the last of his bagel, then he nodded faintly. "Very well. But call me if there is a problem."

"You got it."

Tate invited Laurence to meet her at the Harbor House in Seaport Village, and he arrived at a quarter past six. Seaport Village was only about a mile from the Jack in the Green, so he jogged there, since parking cost money and his legs were free. It was bad enough meeting at a place where appetizers were nearly twenty bucks without adding avoidable expenses on top.

He made his way through the mini-mall that was the Village. Strains of terrible singing wafted from the bandstand, seemingly determined to counteract the beautiful early-evening sky and warm salt air from the sea. He hurried toward the dark wood and gleaming windows of the Harbor House restaurant. It was always a popular place, both with locals and tourists, mainly for the view from those tall windows out over the bay. He'd heard they did pretty good oysters, but he wasn't a fan of the prices.

He fixed a polite smile onto his face and assured the maitre d' that he was joining someone who already had a table just as Tate waved to him from across the room.

He hurried toward her and his smile became less forced. "Hey. Sorry if I'm late."

"No, you're good." She stood to shake his hand, then sat again, and waited for the maitre d' to finish pouring water and putting a menu in Laurence's hands. "Glad you came."

Laurence skimmed the menu, but as expected, this was firmly in the zone of places he'd gripe about if Quentin brought him to them. He tried not to let his eyes bulge when he saw the cost of the steaks, and put the menu down.

This was eerie. He'd watched the whole meeting last night, and now that he was living it through, he had to remind himself to act like he didn't know what this was all about, so he looked around, then leaned in. "You're sure this is the place to talk? It's kinda busy."

Tate shrugged. "We're just meeting, that's all. The noise level works in our favor, but we don't have to talk about anything we don't want to."

Laurence nodded slowly. His discomfort was slowly crawling up his spine, and he couldn't put a finger on where it had come from. Maybe it was the combination of subject matter and location, or it could be the way time seemed to be bleeding over until he couldn't tell vision from present. He shifted in his seat, trying to get more comfortable, then dug the envelope out of his pocket and offered it to her. "This is yours."

"Thanks." She took it and dropped it into her purse without a second glance. She didn't even bother to check that her pendant was inside.

Did she trust him? Or was it a trinket that meant nothing to her?

Laurence wondered whether this was how spies felt. He was in a restaurant with a total stranger, surrounded by diners who had no idea there were two witches in their midst. Would anyone who overheard them think they were talking in code?

Was she on his side, or was this a modern-day Cold War?

He tried to play it cool, and looked at his menu again. "You knew my dad?"

"No." Tate shook her head. "I knew *of* him, but only by reputation. I heard he traveled a lot, that he didn't use his magic much once he settled down." She kept her voice low, and faced him directly, but didn't act at all suspiciously.

He knew part of getting away with crap was behaving like you belonged, like you weren't doing anything out of the ordinary. Usually he'd applied that knowledge to buying drugs, but it was jarring to hear her say 'magic' so calmly out in the open. Would it be so strange to anyone else, though? People talked about illusionists without acting weird about it. Who here was going to clutch their pearls at anything Tate was saying?

Goddess, he needed to get a grip.

"So what made you reach out?" He closed the menu and pushed it aside.

She shrugged. "I was asked to. A contact told me about your father's death and suggested you might need a tutor if you shared his talents." She rested her fingers around the stem of her glass and twirled it idly, not looking away from Laurence.

"And who is this contact?" Laurence leaned back in his chair and stretched his legs a little, acting relaxed and feeling anything but. The deja vu was constant, even while he tried to forget he'd foreseen this whole conversation so that he could enact it for the first time.

It was harder than he hoped he made it look.

"Can't tell you," she said simply. "You know how it is. We

protect each other, potentially at the cost of making new friends, because the ones we already have are too rare and too valuable." She licked her lips, then made eye contact with a waiter. "What did you think of the pendant?"

"I figure you probably know what I thought of it," he said with care. The waiter was on them in a flash, and Laurence waited until they'd ordered before he continued. "I can't see how it glows. I don't understand what's written on it."

Tate drank some of her water before she answered. "Then you do see it?"

"See what?" He played dumb.

"The glow."

"I mean, it's right there." He laughed a little and shrugged, then picked up his own water. "How does it work? You're going to say magic, aren't you?"

She shrugged right back at him. "I'll be honest. Plenty of people wouldn't be able to see that spell even if they *were* capable of magic. They might feel something was unusual about it, but spells like that are subtle and can't usually be seen by anybody other than the caster, without specifically using a different spell to give themselves that sight."

"I didn't do anything weird, if that's what you're asking me," Laurence said.

This *felt* weird, though. Now that he was present, in the moment, it was like they were playing chess. She was probing him without giving anything of herself away, he was ducking and weaving and hopefully giving away just as little, and when he'd looked forward to this meeting yesterday he was only an outside observer. He hadn't picked up on any of this undercurrent.

His acting was good enough to fool his past self.

Was hers?

She hadn't said anything that made him think it might be a lie. She might be hiding things, but at least she stated outright that she was keeping those secrets, and her words all rang true.

It felt like a game of cat and mouse, except Laurence couldn't figure out which one of them was the mouse.

"No," Tate agreed. "Probably not. But since you have the aptitude, the ability to learn magic is yours. It's down to whether or not you want to."

He was still giving her a speculative eye when their entrees arrived, and he dug in to his shrimp salad while she started on her risotto.

"What if I say no?" he eventually asked.

Tate laughed and shook her head. "Do what you will, as the saying goes. If you say no, I go back to my life and you go back to yours. I only have to do anything if you say yes. Honestly, if I were in your shoes, I'd think it over, but then I'd say yes." She paused to eat a mouthful of her lobster. Laurence couldn't even tell whether she enjoyed it. "You have no idea what magic can achieve. I'm not talking about the meaningless things like money or sex, though obviously those are possible." She sniffed like she thought little of either. "It can make your life comfortable, if that's all you want."

Laurence laughed. So far he hadn't found any magic that made him wealthier. The best spell he knew was how to teleport a raven-sized bird from one place to another to avoid trying to sneak Windsor through airport x-ray luggage scanners. The idea that there were spells concerned with gaining riches beyond his wildest dreams didn't surprise him, and maybe if he wasn't living in a huge La Jolla mansion with a British aristocrat he'd be reaching for them, but he doubted Rufus would teach him.

Though maybe that was how Rufus' parents had gotten so rich in the first place.

His laughter faded and he leaned in. "Then what's it for?"

Her eyes glinted. It was the first real glimmer of emotion Laurence had seen her display this evening, and he still couldn't read it. Was it excitement? Greed?

She was throwing his perception for a loop, and the longer it went on, the more deeply unsettled he got.

"Secrets of the universe. Unrivaled knowledge. Communing with the gods themselves. There are many ways to be rich, but most of them are out of reach to everyone else in this restaurant. They scramble for money without even understanding that money is a lie." Tate popped another bite into her mouth.

Laurence parted his lips, but all he could think of was how Herne considered money to be a particularly clever type of magic. "You think you're above them," he realized.

Tate arched her eyebrow. "I know I'm above them," she countered. "That's the crux of your choice. Do you want to stay in the gutter gazing at the stars, or do you want to walk among the stars and know you won't ever return to the gutter?"

He puffed his cheeks out and shook his head slowly, then released the air. "That's... some perspective," he said slowly. "Do I get to think it over?"

"Obviously," she chuckled, but even that didn't seem to convey any real emotion. "Otherwise what's the point of offering? Take your time, make your mind up, call me when you decide. Even if you say no."

A conversation with Tate was like trying to get a read on a brick wall.

"You won't make me forget this conversation or anything like that?"

"If you want me to?" Tate chewed. "Seems cruel to go on with your life knowing that you actively chose to reject your own potential, but some people like that kind of misery. I'm not going to kink shame."

Laurence coughed and reached for his water. "What if I have more questions later?" he eventually managed to ask.

"Ask them. You've got my number. Just bear in mind that if you say no, I'll get a new one, and you might end up calling a used car salesman in Del Mar. You don't get to jerk me around. You'll never see or hear from me again."

Laurence nodded and fell silent while he mulled it over. He

couldn't ask her what kind of magic she taught, because that showed his hand, but she also made it sound like she was interested in knowledge, not demanding the universe do her bidding. She hadn't so much as hinted at ghosts. Hopefully that meant she was neither a warlock nor a necromancer.

The only way he was really going to find out was if he said yes, but if he leaped to it right now it might give his game away. Besides, that creepy-crawly feeling had settled in between his shoulders and made itself at home, occasionally stretching tendrils of discomfort up the back of his neck and into his hairline. His skin tingled, and not in a good way. If he couldn't read her emotionally, how could he be so sure he was doing a great job at detecting whether or not she was lying?

The doubt alone was enough to make him want to say no. He should walk away, forget he ever met her, and get on with his life.

"I'll think it over," he said.

"You do that," she replied.

Laurence didn't feel any better for having come to this meeting, and maybe that was her intent. Like a dealer, she was offering him something more than a mundane human life, but he had no way of knowing yet whether what she had was every bit as bad as what he'd gotten hooked on in the past.

He was at least sure now that he needed to move carefully, whatever direction he took, and that meant checking the potential outcomes before he chose one.

He could do it. He was the hunter.

He'd find the truth.

7

QUENTIN

HALFWAY THROUGH MARCH, LAURENCE WAS STILL deliberating Tate's offer. In a way, Quentin was grateful for that. He vastly preferred when changes came slowly and with plenty of forewarning.

He would have appreciated a change in Violeta's office, too, but alas, this week they still had the view, and he found himself being quite unhelpful for the first half hour, answering questions mechanically and trying his best to steer away from risky subjects.

"Is it the window?" she asked.

Quentin blinked and tore himself away from it for what had to be the tenth time today. "I'm sorry," he said automatically. "Is what the window?"

Violeta gave the faintest of smiles. "Most of my clients look through it as a way to distract themselves, but not you. You look *at* it. Why is that, do you think?"

Quentin slowly unfurled his legs and rose to his feet. He wandered to the window and placed his hand flat against it, fingers splayed slightly. It was cold, as he would expect.

This close, he could see that the faint reflection of his hand was over a centimeter away. The glass was thick, then, or perhaps double-glazed. It was difficult to tell. He was hardly an expert.

He knew why he kept looking to it, of course. And he would have presumed that Violeta had deduced it also. It was possible that she had, and wanted him to speak the words out loud, so he glanced toward her and found her paying polite attention.

"Because it is a danger to you," he sighed. "We should not be here."

Violeta nodded. "Where would you suggest we talk?"

"I don't know." He lowered his hand and turned his back to the view. "There are subjects I am avoiding lest I lose control."

She pursed her lips and stood, walking over to join him at the window, and she looked out toward the bay. "Have you broken glass that way before?"

"Several times." Quentin turned around to watch the bay with her, and clasped his hands together behind his back. "The results are less than optimal, and either I speak to you about the very things I require therapy for, or I..." He shrugged. "I don't, and you remain safe."

"And that doesn't help you at all," she mused. "Well, if this room isn't suitable, we'll need a new one for next week. Nothing breakable, I assume?"

He inclined his head. "I'm afraid not."

"That could be tricky, but I'll see what I can do. When your power goes off like that, does it spread to other rooms?" She looked up at him, her eyebrows raised.

Quentin shook his head. "It does not seem to." Even when he had destroyed Myriam's shop last year, the back room had remained intact. Well, until he'd destroyed that, too, but that was on a separate occasion.

"And how is your mobility?"

He frowned at her, not quite sure of her meaning.

"Physically," Violeta explained. "Are you able to get down to and up from the floor? You said you do martial arts, right?"

"Oh. Yes." He hesitated. "Why do you ask?"

Violeta gave him the first wide smile he'd seen, flashing neat, white teeth for a moment. "I'm just thinking on what we can do. Maybe some cushions on the floor instead of breakable furniture. A different location, sure, but I'll need to work out how to organize it so that you don't throw a couch at my head. I think a few cushions are a good compromise. Would that work for you?"

His own eyebrows lifted, and he allowed himself a small smile. "I think that would work wonderfully," he admitted.

"Great. You won't actually, you know," she raised her hands into loose fists, "come at me?"

"Oh, goodness, no!" Quentin lifted his own hands, as though showing her empty palms could convince her that he was harmless. "Absolutely not!"

"Perfect!" She beamed, and her nose crinkled with cheer. "Leave it to me. I'll figure something out and text you the new address before next week's appointment. If you like it, we can carry on there instead of here."

The relief was like a tightness leaving his whole body with a single breath. He hadn't realized how tense he was, and now the strain was gone he felt lighter for it. "Thank you."

"It's my job." She gestured to the armchairs. "Why don't we sit back down, and we can talk about what it's like for you to have all this power bottled up inside?"

He nodded and moved back to his chair, then waited for her to sit before he did the same.

This was, at least, something he could cover without risk of any untoward hurricanes inside the office, and so he rested his hands together in his lap and considered the question.

"It's like," he finally began, "carrying a dreadful secret. I think that were it something everyone could do, it would be absolutely fine, but…" He leaned his head back to look at the ceiling briefly. "Instead I am a danger to all, not least myself."

"Because of your emotions?"

"Because if it becomes common knowledge that people like me exist, it could set off all sorts of mass panic, attacks against innocents, and goodness knows what else." He hated to sound as pessimistic as Freddy, but his twin did have a point. "I have power I knew nothing about a year ago, and I must keep a lid on it at all times. I suppose that other people have similar feelings about other things."

"Maybe, but we're not here to talk about their feelings. We're here to talk about yours." Violeta's faint semi-smile was back.

Quentin leaned back.

Talking about his feelings was hardly his favorite pastime.

HE WONDERED what solution Violeta would come up with by next week as he strolled up Ninth Avenue. How would she find a room with no windows? Perhaps other properties had bunkers, but if they were people's homes, Violeta could hardly borrow one, surely?

He remained alert as he walked. This wasn't his usual stretch of the Gaslamp, but it was a shorter route to The Jack in the Green than he had taken last week, and so he imagined he looked much like a tourist as he gazed up at the tall apartment buildings and down again at each intersection. Traffic was reasonably light during the early afternoon, and what little of it there was all travelled northbound. There was even the occasional empty on-street parking spot, though the apartment buildings all seemed to have their own parking garages or lots.

It wasn't an exciting route. He might try Tenth Avenue next week to see what was there; the only thing that broke up the apartment blocks on Ninth was the occasional bar.

He was approaching the intersection with G Street when he heard a rasp of rubber against asphalt, just as a shadow cut across and shielded him from the sun. He turned quickly, in case he needed to dive out of the way of an accident, in time to see a black van stop beside him.

At first he was about to write it off as coincidence. A sloppy driver dropping friends off, or faulty brakes. But the side door slid open, two young men leaped out, and they were looking right at him. One even held up a phone, sideways rather than vertical, as though he were recording.

Quentin frowned faintly. He wasn't at all certain what to make of this.

Both young men were white, dressed casually in jeans and hoodies. Usually he found himself amused by the sorts of temperatures locals would consider to be cold, but humor was the last thing on his mind right this very second.

"Quentin d'Arcy, right?" barked the man in front, the one not holding the phone. They both hurried toward him, leaping onto the pavement and closing the distance.

Quentin stepped toward the center of the pavement to give himself space in which to maneuver, loosened his posture, and immediately dispelled his cocoon of cool air. "May I help you?"

Surely if they were filming, they were hardly about to assault him? Why would they want evidence of their own lawlessness on camera? Still, he adjusted his stance casually, sliding a foot back to improve his stability.

"Cameron Delaney," said the one in front. He thrust his hand forward aggressively, but only to offer for a handshake. "Have you got time for some questions?"

Quentin blinked briefly, trusting his sunglasses to hide his surprise. He shook the offered hand, though. "Regarding what?"

This was most unorthodox. Film crews carried much larger cameras, and journalists had microphones. These were two boys in their late teens, no older than Felipe or Clifton, pointing a phone at him.

"Your hand's pretty cold, you know?" Cameron held onto it far longer than was polite. "What, you got circulation problems, or something?"

"Is there something that I can actually assist you with?"

Quentin bit back his sarcasm. Perhaps they were simply students.

Inept ones.

"I run a YouTube channel," Cameron said airily as he finally let go of Quentin's hand. "Maybe you've heard of it."

"I doubt it—" Quentin began.

"Cameron After Dark," Cameron interrupted. "I've got over a million subscribers."

"That's nice." Quentin folded his hands together behind his back. A million subscribers sounded like it was probably a good thing, whatever YouTube was. "Forgive me, but it isn't terribly dark at the moment, and I have somewhere to be."

"We're a paranormal investigation channel," Cameron continued with a gleam in his brown eyes. "And I thought you could answer a few questions for us."

Quentin blinked again, then looked past them to their van. It remained there, driver alternating between checking his mirrors and the situation with Quentin.

"Why on earth do you think I have answers for you? To anything?" he added.

Good God, what was Laurence's advice on lying? Ah, yes. *Stick to the truth wherever possible.*

Now his sunglasses became a disadvantage. He could not stare Delaney down with them in place, but removing them to do so seemed overly dramatic.

"Rumor has it you were on the *Theophrastus* when it sank last year. Is that true?"

Quentin cocked his head and waited.

"That yacht was worth millions of dollars, and it sank right off Shelter Island. It took them weeks to dredge it all up."

"So?"

Delaney turned and nodded toward the phone as though he'd caught Quentin in some exciting scandal, then looked at Quentin again. "And you were there when your boyfriend's shop got wrecked last year, weren't you?"

Quentin gave a deep sigh that was only partially put on. "If you have nothing worthwhile to say, then I'm afraid that I really must be going." He nodded politely and turned on the balls of his feet.

"You saw it, didn't you?" Delaney hurried to keep up with him, trying to cut in front and get in his way.

"What? What the hell are you even talking about?" Quentin slipped easily past Delaney, and Cameron had to run around him again.

"The ghost of your mother!"

Quentin stopped dead in his tracks. His body was rigid.

This was worse than any paparazzi nonsense.

"The *what*?" he snarled, not even trying to keep his disbelief from his tone.

"That's what wrecked the store!" Delaney crowed in triumph. "What sank the *Theophrastus*! It even happened at your mom's funeral! Disaster follows you because your mother is a poltergeist and she's haunting you, isn't that right?"

Quentin's jaw actually fell open. He was at a complete loss for words.

What kind of idiocy *was* this?

"I knew it!" Delaney waved his cameraman closer. "How long have you known she was with you?"

"This is absurd," he breathed faintly.

"That's why your skin is so cold! She's here right now, isn't she!"

What was he to do? He could hardly run. They had a van. But if he walked away, Delaney had shown that he was more than willing to obstruct Quentin's path. How long would they dance along the pavement like fools? If he went into a bar, they could simply follow him. Bloody hell, why hadn't he installed that Uber thing Laurence kept telling him to?

Well, because whenever they needed to, Laurence used it, that was why.

"I can't believe you have a million subscribers for this nonsense," he said. Not for the first time, he wondered how bad it would be to simply destroy a camera, but that would only lend credence to this idea that he was haunted. "My God, are you utterly insensitive? My mother is *dead*, Delaney!" He sucked in a breath to prevent himself from losing his temper. "Have some bloody decency!"

"And I'm sorry for your loss, I really am. But if I'm right, you haven't *lost* her—"

Quentin set off at a brisk pace. The crossing light was white, and he intended to use it before it turned red again.

"She's still with—"

"Mr. Delaney," Quentin seethed without turning to face him, "if you do not cease this harassment immediately, I shall be forced to call for the police. If I see you *again*, I shall seek a restraining order. Neither one subscriber nor one million gives you the right to be cruel to people."

The footsteps behind him stopped. Delaney yelled, "If you wanna talk about it, you can Google me!"

Quentin said nothing. He didn't look back.

His sole focus was on reigning in his anger before it slipped through his fingers and gave Delaney the exact evidence he was looking for.

8

LAURENCE

THE BACK DOOR FROM THE ALLEYWAY OPENED SO HARD THAT IT rattled, and Laurence nearly knocked over his mug of tea in surprise. Windsor hopped back, wings flapping so he could move faster, which sent a few loose sprigs of lavender flying off the bench.

Laurence was about to ask what the hell was going on when he caught sight of Quentin's face, and his voice died before it was even born.

He'd only seen Quentin this angry in Annwn, and even though he hated himself for it, he felt a quick flicker of panic. What if Gwyn *had* done lasting damage? What if Quentin had reverted back to the rage-controlled man he'd been turned into in Otherworld?

Goddess, Quentin's therapy couldn't have gone *that* badly, could it?

Quentin managed to close the door more gently than he'd opened it, and he pulled his sunglasses off, then tossed them onto the bench among the half-completed flower displays Laurence was working on.

Laurence pushed his tea aside as he packed the worry away, then stood. "Baby?"

"Cameron Delaney," Quentin seethed. His whole body was

taut as a bowstring, and his eyes were like clouds before a storm. "Who the hell is he?"

"Never heard of him." Laurence was relieved, in a way. Whoever had pissed Quentin off, it was something recent, not a resurgence of an older wound, and so far nothing in the back room had broken as a result of Quentin's arrival. "What's going on?"

"He said that I could Google him." Quentin finally came nearer and reached for Laurence's tea, then drank half of it before he put it down again and briefly patted Windsor's head with a fingertip. "Says that he has a million subscribers on YouTube."

"O…kay?" Laurence didn't know how this conversation was going to go, but Quentin was clearly working his ass off at bringing his anger under control. Laurence swallowed his relief, pulled his phone out and quickly searched, then scrolled through the results. "Yeah. Cameron After Dark. He's nineteen, a student at SDSU, has a channel about…" He trailed off, still confused. How had a ghost hunter angered Quentin so much? "You met him? I thought you were at your therapist today?"

"I was. And it went very well. And then this cretin—" Quentin jabbed a finger toward Laurence's phone "—ambushed me on Ninth Avenue and began interrogating me about…" He sucked in a deep breath. "About my mother."

Laurence's breath caught. Quentin's mom had died before they'd met, and Laurence knew how much the Duchess meant to at least two of her sons. They'd gone to war with each other to find the truth about her murder. "Whoa. What the fuck?"

Windsor clattered his beak in irritation, agreeing with Laurence.

No wonder Quentin was livid. Laurence was quickly getting that way, too. Whatever Delaney had said was obviously deeply upsetting, and Laurence's protectiveness reared its head, quickly followed by mental images of what his vengeance might look like.

Entrails, he thought. *It's always entrails.* His brain seemed really into the idea of plunging his hands into his enemies' guts and pulling out whatever was inside.

He shook his head quickly and finished off his tea. The action helped him simmer down a bit, and he took Quentin's hand. "C'mon. Come with me."

I come? Windsor hopped toward the edge of the bench.

No, it's okay. Wait here, Laurence replied.

Quentin strode after him as Laurence led him up the stairs, and Laurence let go of his hand to unlock the apartment door. Once they were in, he closed it, then waved toward the dining table. At least if Quentin wrecked everything up here, they could replace it without costing the shop a fortune.

Quentin marched to the table and gripped the back of a chair so hard that his knuckles slowly whitened. A few things around the apartment began to jitter and skip, but nothing broke.

Laurence waited. Quentin would talk when he was ready, when he was sure of himself.

"He had two friends with him," Quentin said through gritted teeth. "One to drive, and one to record everything on a phone. They pulled up alongside me as I was walking here, and Delaney launched into demanding answers about the *Theophrastus*, about Myriam's Valentine's party last year, and about..." He took deep breaths. "About Mother's funeral. He said that he is a paranormal investigator, and that those events were evidence of Mother's ghost haunting me."

Laurence listened in mounting horror. "What, he just, like, came out with all that?"

"Quite literally, yes."

"What the hell, man!" He shook his head numbly. "What then?"

"I told him that if he did not leave me be I would call the police," Quentin answered. "And that I would seek a restraining order if I saw him again. After that, I was able to make my escape."

"Fuck," Laurence whispered. "I'm so sorry, Quen. He's obviously an asshole. Do you want tea? I can make some fresh?"

"No." Quentin screwed his eyes shut, and took on the slow breathing of meditation.

Laurence gnawed his lip, then tapped his phone and started scrolling through Delaney's YouTube channel. The kid wasn't lying, that was for sure. He did have over a million subscribers, and his channel had been running for more than three years. Delaney must've started it while he was still in high school, and he seemed to have something new to say at least once a week.

He didn't want to play any of them. Not until Quentin was less upset. So he pocketed the phone, moved to the table to take a seat, and waited for the stuff on his shelves to stop bouncing. If his dad's Book of Shadows came loose, Laurence was ready to dive across the room to save it, but otherwise, he was willing to sit this one out.

It was a couple more minutes before Quentin released his death grip on the chair and slowly opened his eyes. A couple of pot plants had tipped over and the salt and pepper had both rolled off the dining table, but everything else was surprisingly good, so Laurence offered a soft smile.

Quentin pulled his hands free and slipped down into the seat, then plonked his elbows on the table and sank his face into his hands. "Christ," he whispered, "I'm sorry. I shouldn't have let him get to me."

"You'd just left your therapist, Quen," Laurence murmured. "You might have been... I don't know. Open, or vulnerable. Relaxed. Whatever state you were in when you were walking back, you obviously weren't ready to have some kid spring this bullshit on you. That was a dick move. You didn't... you know..." He licked his lips. "You didn't do anything on camera, did you?"

"No." Quentin shook his head. "Thankfully. I was more

flabbergasted than angry at the time. It was only as I walked away that it began to sink in."

"Yeah. I know what you mean." He slid his hand across the table and offered it to Quentin, content to wait for Quentin to notice that it was there. "You've got every right to be upset. He might even have been trying to antagonize you deliberately."

Quentin dropped his hands and blinked at Laurence in shock. "Why?"

"If he thinks you're haunted, maybe he hoped to catch proof on camera, and if he thinks your mom's the one doing it all, he might think she'd come to your rescue if he put you under pressure. I don't know." He glanced down as Quentin slipped a hand into his, and he squeezed gently. "Do you want to hide out up here for a bit while I go back to work, or do you want me to leave early and take you home?"

Quentin returned the squeeze, and sagged a little. "I'd like to remain here a while, if you do not mind. May I use your room?"

Laurence looked over his shoulder toward the closed bedroom door, then laughed a little. "Of course you can." He raised Quentin's hand to his lips and kissed his knuckles. "I'll be downstairs if you need me. You can just text me if you want, you don't even have to come down, okay?"

Quentin sighed and nodded. "Thank you. I'm sorry. I didn't mean to be so abrupt."

"You're allowed to be upset," Laurence said dryly. "Get some rest, then we'll head home and I'll make dinner. Nuh-uh, no argument." He grinned and leaned in for a kiss, then held it a moment before letting it go. He stood, then added, "And no Googling this asshole. Leave it to me."

Quentin crinkled his nose, then leaned back. "Very well."

"Great. Then enjoy my apartment, and don't wreck anything." He brushed his fingers tenderly across the back of Quentin's hand, then headed for the door.

LAURENCE FIGURED it would be a good idea to watch some of Delaney's videos of different ages so that he could pick up the ghost-hunter's style and whether it had matured or shifted over the years, so he scrolled all the way back to the very first video, tidied up the dropped lavender stalks, made himself a fresh mug of tea, then sat at the bench. He propped the phone against a vase and hit play, and went back to work while he occasionally looked at the screen.

Windsor hopped across to settle in front of the phone, watching it with his head tipped aside. Now that Laurence had seen through Windsor's eyes, he understood how Windsor had to turn to focus on the things he wanted to see. Having eyes on the sides of his head gave him a far wider field of view than Laurence had, though.

He smiled fondly and petted Windsor's feathers in between snipping or arranging stems.

"Oh my God, did you hear that?" Delaney's voice whispered from the phone. "I definitely heard footsteps! I'm gonna… yeah, I'm gonna go up the stairs, hopefully it's just a tourist, but I could swear there was no one in front of me on the trail up here. It's pretty deserted most mornings. Oh, God, this is so scary!"

Laurence paused after finishing another arrangement and watched the video. The camera was mostly focused on Delaney's face, and he was looking around himself like he was terrified. Wherever he was, it was dimly lit, but a strong line of sunlight cut across a wall in the background.

"There! There it is again!" Delaney looked about seventeen in the video, and Laurence prodded the screen to check the time remaining.

Goddess, this video was over an hour long!

He watched as Delaney slowly climbed a narrow, circular-looking staircase, and it wasn't until the camera was overloaded with sunlight from a window that Laurence worked out where Delaney was. This was the old lighthouse over on Point Loma, part of the Cabrillo National Monument park.

"This is terrifying," Delaney insisted as he climbed up to the bedrooms of a perfectly safe tourist attraction. He was acting like he'd get murdered any moment now and his phone would be the only evidence, like a real-life Blair Witch recording.

Laurence scoffed and took the arrangement over to a shelf and placed it with the rest, then went back to the bench.

"Dude, what're you watching back here?" Ethan brushed through the bead curtain with a bemused smile on his face. "Are you into ghost-hunting now?"

"No way." Laurence sat again and pulled the next vase closer. "This douchebag harassed Quentin on the street earlier. Figured I'd try to work out what his angle was."

Ethan came around and petted Windsor as he watched the screen for a moment, then snorted. "Too much time, not enough going on in his life, that's his problem."

"Yeah, probably."

"Oh shit," Delaney whimpered. The camera angle was a great close-up of his chin. "I can hear footsteps again, and they're definitely upstairs." He paused for dramatic effect. "But there's no more upstairs. I mean, there's the lighthouse tower, but it's only open to the public twice a year, and I'm here right at the start of January. There is no way — *no way* — that there's anyone up there. Oh, shit! Oh shit, did you hear that? I heard a scream! Oh, God, I gotta get out of here!"

"This is better than Storage Wars," Ethan laughed. "Look at him! Does he think he's convincing?"

"A million people believe him," Laurence mused as he went back to snipping stems.

"You're not one of them, huh?" Ethan filled the kettle.

"No way, man." Laurence glanced to the phone as Delaney managed to run in fake terror down to the ground floor of the lighthouse, yet somehow managed not to make it out into the glorious sunshine beyond the front door.

San Diego could usually be relied on for sunny skies, and filming a spooky, scary segment during the day had to be a lot of hard work.

Laurence frowned and picked up the phone, killing the video and scrolling forward through the list. As he figured, the more recent Delaney's work got, the more he seemed to shoot at night, if thumbnails were any indicator. He'd have to watch a few to be sure, though.

"There's a lot of gullible people," Ethan said as he turned the kettle on. "But why was he harassing Quentin? I mean, he's British, not dead."

"He thinks Quentin's haunted by the ghost of his mom," Laurence muttered. "It's all just channel bait for him. I figured I could look through his other stuff and find out what he's like, but there's a lot of material here, and some of it's like a full length TV show."

"So just read through the comments sections instead." Ethan shrugged. "Maybe you'll get some idea of what's going on there."

Laurence mulled it over while Ethan finished making more tea, then sat up slowly. "Or I could just ask someone who might know."

Ethan put a fresh mug down by Laurence, then sat opposite him. "Like who?"

There was only one person Laurence knew who had probably watched a whole bunch of channels just like Delaney's, and maybe even Cameron After Dark itself. He checked the time, then did the math — since New York was three hours ahead of San Diego — and smiled slowly at Ethan.

"His name's Basil," Laurence said.

"Like, the Great Mouse Detective?" Ethan snorted. "Who is he?"

"He's a ghost hunter." Laurence's smile became a smirk. "But he's way better than Delaney."

Ethan blew on his tea. "How can anyone be better than this genius?" He thumbed toward the phone.

"Because he does it for real."

Windsor clacked his beak and ruffled his feathers like he was preparing for some big announcement. Instead, the only word that came out of his beak was a loud, clear, "Shit!"

Laurence sank forward and banged his forehead against the bench while Ethan burst out laughing.

9

QUENTIN

LAURENCE'S BED WAS PERFECTLY MADE, AND AS QUENTIN settled down onto it, he wondered how long it had been since Laurence last slept here.

All he removed was his shoes. There was no need to track muck across Laurence's pristine sheets, but there was also no requirement to shed any more than that. He just needed a few moments' peace and quiet, some meditation time before he reentered the world.

Eyes closed, head against the pillow, he laid his hands down by his sides and focused on the sounds and smells around himself, cataloging them so that he could choose which ones to eliminate. The scents of fruit and mint were, he supposed, from the bathroom, so faint that he was barely able to detect them. Otherwise, the bedroom had no particular odors that stood out to him, and he wondered whether Laurence was able to detect more than Quentin could.

No. He had to stop that train of thought. He was supposed to be weeding out stray ideas, not adding to them.

He could hear an electric hum from the apartment, and occasionally the faintest of mumbles from downstairs, though nowhere near loud enough to work out who might have been speaking. He thought he could make out the faint tick of a clock, but it wasn't in here with him. He was alone, which suited him perfectly well.

The final sensation, a mixture of sound and feeling, was his own breathing. As he honed in on it, practice took over, and piece by piece he was able to slough away all the other distractions until there was only his own breath.

In. Two. Three. Four.

Out. Two. Three. Four.

The most fundamental thing that he had come to accept about meditation was that, once it began, there was no way short of setting an external timer to know when it might end. Rarely, when utterly exhausted, he might even drift off into sleep at some point, but more usually — as he did now — he would simply float to the surface of his own consciousness as though waking from a light nap, aware that he was finished without any grasp of how much time it might have taken.

He took the time to stretch, then sat up, swinging his legs off the bed and sitting on the edge while he assessed himself to be sure that he truly was calm once more.

There was no anger. Not even frustration. Perhaps a little tiredness, but he had received quite the shock today. He could forgive himself for being a little drained by it.

Satisfied that he was fit for human interaction once more, he eased his shoes on, then stood and adjusted his clothing with the aid of Laurence's mirror.

It would do. This spring the trend was for denim or pinstripes, but he had never worn jeans in his life, and so he'd skipped that look and gone for the pinstripes instead. They flattered him tremendously, and he instantly regretted the fact that they'd likely be gone again in a year's time.

He was as though nothing had gone awry with his day. He slipped fingers through his hair to neaten it up, then made his way from the bedroom and toward the front door.

A soft glow caught his eye.

Quentin hesitated.

He was used to the glow around the windows. Laurence

had warded Myriam's shop as well as her farm and the mansion in La Jolla. It was horrible, but ever-present, and he just had to deal with it. But this glow was out of place, and he was torn between seeking it out and looking the other way.

It really was best to confront his fears, so he turned toward the shelves and eyed the handful of books that were propped up in one of the cubbyholes, half hidden by the fronds of some sprawling plant.

He didn't know what it was about books stuffed with spells that made them glow. Was there something about having so many powerful words crammed into such a tiny space that made them somehow magical in and of themselves, or did they have spells cast upon them to protect the books from damage or circumstance?

It was tempting to look, to see if he could work out the source of the glow, but he had had quite enough of a challenge for one day. And one of these books could well be Eric's book of shadows, a personal journal which he had wanted Laurence to have. It was none of Quentin's business.

This wasn't cowardice. It was respecting Laurence's boundaries and property. If Laurence wished for Quentin to nose through these things, he would have brought them home and offered them up, not tucked them away in an apartment Laurence only used during his lunch breaks.

There. Now he could leave without taking any further notice of the nasty books and without actually running away from them. He was almost proud of his logical reasoning, and he let himself out of the apartment with a spring in his step.

He was back where he needed to be: in control.

He heard laughter as he descended the stairs, but it wasn't Laurence's, and he lifted his eyebrows at the scene that came into view once he was halfway down.

Ethan was the one doubled over, while Laurence's face was

resting against the bench he used for flower arranging. Windsor stood on the bench with his head held high.

"Is everything quite all right?" Quentin murmured as he alighted from the bottom step and into the room.

"Shit," Windsor said, evidently pleased with himself.

Quentin eyed the bird. "I see."

"Don't encourage him," Laurence mumbled, head still down.

"I don't believe he requires any encouragement," Quentin sighed, reaching out to gently stroke Windsor's head. "You're quite capable of being a reprobate of your own free will, aren't you?"

Windsor cackled and waggled his tail.

"Oh, hey!" Ethan managed to straighten himself up and rub his face, then nodded past Quentin toward the window. "Maria's here. I'm gonna go see if she needs a hand."

"Huh?" Laurence finally lifted his head from the bench and swept his hair back, then ran fingers over his stubble. His face was pink from having been bent over for a while, and he flashed a warm smile at Quentin once their eyes met. "Feeling better?"

"Yes. Thank you." His fingers briefly checked that his cuffs were aligned correctly within the sleeves of his jacket, and he circled the bench to perch on a stool by Laurence's side.

Laurence reached out for his phone, which was currently propped against a vase, and drew it closer to himself. "I was just going to text Basil to see if he's free to talk," he explained as he thumbed the screen to wake it up. "I thought I'd ask what he knows about this Delaney guy."

Quentin pursed his lips, faintly irked at not having thought of it himself. He had been too consumed by anger to think straight, and if it had been a more dangerous situation, he could well have lost more than merely his temper because of it.

How could he have dedicated so much time to improving himself, and yet be so easily wrong-footed?

"That's an excellent idea," he said. "I would like to be present for that call, if that's all right?"

"Sure. Of course!" Laurence turned toward the door as Maria breezed in.

Quentin looked, too. Ethan was out in the alley, loading a dumpster with cardboard from Maria's truck, and Maria's hair had worked out of her plait and into a halo of frizz around her head.

"Hey, how'd it go?" Laurence asked her.

"Fine, no problems." Maria cast Quentin a quick smile, then turned to hang the truck keys up by the door. She pulled her apron off and walked to the hooks near the bead curtain, gesturing to Windsor on his way past. "He doesn't want to leave, huh?"

"Naw, I think he likes the sandwiches." Laurence grinned. "How're the kids?"

"Oh, you would think I was the best mom in the world!" She sighed as she hung the apron up, then took a small wallet from the pocket of her jeans and checked through it for something. "Now Alejandro wants to be a rock star just like Neil Storm, and he's asking me for an electric guitar for his birthday. Do not," she added as she put her wallet away again, "get him an electric guitar. He can learn on an acoustic. Only when he can play will I let him play even louder."

"For what it is worth, I concur wholeheartedly," Quentin chuckled.

"Thank you. You see, a musician understands." Maria smiled at him. "I'm running late. Is there anything you need before I go?"

"No, we'll take care of the truck. Thanks, Maria. See you tomorrow." Laurence grinned at her.

Maria blew Laurence a kiss, then disappeared through the bead curtain.

It dawned on Quentin that, despite having four children, Maria never drove to the Jack in the Green. She always came and went on foot.

"How does she get home?" he asked of Laurence.

"The trolley." Laurence blinked, then snorted. "Fifth Avenue down to National City."

"Oh." Quentin had seen the tram — or trolley, as Laurence called it — now and then during his exploration of the city, but he had never ridden it. It looked perfectly nice in passing, but he wasn't one for public transport. That, and he wasn't sure where it actually went.

Laurence just smirked as he tapped out a text message.

"I should head home," Quentin mused. "Oh! Actually, I had meant to pick Myriam's brain about something." He half-rose from his stool. "Is she here today?"

"Uh huh. Out front." Laurence eyed him. "Are you up to something?"

"Possibly." He leaned in to kiss Laurence's cheek, then backed away before Laurence could snag hold of him. "I shan't be long."

"Quennnnn," Laurence said, wheedling a little.

Quentin just chuckled and nipped through the bead curtain, taking stock of the shop quickly to see whether he would be a bother.

Rodger was tweaking a display, and Myriam was at the counter, which meant that Aiden had to be out on his own deliveries. There was a browsing customer near the door, but he seemed more interested in his phone than the flowers.

"Quentin!" Myriam came over to hug him tightly. "Are you heading home now?"

He returned the hug with a smile. "Not yet. Actually, I wondered whether you might have a moment?"

"Of course, dear. What can I help you with?"

"Staff," he said simply. "And how I might hire some."

She leaned back and looked up at him, eyebrows scrunched together quizzically over hazel eyes. "Are you opening a business?"

"Not that I know of." Quentin rested one hip against the counter and loosely crossed his arms. "I think we need some domestic assistance at the house, but I'm not sure how one would go about that in the United States."

"Oh!" Myriam chuckled and patted his arm. "Well, that's no different from hiring Mia or Sebastian. You are not the employer, you are a customer. So you have no need to take on employees, even if you think of them as your staff. Do you see?"

He blinked. Was it really that simple? "So all I need do is… find one?"

"Usually through an agency, yes. You become a customer of the agency, the agency is the employer for the staff, and the agency sends you the staff and the check."

"But what if I were to employ staff full-time?"

Myriam shrugged. "It still works the same way, though I can't imagine you'd want staff in that house all day, every day." At his raised eyebrow, she added, "it can sometimes get a bit weird there, can't it?"

He nodded slowly. "I understand. Thank you."

"You're welcome."

Quentin took his leave, retreating back through the curtain while he mulled it over. Myriam was quite right. The house was full of teenagers who practiced their psychic gifts after school. There was a talking bird, who seemed to favor swear words, but who would be considered a wild animal by most. There was a room for martial arts practice, and another that Laurence used for magic and prayer.

All told, a cleaner would not suffice. He required more than someone who could cook or tidy up. What he would need, first and foremost, was utter discretion.

And the only place he knew to find someone who was well versed in such things was London.

Ethan came inside and closed the back door; Laurence was watching Quentin.

"Nothing important," Quentin assured Laurence. "Just something I'd been meaning to ask."

"About?" Laurence began, but then his phone rang, and he looked at it. "Oh, it's Basil."

Quentin came closer and reclaimed his perch on the stool beside Laurence just as Laurence answered the phone.

He had no idea whether Basil might know anything, but if he did, Quentin wanted to hear it firsthand, so he made himself comfortable.

With any luck, this phone call would solve everything with Delaney, and Quentin could get on with his life without ever having to deal with the student again.

10

LAURENCE

"Hey, Basil. Want me to call you back?" Laurence held the phone to his ear and rested his knee against Quentin's while Ethan filled the kettle.

"No, it's okay. This phone is covered by expenses." Basil chuckled. "What's up?"

"I've got Quentin with me. Are you okay if I put you on speaker?"

"Sure!"

"Great. Hold on." Laurence lowered the phone and tapped the speaker button, then put the phone screen-up on the bench between himself and Quentin. "Can you hear me?"

"I can. Hi, Quentin," Basil chirped.

"Good afternoon." Quentin paused. "Or evening, I suppose?"

"Yeah, evening," Basil agreed. "Is everything okay?"

Laurence dropped his hand to Quentin's thigh and rested it there. As much as he might have liked to run his thumb across Quentin's pants, he didn't want to cause any discomfort for the scars beneath the material, so he held still. "Not really. You do ghost-hunting, right?"

"Oh, have you got a ghost?" Basil's excitement was palpable.

"No, but I've got a ghost hunter, and I was wondering if you'd heard of him." Laurence licked his lips. "Cameron Delaney?"

Basil laughed. It wasn't a mean sound, but Laurence wasn't sure Basil even knew how to be mean. "Cameron After Dark? Of course. He's hilarious!"

Laurence propped his elbow against the bench and looked at Quentin, who seemed mildly affronted. "Why do you say that?"

"Oh there's so many of these guys," Basil replied, still chuckling. "They all want to make a name for themselves, but they're all fake. There's one in England who makes videos that are like two hours long and it's just him and a flashlight in some woods every time, acting like he's going to die. People love it." Basil paused. "Why're you asking?"

Laurence parted his lips and took a breath, but Quentin got there before him.

"Because he accosted me in the street and began harassing me," Quentin said, far more calmly now than he had earlier. "He believes that I am haunted."

"If you were, I would've noticed." Basil huffed like his professional reputation was on the line. "How rude!"

"Yeah," Laurence agreed. "That's one way to put it for sure. Quentin's threatened him with a restraining order. Will he back off, do you think, or is he the kind of asshole who doubles down on that shit?"

"He's pretty light," Basil said. "He won't want to face legal action. He's just a kid having fun making videos. There are a few places he's active, though. I'll check them out, see if he's said anything."

Laurence breathed a sigh of relief. "That'd be awesome. Thanks, man. How are you guys, anyway?"

"Doing okay, thanks! Oh, hey, guess what? We haven't seen that black dog around since you guys were here. Jon's theory is all the ghosts it was made up of got destroyed when they touched his badass corpse-form."

Quentin tilted his head.

"Maybe come up with a better name for it than that?" Laurence smiled dryly. "Okay, I should let you two get some sleep. Let me know if you find anything, yeah?"

"No problem! Take care, Laurence. Bye, Quentin!"

They said their farewells and Laurence hung up, then puffed his cheeks out just as Ethan put a mug of tea in front of him and another by Quentin.

"So it sounds like it's all taken care of?" Ethan offered while he walked back to fetch his own tea.

Laurence nodded absently and reached for his mug. Basil's laughter seemed disarming, but Laurence's hackles were still firmly raised, and it took him a moment to figure out why.

"What do you think?" Quentin asked gently as he picked up his own tea.

"I think," Laurence began slowly, forming his thoughts into words as he went, "that just because Delaney's a faker, doesn't mean his audience doesn't believe every word of it. I mean, sure, most of them probably just watch because it's entertaining, but all it takes is someone who really believes in it all, and…" He tailed off.

"Right," Ethan agreed. "But it sounds like he doesn't have anywhere near enough footage of Quentin to make a whole episode out of."

"You think he might try again?" Quentin turned to face Ethan.

Ethan shrugged. "Depends on whether he really thinks you're haunted, or if he's just messing around."

Laurence blew on his tea. It felt like there was a knot tightening in his gut, and Ethan's words hadn't helped it any. "If he thinks he's onto something," he said, "he might come back. Imagine if, after three years of making up content, you thought you had access to the real thing? Wouldn't you ignore a threat like a restraining order? Especially if you don't actually receive one?"

Quentin frowned faintly. "If he were to corner me again, I

would hopefully endure it with greater composure, now that I know what it is that he wants."

"But that still gives him more footage to string together, even if it's only another five minutes' worth," Ethan reasoned. "Maybe you should just get the restraining order. Let him know you're not fucking around."

"I don't wish to engage the services of a lawyer unless I absolutely must," Quentin said.

"That's pretty much everyone's opinion of lawyers, dude."

Laurence had to agree, but perhaps it ran deeper. After all, Frederick was a lawyer — or, at the very least, training to become one — and he wondered whether that might have anything to do with Quentin's aversion. It could just as easily be because Quentin didn't know how to go about finding one, though. He made a mental note to ask later.

"Well, I'm quite content to see how it goes, and pursue the matter further should he refuse to drop it," Quentin murmured after a sip of tea. "Thank you," he added, "for your help."

"Hey, it's what I'm here for." Laurence grinned.

Windsor cawed his agreement, and even hopped over to rest his chin on Quentin's forearm, though Laurence was half sure it was a ploy to get Quentin to pet him, which succeeded.

"I'm just here to make the tea," Ethan said, raising his cup like he was toasting the room.

"All right." Laurence eyed his half-finished arrangements. "I better get these done. Do you want to head home, hon, or are you going to stay a while?"

"I suppose that I had best return home." Quentin gazed at Laurence, then finished his tea and leaned over to kiss him.

His lips were hot, wet, and distinctly tea-flavored, and Laurence's eyes fluttered closed until the kiss was broken.

He considered dragging Quentin upstairs, but he really did need to finish his work, so he groaned in frustration. "Go on," he muttered, "stop teasing me."

"But I do enjoy it so." Quentin smirked. He took his cup to

the sink, then made his way to the curtain. "Good day, Ethan," he added.

"Yeah. You too, man," Ethan said with a wave. The moment Quentin was gone, he eyed Laurence. "You're gonna get some tonight," he crowed.

Laurence was tempted to tell Ethan to get lost, but the taste of Quentin lingered on his lips, and he gave a sly grin.

"Yeah, I am," he agreed.

———

TWO DAYS LATER, Laurence hadn't heard back from Basil, and he hoped that was good news, but he figured if he didn't hear anything by closing time, he'd call on his way home after work.

He had his own therapy each week during an extended lunch break, because it was the only way to cram it in, and he'd given in to allow Quentin to pay for it all, otherwise he'd only be able to afford once a month. Maybe one day he'd only want to go monthly, but for now he had a lot to work on, and not enough time to do it all in.

His therapist was a lady in her thirties working out of an office building in the East Village, just a couple of blocks beyond Quentin's, and Laurence was happy to jog there and back. Parking in San Diego, especially downtown, was a joke that had stopped being funny years ago, and he didn't want to risk missing an appointment because there wasn't an on-street parking spot.

He made sure to get there early enough that he could cool off, then smiled when he was called through to Dr. Hammond's office. Not out of any great pleasure at being there, but because it was polite.

The office was on the top floor of the three-story building, and spacious, with tall windows and leather couches so comfortable that Laurence always regretted leaving them.

"Hey, Laurence. How're you doing today?"

Laurence shrugged and sat on the couch, up at one end so that he could lean on the arm if he wanted to. "Okay, I guess. How about you?"

"It's my sister's birthday this weekend, so everything's hectic." Pauline Hammond laughed as she settled into the chair facing Laurence and reached for her notepad. "How has your week been?"

He blew air in a huff so strong that it made his curls flutter over his eyes, and leaned back into the cushions.

"That good, huh?" Pauline nodded, and her smile melted away into studied concern. Not so studied that it was false, but Laurence knew it was a practiced expression. She used it a lot, and it gave him a nice blank canvas to dump his words out in front of. "What's going on?"

"Urgh, it's just..." Laurence sprawled slowly, sinking into the couch like it could support him more than just physically. "Quentin got some street harassment and it pissed me off."

"Quentin is your boyfriend, right?" Pauline glanced to her notepad.

He nodded. "Yeah. Some wannabe paparazzi douchebag leaped out at him and tried to do an on-the-spot interview, and got pretty rude about the whole thing. I wasn't there," he added. "Quen told me about it after."

Pauline nodded slowly. "Which kind of doubles down on the powerlessness, doesn't it? It happened while you weren't there, and you might not have been able to stop it even if you were?"

"Ouch." Laurence winced and drew a cushion into his lap, holding it there loosely with one arm. "Getting personally attacked here." It usually took them at least half an hour to get to this point, but then Laurence was the one who strung it out for that long most of the time. Was this some kind of Stage Two, where they were past all the introductions and fact-finding, and onto the harder part?

Pauline nodded. "It can feel like that sometimes, can't it? I'm sorry, I'll take it more gently."

"No." Laurence regretted it the moment he said it, but he shook his head with a sigh. "No. I mean, the whole point of coming here is to figure out all this—" he raised his hands either side of his head and waved them a couple of times "—mess, and, I don't know. I've got so much going for me, and then I feel helpless just because something dumb like this happens." He let his hands fall to his lap. "It's stupid. Quen didn't even get hurt. He's an adult, he doesn't need..." He puffed out his cheeks.

He couldn't finish that sentence, because it wasn't true. Sometimes Quentin *did* need Laurence's protection, just like Laurence needed his.

"There's nothing wrong with caring about the people we love," Pauline murmured. "But this was beyond your control." She put her notepad aside so that she could lean in a little. "And you've had so much of that already in your life, haven't you?"

Laurence crossed his legs and held the pillow more tightly. He felt his frown form as he looked out the window, and debated whether this was getting too close for comfort.

But she was right, and she was only doing her job.

"Yeah," he said thickly.

"You said last week you were starting to feel..." She reached for her notepad and consulted it, then raised her head. "Numb. Disconnected. Is that still the case?"

"I don't know." Laurence took a deep breath, then let it out slowly. "Maybe. Yeah. I just..." He tailed off and licked his lips. "Something happened between us a couple of months back. Me and Quen," he added. "He's got his own shit, and... he kind of lost it, and it..." He swallowed. "It scared the fuck out of me."

Pauline nodded kindly. "Were you hurt?"

He bounced his foot and stared sullenly at the skyline. How was he going to answer that one? If he told the truth, it sounded like he was in love with a guy who abused him. If he lied, what was the point of coming here at all?

Laurence rubbed his wrist at the memory of how it had broken.

"Yes," he breathed.

"What brings it to mind today?"

"Because that's…" Laurence ground to a halt.

There was no way to say this without it sounding awful, but he needed to hear it out loud, to get it off his chest and stop it playing on his mind in the dark.

"Because when he got harassed," he sighed, "it reminded me of how angry he was in New York. I know he's dealing with that, I know he's seeing his own therapist, but it just…" Laurence raised a hand and gnawed on his thumb. "It wasn't the same. I knew he wasn't angry at me, he wasn't going to hurt me, but my brain just went right back there, you know? Acting like I should be scared of him, and I'm not. I'm *not*." He sucked in air too fast, and it made him hiccup. "And he wasn't angry at me in New York, either. That was… someone hurt him, bad, and he wasn't himself."

He heard movement, and turned toward her in time to catch Pauline nudging a box of tissues toward him across the table.

Another hiccup.

Laurence caved and grabbed a tissue from the box, then scrunched it in his hand as he began to cry. "It's not fair," he whimpered. "None of it's his fault. I don't want to be scared of him. I *love* him."

It was like the dam had burst, and he reached over to take the whole box from the table. One tissue wasn't going to cut it. He blew his nose, but now tears were coming, and he ended up with a fistful of used tissues and a dull ache in his chest.

He felt so tired all of a sudden. Exhausted and empty.

But he'd had a *feeling*. Something other than the creeping numbness he'd hidden in since New York.

"Would you like to talk about that?" Pauline's nudge was gentle, her voice soft. She hadn't moved an inch.

Laurence dabbed at the tears on his cheeks and looked for

somewhere to put all his used tissues, then found the little trash can to the side of the couch and dropped them all in there. He hiccuped again, and he was so worn thin that it almost hurt.

"I don't know," he croaked.

She nodded. "Would you like some water?"

"Yes. Please."

She stood and moved to a water fountain tucked into the corner of the room, and he listened to it bubbling like a fart in a bathtub while she poured him a cup. By the time she placed the water on the table within his reach, his hiccups had subsided. If he'd been anywhere but here, he probably would have taken himself away for a nap, but he had to push on through. All this talking cost a fortune, and he wasn't going to waste it.

He sipped the cold water to begin with, then gulped it down as it eased the scratch in his throat.

"All right," Pauline murmured. "Walk me through what you're thinking."

Laurence put the cup back down and pinched the bridge of his nose, then rubbed his eyes. "I'm worried you might think I'm living with an abuser," he admitted. "And I'm really not. And you've probably heard that so many times, but Quen, he's... he's the gentlest guy. He wouldn't hurt anyone."

"Not like his brother?" Pauline had her notes to hand again.

Laurence curled his lip and clutched his cushion tight to his gut. "No. Not like Freddy. Not at all." He chewed his lip. "He fucking drugged me. He's... he's not okay. And I can't tell Quen what happened, because it'll break his heart."

"So you hold on to these secrets," she surmised. "What do you think will come from doing that?"

Laurence grit his teeth and crushed the cushion between his hands.

This was *not* how he'd wanted to spend his lunchtime, and

he wasn't sure he'd be in any fit state to go back to work after this.

He sucked in air and shook his head. "I think it'll ruin us," he whispered.

And after that, he couldn't find anything more to say. Nothing that made sense or had meaning, because he was too busy struggling to carry the weight of his own admission.

It couldn't end. They'd promised each other it wouldn't. They'd been in the worst situations imaginable and clutched each others' hands, swearing their lives to one another. Quentin had made a deal with Arawn to be there for Laurence in the afterlife. They were so utterly committed that a split didn't bear thinking about.

But how could they survive with such a huge Catch-22 between them?

He clung to the hope that it couldn't possibly be over, but that hope spent the next half hour slipping through his fingers.

11

QUENTIN

LAURENCE SEEMED QUITE SUBDUED THROUGHOUT DINNER, AND even into the evening, eventually claiming that he felt unwell and wished to go to bed early. Quentin's initial worry was for a resurgence of post-acute withdrawal syndrome, since Laurence fought off everyday illnesses with ease, but it seemed more a general lethargy, and so he remained available for the children until eight o'clock, then made his own excuses and reminded them to be in bed at a decent time.

He slipped into the bedroom and found Laurence in a chair by the window, hugging Windsor while he gazed into space, and it was only when Quentin closed the door that Laurence blinked and looked over.

"Oh. Hey."

Quentin tilted his head faintly and approached. "Is everything all right?"

Laurence sighed and put Windsor on the table, where the bird hopped along to the other chair and leaped onto the armrest. "I guess. I don't know." He rubbed his stubble with both palms. "Just a rough time with my therapist today, that's all."

Quentin frowned and carefully lowered himself into the chair, giving Windsor enough room to hop up onto the back and out of the way. "I'm sorry," he murmured. "Is there anything I can do for you?"

"No, I'm… working some stuff out, I guess." Laurence bit his lip, and shook his head. "I'll be okay. I just need to sleep on it." His eyes flit in Quentin's direction, and he mustered a brief smile. "I didn't mean for you to worry."

"I always worry," Quentin said dryly. "So long as—"

He was cut off by the ring of Laurence's phone, some sort of pop song that he wasn't familiar with, and so he leaned back and waited patiently for Laurence to attend to it.

"Oh. It's Basil!" Laurence tapped it once it was out of his pocket, and he put it on the table. "Hey, Basil. You're on speaker. Quentin's here. What's up?"

"Hey Laurence, Quentin." Basil's voice lacked any cheer. He sounded flustered, even.

Quentin leaned in, but Basil continued without pause.

"It's late. Sorry about that. I mean, it's later here, obviously, but it's late there, right? But I've been checking out everywhere I could think of for a couple of days and I've got bad news."

"Bad in what regard?" Quentin kept his voice steady even as his pulse quickened.

"Cameron Delaney," Basil breathed. "Okay, so, I'm on a lot of ghost-hunting forums and Facebook groups and Slack groups and… I mean, you get the idea. Some of these things are viewable to the public, some are closed. Delaney's talking a lot in the closed groups about how he's scored this huge scoop of a lifetime story, which is how everyone talks around here, but he's been saying for a few weeks he's got something huge in San Diego, then last night he said he's got footage."

Laurence curled his lip and rubbed at his forehead. "All he's got is some back and forth with Quentin on the street. He hasn't got anything good."

"I don't know. Okay, so let me explain this. On the public forums, people will talk openly about hauntings they think have happened or are in progress. They'll list the location, address, whatever, and other ghost-hunters go over and check it out. But when they're convinced they've got something real, they take it to closed forums, and they don't give anything away, because they don't want to lose the exclusivity. It's almost like real, actual journalism, except it's usually also fake. But, uh." Basil hesitated. "Tonight he straight-up named Quentin."

Quentin exchanged a look of confusion with Laurence. "I don't understand," he said. "Is he not giving his so-called story away by doing so?"

"It gets worse. He's suggesting that anyone near San Diego get together with him to help catch you out on camera. He's posted this video of you where you're threatening to call the cops on him. He's basically attempting to crowdsource his exposé because he can't get close to you himself. He's calling on everyone in the area to get in touch with him to coordinate an attempt to question you without ever using the same interviewer twice." Basil hissed. "He's stirring up a mob."

Quentin had to quash his initial stirring of disquiet. There was no need to hide from the media any longer. His father already knew where he lived, and had agreed to leave him to it, so the fear that had chased him from one city to the next had no use any longer, no matter how relevant it still seemed to consider itself.

And now that he knew what was coming, he could brace for it. He would simply stick to the threat of legal action, and eventually the attention would die away.

Laurence's features indicated that he was far angrier than Quentin. His cheeks had flushed pink, and his eyes were wide. "He can't do that!" he snapped at the phone.

"He's got whole folders of documents he's posted to go with the video," Basil said. "Screenshots from news sites, scans of magazine clippings, you name it. I don't know how long he's been working on this, but his 'evidence' of your so-called haunting is pretty compelling, and I'm saying this as someone who knows for sure you're absolutely not haunted. If I was down there in SoCal I would totally come and look into this."

"Well, just how many ghost hunters can there be here, anyway?" Quentin sniffed.

"It doesn't matter," Basil said. "I mean, there's a bunch in LA, and all they have to do is drive, but you're also within a few hours of Nevada, and there's a whole lot of paranormal investigators out near Vegas who wouldn't say no to a road trip. This is what I'd call really good research material. It'd be more than enough to interest me, and most of these people take way less convincing than I do." Quentin heard Basil suck in a breath. "I figure all this evidence is actually psychokinetic, right?"

Quentin winced softly. "I'm afraid so, yes."

"Then maybe if you don't use it for a while, they won't get anything new, and will move off. I'm really sorry. You might just have to be extra careful for a few weeks until this blows over."

"That shouldn't be too—" An incessant knock at the door interrupted him, and Quentin broke off. "I need to leave you with Laurence for a moment," he explained to Basil, then hurried to open the door.

Felipe was there, his fist raised to knock again, but he snapped his hand back and gestured to the stairs. "Problem," he said.

Quentin slipped out into the corridor and drew the door closed. "What kind?"

"Don't know. Estelita and Soraya are looking into it; Kim went to go check it out."

Quentin hurried after Felipe. "Where is Mia?"

"In bed, probably. Soraya told me to come get you."

"All right. She's in her room?"

Felipe nodded. "You want me to get Mia?"

"If you would be so kind."

They sprinted up the stairs, and Quentin peeled off toward Soraya's room while Felipe darted on down the corridor.

Estelita called out "Come in" before he could even knock on the door, so Quentin barged in like a freight train.

"What's wrong?" he demanded. He hadn't intended for it to sound so harsh, but anything which had ruffled the children enough for them to send for him was cause for alarm.

The scene that met his eyes didn't seem too peculiar. Soraya was sitting up in bed, sheets over her lap, staring off into the distance. She was watching something that wasn't in the room. Estelita was perched on Kimberly's bed, dressed in pajamas, her feet grazing the carpet as she swung them back and forth. Her head was tilted as though she were listening, and Quentin supposed it might well have been to whatever Soraya was watching.

He looked at Estelita. "Where is Kimberly?"

"Outside," she breathed. "There's something really weird out on the street. I heard all these…"

"Trucks," Soraya said. "Mostly."

"They pulled up and just stopped out there with their engines running, and people were talking to each other about you and whether or not this was the right house."

His gut clenched. Was this the result of Delaney's internet activity, or something unrelated?

"And Kimberly has gone to take a closer look?" he surmised.

"Yeah."

Quentin bobbed his head and darted out, where he almost collided with Mia coming the other way.

"Where's the fire?" she said.

"Outside, and potentially invasive. Could you check the grounds, please?" He ran down the stairs two at a time.

"You think someone might have gotten in?" Mia sprinted after him, hot on his heels.

"I think it's safest to be sure that they don't."

They parted ways, Mia continuing on toward the kitchen as Quentin broke off to get to the front door. He tugged it open, then slowed himself, attempting to appear less irate than he felt.

There was no sign of Kimberly in the courtyard, so he strode through it and up the steps to the front gate.

By now, he could hear it. Running engines, low chatter, muffled by the tall wall and the trees and vines that overgrew it. He eyed them and called softly, "Kimberly?"

If she was present, she didn't answer.

There was nothing for it. He couldn't see over a wall, and if Kimberly had already gone over it, he wasn't satisfied with leaving her alone among people who were eagerly awaiting any sign of paranormal activity whatsoever. He drew himself to his full height, turned the handle, and pulled the gate open.

The reaction from the waiting crowd was immediate. Voices hushed, then bodies surged toward him in true paparazzi-huddle style, cameras hiding faces in an ever-present irony. These people always wanted to expose others while remaining hidden themselves.

Quentin stepped up onto the pavement and drew the gate almost closed at his back, leaving it ajar but blocking it with his body. He swept his gaze around to assess the situation.

The house was situated perhaps fifty yards from a bend in the Camino de la Costa to his left, almost at the top of the hill, which continued down to his right. The curb along this side of the street was painted red, which Laurence had informed him meant that parking was not allowed there — or, in fact, stopping of any kind — but the curb opposite was not, and that was where a sudden glut of vehicles had accumulated, stretching from the top of the hill to the bottom, so far as he could see.

It was not unusual for neighbors or visitors to park there for short periods of time, but most of these vehicles were dusty or battered, and their engines rumbled. There were what Laurence would call trucks — enormous things with flat-bed rear ends for hauling heavy weights around — as well as what Quentin considered to be vans, though Laurence seemed to call those trucks too. Some even had dishes or aerials sprouting along their rooftops. Their headlights pierced the night and lit the area up like a football pitch.

Surrounding him were easily ten people, though it was difficult to count them at speed, since they were jostling each other in their attempts to get the best position. Only two held mobile phones. The others used what he considered to be proper cameras, with bulky bodies and even bulkier lenses. One even had a film camera with built-in boom resting on his shoulder.

Quentin maintained a placid exterior while he waited for them to stop pushing each other around, but after thirty seconds it was clear that he would likely wait all night, so he barked out, "What is the meaning of this?"

A glut of them answered at once, so he raised his hands.

"No. Let's try again." He selected one and pointed directly at him. "You. Explain yourself."

"Mr. d'Arcy!" another one yelled. "Mr. d'Arcy, is it true that—"

"Hey, hey, it's Quentin, right? Quentin, did you—"

"What are you hiding behind that—"

Quentin pointedly ignored them all, and gazed directly at the one he'd singled out.

"The hauntings," the target of his stare managed to blurt out.

Quentin inclined his head, then placed his palm against the gate, turning side-on toward the mob. "You have five minutes to clear off before I call the police," he said, raising his voice to be heard above the din, but stopping short of a shout. "That's assuming the neighbors haven't already, what with the racket you're making. It's late. People are trying to sleep." He pushed the gate open, but stepped away from it.

As he anticipated, the group stuck with him. Wherever Kimberly was, he hoped he'd cleared enough space for her to retreat without being noticed.

"Allow me to reiterate," he said, lowering his voice. If they hoped to catch a scoop, they'd have to shut up and let him speak. "Five minutes." Then he pulled his phone out and idly glanced to the screen. "Let's call it four. Off you pop." He looked up to them, then quirked an eyebrow. "Shoo."

"This is just the beginning," one of them called out from the back of the crowd. "You can't stop all of us forever, Mr. d'Arcy! Sooner or later we'll find the truth, and then the world will know!"

He checked his phone again. He had to hope he'd given Kimberly enough time to make her escape, and he turned his back on the mob, then stepped to the gate and through it. He even got it half-closed before a body thudded into it from the other side and knocked him back a few inches.

The gate flew open, and Quentin was debating whether to use more force when Laurence sped past him and rammed himself up against the gate to shut it. "Fuck off!"

Quentin's wrist throbbed, and he rotated it slowly, rubbing at it as he checked it for injury. He glanced around, down the steps toward the courtyard, where Kimberly stood with her eyes wide and her arms wrapped around herself.

"Are you okay, hon?" Laurence gasped.

"I think so, yes." Quentin lowered his arm, then eyed the gate. "But we should contact the police."

"Yeah. I'll do it. C'mon, let's get inside." Laurence stepped away from the gate as though it might give way without him there to prop it up, but the lock held against the forces clamoring beyond it.

Quentin headed down the steps and across the courtyard, ushering Kimberly quietly inside. He didn't wish to say anything out here that could be overheard, but that left time for his brain to churn over the threat that had been made.

You can't stop all of us forever.

He knew a declaration of war when he heard one.

QUENTIN

SORAYA AND ESTELITA WERE ALREADY DOWNSTAIRS BY THE TIME Quentin got back inside. Felipe was there, too, pacing in the living room, hands in his pockets. Clifton had made it out of bed, and looked confused as he sat on one of the couches. Pepper and Grace had managed to wake up enough to join the group, but had curled up by Clifton and fallen asleep again. Kimberly hurried over to Soraya and sat beside her.

"I didn't see anything," Mia announced as she hurried inside. "What's happening?"

"Hang on," Laurence said. "I'm gonna call the cops. I'll catch up." He squeezed Quentin's hand, then darted toward the stairs.

Quentin watched him go, then entered the living room and closed the door behind himself.

"All right," he said softly. "I think we have a problem."

"Why do they want you?" Soraya raised her chin like he'd done something to warrant this circus, and he couldn't blame her. It must seem to her as though he'd messed everything up yet again.

"They do?" Felipe blinked. "So what's the big meeting for? We can just go to bed, right?"

Quentin raised his hands to try and calm the teenagers. "A

paranormal investigator has made it his business to get involved in *my* business," he sighed. "After I threatened him with a restraining order, he released my details on the internet to other ghost hunters and the like, which is who we have outside the house at present."

Soraya released a low whistle. "He doxxed you?"

"I'm sorry," Quentin murmured. "I don't know what that means."

"It means he posted your name and address online," Mia explained. "Which, yeah, sounds exactly like what he did."

Quentin pursed his lips and lowered his hands. "Then, yes. He doxxed me, and now we are effectively under siege. Laurence is calling the police, but I doubt that what these people are doing is illegal in any way. They are simply..." he shrugged. "Parked."

Mia scowled and crossed her arms. "This is a big problem."

"Agreed." Quentin sighed. "Kimberly, I appreciate you taking the initiative, but I would prefer that you not place yourself at risk in the future. Are you all right?"

She bobbed her head quickly. "They didn't see me."

"No," he agreed. "Thank goodness. All right. More importantly, we need a plan for getting you all to and from school and other activities without encountering the mob."

"I can drive them," Mia offered. "At least to and from the bus stops?"

Quentin eyed the teenagers and considered how many of them could fit into the big black truck in the garage. He wasn't terribly satisfied with the answer.

"I can drive," Soraya piped up.

"Do you have a license?" Felipe asked.

"I mean, no, but—"

"Perhaps it is best if we avoid doing anything illegal for the time being," Quentin offered.

"Maybe we need to relocate Estelita until this blows over." Mia sighed. "She's under eighteen. If the cops get involved and find out we're not her legal guardians, all hell could break loose."

Estelita sat forward, her eyes widening. "I don't want to go anywhere else!"

Quentin nodded. He understood completely. All the children in this room had chosen to remain in the house after Kane's death, even though they had been freed from his control. Quentin had never asked for their reasons, though he suspected that Soraya simply didn't have a home to return to, but they had wanted to stay and he had assured them that they could. To be faced with having to move away from her friends and adoptive family just because of Delaney's actions had to be terrifying.

"We'll think of something," he assured her. "But for now I would strongly suggest that nobody leaves the house on foot, and absolutely nobody uses their gifts outside the property. It's me they appear to be interested in, but if they catch a whiff of anything unusual, I don't doubt that they will happily transfer that interest to you. I'll speak to Sebastian tomorrow and see if he has better security suggestions, but I think we'll have to work on that basis for now. Agreed?"

The teenagers all nodded and muttered affirmatives.

"All right. Get some sleep. If you need to get to school or work tomorrow, perhaps Laurence and Mia can drop you off wherever you need to be, and then we can work out the rest later in the day. Try not to worry. Sleep well."

"Okay."

"All right."

"G'night."

"Good night." Quentin opened the door and watched them file out, then looked worriedly to Mia.

Mia pursed her lips. "Are you okay?"

"Somewhat taken aback," he admitted. "I shall have to contact Myriam and let her know that it's not safe for Lisa here right now."

Mia dipped her head. "Agreed. You know you can't walk the dogs with them waiting for you out there?"

Quentin grimaced and glanced to the girls, fast asleep still. "It would not be ideal, no," he sighed. "But Laurence has to work, and I cannot ask you to do it. That isn't fair on you."

"Then you need a plan." She looked at Laurence as he came into the room. "Have they gone?"

"No." Laurence shook his head and came over to slide his arm around Quentin's waist. "Cops say they'll send a patrol car, but the only way anything becomes enforceable is if they park more than three days, or if Quentin gets restraining orders."

"And all the while the numbers grow." Quentin sighed and leaned against Laurence. "All right, well. I'll contact Sebastian in the morning and seek his advice. I'll see if Neil has anything to offer on the subject, too."

Mia nodded. "And hire a maid," she added with a wag of her finger.

"Top of the list," he assured her.

"Okay," Laurence said as they finally got into bed. "What if Mia drops the kids at the bus stop tomorrow morning, then we figure it out from there?"

Quentin sighed as he eased his legs beneath the sheets. He eyed the windows, whose soft green glow was visible even around the closed curtains. "It is not ideal," he said.

Nothing about any of this was ideal, though, and he was left wondering how much of it was on his shoulders.

No. He couldn't go down that road. He had once asked Laurence whose fault it would be if Quentin were to hit him, and Laurence had suggested that he could be the one to blame, depending on what he had said to deserve such a thing. Now Quentin was attempting to accept responsibility for the actions of others.

Quentin had lost control of his gift before he was even aware that he had it, and that was not his fault. He had been accosted in the street by a young man who used that against him, and he had defended himself without revealing further proof of said gifts, to the full extent available to him within the law. Delaney's subsequent attack — and its results — were not justified. They were not reasonable. And they certainly were not Quentin's fault.

Those actions were Delaney's. The self-styled paranormal investigator had chosen to doxx him, as Soraya had put it, and from the reactions in the room this was considered bad form. Perhaps Delaney even believed that he was doing the right thing, although from the way Basil had described Delaney's internet diatribe, Quentin suspected it was more down to bitterness and anger at being rebuked than any real desire to get to the truth of the alleged haunting.

"What are you going to do about the girls?" Laurence sighed as he slipped his arm across Quentin's waist.

"I'll walk them as usual," Quentin decided. He eased his arm around Laurence's and turned to face him in the dark. "I'm not about to allow these people to dictate how I spend my time. I have things to do, and I intend to continue doing them."

Laurence's chuckle was low, throaty, and he leaned in to kiss Quentin. "Good idea, my lord. Give them so much stiff upper lip they don't know what to do with it."

Quentin blinked, then laughed. "I thought you weren't ever going to call me that," he teased.

He felt Laurence's shrug, the movement of it against the sheets and his arm. "I don't know. It's kinda growing on me." Then he leaned closer, until his breath warmed Quentin's ear, and whispered, "My lord."

That put paid to them getting to sleep any time soon.

LEAVING the house the next morning was something of a farce. Quentin led the girls out through the gate and drew it closed behind himself, and some vehicles almost immediately disgorged disheveled men, but the others remained silent.

Most of these birds apparently could not rise early enough to catch the worm, and Quentin kept his eye-roll to himself lest the few who were awake record it for posterity.

He pressed against the gate to ensure that it had locked behind him, then turned left and made his way toward the little sea-view lookout spot which was just on the other side of the bend in the road. As predicted, the dawn chorus of shouting broke out almost immediately.

"Mr. d'Arcy, I'll give you a hundred bucks for an exclusive interview!"

"Two hundred!"

"Where are you going?"

Quentin adjusted the strap of the courier bag slung across his chest, then picked up the pace. He wouldn't jog until they reached the beach, and he preferred not to use the crumbling concrete steps by the lookout spot, as not only were they in an advanced state of disrepair, with cracks in the stairs and a handrail that was more rust than metal, but they also led down to smooth boulders and rock pools from which it was difficult for Grace to descend to the beach. He preferred to stick with the Camino de la Costa all the way down to Neptune Place, where he could head down steps that were in considerably better condition and run the girls along Windansea Beach. When the tide was out, there was enough exposed sand to lead Grace around all the rock formations, though he made sure to give any seals or sea lions a wide berth, particularly as they had pups at this time of year.

Adorable, playful pups.

There were footsteps behind him. Less shouting, but presumably they were conserving breath while they trotted along. He didn't turn to look. That would give them the attention they craved, and he had no interest in feeding the beast.

It was of abstract interest to him that there were, thus far, no women among the crowd. They all appeared to be men, and each and every one of them was white. Quentin wondered whether the rest of the world had better things to do with their time, but it did strike him as peculiar that in a city with a population that seemed almost as diverse as that of London or New York, harassing people about ghosts seemed to be a thing that only white men did. Perhaps he could talk to Basil about it later, to see if there were some cultural factor at play that he was unaware of.

"Your dogs are beautiful," a voice gasped from just behind him. There was a burst of activity, and one man twice his age caught up, jogging onto the road to get alongside him. "What're their names?"

Quentin spared him a glance, if only to ensure that he wasn't about to do anything foolish. His natural inclination was to answer the question, and the words were even halfway to his lips before he cut himself off and looked straight ahead once more.

Bloody hell, this was trickier than it looked.

He plowed ahead, disregarding all other attempts to snare his attention or prompt an outburst, and by the time he reached the beach and broke into a jog, he had lost the very last of them, which meant that he had at least a couple of hours' peace and quiet ahead of him.

Alas, it also ensured that he would have a full complement of investigators awaiting his return, but he would have to cross that bridge when he arrived at it.

He would take his small victories wherever he could find them.

13

QUENTIN

HE RAN ALL THE WAY ALONG THE COAST, FROM WINDANSEA Beach up and around La Jolla Cove, until he reached Scripps Beach. By the time he made it to the pier, the girls were flagging somewhat, and so he stopped in the shade of the pier and dug their pop-up bowl and water bottle from his bag, and he took his time to dig the bowl into the sand a little so that it wouldn't tip over when he filled it.

Quentin stretched gently while the dogs drank their fill, and looked out toward the water. The parallel lines of the wooden support struts made the sea look as though it had been framed, and for a while it felt as though there were no one here but himself and the girls, and the rest of the world had fallen away into the soft sloshing of the waves.

He refilled the bowl once it was empty, then dug out his own water and drank some. The day was already warm, but not uncomfortably so, and he had no desire to drag his own personal cold spot around while he was being tailed by people without anything better to do with their time, who were looking for the slightest excuse to declare him haunted. He could keep cool the old-fashioned way.

As the girls began to putter around and play in the low tide, he tucked everything back into his bag, then retrieved his phone. It was almost exactly eight o'clock, which seemed a much more reasonable time of day to call people. He thumbed through his limited phone book until he found Sebastian, right at the end of the list, then tapped it as he watched the girls to ensure that they weren't going too far out or likely to encounter any protective sea lions.

"Quentin?" Sebastian sounded like he had a mouthful of food when he picked up. "What's up?"

"I'm sorry to trouble you over breakfast." Quentin gestured for Pepper to come closer. "I wondered whether you had a moment?"

"Wouldn't have answered the phone if I didn't," Sebastian said. Then his voice cleared, and he added, "What do you need?"

"A spot of advice, I'm afraid." He crouched down to fish Pepper's leash out of the water, then snared Grace's when it came near enough, and shook them both to dislodge a little seaweed. "I've been doxxed, and now there are a slew of paranormal investigators on my doorstep. The police won't clear them."

"Right, because they're not breaking any laws yet." Sebastian hummed briefly. "You need a bodyguard, and I'm not available. I have a contract this week. Let me make a few calls, see if I can put you in touch with someone who's free today. Are you okay with me passing your number on so they can contact you directly?"

Quentin crinkled his nose faintly, then sighed. One way or another, they would have his phone number in the end, so he gave in. "Of course."

"Okay. Are you safe right now, or are you out with the dogs?"

"The latter," he admitted.

"Not a problem," Sebastian assured him. "They're still at the house? Or did any of them follow you?"

Quentin glanced along the beach in the direction he'd come, but there were only joggers and other dog-walkers, as well as the occasional morning swimmer. "Not this far," he said.

"Okay. And you've got..." Sebastian paused briefly, "an hour before you have to be off the beaches. Okay. Stay away from the house; I'll find you someone and get them to call you as soon as they can. With any luck, they can come meet you and escort you back home, okay?"

Quentin sighed with relief. "That sounds ideal. Thank you so much."

"No problem. And when I get off work tonight, I'll come over and you can tell me what the hell is going on. Be careful. Whoever I can find won't know a damn thing about your gifts, so you can't flash them around."

"I can't anyway," Quentin murmured.

"True. Okay. I'll see you tonight."

"Thank you again."

He hung up and slipped his phone away, then began the jog back the way he had come. From Windansea Beach he could potentially make his way to a dog-friendly cafe, with Siri's assistance.

No wonder Laurence had once been so confused that Quentin didn't have a phone. The bloody thing was indispensable.

———

HE WAS JUST APPROACHING La Jolla cove when his phone rang, so he slowed to a stroll before he answered.

"Quentin d'Arcy?"

The voice was brusque, American, and sounded like a woman.

"May I ask who is calling?" he said.

"Carolina Vargas. Sebastian Wagner gave me your number."

Quentin exhaled softly. "Then, yes. Thank you for contacting me so quickly."

"No problem. Are you in any immediate danger?"

"No." He scouted around himself just to be sure. "And I don't believe that I am in danger, per se."

"Better safe than sorry." But her tone relaxed as she spoke. "I understand you're in La Jolla?"

"That's correct."

"Okay. I can meet you in thirty minutes. Where will you be?"

He considered. Thirty minutes would give him time to complete his run. "At the corner of Neptune Place and Palomar Avenue, at the southern end of Windansea Beach."

"Perfect. I'll pick you up there. I'll be in a black Lincoln Navigator."

Quentin blinked. "I'm afraid I have no idea what that is."

"No problem. I'll send you a message with a photo and the license plate. Text me back when you get it to confirm receipt, okay?"

"I will."

"Great. Don't get in any vehicle that doesn't match that license plate, and wait until I show you my ID."

He nodded to himself. "Understood. Thank you, Miss Vargas."

"You're welcome. See you in thirty."

She hung up, and Quentin waited for the message, then replied to it as agreed.

Now all he had to do was get there on time.

***

THERE WAS a bench right at the corner where Palomar Avenue made a ninety degree turn to become Neptune Place, and Quentin sat with the girls as he waited for Vargas. Here, Windansea Beach stretched out in front of him from his left, and Neptune Place ran alongside it from his right. A white wooden fence protected pedestrians from falling down the small but steep embankment from the narrow pavement on his side of the street.

This was, he noted, a tactically decent position. He had a low wall at his back, he could see up the gentle hill of Palomar Avenue to his right even with only his peripheral vision, and the steps that descended to the beach were right in front of him.

He clicked his tongue. Ever since Mia had put Musashi's *Book of Five Rings* on his phone, he had read and re-read it so often that he had lost count, and something Musashi wrote had stuck with him.

He was always at war.

Quentin sighed faintly and leaned back against the bench. Even here, he had assessed his surroundings. It had come naturally. He hadn't intended it.

He'd claimed the mantle of Warrior, and now he couldn't shake it. He didn't want to. Not that he was itching to fight anyone or anything. The opposite, in fact. And if by paying attention to his surroundings he was more able to avoid a conflict, so much the better.

He heard the vehicle before he saw it, and turned toward the rasp of tires against asphalt. It crested the hill of Palomar Avenue and came toward him at a sedate pace, looking very much like the photograph Vargas had sent him, although he didn't think the picture had done the size of the vehicle any justice. Apparently a Lincoln Navigator was a glossy black tank of a car. It looked like it could plough through any of the houses around here without sustaining a bloody scratch, and when it stopped around fifty feet away, he remained seated while he double-checked the license plate against the number that Vargas had texted him.

They were a match.

Quentin stood and urged the girls to their feet, then crossed the street and made his way up the hill toward Vargas, crossing again at Vista Del Mar Avenue. As he approached the car, the darkened passenger side window wound down, and the driver leaned across with her driver's license held where he could see it.

He read it, then looked at Vargas. Everything matched, from her short-cropped dark brown hair to her pixie-like rounded face. She looked even more tiny when compared to the size of the car she was inside.

"Quentin d'Arcy?" she said with a bright smile, and the voice matched that of his phone call.

"It's a pleasure to meet you, Miss Vargas."

"Oh, you say that now." She hopped out of her side of the car and strode quickly to the rear to open the boot. "Dogs in here, please."

He walked along the pavement to meet her, and eyed the inside of the vehicle, but this was bigger even than a Range Rover. There was more than enough space for the dogs in the back, so he patted the floor of the boot and urged Pepper inside, then lifted Grace to sit beside her. It wasn't terribly easy without the aid of his gift, but she was perhaps eighteen kilograms at most. He could manage for a few seconds.

Still, he huffed when he set her down, and began patting fur from his clothes as Vargas shut the boot. "Thank you."

"You're welcome. Have you worked with personal security before?"

Quentin inclined his head. "Do as you say, waste no time, ask no questions?"

She smiled faintly. "Those are the basics. Good. I'd like you in the back, please. The window tints are stronger there."

Quentin inclined his head and did as she asked, slipping into the seat behind her so that her body would obscure him from any direct onlookers in front of the car. Not that there was a great deal of body for her to use. He had at least six inches on her, and she even managed to be about as narrow as he was. He suspected that she was ten times as formidable as Sebastian to make up for the lack of body mass.

"All right." Vargas started the car and eased it away from

the curb, turning down the Camino de la Costa. "Wagner gave me your address. I assume we're going there first?"

"If you would be so kind?"

"Sure thing. You can brief me fully once we're there. Until then, tell me what's waiting for us outside."

Quentin leaned back and glanced out of the windows as they trundled slowly along. "A variety of vehicles parked along the street," he murmured. "Most only seem to have one person in them, but I think two or three came in pairs. They are, effectively, untrained paparazzi. Not that I am certain paparazzi undergo any training, exactly." He met her eyes briefly in the rearview mirror. "I didn't notice any weapons. Most are armed with cameras and a lack of respect for privacy or personal space. They are more of a nuisance than a threat."

"Got it," Vargas said. "So for the most part the job is to get you in and out of the property without any unnecessary encounters?"

"Essentially, yes."

"Great. You got a garage, or are we parking out with the mob?"

"We have a garage." He pulled his phone out. "Let me get it opened for us." He tapped out a message for Mia and sent it.

"You don't have a remote for it?"

"No. I don't drive."

Her head bobbed briefly. "No problem. We'll get that arranged as a priority."

They rounded the bend where the viewpoint overlooked the sea, and the parked cars, trucks, and RVs stretched all the way down the hill in front of them.

"Is it usually like this?" Vargas commented.

"No." Quentin shook his head as his eyes widened. "No, and in fact this is worse than when I left the house this morning."

Vargas tutted faintly. "White garage doors?"

"Correct."

She skewed the car toward them and waited, and the

moment one of the doors opened enough for her to get the tank-like car inside, she tapped the pedal. "Wait until the door's down," she instructed.

Then she leaped out of the car and walked around it to stop anyone sneaking inside the garage before the door had closed.

Quentin sat and waited, reaching over the back seat to pet the dogs and watching through the dark rear window until the last sliver of light from the outside world had cut out.

How long would he have to do this? Enter and leave the house like smuggled cargo while other people kept the mob at bay? How soon before they began to give up and go home?

There was nothing for it but to be patient. It was the doing as he was told part that would chafe.

14

LAURENCE

"So these guys just, what, camped outside your house last night and haven't gone yet?" Ethan put his fists on his hips and scowled.

Laurence knew the scowl wasn't directed at him, but at the ghost hunters they were discussing. "Yeah that's about it."

"What will you do?" Myriam finished washing her hands, and patted them dry on her apron as she turned away from the sink to face him.

Laurence sighed and waved his hands in the air, and Windsor hopped back from the gesture. "I don't know. Quentin's calling Sebastian today, so maybe he'll have ideas. Otherwise we'd have to find out who they are, get restraining orders, all that crap, and that's a whole lot of time, money, and effort we shouldn't have to spend in the first place."

"Yeah," Ethan agreed. "How even is this Delaney asshole allowed to ruin your lives like this?"

"He'll reap what he sows in the end," Myriam murmured. "Threefold."

"Shit," Windsor chimed in. He seemed to agree that Delaney should be drowned in a mountain of it.

Laurence sighed. The threefold law usually did pan out,

but in the meantime he had a house full of people who were going to suffer while they waited for it to happen.

An idea struck, and he sat up slowly, tilting his head while he tried to work out how he felt about it.

Myriam narrowed her eyes. "What is it?"

Laurence idly scratched at his stubble, then ran fingers through his hair, tugging a little at it, as though that could persuade him that he should stop thinking down the path he'd set out on.

"Uh oh," Ethan muttered.

"No, hear me out." Laurence licked his lips. His hand remained clutching his curls. "Frederick could make this all go away."

Ethan and Myriam immediately made a variety of noises that, when taken together, sounded a hundred percent disapproving. Only Windsor was on board with the idea, but he was a bird, and had a very loose grip on the whole ethics thing.

"Is that okay?" Ethan mused.

"Bambi, I don't know whether that's reasonable," Myriam agreed.

Laurence shrugged at them. "Hey, he can mold thoughts like putty. He can make them all go away and never come back."

"And what then?" Myriam settled down on a stool across the bench and laid her hands on the wooden surface. "What happens to all the other people on these websites who realize that everyone who came to investigate Cameron Delaney's information has either gone silent or is suddenly denying everything? Do you think Quentin's brother has the time to spend constantly sitting on this until it eventually dies down?"

"He says he'll do anything to protect Quen," Laurence argued.

"Then ask him." Ethan shrugged. "Give him a call, get his opinion. But let me put it this way, Laur. If you were onto something big, and some asshole came over and wiped your memories and sent you on your way, wouldn't you be pissed about that?"

Laurence lowered his hand and chewed on his lip instead.

Fuck it. Ethan and Mom, they were both right. Laurence had endured Freddy rampaging through his head more than enough. Could he inflict that on other people, just for being a mild nuisance?

He sighed and sprawled across the bench, arms spread wide. "Fine," he groaned. "You're right."

That didn't mean he had to like it.

Rodger breezed in through the curtain, and thumbed toward it over his shoulder. "Customer," he said.

Myriam sighed and stood, eyeing Rodger as though she might be able to get him to actually do some work; but it washed off him like he was Teflon-coated, and she strode out through the curtain.

Rodger shrugged, then looked between Laurence and Ethan. "So," he said. "Crazy stalkers, huh?"

Laurence exchanged a wary glance with Ethan, then sat up straight. "Were you eavesdropping?"

"Yep. I'm pretty sure you forget I even work here, you know." Rodger sat down on Myriam's recently-vacated stool.

"I mean, it's not like you do any actual work," Ethan snorted.

Rodger shrugged. "You're welcome to do my deliveries one day and see how that works out for you." He tapped the bench with his fingertip. "I was here for the party last year. I cleared this place out for you after you had a fucking hurricane inside. I washed up all of Banbury's blood for you. I took a chainsaw to a tree that appeared overnight and looked a hell of a lot like your ex boyfriend. I'm the delivery boy, not the black ops cleaning crew, and I think it's about time we talked about all of this, because I'm not stupid. I can see all the weird shit that goes on around here."

Laurence's jaw worked briefly, and he blinked.

Ethan burst out laughing and patted Rodger's shoulder. "You're gonna regret this."

"Maybe." Rodger shrugged. "But not as much as I'd regret keeping my mouth shut any longer. I'm here, Laurence. Tag me in."

"Sure." Laurence glanced to Ethan, then to Rodger again. "Let's start with what you know, and take it from there."

Rodger nodded to him. "Seems fair. Okay. I know you and Banbury are, like, mutants or whatever. I know this bird—" he nodded to Windsor "—isn't normal. I know you keep disappearing to have adventures and stuff and we all get to cover the workload when you're gone, or injured, or not even in the country."

Laurence puffed out his cheeks and reached for Windsor, who hopped onto his arm and then all the way up to his shoulder to preen himself. The bird didn't seem to have realized that *not normal* wasn't usually a compliment.

"I mean, that pretty much covers all of it, right?" Ethan shrugged. "Welcome to the team, I guess?"

"Maria doesn't know anything," Rodger added. "She comes and goes, she's not in the store enough to hear you being subtle as a brick back here. So, what's the deal with all these people creeping on your house?"

Windsor clacked his beak, and Laurence clicked his tongue in response.

Is bad?

Don't know.

"Fine," Laurence finally murmured. "Because of all that stuff — things like the party blowing up — a paranormal investigator is on Quentin's tail, and since Quentin told him to get lost or face a lawsuit, that investigator has gone online and given all his collected evidence to every other ghost hunter out there, and now a bunch of them are camped out on my doorstep trying to interview Quentin about it."

Rodger nodded to himself. "What you need is a guy on the inside."

"I've got one. He's on all these forums and groups and whatever else."

"But is he here in San Diego?"

Laurence had to shake his head. "No, he's the other side of the country."

"So he can only tell you whatever these losers choose to report back online. But scuttlebutt goes way faster in person." Rodger tapped the side of his nose. "Okay, I'll do it."

Ethan leaned his hip against the bench and crossed his arms. "Do what? Are you seriously suggesting you go infiltrate these guys and report back on their gossip?"

"That's totally what I'm suggesting, yeah." Rodger began to unhook his apron over his head. "You have no idea what they know other than what's online. I'm going in. I don't have crazy superpowers, I'm perfect for the job."

"Dude, you can't just—" Ethan began.

Laurence raised a hand slowly. "Wait." He dropped it and watched Rodger take his apron off and hang it by the door, and mulled it over.

Was it such a bad idea? These investigators weren't dangerous. Not in the conventional sense. They hadn't shown any signs of wanting to hurt anyone; they just didn't seem to know what dangers they could pose if they did happen to get the scoop they were all chasing. It was noble enough to want to find the truth and share it with others, but Laurence knew damn well that some people just hated what they didn't understand and would happily go all vigilante action about it.

And this was way less invasive than asking Freddy to mess with people's thoughts.

"Okay," he said. "You're on. But be careful, okay? And if you get into any trouble, get out of there. Your own safety is your number one priority, got it?"

Rodger snorted at him. "You bet your ass it is."

Laurence watched him slip out the back door, then gazed up at Ethan. "What just happened?"

Ethan shrugged. "You got owned is what happened. He

could've walked and found another job after the party, but he stuck around, and it turns out he's been paying attention, too."

"Sneaky asshole." Laurence petted Windsor's head. "Gotta admire that."

"What I'd admire more," said Myriam as she came in through the curtain, "is if you'd discussed whether or not I'm paying him for this side project. Who's going to do his deliveries?"

"I'm on it, Mrs. R," Ethan grinned. He grabbed the keys to Rodger's truck. "Let's get loaded up!"

Laurence stood and let Windsor down onto the bench, then headed to the stairs, since Rodger's deliveries today were all potted plants. "I'll go get everything."

It wasn't how he'd expected to spend his morning, and now he would have to stay in the shop to cover for Ethan instead of slip away to go speak to Rufus — and that just reinforced how much Rodger had been covering for him all these months.

He sighed and jogged up to the roof to start collecting the plants from the greenhouse.

LAURENCE FIGURED that if he worked through his lunch, he could stop off to visit Rufus on his way home that evening, so he'd texted Quentin to let him know, then knuckled down to get as many arrangements done as he could without screwing any of them up.

He checked through his list and made sure he'd only marked off the completed ones, then checked he had what he needed to hand for the next batch, and got to work while Windsor stood on the windowsill and eyed the alleyway.

When his cell rang, he was so deep in the zone that he almost jumped out of his skin. He checked it, then put it on speaker. "Hey, Basil. What's up?"

"Laurence. How's it going?" Basil's light voice was tense, despite his attempt to sound cheerful.

"You want to spit it out?" Laurence snipped a couple of stems and placed them.

"Wow. Okay." Basil cleared his throat. "There are still a few people on their way to La Jolla, but I think you've got almost as many as you're gonna get for now. They're all in that early excitement stage, but if you keep clean it'll wear off after a few days."

Laurence nodded thoughtfully as he kept working. "Say, a week?"

"That should do it for the less persistent ones," Basil agreed.

Laurence smirked to himself. "But?"

"Buuuuut," Basil echoed slowly, "you've got a couple of the persistent ones, too. The only thing that'll pull them away is news of a sighting somewhere else."

"Okay. And how do we make that happen?"

He heard Basil's voice hitch. "How do we... what?"

"I mean, if all it takes is some kind of ghost news to make them go away, it seems obvious; all we have to do is actually post the ghost news and they'll go look into it, right?" Laurence finally glanced at the phone, even though Basil couldn't see him.

"It's not that easy."

"Never is," Laurence sighed.

Basil huffed. "It would have to come from a good source. Someone who has been around for a few years, part of the community. Someone who's known. You can't just make up a new user, join up, then start posting wild shit. It'll either get ignored, or be really obvious that it's you trying to pull attention away from Quentin."

"Or a rival ghost hunter trying to do it." Laurence went back to finalizing the arrangements on the bench, snipping rose stems with care so he didn't stick his fingers on the thorns.

"Not impossible. But still not going to draw them away."

"So you do it?" Laurence murmured.

"I can't. I don't interact enough. I'm mostly a lurker in these places." Basil huffed softly. "I'm sorry," he added. "If I could say anything to them that'd make them move, I would, but I'm literally a nobody to these people."

Laurence let out a breath slowly and leaned his elbows on the bench. "Yeah," he mused. "Yeah, that makes sense. I'm sorry, Basil. I shouldn't have asked."

"Asking is never a problem," Basil insisted. "I wish I *could* get them to leave you alone. Honestly, though, half these guys don't even have their own channel, blog, or any other kind of platform. They're just lookie-loos who were in the area and thought they'd see if they could find anything. They're not the dedicated ones, and they're the most likely to have jobs and families to get back to. I suggest we leave it a few days, then see who's still there, and I can start digging up names for you if you want to take legal action?"

"Oh, man." Laurence put his pruning shears down and sat. He'd only met Basil in New York, but they'd gone to Otherworld together in search of Quentin, and had wound up working side by side to defeat Gwyn ap Nudd. In all of that, what Laurence had seen of Basil was a small but plucky femme Necromancer.

What he'd forgotten was that Basil was also a journalist.

"That would be great," he said, reaching for the phone. He picked it up and took it off speaker as he held it to his ear. "And it sounds like a plan," he added, "which is a hundred percent more than what I've got right now."

"Perfect!" Basil almost squeaked. "Okay. I'll call you if anything else crops up, and you call me if things get worse. We'll fix it, Laurence. Teamwork!"

"Yeah. Teamwork," Laurence agreed. "Thanks. I owe you."

"I'll open a tab!"

Laurence laughed as they said their goodbyes, then hung

up and put his phone down, twirling it around in circles on the bench.

He felt like a weight was lifting from his shoulders. A few days, and the worst of this would be over. Then, if there were any vultures left, Basil could get names, and Quentin could seek restraining orders. Laurence might get back to his life as early as next week without too much trouble. All he had to do in the meantime was ignore the mob and make sure Quentin was okay.

Which meant he could focus on his previous problem. Did he want to get in touch with Angela Tate and continue to pretend he didn't know anything about magic so that he could find out who she was working for, or did he want to let it go?

For now, all he could do was finish getting these arrangements ready for Maria to take out first thing in the morning, so he put his phone away, picked up the shears, and got back to work.

Angela would have to wait.

15

QUENTIN

Once he and Vargas were safely inside, Quentin had enlisted Mia's assistance in briefing the bodyguard, since Mia was not only one herself, she also knew the ebb and flow of the mansion and could couch it in professional terms that Quentin could only deduce through context.

Vargas also discussed her rates, and how invoices could be paid, and then suggested she stay until Sebastian came over so that she could get his input too.

Quentin outlined the children's schedules, and once all the teens were home and had met Vargas, they worked out a more balanced method for getting each of them where they needed to go in the mornings and then back home again once school or work was finished. All things considered, he was rather pleased that he needn't have troubled Neil with questions after all.

Laurence didn't make it home until well after Sebastian and Carolina had gone, barely in time for bed, but when he did arrive he mentioned speaking with Basil, and Basil's hopes that this would all blow over within a week or so.

By the time his head hit the pillow, Quentin felt considerably better about the whole affair.

THE NEW ROUTINE was surprisingly easy to settle into. It meant that Quentin had to walk the dogs later than he would usually so that Carolina could take some of the children to their bus stops. Because the beaches didn't allow dogs to run free after 9AM, she drove him down to Balboa Park.

Carolina had found a couple of acres that were fully enclosed and complete with water fountains for the dogs to drink from, so they arrived at about half past nine and then ran with the girls for a couple of hours before they headed back to the house. Once they were home, Carolina could pop out again to collect teens from wherever they needed to be picked up, and then she was on hand for the remainder of the day should anyone wish to leave again. It was almost as good as having a chauffeur on hand, except that a chauffeur wouldn't expect Quentin to dive to the ground if he was told to.

It wouldn't come to that, hopefully. Now and then one of the vehicles attempted to follow them to Balboa Park, but Carolina was a skilled driver, expert at using trucks and lorries to hide her vehicle and dart down exit ramps before their tail could realize where they'd gone. After the weekend, at least half of the waiting cars disappeared overnight, gone by Monday morning as though they had never been there at all. The others shuffled up and down the street, presumably in an attempt to avoid breaking any parking laws.

Dr. Núñez had sent him a message with the address for this week's appointment, which he had almost forgotten about in all the fuss over the ghost hunters. It wasn't until he spoke to Carolina about it that he found out where it was.

Carolina crinkled her nose. "You want to go *where?*"

"2245 Hotel Circle South?" he repeated, confused by her response. "Is that bad?"

"I mean, it's all in the name. Hotels." She pulled out her

phone to tap at, then raised an eyebrow. "Except that address, 'cause it's a storage unit."

"Oh!" Quentin smiled slowly. "That's rather…"

He tailed off. If he admitted that Núñez's choice of venue was ingenious, he would need to explain why. Within an enclosed unit, there would be nothing for Quentin to damage, and no windows for him to break. No wonder Núñez had wanted to know whether he could sit on the floor without any difficulty.

"Weird?" Carolina prompted.

"I was… not comfortable with her office," he explained, cutting out just enough of the truth without turning it into a lie. "Do we have time?"

"Plenty. Let's roll out."

He met Violeta in the storage building's reception, where he briefly introduced Carolina, and then Violeta handed him a cushion and carried her own as she led the way up to the top floor and unlocked a solid white door.

"What do you think?" she said as they stepped inside.

The room was smaller than those Quentin had sometimes hired when he moved from one city to the next, perhaps ten feet wide in either direction, and was lit by a single plastic lightbulb embedded in the ceiling. The worst he could do in here was plunge them into darkness.

"I think it's ideal," he breathed with relief.

"Perfect!" Violeta drew the door shut, then walked past him to drop her cushion onto the floor. She lowered herself to it, folding her legs to the side and checking that her skirt lay neatly.

Quentin set his own cushion down, then debated how exactly to sit. Was it acceptable to sit cross-legged with a lady present, or should he emulate her position?

Ultimately, he was supposed to be comfortable, and he

suspected he wouldn't be so if he sat with his legs to one side, so he sank down and crossed his legs as though he intended to meditate, and lightly rested his hands on his knees.

"Now," Violeta murmured. "How about you let me know what subjects you were avoiding?"

"Goodness." He winced. "That's direct."

Violeta nodded. "How was your week?"

He took a deep breath, ready to let the answer to that pour out of him, but then he just let the air go and slid forward until it was his elbows on his knees instead of his hands. "Taxing," he admitted. "I'm being hounded by people who believe that my handful of lapses in self-control are indicative of a haunting, and wish to catch further proof of ghosts on camera."

"Hence Ms. Vargas?"

"Indeed. She ensures that we are able to come and go without too much trouble."

"We?" Violeta tilted her head slightly.

"The children and I, since we cannot drive. Laurence is all right."

Violeta nodded again. "Tell me about the children."

Quentin knew that she was throwing him a lifeline, giving him a safe topic to discuss until he was more settled. They'd come back to the elephant in the room soon, and he could avoid it if he wished to, but to do so would be fruitless. He was paying for Violeta's help. The least he could do was let her provide it.

So he talked about the teens for a while. He explained how he had come to be their de facto guardian after Wilson's death, how some had returned to families while others chose to remain even though they were free to leave. By the time Violeta steered him back to her original question, he was far more ready to deal with it.

He pursed his lips and sat up straighter, folding his hands together in his lap and glancing past her to the wall. "I was—"

The word stuck in his throat.

He'd thought he was prepared, but it didn't come out. It stalled, and ice settled into the pit of his stomach at the thought of what he'd nearly done.

What he *had* to do.

"My—"

The word was nothing more than a light croak, and he closed his eyes so that he could focus on his breathing for a few seconds.

Violeta didn't interrupt.

Perhaps if he kept his eyes closed, this would be easier. He could pretend that he was talking to Laurence, or even to himself. It was like any other hurdle. If he built little steps, he could climb over and not notice the enormity of the task until it was completed. He absolutely, under any circumstance, was not a coward, and he knew deep down that he could do this. Laurence had already shown him that he could do this. And if he snuck up on it, he might be able to lay it all out before his brain could stop him.

"Magic is real," he said calmly. He would begin with the basics. "I was born without the capacity for it. My father chose to undertake a series of rituals over the course of—"

"*Thirteen years! Jesus Christ, Icky, aren't you the least bit angry?*"

Quentin drew another breath.

"Over the course of thirteen years," he breathed, "to bestow that capacity upon me."

"A magical ritual?" To her credit, there wasn't a trace of disbelief in Violeta's tone.

"Correct. He possessed magic, and I did not. And until recently I was… unaware of this. I recalled nothing of it."

There was silence in the room. He was glad for that. It allowed him to pretend that he was barely even here. In fact, if he were able to harness his brain's ability to detach itself from his body, perhaps it could be put to good use and allow his mouth to carry on this conversation without the need for him to be present in the slightest.

He doubted that it worked that way.

"This has been passed down," he finally breathed. "For generations. It seems we are all born without magic, and receive it on our eighteenth birthday. A gift from our fathers."

Quentin bit the words off as they turned savage on his tongue.

"Do you know when it began?" Violeta asked softly.

His eyes fluttered open in confusion. "Um."

"As I understand it, it takes magic to use this ritual."

He bobbed his head briefly. "Yes."

"Then at one point, someone must have been born with magic to have been able to pass it on."

Quentin worked his jaw slowly. He hadn't thought especially hard about all of this, but Violeta's deduction made sense. His family had bred for psychokinetic strength, and it would be lax to believe they hadn't also bred for magical power. Laurence's magic came through his father. It seemed to be hereditary.

Where had it broken down for the d'Arcy line?

Why?

"I don't know," he admitted.

"Do you know now what happens during this ritual?" she murmured.

"Yes." Quentin licked his lips and closed his eyes. His fingers held so tightly to each other that they ached.

He *would* do this.

"Torture," he said. It came out of him almost calmly now that the decision was made. He had that peculiar feeling once more, like he wasn't quite in his body, merely observing it from somewhere deep inside.

He'd disconnected somehow, and the odd thing was that the realization didn't even surprise or shock him. It simply existed, devoid of emotion.

"He beat me," his mouth continued. "Every birthday until I was eighteen. He beat me until I was bloody, sometimes until bones were broken, and once he finished beating me, he—"

No.

The wind whipped at his hair. It tore around them even though he felt nothing, and he sat still.

If he sat still, it would go away.

"Quentin."

He didn't have to answer. Even once the light went out, once the winds had taken over, he didn't have to say a word.

But the voice didn't go away.

"Quentin," it said again. No fear. No alarm. Just soft, calm, and feminine. "Can you hear me?"

It was okay. He was safe. The voice would leave in the end.

"Quentin, this is Dr. Violeta Núñez. We're in San Diego. You and I are sitting in a storage unit on the Hotel Circle. Your bodyguard, Ms. Vargas, is downstairs in reception. Does she know that you are psychokinetic?"

No.

Were his lips moving? He didn't know, but Carolina couldn't know about this.

"Does Ms. Vargas know that you are psychokinetic, Quentin?" Violeta repeated.

He sucked in a deep breath. "No," he croaked.

Oh god.

He was back in his body, inhabiting every inch of it, aware of every point of contact between himself and his clothes, the floor, his fingers, all of it. His hands were sweating and clasped too tightly together. The wind was whistling around them in fury.

"I can…" Quentin forced his hands apart and clutched his knees instead. "One moment."

In. Two. Three. Four.

Out. Two. Three. Four.

He took control. It was what he had been bred for, and trained his whole life to accomplish. The lapse was inexcusable.

The wind sputtered out of existence.

When he opened his eyes, the room was still pitch black.

He'd evidently broken the only light they'd had, and the door fit so well in the frame that none crept in from outside, either.

"Quentin?" Violeta asked again, her voice still as steady and calm as it had been during his disconnect.

"I'm here," he breathed. "I apologize."

"It's okay. Although we do now get to pretend we're in a much bigger unit, I guess."

He blinked, then laughed weakly. "Would you like some light?"

"Would you?" she countered.

He mulled it over, then shook his head. "Not especially."

"Then let's not worry about it. Can you describe to me how that felt, just now? What you were thinking?"

Quentin absently wiped the sweat from his palms, then hung his hands forward over his knees, resting on his elbows once more. "Nothing," he admitted. "I do this. I suppose it is how I... survived. Protected myself. I don't know. Laurence calls it shutting down; he says I go to my 'happy place,' but truth be told there is no happiness there. There's simply... nothing at all. If I am pulled back from it, I seem to recall what set it off, but if I go all the way, then..." He sighed. "I forget."

"And so you forgot these rituals," Violeta surmised.

"That is correct."

"I think that next week I'd like to hear about how you uncovered those memories. If you like, you can think about how you'd like to speak to me about that. Or you can even write it down ahead of time, if you'd prefer. This is in your hands." She paused. "I'm hesitant to offer a diagnosis so soon, but it seems to me as though you enter a dissociative state. It's something our brains can do if we're overloaded with stress," she added. "You feel disconnected from yourself, and the world around you, and it generally lasts until the source of the stress has gone away. Does that sound accurate?"

Quentin blinked into the darkness. "Yes. That's... eerily accurate, yes."

"It's a natural occurrence," she said. "Your brain is trying to protect you by removing you from the stress, that's all. We can talk about it some more next week, and if everything fits together, we can start helping you come up with some coping strategies. Does that sound useful?"

"It does," he breathed. "That's possible? To get on top of this?"

"It isn't easy," she warned him. "But hopefully we can see some results. There's light at the end of the tunnel, Quentin. It just might take a while to reach it."

He let his head fall forward, and closed his eyes.

One more thing to master.

He'd do it. He couldn't doubt that. Of all the things he had achieved in his life, this might prove the most challenging yet, but he *would* do it.

Nothing could stand in his way.

16

LAURENCE

"How many spells can be imbued into an object?"

"One," Laurence answered.

"And how are they tethered?"

"Usually with sigils, but they might not be necessary if the spell is common enough."

"Is it possible to work out what an imbued spell is?" Rufus' questions were like a barrage, issued by someone who already knew the answers. Which, of course, he did.

"If it's tethered by sigils and you understand the sigils," Laurence said. "Or can look them up. But if there aren't any sigils, you're going to need to cast some kind of identification spell on it."

"Nice." Rufus leaned back in his chair and raised a leg to drape it across the tabletop. "Okay. There are a lot of basic protection spells that don't require sigils because they're so common, the universe knows them inside out. Personal defense, mostly. You've cast a couple of those already, you know how they go. Then there are the spells that aren't imbuing an item, but are being cast like a net over an area. Don't mistake anchors for tethers, though if it comes down to it, you can just fuck up the sigils to dissipate the spell if it's a problem."

Laurence nodded. "Got it." He straightened in his seat and petted Windsor, who was snuggled in his lap radiating pure smug satisfaction at being fussed over. "What'm I gonna imbue?"

Rufus chuckled. "Whatever you want. Your only real limit is how much shit you want to carry around with you wherever you go. Whatever item you pick needs to be at least tangentially related to the spell you choose to imbue into it, and an item can be a discrete unit or a thing made out of many parts, so long as those parts don't separate."

Laurence let go of Windsor to push his sleeve up his left arm enough to reveal his bracelet, and the softly glowing pentagrams knotted together with a strip of leather. "That's why protective spells need to be imbued into things that represent protection, right?"

"One hundred percent. And that means you first have to decide what spell you want to imbue, and then choose what to stick it to, and not the other way around. If you cram a fire spell onto a brick, it's not going to last, even if the sigils don't get damaged."

"Huh." That part made sense, but it was new to Laurence, so he made a mental note of it before he started wondering what kinds of spells he might want to attach to things.

The whole point of imbuing was either so that a spell was constantly running, or that it was immediately available without any need to stop and cast it. Depending on the complexity of the spell, it could save anywhere from a few seconds to several minutes, and Laurence liked the idea of having access to magic in an emergency. For a start, it meant that he wouldn't be fumbling through a book of shadows the way Basil had been forced to in Otherworld. All Laurence would have to do was pull out the right item and trigger it, and it would replace the whole casting process with a single word or a gesture.

That was the other advantage to an imbued spell. Laurence could choose the trigger, and that was all he needed to remember. Even if the item fell into someone else's hands, it wouldn't work for them. Unlike anchored spells, like the wards over the house and shop, tethered spells still required that connection to the caster's aura.

That was why Basil's ring had stopped glowing once he handed it to Laurence, and why Laurence's own amulet didn't work after Annis had cut it off him. But Laurence would be able to quick-cast, and the item was inert and useless to anyone else, even if they'd figured out the trigger.

He turned slightly in his chair and let his gaze roam over Ru's bookshelves.

There were a lot.

Rufus seemed to have an even bigger library than Quentin's dad, though a large percentage of Ru's books weren't spellbooks. There were books on lore, mythology, history, and theory. There were diaries and journals, too. Laurence couldn't begin to imagine how long it had taken to amass, or what spells it might contain.

He scritched at his jaw and mulled over something Basil had said in New York. "Got anything for controlling weather?"

"We're going full traditional witchcraft, huh?" Rufus grinned like his birthday had come early. "Do you think making some rain is going to be a thing you have to do urgently and often?"

"I don't know." Laurence lifted Windsor onto the desk so that he could stand, then he began to pace alongside the bookshelves, letting his gaze roam across spines and trinkets. "Literally no idea, Ru. You're asking me to pick a spell, but I don't even know what's possible, or what you have here that I might need. Have you ever considered making a directory? Some kind of index?"

"Why bother? It's all up here." Rufus tapped his temple with his index finger.

"You say that, but even you have to try to remember where you read something. If you had an index you could just look it up." Laurence paused and turned toward the windows with their slightly golden-tinged view out over the ocean, and he straightened himself up. "You know, when I first met you, I thought you'd turned your whole house into a sanctum, but you didn't, did you?"

Rufus lowered his leg so he could twist in his chair and look outside, then he snorted. "You noticed, huh?"

Laurence raised his chin. He supposed he'd kind of known it, but it hadn't been important enough to click together. Rufus' magic was turquoise, but the spell that took his house out of reality and tucked it away in another realm was golden. At first, Laurence had figured that was just color from the brass the spell was anchored to.

"How do you get water?" Laurence wondered out loud. "Light? Electricity? Air?"

"Magic," Rufus said.

"Ha fucking ha. I'm serious."

"When my parents took the house out of the physical world and shunted it into its own realm, they took a whole chunk of land with it." Rufus stood and turned to face the window too, pointing out toward the sea. "All the way to the boundaries of the property. But to take all that, they had to replace it with something. They had to install things in the physical world that stopped the pipes left behind from leaking, and so they put terminals on everything, then anchored spells to work as pass-throughs. Water from the pipes in the physical world is routed through to the corresponding pipes here, and the waste from here is routed back. The pipes in the real world think everything's working like it always did. Same with the electricity. The air is exchanged every time the gate opens. The light is an illusion passed through from the brass you cross over to get in here."

Laurence blinked slowly. "That's..." He took a breath.

That was way more complicated than the duke's sanctum, a single chamber with no air supply and whose only light came from candles. There was no water in there, no electricity. It was just a little room separated from reality by a single door.

But this?

This was a feat of magical engineering, and Rufus hid out in it every single day of his life.

"That's complex," he breathed. "Why'd they do it?"

Rufus shrugged. "I don't know. Maybe they already knew they were in danger. Or they just wanted to prove it could be done."

Laurence slid his hands into his pockets. "If you can't cross the brass ring without getting transported into the sanctum, how do you make sure the pipes and cables and whatever don't get tampered with before they reach you? How do you maintain them?"

"There's a way down below the ring that passes you into a room they dug out where all the pipes and cables are positioned. No, I'm not showing it to you." Rufus turned his back on the view and crossed his arms. "The only way to reach it is through the house. It's inaccessible from the physical world."

"Unless someone tunnels their way in."

Rufus snorted at him. "Why would they?"

"I don't know, man." Laurence turned toward the shelves again. "They seemed really paranoid, and in the end…"

In the end they'd been killed in an auto wreck, and Rufus had been the only survivor.

"I'm sorry," he added. "Just thinking out loud, that's all."

Rufus eyed him. "You want to make a sanctum," he concluded.

"Yeah." Laurence sighed and reached for a vial, twirling it between his fingers and watching the golden liquid inside slosh around. "We've got these ghost hunters camped outside the house right now, and we're having to treat going outside like it's a special ops maneuver or something. It's a military operation just getting to work in the morning."

"How long have they been there?"

"About a week?" Laurence put the vial back where it came from. "It's Quen they're after. They've got this idea that all his telekinetic meltdowns were actually the ghost of his mom, but it just got me thinking, like, what if they send drones over the wall? What if they find some way of listening in to what goes on inside the house?"

"What's a drone?"

"What's a—" Laurence broke off midway through spinning on his heel to gawp at Rufus, and quickly fixed his expression so it didn't look like he thought Rufus might be pulling his leg.

Rufus' parents had died over ten years ago, and Ru had been trapped in here ever since in a mostly self-imposed exile. No phone, no internet, only books, and a pagan potter as a surrogate mom until he was old enough to take care of himself. Amy Jenkins had dedicated years of her life to raising her best friends' son as her own, but Rufus was in many ways as cut off from the world as Quentin had been when Laurence first met him, if not more so.

"It's a little mini helicopter, kind of," Laurence said, taking his hands from his pockets and holding them inches apart. "You get a few rotors for lift, and it's remote controlled, and most of them have a camera on them that transmits back to whoever's flying it. Some have microphones, too."

"Huh." Rufus seemed unimpressed. "Weird. But okay, so a sanctum sounds like a good idea. I don't recommend you take a whole house, though. Like you've already realized, it's got security risks. The safest sanctum is a small one, with enough barriers in the physical world to stop people even getting that far."

Laurence nodded slowly and wandered back to the table to fuss Windsor. "Like a single room in a castle, behind acres of land and miles of stone wall," he mused.

"That'd be great, but I doubt that's what you've got. I do recommend the first floor, or underground if you can. That way nobody wrecks your doorway by knocking a building out from under you."

"I can do underground," Laurence said.

"Great. Then let's go through sanctum building 101 and take it from there!" Rufus made his way to shelves near the door and began to pluck books down into his arms.

Laurence kept his groan to himself. He should've learned by now that he couldn't just pick out the right spell and rush off home to cast it.

Still, he'd got the afternoon off to come and learn, so learn he was going to do.

He drew Windsor into his arms and braced himself as best as he could for the coming hours of lectures.

17

QUENTIN

VARGAS WAS A CONSUMMATE PROFESSIONAL. SHE DIDN'T ASK him how his therapy had gone, or even try to tease him about why he was seeing a therapist at all. She simply stood once he returned to reception, and asked him whether they were going straight home.

"Yes. Thank you." Quentin had already checked that he was presentable before he came downstairs, but his fingers still darted to his cuffs to tug his sleeves into place and ensure they were straight. He couldn't help it.

"No problem." Carolina made her way to the door and checked outside, then held it open for him, and she constantly scanned their surroundings as she made her way toward the car, even though those surroundings were a car park.

It wasn't until they got into the car that Quentin realized he recognized the area. This was close to the Fashion Valley Mall, and he idly considered popping over there to do a little shopping. Not right now, of course. That would make Carolina's job far harder than it needed to be, and for no good cause. He could wait until this nonsense with the ghost hunters had blown over.

Instead, he decided to use the drive home to figure out how to hire a butler, but by the time they were halfway to La

Jolla he'd grown so confused by the variety of options Siri found that he decided to swallow some pride and text Freddy for help, but it was far too early in the day for Freddy to be awake yet — assuming that he was currently in London — so Quentin tucked his phone away once he sent the message, and watched the outside world go by.

Carolina liked to stick to wide roads for as long as possible, he'd noticed, whereas Laurence might choose to weave through narrower streets to take more direct routes. Still, as they pulled off La Jolla Boulevard and onto the Camino de la Costa, the difference was stark. Where the Boulevard had been wide enough for diagonal parking either side of the street, the road Quentin lived on was residential, and therefore much narrower. There always seemed to be some construction work in progress at one house or another, too, so when they rounded a bend and found a lorry blocking the road while it offloaded bricks, Quentin wasn't too concerned.

Carolina tutted faintly and began to turn the car, though it was so large that she'd need to go back and forth a couple of times to make it. "I don't like this," she muttered.

"Alas, building work seems to be a year-round pastime in La Jolla," Quentin said.

"Yeah, but they're blocking the street right after a sharp bend, with no warning signs. It stinks." Carolina pulled forward and spun the wheel.

They were halfway through the turn, stranded across both carriageways, when a big grey truck came speeding around the bend and rammed straight into the side of Carolina's car.

There was barely any time to spot the danger, let alone react to it. Quentin raised his arms to protect his head as he was thrown against the window, and attempted to telekinetically buffer himself at the same time, but it all happened so fast and he wasn't sure whether his telekinesis had even worked. He didn't feel anything from it, either through the numb feedback it offered, or from his own body.

His arm slammed against the window, just in time to cushion his head from the glass, and he fumbled to unfasten his seatbelt as soon as he was upright again.

"No," Carolina rasped. "Stay where you are."

He was about to argue, to tell her he was capable of taking care of himself, but stopped before the words came out.

This was her job, and she couldn't do it if he got in her way.

She wrenched on the wheel and hit the accelerator. The scream of metal against metal made him flinch, and he heard the dull roar of tires against the road. Carolina's car moved several inches before the truck pushed forward again, then everything ground to a halt.

Quentin looked at the truck. The driver was facing him, still behind the wheel, but people were jumping out while Carolina's car was pinned down. One held some sort of metal bar. Another had a baseball bat.

Carolina let out a low whistle. "Well, they mean to do some damage." She thumbed the steering wheel, and a beep came from the car's speakers. "Call 911," she said.

"Calling 911," came a Siri-like voice. Then a ringtone.

The third person to leave the truck, Quentin noticed, was a white woman in her forties. She had short, close-cropped grey hair and her hands were empty, but she was the first woman Quentin had seen among all these investigators lining his street, and he began to doubt that this was at all connected to the reason he'd hired Carolina to begin with.

Carolina spoke efficiently to the 911 operator, outlining their position and requesting urgent assistance, but her words were soon drowned out when their assailants began to hammer at the glass by Quentin's head, taking it in turns with the metal bar and the bat.

The glass began to show signs of hair-thin cracks, but it held fast.

This situation was untenable. Sooner or later, even

toughened glass would give way, surely? And how long would it take for the police to arrive?

Carolina seemed to have the same thought, and she threw the car into reverse, still talking to the operator as she hit the gas, but all that happened was the truck shoving into them pushed harder, lifting the passenger side of the car slightly into the air.

"I'm going to have to get out," Carolina sighed. "Stay inside, okay? Even if I go down. Cops should be five minutes at the latest. Just hang tight."

"Carolina—"

"You know the rules," she barked.

Moments later, she'd thrown off her seatbelt and kicked her door open to spring outside and kick the leg out from under the fellow wielding the baseball bat, all while slamming her door shut behind her.

Quentin looked back to the woman on his right. She was standing, arms crossed, waiting. She didn't seem at all concerned that this might not go the way she wanted.

Behind her, a black van came around the corner. It skewed to the side of the truck, parking alongside it, and the driver hopped out to slide the side door open.

Delaney.

Quentin gritted his teeth.

So much for this not being connected. What could they possibly hope to achieve? Did they think that by threatening him, the ghost of his dead mother would suddenly materialize to prove them all right?

This was utter madness.

He turned back toward Carolina. She'd knocked the baseball bat aside and left one man on the ground. Now she was sidestepping the one with the metal bar, her hands up defensively. She was waiting for the right moment to strike. He didn't know that exact stance, but he had practiced plenty like it.

Something caught his eye. A flash of yellow. He looked at it and saw that the man on his back had drawn a plasticky gun-shaped object out and was aiming it at Carolina's back.

He squeezed the trigger.

Quentin didn't even think. He attempted to reach out, to knock the weapon aside just enough for it to miss Carolina, and to hell with the consequences.

But nothing happened.

His telekinesis didn't respond.

Carolina jerked and fell to the ground, spasming as though she were being electrocuted. In the sunlight, Quentin thought he saw wires in the space between the weapon and the back of her thigh.

The man with the iron bar raised it over his head, poised to strike down with it, then he looked toward Quentin.

"Get out of the car." He shouted it, but the soundproofing was mostly intact, and Quentin only heard it as a muffled cry.

But the message was clear.

The man hefted the bar. "Three," he yelled.

Carolina's body was shuddering, beyond her control.

Quentin reached for the handle and pulled on it. He eased out of the car just as the man shouted, "Two!"

"Enough," Quentin barked. "Let her go."

"Come with me," the woman called from the other side of Carolina's car, "or we cave her head in."

He curled his lip and stepped toward the man with the metal bar, who shifted his grip. "Come any closer and she dies right now."

Quentin drew a deep breath and raised his head, then lifted his hands in surrender and backed away. He'd been electrocuted, and it had stopped his heart. If Carolina endured for much longer, who knew what the damage might be?

But if he went now, she stayed alive, and she could describe their attackers to the police. She could share the license plate numbers and tell Laurence what had happened.

If he delayed, he had no idea whether the weapon they were using would kill her over time.

"Very well," he muttered. "Let her go."

"She'll be released the moment you get in the truck, and not a second before," the woman said. "Stop wasting time. We just want to talk; then we'll take you home ourselves."

Nobody went to all this trouble just to talk. He was quite sure of that. But he could work out what they wanted once he knew Carolina was safe.

He dropped his hands to his sides and strode toward the white van, meeting the steel-blue eyes of the grey-haired woman as he passed her.

She gazed at him in return, then followed him into the back of the van, and the moment she slammed the door shut, Delaney reversed it all the way back up to the roundabout.

Quentin sat in stony silence and settled in to wait for an opportune moment in which to make his escape.

18

QUENTIN

THEY WERE TRAVELING SOUTH, HE KNEW THAT MUCH. BACK toward San Diego. Delaney was avoiding the interstate, most likely because that's where the police would look first, but it was also slowing them down. The speed limits were lower, the roads often only had single lanes, and there was more traffic than they might have encountered if they'd taken faster roads.

It was, Quentin presumed, far safer to jump out of a moving vehicle on these streets than it would be on the interstate, so he had that to thank them for, too.

Nobody spoke. Delaney was focused on driving, and the woman to Quentin's left was watching him with a blank expression. They were the only two people in the van besides himself.

This was not remotely beyond his capabilities. Even if his telekinesis was, for whatever reason, not cooperating at this very moment, he could still potentially have his door open and leap out of it before either of them could stop him. He wasn't wearing a seatbelt, and neither was his guard, but even if she jumped out after him he would have space in which to act, which would be better than his current position.

He felt better for having pulled his observations together into a plan, and he waited for his best possible chance. His side of the vehicle was closest to the curb, so he would have to ensure he wasn't jumping out onto a lamp post or a bin.

"Don't." The single word, spoken by the woman on his left, sounded bored.

Quentin glanced at her. "Don't what?"

"Don't do anything foolish," she said.

He looked forward again. Assessing their surroundings.

The traffic lights at the next intersection were red. Delaney was slowing down. Quentin supposed they would expect him to make his attempt when they stopped, but he remained still.

Waiting.

Hopefully it would put them at ease. The moment would pass, they would let their guard down.

When the light turned green, Delaney pulled forward, and Quentin grabbed the door handle.

He was only halfway through wrenching the door aside when his muscles went into spasm. It started in his back, but a second later had radiated throughout his entire body, and everything from his neck to his toes cramped as though he'd pulled all of his muscles and failed to stretch properly. As he slid off the seat he was only dimly aware of the ratchet of metal and the cold touch of handcuffs around his wrists.

When the spasm died away, he was left dizzy and gasping on the floor, staring up at the ceiling, with the woman leaning over him. She planted a booted foot on his chest, and dropped another of those plastic gun-shaped weapons by his shoulder.

"Now you get to ride the rest of the way on the floor," she said, as though addressing a misbehaving child. "Maybe next time you'll do what you're told."

"I wouldn't count on it," he muttered.

Her boot pressed down hard as she leaned over his body to drag the door handle back into place, and he barely managed to pull his feet back inside before she could crush them in the closing door. "The wires are still in you," she said when she sat back down. "All I have to do is hit the trigger, and you get another 50,000 volts."

Quentin eyed the weapon by his shoulder. He couldn't see where the wires went, but there was a pain digging into his back that was exacerbated by her boot pressing him down on it, and her leg was between his cuffed hands and the plastic gun.

He ground his teeth and went back to gazing up at the ceiling of the van.

All he had to do was wait until Laurence heard of this, and all hell would break loose.

THEY DROVE for so long that the pain in his back had become a bone-deep soreness. Every time they hit a bump or dip in the road, whatever was there seemed to dig into him just a little deeper, but the boot that pressed down on his chest made it impossible for him to find a more comfortable position. At some point his phone had buzzed, so the woman emptied his pockets, removing everything she could find and tucking them into the back of the driver's seat.

"You could at least let me sit up," Quentin eventually groaned.

"You lost that privilege," she answered, not even looking down to him.

"The police are already looking for you."

"People go missing all the time. Even rich ones."

"Bet you wish you'd just talked to me like an adult when I asked, huh?" It was the first time Delaney had said anything, and his words carried malicious glee the like of which Quentin hadn't heard since he was a child.

Quentin continued to gaze at the ceiling. He couldn't possibly see Delaney from down here, so he didn't try. "You were an imbecile then, and you're even more of one now," he retorted. "This is madness. Where are we going?"

"You don't need to know," Delaney snapped.

"Naturally." Quentin sighed and crossed his legs. He

couldn't get comfortable, but he could at least give off an air of insouciance. It might provoke Delaney into giving more away. "But we can't go to your home, can we? This is your van. The police will find you from the license plate. So where *are* we headed? Somewhere with a view, I hope?"

"Can't you shut him up?" Delaney spat.

"Sure." The woman shrugged. "If that's what you want."

"It is."

Quentin shifted his gaze to her as she dug through her pockets, then quirked his eyebrows as she withdrew a roll of black tape.

"You can't be serious," he snorted.

She didn't answer. Instead, she used her teeth to tear off a strip, and then she leaned down and used her other foot to stamp his hair to the floor of the van when he tried to jerk away.

With brutal efficiency, she taped over his mouth, but didn't move either of her feet once she was done.

QUENTIN HAD no idea how long they drove. The soreness in his back transformed into a frustrating irritation, and the constant pull on his scalp from the boot trapping his hair to the ground was equally painful. The vehicle stopped several times, for intersections and the like he assumed, but eventually a stop was accompanied by the creak of a handbrake, too.

The van shifted as Delaney jumped out, and then Quentin heard the door at his feet slide open. Boots lifted off his chest and hair, but before he could lash a kick at Delaney's face, his muscles seized up, and he struggled to breathe with the tape over his mouth.

His body moved without his volition. The shock from the plastic weapon went away, but by the time it did he was in the back of another vehicle, on the floor once more.

The woman got in the back with him, and Delaney drove. She returned her boot to his chest, potentially to keep him from reaching the tape and taking it off, but at least she left his hair alone this time.

As they drove away, Quentin could only wonder at how deeply they'd all underestimated Delaney.

HE RESORTED to meditation throughout the journey. It helped to control his temper, to keep a lid on his anger and pain and prevent him from taking foolish actions. Until this voltage delivery system was removed from him, it was clear that any attempt at resistance would lead to his immediate electrocution. Instead, he closed his eyes, and focused on his breathing.

The road beneath the van was uneven. Pitted. The vehicle rocked as it traveled, and it was all Quentin could do to remain calm and collected, but the longer it went on, the more used to it he became. By the time the handbrake sounded once more, he was half asleep.

"Up," the woman ordered. She grabbed his shoulders and heaved him toward the door as Delaney slid it open.

He didn't so much leave the van as get dragged out of it, and when he stood, he wavered slightly until he regained equilibrium in the cold night air.

It was dark. So dark that he could make out the faintest of stars overhead, as well as what looked like a beautiful sprinkling of dust across the night sky. He was so startled by it that his eyes widened and he raised his head to try and take it all in.

He'd never seen such a sky, not even in Hellhole Canyon. Here was utter darkness, and it allowed the stars to truly shine without competition from cities or roads.

Wherever he was, it was miles from civilization.

"That's enough sightseeing," Delaney muttered as he stomped away from Quentin. "Let's go."

Quentin blinked and refocused on Delaney's back, then on the building beyond him. It was low, made of uneven rocks, and looked like a little house in the middle of nowhere. The woman grabbed his cuffs and used them to drag him toward it, and he had to pay attention to the uneven, rubble-strewn ground to keep from falling over.

"Pick your feet up," she said idly as she drew him nearer to the house's front door, made from wood bleached almost as pale as the rocks.

He glowered at her and kicked a rock in her direction, but all she did was speed up, and he vastly preferred remaining on his feet to being dragged along face down, so he resumed walking until they were inside.

It was no warmer indoors. Delaney used a flashlight to light their way, and Quentin had no choice but to follow. It was difficult to make out his surroundings, since there were two other bodies between him and the light; but from what he could glean, the interior was the same stone wall as the exterior, with no insulation or lining, or even much in the way of decor. Underfoot was bare stone, too, though it was at least rubble-free.

The building was small, although he supposed that compared to Laurence's apartment over the Jack in the Green, it was decent. He saw no evidence of furniture, though he didn't get too much time to dwell on it. Darkness opened up ahead of him, and he was dragged down stone stairs into an even colder basement, but they were so deep in desert that there wasn't the slightest hint of humidity in the air.

Finally, the woman let go of his handcuffs and yanked the wires out of his back. It set off a fresh wave of pain as wounds he'd worked hard to ignore flared back into his consciousness, and while he was gritting his teeth against the resurgence, she kicked him viciously in the back of one knee.

He dropped forward, landing on that knee first, and he

heard the clank of metal. She manhandled his leg and closed something more substantial than the handcuffs around his ankle, then the flashlight bounced away toward the stairs.

Quentin managed to tear the tape from his mouth at last, gasping for air and trying his damnedest not to let them hear it. "What do you want?"

The light switched directions and blinded him, and he raised his hands too slowly to stop it, hissing softly as he ducked his head.

"I just want some answers," Delaney said, sounding like he thought he was being reasonable. "And you're not leaving until I get them. So why don't you sit down and think about your life choices, and how all this could have been avoided if you'd just treated me with some respect."

Quentin grit his teeth and tried to peer toward Delaney, but the light was far too bright. "You're making a mistake," he rasped. "I don't know what you think is going to happen here, but I can assure you that you aren't going to get what you want out of this."

"We'll see. I'm gonna get some rest. You should do the same." The light went away, but the after-image of it left Quentin just as blind as if it were still there. "Good luck with that. It's kinda cold down here."

He heard footsteps, then the heavy slam of a door, and he was alone, down on one knee, in utter darkness. He dropped the tape to the floor and attempted to release some fire into the air to provide light, but it didn't come.

Quentin sucked his teeth and tried to reach out telekinetically instead, to feel the extent of his surroundings.

Nothing.

Absolutely nothing.

He sat so that he could turn around and run fingers over his ankle, but what he found made as little sense as the rest of this whole debacle. There was metal, like a cuff, and it was barely big enough for him. A loop protruded from it and attached to the link of a chain.

A thick, heavy chain.

This was madness. He had to be dreaming. The sensible response to the threat of legal action wasn't a bloody kidnapping.

He tugged on the chain, but it was fastened securely to something he couldn't see and had no inclination to investigate with his fingers.

It took a little while for the reality of his situation to sink in. He'd been attacked by gods, transported to Otherworld, and faced off against his own father, but this? This was so shockingly mundane that it beggared belief.

Kidnapped, driven out into the desert, then manacled to a bloody floor in a basement, of all things. An actual manacle! Who owned those, outside of a museum?

He untied the laces of his shoe and pulled it off, then removed his sock for good measure. If he could just wriggle the manacle over his ankle, he could take the stairs like a rat up a drainpipe; but it was too damn small, no matter which way he twisted either it or himself.

This was like no nightmare he'd had before. Perhaps therapy had stirred up old fears and given him new things to have awful dreams about. Or maybe he didn't know as much about his gifts as he thought he did.

It really was damn cold down here. He shivered, and tried to draw some warmth into his body, but that didn't work either. He pulled sock and shoe back on, and huddled down inside his coat, drawing his knees close to his chest. He was stuck here for the time being, and if he was to have any hope of escape he would need to conserve his energy.

Either he would find an opportunity, or he would make one, but one way or another he would get out of here, and then he'd damn well make sure Delaney went to prison for this.

But for now, all he could do was try to make himself comfortable.

19

LAURENCE

CREATING A SANCTUM NEEDED A LONG AND IN-DEPTH LOOK AT planar mechanics, according to Rufus, and Laurence deeply regretted not having found his dad's book of shadows before he'd sought out a mentor.

Basil had it easy. All he had to do was check his spellbook and cast one. If he didn't have a spell, he couldn't use it, and that was the end of it.

Laurence had access to a hermit whose whole library was overflowing with facts, theories, and spells from different eras and magical styles, and sometimes it seemed like that amount of choice just led to paralysis. Even Windsor had gotten bored and fallen asleep in Laurence's arms with his feet up in the air and his beak resting on the table edge.

"Nodding off?" Rufus cut in.

"I mean, why do I even need to know all this?" Laurence could hear the plaintive whine in his own voice, but didn't care. "I've got an underground bunker; I just wanna put a sanctum in it. Nothing fancy. I'm not looking to do interdimensional plumbing."

Rufus blinked slowly at him, then let out a long-suffering sigh and closed the book he'd been consulting. "Because—"

"I gotta learn to walk before I run?" Laurence cut in. It was Rufus' usual excuse.

Ru got up and walked around the table, then perched on it by Laurence's side. He rested his hands together on one thigh and gazed down at Laurence.

Laurence leaned back and looked up. He had no idea where this was going. Rufus usually just told him to shut up and they got back to it.

Windsor stirred and wriggled onto his front, then hopped onto the table, where he stretched and yawned.

"I teach you," Rufus said calmly, "in the hope that, sooner or later, you'll uphold your end of the bargain and do what you promised to do. I've been patient. I've been understanding of the fact that you have problems to deal with that have delayed your willingness to help me. And I keep teaching you, even though you're an ungrateful asshole who fights me the whole way, like I'm asking so much of you. You're welcome to leave at any time. You're not a prisoner here. But you keep coming back, and then you complain about being taught the very things you asked to learn."

Laurence's jaw fell open. The way Rufus laid it all out like it was just some daily fact that constantly disappointed him made Laurence feel like he'd been hauled up in front of the principal.

"You're a brat," Rufus concluded. "And maybe if you were less of a brat, I'd answer facetious questions. But you're not, and so here we are, with you in my hair, and me with nothing to show for it. And that is why you have to learn about planar mechanics instead of jumping straight to the fun stuff."

Shame burned Laurence's cheeks.

He *had* promised to investigate the death of Rufus' parents, but whenever he had the time, he didn't feel strong enough to watch two people die in a car crash, and when he felt robust, he was busy fighting for his life or trying to save Quentin's ass. But from Rufus' perspective, Laurence hadn't done jack shit to help out like he'd sworn he would.

He swallowed down his pride, the part of him that wanted to shout in Rufus' face about how unfair Ru was being.

"You're right," he sighed. "I'm sorry. How about we do that now, and—"

Rufus hissed between clenched teeth and his head snapped toward the library door.

Laurence frowned and waited.

Rufus did this whenever someone opened the gate to his sanctum. There were some kind of magical alarm bells on it that they hadn't even begun to cover in today's lesson, and that person — at least in Laurence's presence — was always Amy Jenkins. Nobody but her or Laurence ever came here.

"It's Amy," Rufus said after a minute. He slid off the table and marched toward the door. "She looks worried."

Laurence waited for Windsor to hop up onto his shoulder, then sprinted after Rufus, who was already halfway down the wide staircase.

The doorbell rang moments before Rufus pulled the door open, and Amy spilled over the threshold, her auburn curls every bit as frazzled as she looked.

"Laurence!" She called out as she bypassed Rufus.

It had to be bad. She hadn't even brought any cookies with her.

He hopped off the last step and moved in for a quick hug. "What is it?"

She squeezed him for a second. "Myriam called me. She says Quentin's gone missing." Her cheeks were almost as red as her hair, and it made her blue eyes seem even brighter.

Laurence opened his mouth and blinked. There were too many questions trying to cram themselves out of him all at the same time, and he fought to try and pick one. "Like... how?" seemed to sum up most of them in one go.

Rufus shut the door and stuffed his hands in his pockets, head tipping to the side as he listened in.

"Honestly?" Amy looked skeptical. "She says he's been kidnapped."

Laurence stared at her. Amy hadn't ever met Quentin, so he figured the skepticism came from the fact that most people just didn't get kidnapped. "What, like..." He struggled to wrap his head around it. "Like, by a daemon or something?"

Amy shook her head quickly, and her frizz bounced over her shoulders. "Didn't sound like it. She's been trying to call you." She hesitated. "You don't look all that worried."

He puffed out his cheeks, and Windsor cawed in amusement. "I've gotta say," he admitted as he planted his fists on his hips, "if anyone's dumb enough to try and kidnap Quen, they kind of deserve whatever they get." Laurence drew his phone out of his pocket, and headed for the door. "I'm just going to go get signal. Be right back."

Amy cast a worried look to Rufus, who just shrugged at her.

Laurence made his way out the door and jogged around both his own and Amy's vehicles, then heaved the heavy wooden gate aside and slipped out onto the sidewalk. He drew the gate back into place and strolled away, eyeing his phone, waiting for it to show bars and pick up on the missed calls.

Thirty seconds later, his phone all but melted in his hand. Notifications filled the screen, then scrolled older ones off the top, while each one came with a *bing* and a buzz.

Laurence came to a halt. This wasn't just his mom trying to reach him. He had missed calls from Sebastian, Mia, Ethan, Rodger, even Frederick of all people, and Laurence wasn't convinced he'd ever given Freddy his number. Text messages that mostly seemed to contain some variant of "call me when you get this" or "urgent" scrolled by in all the chaos. Some were voicemail notifications.

Worry started to percolate in his gut.

Quentin didn't leave the house without Vargas. Was she missing too? Or — worse — dead?

Once the notification explosion came to an end, he began to scroll through the messages, but in the end gave up and started on his voicemails instead.

"Bambi, it's me," was the first, from his mom. "Sebastian just called. They have police at the house. Quentin's… I don't know how, but Sebastian says Quentin's been kidnapped. I think you need to go home."

"Laurence, it's Sebastian," was the next. "Quentin's been taken. Professional job. Vargas is alive, she's here giving her statement to the cops. Sounds like a set-up. Call me, I'll fill you in." Sebastian hesitated. "Unless by the time you get this he's already come home," he added, sounded as unruffled as Laurence had initially felt.

"I have no idea what the fuck is going on, but your place is crawling with cops," was Rodger's voicemail.

"Sebastian," was the next one. He sounded more grim this time. "Haven't heard from him yet. Call me when you get this."

Three more messages, and then his mom's last was, "Bambi, I'm calling Amy to see if she can come find you at Rufus'. She's much closer than me. Call me."

He felt increasingly confused, even while his panic turned the worry to sickness in his gut.

Who the hell could possibly kidnap Quentin?

Laurence was torn between calling his mom and just looking back in time to find out what had happened, but his mom would be worrying and waiting on him, so he tapped the callback next to her notification and held the phone to his ear as he started pacing back toward the gate.

"Bambi!" She answered almost immediately. "Thank the Goddess! Did Amy reach you?"

"Yeah. What's happening?"

"Sebastian tells me Carolina was driving Quentin home after an appointment, and they hit a blocked road. He assumes the roadblock was intentional. Apparently then Carolina tried to pull a u-turn and got t-boned halfway through the maneuver. She told Quentin to stay in the car, but she got hit with a taser, and they managed to convince Quentin to go with them by threatening to kill her if he didn't."

"Oh!" He almost felt relieved. At least that answered the

immediate question. Of course Quentin would do whatever it took to save someone else's life. "So he's probably still with them trying to figure out why they want him, I guess."

Myriam sighed. "Possibly. It may be best if you go home, though. It's even on the news."

Laurence groaned. That might be why Freddy had tried to call him. "Okay. Thanks, Mom. Can you let Sebastian know I'm on my way?"

"Sure thing, dear." She still sounded concerned. "Be careful."

"Yeah. I will. Merry part, Mom."

"Merry part."

He re-entered Rufus' sanctum, jogging to close the distance, and Windsor flapped off his shoulder to go land on the roof of the van.

"Not yet, Win," he said. "Gotta do something first."

Windsor clacked his beak and took off, landing on his shoulder again just as Rufus opened the door.

"Well?" was all Ru asked.

"I dunno," Laurence had to admit. "Doesn't seem huge, but I'm just going to check."

He could hear them tail him, but didn't wait for them to catch up. He darted through the hallway and into the lounge, and sat in an outdated armchair. Windsor hopped up onto the back of it, and Laurence closed his eyes.

He had more than enough detail to bait his visions with. Quentin had left his therapist and got into Vargas' car, then they headed home.

Laurence knew these streets. La Jolla Boulevard, dotted with roundabouts that even locals got confused by. Vargas drove, and Laurence sat in the back with Quentin, who was gazing out of the window, looking pensive. That didn't surprise Laurence. He figured most people looked pretty thoughtful after seeing their therapist.

There wasn't any conversation. Quentin seemed content to watch the world go by, and Laurence smiled softly.

"C'mon, baby," he murmured. "Why'd you let them take you? Show me."

Vargas turned left at a roundabout onto the Camino de la Costa, the southern end. So far, so good.

Laurence blinked.

He was in Rufus' living room. Rufus and Amy were loitering nearby, watching him.

"What?" Laurence shook his head. "Hold on."

He closed his eyes.

There was no more vision. It was gone. Ended, like the TV had been switched off.

Laurence frowned slowly.

He hadn't meant to drop out of it. He hadn't done anything to make the vision end. Maybe he'd gotten distracted by Amy and Rufus, but he'd had worse visions in the back of a moving limousine before. This was child's play.

He baited time again. Lay exactly the same lures as before.

And received exactly the same vision.

It cut out as the car turned onto the Camino de la Costa.

Laurence ground his teeth. If this wasn't going to work, he'd find another way. He was the Hunter. They'd hit Vargas with a taser, then coerced Quentin into another vehicle.

Time rushed by, and no visions bobbed toward him.

"Come *on*," he snarled. "Where are you, Quen? Show me!"

The harder he tried, the more that flipping in his gut came back to him. He'd done this before! This was how he'd found Quentin after the black dog took him to Annwn. This wasn't like Laurence was trying to push his gift in a direction it couldn't go. This should've been as easy as breathing in and out.

But there was no Quentin.

"Aah!" He sprang from his chair and paced the room, pulling at his curls and trying to push down on the panic that was threatening to overwhelm him. "Fuck! He must be in Otherworld. I can't see him!"

How had this happened again?

And shouldn't he have seen *how* it happened?

Windsor projected doubt across their link, and ruffled his feathers. *Are you sure?* he asked, nothing but skepticism in his tone.

"No, I'm not," he huffed, not caring that Rufus and Amy hadn't heard Win's question. "But if I can't see him, where else could he be?"

Don't know, Windsor admitted.

"What happened?" Rufus finally sat down on an armchair.

Laurence kept pacing, but at least he managed to make himself let go of his hair. "The vision just cuts out," he muttered.

"So you don't actually see the kidnapping?" Rufus narrowed his eyes.

Laurence held his breath and stopped, staring at Rufus. "Oh shit."

Amy sat slowly beside Rufus and folded her hands together in her lap. "So he's *not* in Otherworld?"

"Ru's right," Laurence pushed hair away from his forehead. "Vargas described the whole thing, but I don't even see that happen." He looked at Windsor, then back at Rufus. "You've got spells that can block psychics, right?" He rolled up his left sleeve and tapped his bracelet. "You gave me one to protect myself from telepathy. Is it possible someone's got a spell to protect themselves from me, or a gift like mine?"

"Everything's possible," Rufus admitted. "If it's against you specifically they'll need some of your saliva, if not your blood."

"Which I doubt they have, but it's worth exploring." Laurence only knew one person who had either, and maybe *that* explained Freddy's missed call. He bared his teeth. If the duke had broken his word, Laurence wouldn't cry about having to kill him. "Okay. I've still got other options." He held an arm out for Windsor to fly over to, and the bird came to him, gliding through the air after just a few beats of his huge wings. "But I gotta go home. I'm sorry, Ru," he added.

Rufus nodded. "Another time," he said, like he'd almost expected something to come up and block him yet again.

Laurence sighed and shook the witch's hand, then Amy's too. "Thanks again," he said to her. "I'll let you know what's going on once I know."

"Be careful," she warned.

"Always am."

He hurried out to the truck and let Windsor inside, then moved the gate out of his way. Getting in and out of Rufus' sanctum was always a whole logistical exercise with a vehicle, and he didn't put his seatbelt on until the gate was closed.

"Okay," he said to Windsor as he pulled out into the street. "Let's go find out what the hell is going on."

Windsor cawed softly, then added a quiet "Shit!" for good measure.

Laurence was in total agreement.

20

LAURENCE

By the time Laurence got home, most of the ghost-hunters' vehicles were gone, but the road was just as clogged with news trucks and a couple of cop cars, and he kept a neutral expression as he waited for the garage to open while flashing cameras were thrust up against his window.

Goddess, he was never going to get used to the press.

He saw Sebastian in the garage, revealed slowly by the rising door, and heaved a sigh of relief as they swapped positions, with Laurence pulling off the street, and Sebastian blocking the way for any paparazzi trying to get inside.

Finally, with the door closed, Laurence got out of the truck, and Windsor hopped onto his outstretched forearm. "Thanks," he said, giving Sebastian a nod.

"You're welcome." Sebastian grimaced. "He's not back yet."

"Okay." He licked his lips. "Are there cops inside the house?"

Sebastian nodded. "They're waiting to talk to you."

Laurence grimaced briefly and raised Windsor to the roof of the truck.

I need you to stay here.

Windsor hopped across and cawed softly. *Why? Bad people?*

No. It's illegal to have a pet raven, and I don't have time to get arrested. Just wait here and don't let anyone see you.

I'm not a pet. Windsor eyed Laurence.

They can't tell the difference. He stroked Windsor's head for a few seconds, then headed for the door into the house.

Laurence squared his shoulders as he walked. He resumed his neutral expression. His few run-ins with cops hadn't been great, and he really didn't like the fact that they were inside his home, but he suspected this time would be different. This was La Jolla, after all. The mansion was worth millions of dollars. They were here to help.

Sebastian patted him on the shoulder, and Laurence lifted his chin, then pushed through into the house.

The dogs rushed to greet him, tails wagging, tongues wrapping around his fingers. He didn't need to be Quentin to recognize that they were distressed by all the disruption, and he paused a while to fuss over them while he focused his hearing on the voices coming from the living room.

"And what relation are you to the owners of the property?" That voice was moderate, male, and unknown. Laurence figured he must be a cop.

"Friends," Soraya sniffed.

"You're friends with men several years older than you?" The cop's skepticism rose.

"Yep." Soraya wasn't giving an inch.

Laurence stood and hurried toward the room. There wasn't any need for the police to be interrogating the kids, and they were obviously just killing time until he arrived, so the sooner he got in there the better for everyone.

There were two officers, standing. One was a Hispanic man in his early thirties, lean and fit, with short, neat brown hair. The other was a white woman who was slightly older, and her dark brown hair was also cut short. She stood a few feet away from her colleague, and was the first to look at Laurence when he entered the room.

"Okay," Laurence puffed, drawing himself to his full height. "Where's my boyfriend, and what are you doing to find him?"

The male officer turned toward Laurence, and Laurence didn't have to be psychic to note the slight crinkle in his nose, so Laurence ignored him and looked at the woman.

"You're Bambi Riley, is that right?" she asked as she came toward him. "Quentin d'Arcy is your partner?"

"I go by Laurence." He tilted his head to one side. "I don't want to seem ungrateful, but if there's been a kidnapping, shouldn't there be a detective here?"

She nodded. "We're just here taking statements. The detective assigned to your partner's case is coordinating the search effort right now, but he left his card for you." She reached into one of the pockets on her vest and pulled out a business card. "I'm Fields, this is Garcia," she said as she held the card out. "We're doing everything we can to find Mr. d'Arcy, I promise you."

Laurence skimmed the card. *Detective Martin Hudson.* There was nothing to do but watch Fields again. The card wouldn't give him any answers.

"We just need to ask you a few questions," Fields continued.

Laurence gawped at her. Were they really even considering that he could be remotely connected to this?

"They're just covering every angle," Sebastian rumbled, almost like he'd read Laurence's mind.

It didn't make Laurence any less irritated, but he walked over to a chair and sat. "Okay, ask away."

"Where were you this afternoon, at around four thirty?" Fields pulled a notebook from another pocket and flipped it open, pen in hand.

He knew how this kind of situation went. If he mentioned he'd spent all his time with Rufus, they'd want to talk to Ru to corroborate Laurence's story. If Laurence claimed he'd been out on deliveries, they'd want to see paperwork from the shop to prove it.

"I took the afternoon off and went to the beach," he said.

"Were you alone?"

"Yeah."

She scribbled in her notepad. "Did anyone see you there?"

"Probably?" Laurence shrugged. "I didn't see anyone I knew, but who knows who might have seen me."

"Which beach?"

"The Tamarack."

"Carlsbad?" She squinted at him. "We've got beaches here."

"Yeah, and we've got people who take creepshots of me and put them on Twitter here, too. Fewer people recognize me in Carlsbad, so that's where I go." He shrugged. "I figure you've got cameras up and down the 5. Check my license plate. It's where I went."

He was gambling, and he knew it. He was betting on there being fewer cameras in residential streets, hoping that once the cops saw him come off the I-5 at the right exit and head toward the beach, they'd trust his lie. Once they were out of his hair, he could get on with finding Quentin, and it wouldn't matter any more.

This was a waste of his time, but if he pissed the officers off, they'd hang around longer, and he wanted them gone already.

"Why didn't you answer your phone?"

"Because I left it in my car. I was on a beach," he added, like it was obvious. "I didn't want to lose it or get it wet. I got back to the car, saw all the messages, and I came straight home."

"I understand Mr. d'Arcy is a British citizen?" Fields looked up from her notes.

"Yeah."

"He's here legally?"

Laurence stared at her, then burst out laughing. The idea that a British aristocrat had come to San Diego to live in an eighteen million dollar mansion by the sea without a visa was so preposterous he couldn't help himself. "You can't be serious! Of course he's here legally. He's got a visa! Are you really going to try and find him guilty of something while he's the victim of a kidnapping?"

"It needed to be asked," Garcia finally spoke.

"It really didn't. I'm sure you can just plug his name into a computer and find out." Laurence ran a hand over his stubble to try and help himself stop the laughter. It wasn't appropriate, and if he was honest with himself, Fields' question wasn't at all funny. Were they looking for excuses to not bother investigating? He pushed himself out of his chair. "Okay. I think that's enough. I'd like you to leave now, and I don't want another officer here unless they're escorting Quentin home. Thanks for everything, but if you're not out there looking for him right now, then so far as I'm concerned you're not doing a damn thing to find him."

Fields eyed him, but she tucked her notepad away. "We'll let Detective Hudson know that you're home," she stated.

"You do that. I'm sorry," he added. "I know you're just doing your job. But you're interrogating me, and I don't even know the circumstances of his disappearance yet. Hudson should have been here." He bit off his words before he could add *and the reason he isn't is because we're not straight*, because that'd just make them more antagonistic toward him, whether or not it was true. If it was true, they'd hate to get called out, and if it wasn't, they'd be justifiably upset at their boss getting called a bigot. "The man I love has been taken. Find him, okay? Just…" He exhaled as the fight left him. "Find him."

Fields' gaze was at least sympathetic, to make up for the fact that Garcia's wasn't, as she started toward the door. "Thank you for your time, Mr. Riley. We're sorry to have kept you for so long."

Sebastian led them out, and Laurence collapsed back into his seat, waiting for them to be gone and for Sebastian to return. He exchanged looks with Soraya, who seemed just as annoyed as he felt.

"Okay." Sebastian returned to the room and ran a hand through his hair. "You can come downstairs, they're gone," he said, as though to himself. Laurence figured that meant Estelita was upstairs and eavesdropping, and soon enough he heard the clatter of teenagers rushing down the stairs.

"What happened?" Laurence propped his elbows on his knees and looked at Sebastian.

"Quentin went to his afternoon appointment." Sebastian didn't wait for the kids to arrive. "Vargas drove him straight back here after. No detours, nothing untoward. When she turned onto the Camino de la Costa off La Jolla Boulevard and rounded the corner, there was a construction truck blocking the street, offloading materials."

Mia and the teens clambered into the living room and spread themselves out across chairs as Sebastian talked.

"She smelled a rat and started a three-point turn, but another truck came around the corner and hit her car, and kept the pressure on to stop her pulling away, so she called 911. Two assailants came round to the driver's side. She told Quentin to stay where he was, and went to engage them, and was doing okay until they hit her with a taser. At that point, she was down, but she heard a woman tell Quentin to go with her or the goons would cave Vargas' head in. She says Quentin went with them, and the goons left her on the street. By the time she managed to get to her feet, there was no sign of them and her car was a wreck, so she had to stay there and wait for the cops to arrive. She called me while she was waiting, but I was out on a job." Sebastian sighed. "She did it all by the book, Laurence. Quentin should've been safe in her car."

Laurence nodded. "But he wasn't going to sit there and let them kill her. It's okay. She's not at fault."

"Yeah. We never believe that when we lose a client, though."

He turned to Soraya. Now the cops were gone, he could finally solve all this anyway. It wouldn't be as easy as using his own gift, but they'd combined Soraya and Estelita to triangulate in the past, and Soraya was fond enough of Quentin that she could reach past her expanded two-mile limit for him. "Okay," he breathed. "Let's get this done. Can you see him?"

"I couldn't earlier," she huffed, glancing at Kim. "But I'll try again."

Kim nodded.

Laurence waited, trying to convince himself that it would work. Maybe Soraya had failed earlier because she'd gotten interrupted, or distracted. He couldn't guess at the circumstances of her previous attempt. All he knew was that it had to work now. It *had* to.

He breathed so quietly he wasn't even sure if he heard himself. Everyone from Kim to Felipe was watching Soraya as she closed her eyes and concentrated, but the longer they all waited, the more Laurence started to worry all over again.

It never took her this long.

Soraya snorted and shook her head as she opened her eyes. "I can't find him."

"Why not?" Felipe leaned forward.

"Too far?" Mia suggested.

"How should I know?" Soraya crossed her arms in anger and scowled at Laurence, like it was somehow his fault her gift had failed.

"Okay," Sebastian said, raising his voice a little. "Let's just stay calm. If we can't do this the awesome way, we'll have to do it the old-fashioned way."

Laurence turned to gape up at him. "I really hope you don't mean we sit here and wait for the police to do their jobs?"

Sebastian snorted. "No fucking way. Mia, stay here and look after the kids. Laurence, come with me."

He leaped out of his chair and hurried after Sebastian as the older man strode for the door. "Where are we going?"

"We're going to the scene of the crime, and we'll take it from there."

Laurence glanced back toward Mia, who nodded to him, then he hurried along the corridor and toward the garage.

He wasn't a detective. But Sebastian had a point. If

Laurence could pick up Quentin's scent, there was a chance they could track him.

It was all he had right now, but it was a hundred percent better than sitting around waiting for some detective to give him a call.

21

LAURENCE

Sebastian drove them out to La Jolla Boulevard and stowed the SUV in a parking space outside a building that was up for sale. They hopped out and backtracked to the roundabout on foot, with Windsor soaring ahead to perch on a streetlamp. The short drive got them out past the news crews without too much fuss, and prevented Laurence from punching any of them in the face. Getting arrested wouldn't help Quentin.

Assuming he was still alive.

No. He couldn't afford to start thinking like that. There wasn't any evidence to suggest Quentin had even been hurt, and Laurence couldn't let himself waste time panicking over stupid shit. If they wanted him dead, why take him alive?

So they can dump the body in the desert, where nobody will ever find it.

He snarled under his breath and picked up the pace as Sebastian turned onto the Camino de la Costa.

"Okay," Sebastian breathed as they rounded the corner and crossed Chelsea Avenue. "It was literally…"

"Huh," Laurence said.

They both slowed down.

Windsor caught up and landed in a palm tree, and chattered away to himself.

Law? Windsor queried.

Yeah, that's the PD, he agreed.

The street was blocked off by a cop car, a forensics truck, and a gazebo in the middle of the road. Laurence could make out slow but constant activity with people in white coveralls bagging items, and a photographer moving around to take snapshots. A uniformed cop was this side of the gazebo, probably to direct traffic back the way it came, and Laurence caught sight of another on the far side. Lights from cars and news crews made it bright as day even though the sun had already gone down.

There were a couple of scattered onlookers, some journalists, and an older guy in a suit who was taking a phone call in the middle of it all.

If Laurence started sniffing the crime scene, people were definitely going to notice.

"We better back off, before—" Sebastian broke off when one of the journalists spotted Laurence.

Laurence groaned. Lights flashed toward him, and he had to shield his eyes, which probably wouldn't be a good look on camera. The trouble with having such great eyesight was that he'd been fully attuned to seeing in the low evening light, and now he'd been blinded by everything that got pointed his way. It was too much.

"Mr. Riley?"

"What can you tell us about the disappearance of Quentin d'Arcy, Mr. Riley?"

Footsteps hurried over, and Sebastian stepped between Laurence and the lights. To Laurence's surprise, he heard the uniformed cop intervene, too.

"Hey, back off. Give the guy some room!"

And then there was another voice. Quieter. Closer. Sebastian had let this one through, and Laurence turned his side toward the crime scene to try and recover his eyesight.

"Mr. Riley? I'm Detective Hudson. I was just on my way to see you."

Laurence blinked rapidly and found the blobs on his retinas starting to fade, but for a moment, Hudson's entire head was just a dancing orange dot, which was seriously disconcerting. "Okay."

"Let's go," Hudson murmured. "These vultures have the kinds of microphones that'd get me arrested if I used them without a warrant. You don't want to talk to me right here." He glanced past Laurence, then added, "Your house is in the other direction. Did you drive?"

"ID?" Sebastian cut in before Laurence could answer.

"Sure." The time it took for Hudson to bring out his shield and show it to Sebastian was all the time Laurence needed for the dancing blobs to disappear at last.

"Great," was all Sebastian said after he'd looked it over.

"Let's walk," Hudson said softly as he gestured back the way Laurence had come.

They turned, and the uniformed cops behind them managed to keep the news crews in check until they lost interest and went back to filming the forensic team. Windsor kept an eye on the press people so that Laurence knew where they were, while he strolled back to where Sebastian had parked the SUV.

There was a bench just before the parking spaces, and Hudson wandered over to sit there, so Laurence sat next to him. Even though it was a three-seater, Sebastian remained standing, falling easily into bodyguard mode.

"I'm sorry I wasn't there when you got home," Hudson began. He looked Laurence in the eye as he said it, turning toward him on the bench.

Laurence regarded him skeptically, but didn't pick up an ounce of sarcasm or the faintest trace of a lie. "Yeah. Not as sorry as I am that my boyfriend wasn't there," he muttered.

"I'll bet. Let me tell you where we're at right now." Hudson took out a notebook and paged through it. "We're pulling

CCTV footage from every street in a mile radius. We've requested Mr. d'Arcy's phone data from his service provider. Hopefully we can pair his GPS pings with a license plate, then cast the net wider for the vehicle they used."

Laurence's irritation began to subside. "You can really do that?"

"Sure. It just takes time, that's all. It's not my favorite method, but every scrap of information helps." Hudson licked his lips. "Nobody's contacted you with any kind of demand?"

He shook his head. "What, like a ransom? No. Nothing like that."

The moment he said it, from the way Hudson's lips twitched into a ghost of a frown, Laurence knew that was bad.

"Shame," Hudson mused.

"What does that mean?"

"It means we don't have a motive yet." Hudson met his eye again. "We can't begin to guess at why they took him, or what they want. All we can go on is what was said at the scene, and we're fortunate in that the key eyewitness is trained in observation, so we've already got way more than we would have in similar cases." He paused. "I can't make you any unrealistic promises, Mr. Riley. But I can assure you that this case is my top priority, and I'm doing everything in my power to find your partner as swiftly and efficiently as possible."

Laurence wondered whether this was the kind of police effort all rich people got if they reported a crime. A detective who seemed to want to solve the case. A response that was more than just a note jotted down and a goodbye. Absolutely zero chance that Laurence might get arrested for being queer in the vicinity.

He ran his tongue along his teeth, then nodded. "What happens now?"

"Well, now I go back to my team and we start pulling together everything we've collected and try to build a timeline. Does Mr. d'Arcy have K&R insurance?"

Laurence shook his head. "I don't even know what that is."

"Kidnapping and ransom," Sebastian supplied.

"How do you insure against being kidnapped?" Even the idea of it made no sense to Laurence, and he looked up to Sebastian.

"You don't. Not really. The insurance covers the cost of your ransom *if* you get kidnapped."

Laurence just shook his head, astonished that someone had even come up with the idea. "I don't know."

"Not a problem." Hudson shifted forward in his seat, as if to stand, but he paused before he made it that far. "Can I ask you something?"

"I mean, I guess?" Laurence returned his attention to the detective, who still seemed pensive.

"You don't seem too concerned." Hudson lifted a hand gently. "What I mean is, obviously you're worried. I can tell that. But most partners would be kicking doors down and demanding to see my Lieutenant by now. You're laid back by comparison. What gives?"

Laurence sucked his teeth faintly as he scratched his stubble. There was no way he could say, *Well, he's psychokinetic and pretty good in hand to hand combat, so actually I'm just confused about why he hasn't dealt with it and come home yet*, and he sure as hell couldn't say, *I'm weirded out by the fact that I can't see him and neither can Soraya.*

"I don't know," he breathed as he dropped his hand into his lap. "I don't think it's really hit yet. Like how could anyone just take him off the street in broad daylight, you know? With his bodyguard right there!" Laurence threw his hands up, and he wasn't even half faking it. "It's so weird. It doesn't feel real."

Hudson nodded thoughtfully. "Fields gave you my card?"

"Yeah." Laurence stood as Hudson did. "I've got it."

"Good. Call me if you need anything, or even if you have a question. But for now, I suggest you try and get some sleep."

Laurence laughed bitterly. "You think I can sleep?"

"No." Hudson wasn't unsympathetic. "But you should try."

He held out his hand, and Laurence shook it. "Thank you for your time, Mr. Riley. I'll be in touch."

"Yeah," was all Laurence could think of to say. "Thanks."

He stood with Sebastian and watched Hudson walk away, then waited until Windsor saw the detective pass under his perch.

"That's a problem," Sebastian noted quietly.

"Huh?" Laurence blinked up at him. "What? Why?"

"He's insulating you from the truth," Sebastian mused.

That didn't make a whole lot of sense. Laurence's instincts hadn't picked up a single lie during anything Hudson had said. How could Sebastian have noticed something he hadn't?

"Nah, he didn't lie," Sebastian added. "But there are a few things he didn't tell you."

"Like?"

"Like the fact that in any missing person's case, the first 48 hours are critical," Sebastian explained, keeping his voice quiet. "Or the fact that no ransom so far is highly unusual and suggests they might still be traveling. Quentin could be over the border by now, or out of state, and if that's the case, Hudson's going to have to call in the FBI. That's when it all gets complicated." Sebastian started toward the SUV, but he checked Laurence was with him before he continued. "He wants you to get some sleep because if they haven't called yet, it's unlikely they will until morning."

I come? Windsor had picked up on the fact that Laurence was on the move.

Can you stay there for a while? Watch the cops? I want to know when they're gone. Will you be safe doing that for me?

Yes!

"Okay. Windsor's going to stay and let us know when the cops leave, then we can come back here and try to pick up Quentin's trail."

Sebastian unlocked the SUV and waited for Laurence to get in, then slipped into the drivers's seat. "And until then, maybe some rest isn't that bad an idea."

"Yeah, maybe. But it's not gonna happen."

He felt weird leaving Windsor behind like this, even though they'd been apart plenty of times before. As Sebastian drove away, it felt like Laurence was leaving a little piece of his soul behind. Maybe it was because he was already without Quentin, but as much as he wanted to hug Windsor to convince himself everything would be okay, he needed to know when the cops cleared out, and this was the best way to do it.

Laurence just had to find a way to deal with it.

He looked out the window, then frowned as a question hit him. "What happens after 48 hours?"

"Statistically, the odds of finding the victim alive drop off significantly." Sebastian's voice was level.

They both knew *the victim* in this situation was Quentin. For all that Laurence wanted to scream in Sebastian's face, Quentin needed him, and Laurence didn't know how to help. All he knew was that there was a deadline, and the cops weren't being open with him about the danger or the urgency.

Maybe rich people didn't get better cops after all. They just got more polite ones.

The thought didn't make him feel any better. For all that he had a plan to come back here and try to pick up Quentin's scent, he still had to spend time waiting, and if the scent proved just as useless as the rest of his gifts, he'd be relying on those polite cops to save Quentin's life.

The clock was ticking, and nothing Laurence could do would slow it down.

22

QUENTIN

"The trouble with you, Banbury, is you don't pay attention."

Quentin scowled at Mr. Hargreaves.

It was difficult to pay attention in class while still recovering from his fall, but Mr. Hargreaves had shown little interest in any attempts to explain that to him. The teacher had decided that Quentin was an idiot, and that was that. What use was there in fighting it any more?

"Yes, sir," he said.

Mr. Hargreaves didn't look at all pleased with that answer. He didn't rise from his desk, nor did he give Quentin permission to leave.

He'd held Quentin back as the rest of the class filed out for lunch, purely to berate him, it seemed, and Quentin got quite enough of that from children his own age.

"And because you don't pay attention," Hargreaves finally continued, "you're going to fail all your exams when they come. Is that what you want?"

"No, sir." Though, truth be told, what was the point in trying to pass them? He would be the Duke of Oxford one day. It hardly required a test.

"Your problem is—"

The door to the classroom slammed open so hard that the fixtures on it rattled and the wood itself vibrated.

"There you are, Icky!" Freddy drawled as he entered the classroom. "Oh, hello there, Mr. Hargreaves. Is Icky bothering you?"

Quentin could have leaped out of his skin, and he spun on the balls of his feet to face Freddy, terrified that Fred was going to get into trouble now.

"Not at all, Lord d'Arcy," Hargreaves said smoothly.

Naturally he'd favor Freddy, since Freddy was at the top of almost every class he was in.

"Wonderful. Come on, Icky, let's go get lunch."

Quentin didn't need to be told twice. He scurried out into the corridor with Freddy, and didn't look back.

"Timely rescue?" Freddy offered.

"Honestly, I don't know why he has to be so mean all the time," Quentin huffed in response.

"Because he's a commoner, and he's jealous that half the children in this school outrank him," was Freddy's answer. "He's a nasty little man, and he's beneath you, Icky. Don't let him wear you down. Only a few more months and we'll both be out of here. All you have to do is hold on."

Hold on, and eventually all this would be behind him.

He gasped awake to the sensation of being jostled. There was too much to process all at once: hands on his body, pain in his wrists, his arms being wrenched behind his back, the darkness that surrounded him. If this was another nightmare, it was so thoroughly random in nature that it confounded his ability to comprehend it.

Pressure brought his hands together behind his back and he struggled against it while trying to work out where he was or why he was here, but they were stronger than him, and a metallic *click* sounded.

Handcuffs.

He cursed himself. He must have dozed off, and they'd taken the opportunity to cuff his wrists behind his back instead of in front, as they'd left him. He didn't feel as though he'd had a full night's sleep, either.

Fingers tangled in his hair and pulled his head up, and a bright light shone directly into his eyes a second later.

"Rise and shine," Delaney grunted.

Quentin screwed his eyes shut and tried to turn from the light, but whoever had hold of his hair had a fierce grip. Instead, he assessed what he could of his situation. He was on the floor, still with the pressure of the manacle around his ankle, and sitting upright. Either he'd fallen asleep like this, or they'd moved him so fast that it was what had jolted him awake.

There were legs behind him, knees against his shoulders. He curled his fingers, both to lift them off the floor out of stamping range, and to do what he could to feel for the handcuffs. They were two loops of metal joined by some sort of solid central piece that was coated in hard, textured plastic. It made it next to impossible to get himself any more comfortable, so he balled his hands into loose fists to focus on protecting them, since the woman in the truck seemed quite keen to put her boots on any part of his body.

Despite having shut his eyes, the light was still there, stained deep pink through his eyelids. If he relaxed at all, the pink only got brighter.

While he supposed that it would be fruitless, he attempted to reach out with his gifts and glean some sense of his surroundings, but as before, they utterly failed to respond. Unless the entire previous year of his life had been one long hallucination, he was going to have to accept that he was suddenly without a power he had only recently discovered he possessed, and he would be wholly reliant on his wits.

He was doomed, then.

"All you have to do is hold on."

Freddy's words seemed as relevant now as they had at school, and Quentin took a slow breath to help clear the rest of the cobwebs out of his brain and steady himself.

"All right, Delaney," he sighed as though this were time taken out of his otherwise hectic schedule. "I'm up. What can I do for you?"

"You're going to answer some questions," Delaney said, sounding pleased with himself. "And then, if I like the answers, I'll let you go."

Quentin pursed his lips faintly. "You can't be serious."

Something — he assumed a hand, since it was so sudden and yet not too solid — hit him in his right cheek and wrenched his head aside with the force of the blow, which pulled against the grip on his hair and stabbed more pain through his scalp.

He very much doubted that Delaney could do worse than that, but the woman was a far more dangerous quantity, as were the two thugs who had defeated Carolina, and Quentin had to assume that all four were present.

"You still wanna question how serious I am?" Delaney hissed, inches from his ear.

Very much so. But Quentin would stand a better chance if he held on, kept his sarcasm contained, until an opportunity for escape arose. If he could behave as though he were subdued, he might be left alone with Delaney, and if Delaney could be provoked into coming close enough when there were just two of them in a room together, Quentin should be able to overpower him and search him for keys.

That felt very much like a good, solid plan, so he bit his tongue and stayed silent.

"That's better." Delaney's voice back to a more reasonable, less personal distance now. "Man, all I wanted to do was ask you a few questions about your mom's ghost, but you had to get all holier than thou on me, didn't you? But if you think I'm walking away from the first real evidence of a haunting I've ever found, you're crazy."

Quentin wondered whether Delaney was at all self-aware.

"This is huge," Delaney continued. "You're gonna make me

rich. So why don't you just talk, and we can work this out, yeah?"

He probed the inside of his cheek with his tongue. There wasn't any blood, and he hadn't bitten himself. So far, so good. "And you think that, out of one million subscribers, not a single one of them will contact the police if you record yourself holding me hostage and put it on the internet?"

"No. Because here's what's going to happen." Delaney came close again, and Quentin did his best not to crinkle his nose at having the man in his personal space. "We're going to talk, and you're going to tell me all about this haunting, and then you're going to sign a contract. You're going to agree to not press charges, and then we'll have a conversation on camera where you talk about the hauntings. Once I've got my interview, and your signature to guarantee my safety, everyone gets to go home."

There was the crux of it, then. Delaney was quite bonkers. Either he presumed that Quentin would give him what he wanted and that a piece of paper would genuinely save him from any and all kidnapping charges, or he believed that Quentin would actually trust him to let Quentin go once Delaney had what he wanted. And perhaps Delaney himself even believed it. Maybe he genuinely intended to release Quentin once this was all done, thoroughly wrapped up in his obsession with the notion that Quentin was haunted, desperate to film evidence and show it to the world.

But Quentin wasn't foolish enough to believe that whoever's knees were in his back held the same idea. Delaney's muscle was professional, and far less likely to want their witness to get away.

"All right," Quentin said with care. "What is it that you want to know?"

He had to delay without making Delaney realize that was his tactic. The longer he held, the more likely an opportunity for escape would arise. Quentin simply needed to perform the incredibly dangerous feat of balancing his time against

Delaney's instability to make both last for as long as humanly possible, because the moment Quentin made his move, that would be it. He would have no further chances if he fluffed it.

"I want to know how your mom died."

Quentin gritted his teeth and took another deep breath.

His survival was reliant upon his ability to retain his temper.

Doomed.

23

LAURENCE

Law gone!

Laurence started awake and found himself curled up on a couch, hugging a pillow to his chest. Sebastian had dozed off in an armchair.

All of them? Laurence asked Windsor.

Yes.

Okay. Be there soon.

"Sebastian." Laurence croaked, then cleared his throat. "We gotta move."

Sebastian's eyes opened, then he yawned and stretched his arms overhead. "What time is it?"

"No idea. Uh." Laurence pulled his phone out and checked it, squinting as the bright screen pierced the dimness in the living room. "Ten past two." He swung his legs off the couch and pulled his sneakers on, then stood, putting his phone away in his pants pocket again. Then Sebastian's yawn infected him, and he let it run its course.

By the time the yawn left him, Sebastian had his own shoes on too.

They snuck through to the garage in the hope that they could make it without waking any of the kids, then drove off into the night.

SEBASTIAN PARKED the SUV in the exact same spot as the last time, and Windsor flew over to land on Laurence's shoulder the moment he got out of the car.

"Hey, who's a good bird, huh?" Laurence stroked Windsor's head and tickled under his chin as they set off toward where the forensics team had been a few hours ago.

Windsor chuckled and chattered, making pleased, smug noises at the praise.

"Seriously, Win. Great job," he added. "Thanks."

Windsor cawed. *Yes.*

Yeah, Windsor wasn't great at being humble, and it made Laurence smirk to himself briefly.

They rounded the bend in the street. The only light came from a streetlamp behind them, and the moon and stars overhead, but it was plenty to see by. A house on the right-hand side of the street was masked by a fence covered in plastic sheeting, with a construction company's signage pinned to it. Since that side of the street continued uphill, the house itself was visible past the fence, with a pile of bricks sitting in the yard, waiting to be used. Now the police tent had gone, it was easy to see where the construction truck would have been, but the street was plenty wide enough for passing if it hadn't been parked so as to block the street.

"They must've been paid off," he theorized out loud.

"The construction workers?" Sebastian nodded. "Yeah. You don't park like that unless you want to get a heavy fine if you get caught."

"Yeah." Laurence crossed the street to get closer to where it must have happened, and found chalk marks dotted across the asphalt, and tire marks facing them.

He didn't have to be a crime scene investigator to see how these things added up. The tire marks must have been from the vehicle that rammed Vargas as it wheelspun to keep her from moving. The chalk marks picked out where the fight must have happened, but whatever evidence had been there had been removed.

All he had to do now was pick up Quentin's scent.

Laurence closed his eyes and took slow breaths with his lips parted, drawing the air into his nostrils and over his tongue.

The trace of Quentin in the air was so faint. Hours had passed, and other people hand trampled all over the scene. It took Laurence a minute of slow savoring of the air to pick it out, but then there it was.

Soft musk. Oud wood. Subtle spice.

Laurence latched on and opened his eyes. Scent trails were like synesthesia to him. Once he'd plucked out the one he wanted, they became almost visible, a line of spoor that his nose, his taste buds, and his eyes all worked together to create for him.

This trail appeared out of nowhere, moved one way, then circled around an invisible obstacle. Laurence followed it to where it pooled a second, then petered out to almost nothing.

Almost.

He paced across the street, trusting that Sebastian would alert him if a car came, and for a few minutes his heart sank, growing sure that he'd lost the trail, but there was the most delicate trace of it near the roundabout.

Laurence allowed himself a slow grin. This was going to be hard, but he *could* do it, even if he had to walk the whole way.

Assuming that distance wasn't a thousand miles.

His heart started to sink again. What if Sebastian's theory was right, that the kidnappers hadn't gotten in touch yet because they were still driving to wherever they wanted to go? They could be in Mexico by now, easy, or Sacramento. Phoenix, or Las Vegas. So many potential directions, and that wasn't even including the possibility that Quentin had been taken out to sea.

Was that why he hadn't come back? Did it all come down to the fact that he couldn't swim?

Laurence flexed his fingers in frustration and began to hunt, but that meant crossing La Jolla Boulevard, tracking back and forth until he was sure the scent wasn't there, then moving back to the roundabout and trying the next turning. Thank the Goddess there were pedestrian crossings here.

There wouldn't be if they'd reached an interstate.

The more he searched, the longer it took, the more he was forced to face the sheer futility of it. They were in a vehicle, and Laurence was on foot. They'd had an eight hour head start, Laurence had to wait for the cops to leave the scene just to pick up the trail. They could take whatever turning they wanted, and Laurence had to stop at every single option over a potentially five-hundred-mile journey to find which one they'd chosen, while the trail grew ever colder.

He didn't want to give up. He *couldn't* give up.

But it took him nearly fifteen minutes to find another, even fainter trace of Quentin, and they weren't even a quarter a mile away from where he'd started. This wasn't impossible, but it *was* impossible within the forty hours they had left.

Laurence snarled, helpless. He was damn near right back at the SUV again.

This whole thing was an enormous waste of time. He didn't care about his own. He didn't even care about Sebastian's.

The person whose time was burning away was Quentin.

"It's not going to work," Laurence said thickly. Giving voice to the words only made them more true, but what else could he do? The more time he wallowed in anger and frustration, the more of Quentin's time got eaten up for nothing.

"Okay." Sebastian's voice was level. Calm. "You tried your best, Laurence. It's okay. Have you got any other tricks up your sleeve that can help right now?"

Laurence bit back his immediate *no* and actually

considered the question. His senses weren't any good for this, obviously. His stealth? No. He'd already tried looking through time and got nothing. Plants?

Was there something he could do with plants to find a person?

He shook his head slowly. "No. I don't think I have. I can try to ask Herne, see if there's something he knows that I don't."

Sebastian nodded. "Will he be awake right now?"

"Uh." Laurence bit his lip. "Herne's a god. I don't think he sleeps."

To his credit, all Sebastian did was blink slowly and draw a deep breath, before saying, "Well, okay. Try that, then."

Windsor chattered softly. *I take message.*

Laurence paused and turned to look at his familiar. Windsor's eye was inches from his own, and he felt the bird's excitement thrum across the connection between them.

Born for this! Windsor spread his wings, stretching them. *Given to you for this!*

That *was* what Herne had said. *"When you need him to, he will reach me on your behalf."*

Yeah, well. Laurence needed him to now.

"Okay," he breathed. He scritched the raven's chin while Windsor tucked his wings back in, and thought carefully about what he wanted to say. "Tell him I need to find Quentin, who could be hundreds of miles away. Tell him I don't have long. Another day at most. Ask him for his counsel and his wisdom, for whether there's anything I can do that I haven't uncovered yet. And give him my love and my gratitude, okay?"

Windsor ruffled his feathers. *Yes.*

Laurence held out his arm so that Windsor could hop down it. "Be careful, and stay safe," he added.

I will.

Windsor launched himself into the air with powerful beats of his massive wings, and within moments he had faded out of existence, leaving nothing behind but the afterimage of the blue-purple sheen of his feathers glinting in the moonlight.

Laurence gaped at the spot where Win had disappeared. The bird had really done it. Crossed over into Otherworld like it was nothing, gone from the mortal world in the blink of an eye.

"Fuck," Laurence breathed.

"So that's new to you, too, huh?" Sebastian murmured. "What do we do? Wait until he comes back?"

Laurence nodded weakly, still staring at the spot where his familiar had vanished. He still felt Windsor, but the link was weak, tenuous, the way it was whenever he was separated from Windsor by a sanctum or by being in Otherworld himself.

"I guess," he admitted. "And see if I get a ransom demand in the morning."

It wasn't great, but it was all he had right now.

24

QUENTIN

"You found her body, and that's why she's haunting you!" Delaney crowed his ridiculous statement as though he had solved some universal mystery. "When did you first realize it was her?"

Quentin tried to untangle the question, but he couldn't. His brain was slowly turning to mush. The light against his eyelids was relentless, as were the fingers in his hair. "The body?"

"The ghost, asshole! When did you realize the ghost was her?"

Quentin worked his jaw, as though words might come out that could do what he needed to do, but nothing was forthcoming. All his words had abandoned him. He just wanted to sleep.

"Honestly," he croaked, "I don't know. How do you come to terms with the existence of such things?"

Not *all* his words were gone, then. He sagged with relief.

"I mean, all the evidence is right there," Delaney spat.

"All the evidence is right there for one who is predisposed to believe that ghosts are real," Quentin countered, already weary of this circular conversation. It was worse than feigning extroversion. Here he was talking to total strangers about complete nonsense against his will, and leaving wasn't an option. "Otherwise it is quickly written off."

"But you admit now it's a haunting, right? You *must*!"

Quentin sighed. "Look. Turn this bloody light off, get me a chair, and we can talk."

"You don't get to tell me what to do!" Delaney's voice was almost a scream, and it zoomed in close enough for breath to hit Quentin's cheek.

"Do you want to hear everything, or not?" Quentin shrugged faintly. "For crying out loud, you have a million subscribers. Do you want to give them the very best that you can, or do you want me to fight you every step of the way? I would be more amenable to talking if this light were not in my eyes and I had something decent to sit on. I'm sure you can understand that."

"I *want*," Delaney hissed, "evidence. On camera."

Quentin paused. "Of a ghost," he said with care.

"Yes."

"Do you think that it will manifest on command?"

"I think if we find out what links the manifestations together, we can make it happen." Delaney backed off again.

Quentin pressed his lips together briefly and tried to jolt his brain into action. There was an opportunity here; he just needed to see it, figure out what it was, and take it.

His brain finally obliged.

"All right," he murmured. "If I am allowed to use the lavatory, have a seat, and not have this bloody light constantly, I will work with you on figuring this out."

Delaney snorted at him. "You want the fucking toilet now?"

Quentin shrugged. "I'm afraid so."

It was as though he could hear the cogs turning in Delaney's mind. There was quiet for several moments.

"Okay," Delaney said. "Take him to the bathroom."

"You try anything, and I'll break your arms," the woman stated by his ear, matter of fact, as she let go of his hair and uncuffed his left wrist. The knees in his back moved away, and he swayed at the loss of support while she drew his arms in front and cuffed them together again.

"Wouldn't dream of it," he muttered.

Another clank, and the manacle fell from his ankle. Strong hands dug into his biceps and dragged him to his feet, and the light dimmed so much that he couldn't tell whether it had gone away completely.

She propelled him up the stairs and into a small privy, and it wasn't until his eyesight eventually returned that he was able to use it.

WHEN HE LEFT THE LOO, the two thugs flanked the woman, which made tackling her out of the question. Handcuffed, he could perhaps manage something one-on-one if he had space in which to move, but three people in a cramped hallway who were vastly stronger than himself were out of the question.

He allowed her to lead him back to the basement. He would have to bide his time.

There was a battery-powered lantern on an old, worm-infested table. It allowed Quentin to assess his prison at last.

The walls and floor were stone, just like the house's exterior. There were rusty old chains, hanging from metal loops embedded into the walls or ceiling, or coiled up on the floor. There were hooks without chains in the oddest of spots.

What the hell *was* this place?

He faltered, but she pushed him onward, shoving him down into a chair that faced the table. It, too, likely had woodworm, but it felt solid, and she even went to the trouble of locking the manacle back around his ankle.

Quentin grimaced as the metal settled around him, but he had his hands in front now, where he could use them.

Delaney was in the only other chair, the far side of the table. His thugs remained upstairs.

"Better?" Delaney snorted.

"Absolutely. Thank you."

"Then let's get back to it."

"He's wasting your time," the woman by Quentin's side said. She sounded bored, and when Quentin glanced her way, she looked it, too. "There isn't any ghost, and he knows it."

"What?"

Quentin frowned. He watched Delaney, who seemed every bit as confused as Quentin imagined he must be right now.

The woman moved away from Quentin's side and crossed to the table. She lifted a foot and planted it on Delaney's armrest, forcing him to move his arm out of the way for her, and then she rested an elbow on her knee.

"There is no ghost," she repeated.

"But—"

She cut him off. "But I said I was a ghost hunter and that I could help you get the evidence you needed," she agreed. "I lied."

Quentin sat upright slowly. Was this all some convoluted trick? A joke, even?

Delaney's mouth hung open, but all he managed to say was, "What?"

"You won't get evidence of a ghost, because he's not haunted," she said to Delaney. She paused, and turned to look Quentin in the eye as she added, "He's a witch."

Quentin's heart sank.

If this was a trick, it wasn't about to play out in his favor.

"That's crazy! You answered my posts! You said you could help me get what I needed to prove this was all real!" Delaney looked on the verge of tears. "You fucking lied to me?"

"You're an idiot," she countered. "A stupid child who wants to be famous. Get out of the chair." When Delaney didn't move, she barked, "Get up before I throw you out!"

Delaney jolted to his feet, and she pushed him aside so that she could sit in the chair he'd been ousted from. She leaned forward and rested her elbows on the table, and her attention became laser focused on Quentin.

She looked like she was enjoying herself.

"Delaney is a moron," she said, as though the student wasn't even in the room any more. "Like you said, he's looking for evidence of ghosts, so all he found was what he wanted to see. But I know the truth, d'Arcy. He won't find any ghosts, because all his evidence has nothing to do with them. It's you, isn't it?" She smirked. "It's witchcraft."

"This is insane," Quentin breathed. "I'm no more a witch than I am haunted!"

"You're sitting there wondering why all your power is for nothing," she continued like he hadn't said a word. "You're struggling to understand why the magic the Devil gave you isn't coming to your rescue. You thought this would all be over by now, but instead you're here, stuck, and you can't figure out why, can you?"

Say something, he urged himself. *Deny it, for Christ's sake!*

"What are you even talking about?" Delaney whined.

"Over three hundred and fifty years ago," she continued, "my family were among the most well-paid witch-finders in England. They did God's work, rooting out those who had made pacts with the Devil and putting them to their deaths. They delivered innocents from evil, until your family came along." She pointed at Quentin, and a quiet rage flashed across her features. "A family of powerful witches, in league with both the Devil and the King. They slaughtered as many of us as they could, and drove the rest from England's shores. You forced us into poverty, while you only grew in wealth, prestige, and privilege. You drove us from our home, then profited and proliferated in our absence." Her rage slowly transformed into a triumphant, heartless smile. "There were witches here, too, so we stayed and did our job. But we were ever on the lookout for our enemy, the embodiment of the Nemesis, the Devil's hand on Earth. And then Delaney put his files online. Imagine how amazed I was to find that a d'Arcy was so arrogant as to step foot on *our* turf."

Quentin shook his head faintly. None of this made any sense, short of the fact that his attention had been on Delaney when it should have been on this woman instead.

"Who are you?" he breathed.

"My name is Katharine Marlowe," she answered, "and I'll be the last person who ever saw you alive."

QUENTIN

HIS WHOLE PLAN HAD BEEN BLOWN TO SMITHEREENS IN UNDER A minute. Fooled right from the onset of this nightmare, so convinced that Delaney was in charge, Quentin had built his escape on the certainty that it was Delaney he had to overpower.

In his defense, Delaney seemed like he'd been equally as sure of that. The student was gawping at Marlowe like he couldn't believe what had just happened and his whole life was crumbling down around his ears.

Quentin couldn't help but feel some small measure of sympathy for him. Perhaps reality was rushing in at last, washing away all his dreams of fame and fortune.

"Cat got your tongue?" Marlowe smirked.

Quentin shook his head faintly. "If you wished to kill me, you could have done so several times already. There's something else you want. What is it?"

Marlowe's smirk faded. She rose from the chair she had only just taken from Delaney, and circled the table to lift one booted foot and plant it firmly on Quentin's thigh. He grunted as she leaned forward, her weight against his scars, until she was inches from his nose.

His decision was split-second. As much as he wanted to

know her answer, she'd just made it very clear that she intended to kill him, and she might never come this close again.

Quentin snapped his head forward, aiming for her nose, and jabbed his hands up toward her throat at the same time. He grabbed either side of her neck, and gripped tight, using his hold to pin the bar of his handcuffs against her windpipe. The collision between his forehead and her nose made a god-awful *crunch*, and wetness gushed across his skin.

Delaney screamed, which cut Quentin's time short. That was a bloody klaxon for the thugs waiting upstairs. He had to hurry.

Marlowe scraped her boot along his inner thigh, up toward his groin, and the pressure of it dragged excruciatingly over every scar along the way. Quentin spasmed, unable to stop himself from bucking under the assault, but his grip remained firm around her neck, and he looped his other leg around her only standing one, pulling it forward to shift her centre of balance so that she didn't have the pressure she needed to crush his balls.

She grabbed his arms and pushed one up, the other down. It forced his body to turn in a way that would break his hold on her if he didn't act fast.

Quentin threw his weight backward. With her leaning over him, it only took a quick push to make the chair begin to topple, and he clenched his jaw as he braced for the impact. He kept his leg curled around Marlowe's to stop her from breaking free, and they fell together.

The chair slammed against the hard floor, Marlowe's weight landed on him, and for a split second everything was stars.

Other hands grabbed him and pulled his fingers from her throat, his leg from her thigh. She rolled off him, kicking him in the side either by accident or design as she did so, and he was on his back with his legs in the air and the two heavies pinning him down while Marlowe bounced to her feet, blood streaming from her nose and across her chin.

Her lips curled into a snarl. "Told you if you tried anything, I'd break both your fucking arms," she hissed, then spat blood to one side.

"You're fucking insane!" Delaney hadn't come any closer, and Quentin could hear sobbing in his voice. "You can't just break his arms! What the hell is wrong with you?"

Marlowe turned away from Quentin. "You want me to break yours instead?"

Delaney whimpered in utter terror. "I'm gonna call the cops."

The shadows moved, and Marlowe was gone from his field of view in a heartbeat. Quentin heard a scuffle, and Delaney's cry, and then there was the clanking of another chain, the rasp of more metal.

Bloody hell, had she just chained Delaney up, too?

"Get him up," Marlowe rasped.

The hands on Quentin hauled him to his feet and away from the fallen chair.

Damn it, he'd been so close. If Delaney hadn't screamed, Quentin might have held onto Marlowe long enough to cut off her air, but chokeholds were so difficult from the front, especially without full use of his hands. He'd needed more time, Delaney had robbed him of it, and now they were both buggered.

There was no way Marlowe was going to let Delaney survive this, either. How could she? He was a witness to everything, even if it incriminated himself.

Marlowe was standing with one foot on Delaney's chest now, even though the student was manacled to the floor. She just seemed to like applying her feet to people. Every bully had their own thing, and this was evidently hers.

"Since you care so much," she sneered down at Delaney, "I'm totally willing to break your arms instead. Do you like that? Want to make that trade?"

"You can't!" Delaney squirmed, his eyes wide in panic. "Why would you do that?"

She leaned in. "Do you want to make that trade?" Blood dripped from her nose and onto Delaney's cheek.

"Stop." Quentin straightened himself as best as he could and gazed at her. His heart was racing, in part from the scuffle, but also from the horror of what he was about to say. "Don't hurt him."

Marlowe eyed Quentin, then stepped off Delaney and wiped the blood from her face with her sleeve. "Make him comfortable," she eventually barked. "I'm going back to sleep."

She dug a bundle of keys from her pocket and tossed it to the men, one of whom let go of Quentin enough to snatch it out of the air; then she turned for the stairs as the bruisers dragged Quentin to the edge of the room.

One of them used his shoulder to pin Quentin to the wall as the other unlocked his cuffs, then they turned him and pressed his face into the cold stone as they wrenched his arms around behind him. His heart still hammered, and his limbs were quivering with relief at not having his arms broken just yet, so it was easy for them to twist and turn him like a child's toy. He was only dimly aware of the handcuffs fastening back into place before one of them punched him in the gut, and while he wheezed from that blow, they pulled him to his feet and wrapped something cold and hard around his neck.

Quentin gasped and thrashed in their arms, but a shoulder pinned him again, and he heard the snap of a padlock.

Then they punched him again, for good measure.

He tried to double up, to curl around the pain, but the metal around his neck started to choke him, and his eyes watered. He straightened, his gut cramping, but he could breathe, and the bully boys didn't say a single word as they left him hanging and made their way to the stairs.

The trapdoor slammed shut after them, and Quentin squeezed his eyes shut, taking deep breaths to try and wash away the burning from his thigh, his stomach, and his wrists.

Delaney's wretched crying didn't help matters, and soon Quentin gave up and opened his eyes, blinking tears away.

They were alone down here. The fallen chair lay where Quentin had been dragged away from it. The lantern remained on the table. The other chair was upright.

Delaney's ankle was manacled, and his chain ran to the wall near the table. If he wished to, the student could at least relocate to a chair, or turn off the lantern. His hands weren't bound, and he certainly wasn't being forced to remain standing due to any sort of metal collar around his throat.

Quentin grimaced and twisted on the spot to try and evaluate what exactly was going on. There was a little sway available to him, but not much, and if he tilted his head just so, he could see that he had a chain overhead, connecting the collar to the ceiling.

Comfortable. He curled his lip.

There was no way he could sit. Not even if Delaney threw a chair over to him. If he dipped so much as an inch, he'd begin choking again.

And Marlowe had gone to get some sleep.

He started to grasp the enormity of his current predicament. He'd had barely any rest, he hadn't eaten since lunchtime, and if he began to nod off, he'd choke himself. His hands were where he couldn't use them, and his leg was still manacled to the bloody floor.

Rather than allow himself the luxury of worry, he began to catalogue his assets instead. His own pockets had been emptied, but what about Delaney's? Had the student left his own things upstairs, or did he still have them?

Quentin looked toward Delaney, and found him sniffling into his hands. "Well then," he said, as calmly as he could manage. "This is quite the pickle."

Delaney rubbed his nose and gawped at Quentin. "The what?"

"Do you perhaps have a phone? That would be really rather useful right about now," Quentin murmured.

"Phone?" Delaney echoed, then he sat bolt upright and dug through his pockets. "Yeah, I've got…" He found it and pulled it out, then thumbed at it and started walking around until he ran out of chain, stretching his arm out and waving the phone up near the ceiling. "Fuck. No bars."

Quentin winced. "Where are we?"

"I'm sorry." Delaney clutched his phone to his chest. "I'm so sorry. I just wanted to scare you into talking. I never wanted this to happen."

No, Quentin thought. *Not now that you're caught up in it too.* Delaney had been quite happy for Marlowe to gag Quentin on the way here, and to smack Quentin across the face himself when the student had still believed he was in charge.

"Perhaps not," Quentin murmured. "But here we are, and if we don't get out, she's going to kill us both."

"Me?" Delaney squeaked.

"Yes, you, you bloody idiot." Quentin ground his teeth. "If she lets you go, you'll run straight to the police and tell them everything they need to find and arrest her. She's hardly about to let that happen."

Delaney shuddered, then looked down to his phone. "I should document this," he whispered. "Oh my god, this will get so many views."

Quentin blinked at him with a sinking feeling. The ache in his gut was turning into a dull cramp, and the pain down his thigh was a throbbing burn now. He'd been punched, hit, kicked, and stamped on, wrenched around so much that his shoulders hurt and his wrists felt bruised, and this selfish little imbecile was still fixated on his bloody internet audience.

Not for the first time, he contemplated destruction of a camera from afar, except this time, it wouldn't work even if he tried.

"I would prefer it," Quentin rasped with resignation, quite sure that Delaney wouldn't respect his wishes, "if you did not."

For a moment, it looked like Delaney might surprise him. But it didn't last.

As Delaney held his phone out and started chattering away at it — skipping over a great many incriminating details, Quentin noted, and focusing on his imprisonment rather than how he'd gotten there — Quentin simply turned his back on the student and faced the wall instead. It would be humiliating enough to be filmed in this situation, without it getting plastered all over the internet should they make it out of here alive, and the last thing Quentin wanted the world to see was him looking like this. If Delaney wanted to point the camera toward him, all he'd get was Quentin's back, and that was that.

It was the only thing he had any control over right now, so he would damn well exercise it.

26

QUENTIN

QUENTIN DRIFTED IN AND OUT OF CONSCIOUSNESS. EVERY TIME he swayed on his feet, the collar dug in and jerked him awake before he could even begin to choke. At some point, Delaney had managed to stop bloody talking to his phone, so Quentin turned around and leaned his shoulders against the wall. It provided the faintest respite, but allowed his knees to bend if he began to nod off, and ultimately proved no more restful than facing the stone. Worse, staying in contact with it sapped his warmth more quickly than standing up straight.

His thighs felt like rubber. His stomach had cramped several times as the cold made him shiver and set off a whole new wave of spasms. He couldn't draw on the ambient temperature to keep himself warm, and every now and then his teeth chattered.

The longer it went on, the more sure he was that he was going to go mad long before Marlowe came back.

I have endured worse, he told himself silently, over and over, until it became a mantra. *I can endure this.*

Except usually when he endured worse, he wasn't present. Not really. His mind had shut down and left his body to deal with the pain alone. Perhaps if his situation here grew bad enough, he would slip away once more, safe and distant, but for now he was stuck, floating, half aware and half sinking deeper into wretched, frozen exhaustion.

He slumped against the wall and dozed, then bolted awake the moment he began to slide down the stone and choke.

The madness crept closer.

"What did she mean?" Delaney's voice was like a fever dream. "When she said you were a witch?"

Quentin's eyelids fluttered. Was this really happening?

"What?" he croaked.

"Kathy. All that stuff about witches." Delaney sounded sleepy.

Quentin struggled to pay attention, to open his eyes properly. His jaw itched and his mouth was dry. His eyelids felt like they'd been ironed. "You tell me where we are," he countered, "and we'll take it from there."

Delaney huffed. "You first."

Quentin lifted onto tiptoes so that he could stretch his spine and flex his shoulders back. He heard a series of cracks between his shoulder blades, and they brought temporary relief. "I'm the one chained to the sodding ceiling, Delaney. The least you could do is show some decency — potentially for the first time in your adult life, I realize — and answer a simple question. Where are we?"

Delaney sat up, then crawled to his feet and made his way to the chair he could reach. He sat on it and laid his head in his hands. "Fine," he sighed. "We're in the Colorado Desert, around fifty or sixty miles northeast of Yuma."

Quentin had absolutely no idea where that was. "In relation to La Jolla?" he prompted.

Delaney shrugged. "Maybe two hundred miles east?"

Quentin's eyes widened. "Two *hundred*?"

"Yeah." Delaney shrugged. "This building used to be a general store for an old mining town, but now it's just abandoned in the middle of a nature reserve. Nobody comes up here unless they're real lost."

Quentin tried to tamp down the panic that stirred in him,

but he was too tired to keep it from making him shudder all over again, so he turned away from Delaney and began to inspect the walls more closely. "I don't understand," he breathed. "Why the hell would a shop need quite so many..."

"Chains and shit?" Delaney sniffed. "How should I know? Maybe Kathy installed them. This place has been abandoned for over a century. You know, they used to dig underground and line the hole with stone because it kept things cold. You could store food for longer in a basement like this, or keep fresh, cold water. Might even stay cold enough to store ice, especially in winter."

"You aren't helping," Quentin muttered. He didn't know what he was looking for, if anything at all. While he doubted that there would be a handy loose stone leading to an escape tunnel, failure to bother looking would absolutely lead to a failure in finding one if it *was* there.

There were marks carved into a stone near the ceiling. He squinted at them, hoping that they said *press here to escape*, but they weren't words at all. Instead, so far as he could make out, they were a series of interlocking circles cut into the stone, looking almost like a flower. Precise, too, each one rendered perfectly. There were no signs of age to the marks. They were not softened, nor hidden under dust, so he doubted that they were an original feature.

He frowned and turned slowly, looking for any other odd bricks in the weak light offered by the lantern. They were all rough, and his eyes were so tired that using them so intently made them sore, but he was sure he saw more of the marks around the room, and even etched into the underside of the heavy wooden trapdoor. But if they were magic, should he not be able to see the spell attached to them, the way he could the wards at home?

They didn't look like any sigils he was aware of, although he was forced to admit that he was hardly an authority on these things. Still, from what he had seen at home, and... well, he preferred not to dwell on where else he had seen them, but from what he recalled, sigils were like letters from an alphabet that he didn't recognize, not a cluster of circles drawn together as though by a child doodling with a compass in maths class.

Perhaps they were some maker's mark, and nothing more. His addled brain was trying to find meaning where there was none.

"Your turn," Delaney said.

Quentin turned to face him and slowly flexed his fingers, trying to keep his circulation going while his fingers bathed in the chill that sucked heat toward the brickwork. "For what?"

"Don't give me that bullshit." Delaney sneered at him. "I gave you what you wanted, now you answer my question. What's all this stuff about you being a witch?"

With a sigh, Quentin slowly shrugged. "How should I know?"

It obviously wasn't what Delaney wanted, and Quentin couldn't care less. The boy could rant and rave as much as he wished, and the fact remained that Delaney had a chair and Quentin had been standing in the same spot for several hours with only the briefest of naps. Even though Marlowe had turned the tables on them all, it was Delaney's screaming that had prevented Quentin's escape, and if he gave so much as an inch, Delaney would throw him under the bus to free himself.

He wasn't going to tell Delaney a single damn thing.

Quentin wondered whether this was, in fact, just more sleight of hand. Was this the plan all along? To make him think that Delaney was innocently caught up in Marlowe's crusade, so that he might take pity on Delaney and confess to things he absolutely would not reveal to him under any other circumstances?

It seemed awfully convoluted, but Delaney had been stalking Quentin for goodness knew how long. Was it possible that he'd come up with several stupid plans, and this was the one that had made it through to actualization?

Delaney was still ranting, so Quentin blocked him out.

Instead, he tried to work out if there was some way that he could contact Laurence, or at least make this place easier for Laurence to find. Without his gifts, though, he was utterly useless.

Marlowe knew why they weren't working. She'd as good as said so, though Quentin wasn't in agreement with her on the source of his gifts. The Devil had nothing to do with it, so far as he knew — not that he was convinced the Devil existed at all.

Perhaps he would have to reconsider that stance. Herne existed well enough to have fathered a whole bloodline. If gods came into being through the beliefs of human beings, then did devils and demons also?

Why was humanity so intent on creating all this suffering for itself?

Eric was right. Quentin was a philosopher, even though he'd never thought of himself as one. Here he was, dangling from a chain, ruminating on the nature of humanity's collective psyche instead of trying to escape.

Trying to escape. He snorted. What was he supposed to do? Break the cuffs with his bare hands? Wriggle out of the collar?

God, the outlook got increasingly bleak the more he examined it. He couldn't stand here forever. Sooner or later he'd become so exhausted that it wouldn't matter whether or not falling asleep would choke him.

This collar was a death sentence. A slow, arduous, exhausting death sentence. His only hope was either that Laurence would somehow manage to find him from two hundred miles away, or that he'd get pushed too far and shut down in self-defense.

The best that he could do for now was to close his eyes, try to meditate, and hold out hope that Laurence was already on his way, but that hope gradually coalesced into concern.

If Laurence came, unprepared for his gifts to fail the way that Quentin's had, they'd both end up dead, which brought

Quentin full circle. He had to escape, by himself, before Laurence got here.

He breathed slowly and spread his feet just enough to make it easier to balance without too much attention, then tried to herd his brain toward figuring out how exactly he was going to do this. Thoughts were slippery, and trying to string them together was wearying, but if he couldn't do this, then Marlowe's words would come true, and she really would be the last person to see him alive.

It wasn't good enough. He wasn't bloody dying in a cold desert basement, and that was that.

There was no choice but to come up with a new plan, no matter how long it took.

27

LAURENCE

Laurence woke to the sound of his phone's alarm, beeping at him like he'd be going to work today, except the beeping came from his pocket, and he wasn't even in bed. He managed to turn it off and rub sleep from his eyes, but he wasn't any more alert for it.

His tongue was vacuum-sealed to the roof of his mouth. His ass felt like it had molded to the chair he was in.

Goddess, he'd had maybe four hours of sleep at the most. He wasn't ready to face the day.

He didn't have any choice.

He pried himself to his feet and stumbled toward the bathroom, wobbling as the dogs woke up and crowded around his legs.

Laurence had made it to his bedroom last night and sat by the window, thinking he could maybe pass the time with his phone, but in the end he'd nodded off where he sat, and now he was stiff as a board. He paused to lean down and ruffle the dogs' fur, but finally he made it to where he was going and managed to strip off for a quick shower. There was no way he was going to waste time shaving today, and he barely convinced himself to brush his teeth. There really wasn't any point letting himself go completely just because Quentin wasn't here.

He cursed under his breath. He'd forgotten to charge his phone last night, and if anyone was going to make a ransom demand, Laurence's phone needed to be on to receive it, so he wrapped himself in a towel and pulled the phone out of his pile of discarded clothing, then carried it back out to the bedroom to plug it in.

It rang in his hand a second after he did so, and he yelped, startled.

The caller ID read *Freddy*.

"Shit." Laurence sat and answered the phone. "Yeah?"

"Good, you're awake," Freddy said, his speech clipped. "What's happening with Icky?"

"We're waiting for a ransom demand," Laurence groused, stifling a yawn.

"More data," Freddy demanded. Then he added, "Take your talisman off."

Laurence blinked and sat upright. "No."

"Laurence, my brother is missing. London is eight hours ahead of San Diego. It's mid-afternoon here. I've waited all day to be able to call you so as to not wake you in the middle of the night. I absolutely guarantee that I will make no alterations. I just want to get up to speed without losing any detail." He hesitated. "Please, Laurence. I know I'm asking a lot of you."

Laurence rocked his jaw. The idea of letting Freddy into his head after everything Quentin's twin had done to him was horrendous, but there was no denying that Freddy loved his brother.

He was just really shit at showing it.

Laurence sighed. Every other talisman on his wrist wasn't necessary inside this house. The wards around the mansion protected him from magical attack while he was here.

"Fine," he breathed. "But I swear to the Goddess that if you fucking possess me or mess with my mind, I'll kill you."

"I accept your terms."

Laurence put the phone down, unfastened the thong, and lifted it away from his skin. He put it down on the table so far away from himself that, once he leaned back, it was out of range of his aura.

The glow on the pentagrams faded, and Freddy popped into existence in the chair opposite. If he cared that Laurence was wearing only a towel, he didn't show it.

"Thank you," Freddy murmured.

Laurence ground his teeth and made eye contact with the illusion. "What do you want?"

Freddy held a hand up a moment, then his gaze hardened. "I see," he mused. "The probability is high, then, that whomever has taken Icky is warded in some way?"

"That's the theory," Laurence agreed.

Freddy inclined his head. There was another pause. "You need Icky's blood."

Laurence gawped at him, then shut his mouth again. Blood would enable a tracking spell, possibly even strong enough to bypass whatever wards were in place, but he didn't have Quentin's blood just lying around the house.

He narrowed his eyes. "You still have any of the shirt?"

The shirt Freddy had stolen after all the drama with Kane Wilson. Even though Freddy hadn't known at the time just how bad a betrayal it was, Laurence wasn't willing to let it go.

"No. Father has it." Freddy took a breath. "But I could ask him."

Laurence leaned forward slowly, but sat back in an instant when Freddy's image began to break apart at the same time as Laurence's talismans started to glow on the table. He'd got too close to them.

Freddy reinstated himself with a frown.

"You think he'd help?" Laurence was skeptical. The duke had been willing to kill both of the twins if he couldn't have what he wanted, and Laurence had no reason to believe the old man gave two shits about either of them now.

"I honestly don't know," Freddy admitted. "All I can do is ask. If he won't do the magic himself, the very least I can try for is a piece of the shirt, though I can't get it to you in any less than about fifteen or sixteen hours."

"It's better than nothing." Laurence hesitated, then sighed. "Thanks."

"Thank you," Freddy countered, "for your trust. I'll leave you to it for now, and call you with any new developments." He glanced to the talismans on the table. "Now that I'm up to speed, I doubt you'll need to remove those again," he added.

"Got it. I'll talk to you later."

Freddy nodded and disappeared, and Laurence fastened the thong around his wrist, making sure it was secure before he reached for his phone.

The call had already been cut off.

Laurence headed back to the bathroom to shower as fast as he could so he could start the day.

BREAKFAST WAS A SOLEMN AFFAIR, with people picking at food and not talking a whole hell of a lot. Sebastian was still here, and Laurence figured he'd crashed on a couch overnight, since he looked crumpled.

"Okay," Mia sighed. "How do we solve this?"

"I don't know," Sebastian admitted. He checked his watch. "The cops should get here soon, though, if they're doing the job right."

Felipe snorted. "Then I guess most of us are gonna clear out."

"I don't like having cops here," Soraya agreed.

"Yeah, me either." Laurence sympathized wholeheartedly. "I'll let you know by lunchtime whether they're sticking around."

"What if they do?" Kim mumbled into her toast.

"Then we'll make arrangements. Mom's got a spare room out at the farm, and another over the shop."

"I can sleep on the beach," Clifton drawled.

"No." Laurence shook his head. "Even if we have to get a hotel room for you, nobody sleeps on the beach. Got it?"

Clifton shrugged at him. "Sure, okay."

"I gotta get home and changed," Sebastian muttered. "I have work in an hour and a half and I can't cancel, or I would, believe me."

"It's okay, man." Laurence gave the former soldier a wan smile. "You've done so much already. I don't know where I'd be without you."

"Yeah, well. I'm pissed I can't do more." He looked at Mia. "Keep me in the loop?"

"You got it," she assured him.

Estelita was already out at the farm. So was Lisa. Laurence felt like the kids were being forced out, one by one, and he didn't like it. This was their home for however long they wanted it, and even though Quentin was way more of a dad to them than he was, he still had a responsibility to look after them, make sure they were safe, and the mansion was supposed to be the one place they could hide out from the rest of the world.

It was morning, and there'd been no ransom call. Time was marching on, and Laurence couldn't wait around all day hoping the cops would find Quentin, or that the duke would do what Freddy was asking. He had to keep digging, because if he didn't, and anything happened...

No, he couldn't waste time panicking, either.

"Okay," he breathed. "If they were warded, it's against all of us. That means it's not specific to me, or to Quen. There's some blanket protection against psychics in play, so I'm going to switch to magic instead. That means I have to go see my teacher."

"And *that* means you'll be out of reach if anything happens," Mia scolded. "It's not good."

"I can ask Amy if she'll park outside. That way Mom can call her, and—"

Mia shook her head. "We're not playing telephone, or wasting someone else's day sitting in a car waiting for phone calls. I'll do it."

Laurence opened his mouth to protest. None of them knew where Rufus lived, and Rufus wanted to keep it that way. What Mia was asking was for Laurence to give up where his teacher hid away from the world, and the risk was obvious. Rufus could take it as the last straw and stop teaching him altogether.

"Who's going to answer the door to the cops," he finally blurted.

"Nobody," Mia said. "Fuck 'em, they should be out looking for Quentin anyway." She drained her coffee, then bounced to her feet. "Let's go."

"But—"

"I'll walk the dogs," Clifton offered.

"Plan settled," Sebastian said as he, too, rose from the table. "Call me if it's urgent and I'll do what I can."

The gathering broke apart like everyone was on a mission, and while he didn't like the plan, Laurence had a moment of pride for how eager they all were to do whatever they could to help.

He hurried upstairs to grab his phone and charger, then met Mia in the garage and hopped into the driver's side of the SUV.

"Do you really think magic will work?" Mia asked, once they reached the interstate.

"There are so many options," he said. "One of them has to." Annis had managed to bypass the mansion's magical defenses with a scrap of the shirt Freddy had given the duke. Even if whoever had taken Quentin was behind wards that bounced magic itself away, maybe Rufus' library held a spell that could summon something that could get around them. If that meant sending in a daemon, then that was what Laurence was willing to do, and he'd deal with any consequences after.

His phone rang, and he hit the button on the steering wheel to answer it. "Laurence," he said.

"Mr. Riley. Detective Hudson."

"Great." Laurence pulled toward the center of the interstate to avoid being funneled off over the next few exits. "What's the latest?"

"We've found Mr. d'Arcy's personal effects," Hudson said calmly. "Phone, wallet, what we assume are his keys. They were dumped in a parking lot near the border."

Laurence's heart thudded, and he gripped the wheel tight. "What? Do you think they've taken him into Mexico?"

"I think that's what they wanted us to believe." Hudson paused. "Have you heard the name Cameron Delaney?"

Laurence glanced quickly at Mia. "Yeah. He runs a YouTube channel. He harassed Quen on the street a couple of weeks back. Are you telling me he's got something to do with this?"

"He's a suspect," Hudson agreed. "His cellphone hit the same cell towers as Mr. d'Arcy's, at the same times, yesterday afternoon. His vehicle was picked up by some license plate readers on the way south. But we found Mr. Delaney's vehicle at the scene, along with Mr. d'Arcy's effects."

Laurence shook his head, trying to figure out what Hudson meant, and then it hit him. "They switched vehicles?"

"I believe so, yes. Mr. Delaney's cellphone data heads north again, then east. He's out of state." Hudson sighed faintly. "I've had to call in the FBI."

Laurence snarled. He had to focus on the road, not on yelling at Hudson.

"Don't believe what you've seen on TV," Hudson added. "The FBI are useful in these situations. They've got powers local PD don't, and they're good at this. They've sent us a couple of agents who are already up to speed. I'll remain your main point of contact for now, and my team is still doing everything they can to scrape forensics and pull in Delaney's known associates for questioning. We're not done yet, not by a long shot."

"Okay. Thank you," Laurence said. "I know I'm a bit snippy, but I really appreciate everything you're doing."

It wasn't the whole truth, but Laurence wasn't in any mood to find a better way to phrase all the things he'd wanted to say. And maybe Hudson was a decent cop who genuinely wanted to find Quentin alive, but there was no way Laurence was going to sit back and do nothing in the hope that Hudson was competent.

Keeping Hudson sweet was the sensible thing to do, and Laurence wasn't willing to risk everything by letting his anger out of his mouth.

"You've got every right to be," Hudson said gently. "I take it there's been no ransom call?"

"None," Laurence sighed. "This is bad, right?"

"It's not good, that's for sure, but again, don't panic. I'll call you the moment we have anything, I promise you."

"Thanks."

He hung up, and glanced to Mia again, wanting to get her opinion.

"This is good," Mia assured him. "They've already identified the kidnapper. That's a huge leap forward."

"Yeah." Laurence mulled it over for a while. "And I'm guessing the FBI can track Delaney's cellphone to wherever he is now, if he's dumb enough to still have it on him?"

"You think he's that stupid?"

Laurence snorted. "Oh yeah. He's a real prizewinner. Okay. I'll leave my phone with you, and if anything important happens, just open the gate and come inside to get me. The call will cut out if you bring it with you, though."

"Leave it in the car, come get you," Mia confirmed.

"Yeah. And, uh. Just be aware that the gate leads to a

magical sanctum realm totally removed from the real world, so when a massive house appears out of nowhere, that's what's supposed to happen. Make sure you close the gate after you're inside."

He could feel her staring at him, and managed to flit his eyes toward her for a second.

"Just when I thought my life wasn't going to get any weirder," she finally said.

Laurence raised his chin in sympathy. He knew how she felt, and was about ready to give up on the hope that one day everything could be normal.

This *was* normality now. Gods and magic, daemons and gifts. Kidnappings, psychotic psychics, and murderous faerie kings. He just had to accept that.

If it could all happen a little less often, though, he'd really appreciate it.

QUENTIN

THIS TIME, WHEN THE TRAPDOOR OPENED, HE HEARD IT.

Quentin didn't bother opening his eyes. They were sore, and the thought of forcing them to do any work filled him with horror. Footsteps descended into the basement, more than a single set, and he waited.

"Wake up," Marlowe demanded. She sounded a little congested. Perhaps he'd broken her nose.

"I am awake," Quentin whispered.

She grunted. "Take Delaney upstairs."

Quentin heard chains clink, then clatter. Delaney thanked Marlowe profusely, though Quentin doubted that Delaney was being set free.

Some footsteps receded, while others approached.

He yearned for the warmth of the fingers that touched his neck. He strained to steal it into himself, but it was a waste of time. It was as though he existed solely within his own body, and the external world was no longer a part of him. Or he a part of it.

Christ, he couldn't even get his thoughts to make sense.

The cold metal around his neck withdrew, and he swayed until hands caught him.

Now could be a good time to open his eyes.

He struggled to do it. They were dry, exhausted, and flinched themselves shut again a few times.

The hands moved to his cuffs and unlocked them. When they were removed and Quentin's hands fell to his sides, the pain that suddenly flared in his shoulders made him cry out and his eyes water.

Someone manhandled him into sitting down. They must have brought a chair over for him. He didn't care. His shoulders were on fire, and it felt like he could barely breathe.

The trapdoor slammed shut.

Was he alone? He wasn't sure he cared. The pain radiated up his neck and down his arms, and he couldn't move. If he tried to draw his hands forward, to his lap, the agony grew maddeningly intense, so he leaned back and let his arms dangle.

"I'm hungry," Marlowe said. "Are you hungry?"

It took a few breaths to think that through. *Was* he hungry? He never could tell. His appetite was pure fabrication at the best of times, something he pretended to have so that he could force himself to eat. Right this very moment, he was hurting too much to even try to eat.

"No," he rasped.

She barked a short laugh. "You're tough." She said it as though it was supposed to be a compliment.

Quentin couldn't be bothered to disagree.

"Stay there. I'll be right back."

Where else was he supposed to go? Or was this American humor?

If he could switch off right about now, that would be lovely, but it still didn't happen.

Of course not, he thought. *She hasn't hit any of your triggers.*

He must have lost his mind at last, because hoping that she would assault him in exactly the *right* way was so barmy that he laughed.

Then he stopped, because the movement of his body made his shoulders hurt all over again.

THE BITTER SMELL of coffee stirred him from his daze, and this time when he opened his eyes, it was slightly easier. He should be grateful, he supposed, for the tears that had given them the moisture he needed.

Marlowe came down the stairs, and the trapdoor shut behind her. Even though Quentin had launched himself at her once already, she didn't feel the need to have a guard down here with her.

Why should she? They'd come running at the slightest sound.

She held a mug of coffee in one hand, and a small burrito in the other. Both her eyes were blackened from the headbutt to her nose. She put her breakfast down on the table, dragged the other chair over to it, and sat down. Without looking at him, she reached into her short jacket and pulled out a long shard of brass with a peculiarly ornate handle, and Quentin couldn't tell whether it was a knife, a pair of scissors, or a wand of some sort. It was possible he was wrong on all three counts, since his vision was a little blurry.

Marlowe laid the metal thing on the table, picked up her burrito with both hands, and bit into it.

At first, Quentin wondered how she could eat a burrito at this time of day. But then he realized that he had no idea what time of day it actually was. There was no natural light, not even when the trapdoor opened. The only illumination was from the battery-powered lantern on the table.

She ate the whole thing slowly, like it was delicious. Quentin very much doubted that it was. They were, according to Delaney, in the middle of nowhere, so it was most likely fast food that had been tossed in a microwave, assuming that Marlowe wasn't eating it cold, and the idea of soggy tortilla and mushy rice just made him feel even less interested in eating a damn thing.

Once she finished it, she licked her fingers clean and picked up her coffee, and finally looked over at him.

He didn't like coffee, either. It tasted of bilge water, and the smell was repulsive.

Was she actively trying to make him feel ill? Was the excruciating pain in his shoulders, the bone-deep weariness which consumed him, not enough?

"You're telling the truth, huh?" She finally spoke, still holding the coffee cup in one hand, her fingers wrapped around the body rather than the handle.

Quentin grunted in response. The question merited no more answer than that.

"I guess that's why you're such a skinny asshole. You should eat more."

"I don't care to," he muttered.

"Too late now, I suppose." She took another sip. "My mom always made sure I had a good meal inside me before I went outside. We didn't have much, but she made sure I got to eat. She said to me, 'Kathy, you gotta eat if you want to grow up big and strong like your mama.'"

Quentin squinted, then let his eyes drift closed altogether. This most certainly was not worth the strain of keeping them open.

"You've got two brothers, right?"

He waited.

"What's it like?"

His eyebrows tugged together in his confusion. "What is having brothers like?" he croaked, trying to understand the question.

"Or any siblings, I guess."

Quentin blinked his eyes half open, then turned his head slowly and wriggled his right leg aside far enough that he could look down past his own chest and thigh.

The manacle was still there.

"What do you want?" He sighed the question as he let his head fall back, and he stared up at the ceiling. The shadows cast across it from hanging chains or hooks made a peculiar abstract art which reminded him of tree branches.

Did he hear the trickle of a brook nearby, or was his mind lying to him?

"I want proof," Marlowe said, like it was a simple request. "I'll accept either physical evidence or, if you want to make it easier on both of us, a confession."

"Proof of what?"

"That you are a witch."

Quentin laughed weakly. He did what he could to keep it under control so that he didn't shake his shoulders too much. "You're doing all this *before* you have any proof? What do you intend to do if you find none? Apologize and let me go?"

"I'll find it," she said. "My family has distilled the finding of witches over the centuries into a precise science. Either you confess, or I dig the evidence out of you. Either way, I'll get there, don't you worry about that." He heard her sip more of her coffee. "Do you want to confess?"

He rocked his jaw and tried to sit up straighter. His shoulders protested. He hissed through clenched teeth and the sting as tears returned to his eyes, but leaned forward slowly, taking sharp breaths as his wrists eased past his hips.

He could do this.

He *would* do this.

Adjusting the position of his feet until he was reasonably sure that he wouldn't fall over, he pushed until his backside lifted away from the surface of the chair, and he paused, his breath rasping with pain, his jaw clenched in determination.

He was the fifth earl of Banbury, and this body was the only one he had, so it had better damn well do as he told it.

Quentin leaned further forward. His thighs quivered with strain. His arms moved.

Slowly, so slowly, he managed to pull his hands together in front of himself, and once they were touching, he sat again, letting his legs hold them in place and prevent them from sliding over his lap and back to his sides. Pins and needles emerged from the subsiding burn in his shoulders, and he carefully flexed his fingers, relieved to feel them move, though they were somewhat numb.

He let out a brief, triumphant grunt, and glowered across the room to meet Marlowe's gaze.

"No," he finally breathed.

He would not confess. He wasn't a fool. She'd already said that she intended to kill him, and he knew damn well that the quickest way for that to happen was if he gave her what she wanted. Confession would lead directly to execution, and he was in no state to try and fight her off right this very minute.

He had to buy more time, and that meant refusing to play her game.

Marlowe sat back in her chair and put her coffee down. Her fingers moved from the mug to the brass-colored thing she'd left on the table and closed around it, lifting it so she could look at it. She held it like a dagger, point down from her fist, and the ornate handle fitted around her fingers as though made for them. "Do you know what this is?"

"Pointy," he breathed.

"Oh, you've still got a bit of life in you. I like that." She chuckled. "It's a pricker. Been in my family—"

"—for generations?" Quentin pursed his lips.

"Naturally. The purpose is to find that one spot on a witch's body which is utterly unable to register pain."

Quentin squinted at it. Nothing made a whole lot of sense any more, least of all this. How on Earth would a pointy bit of metal...

Pointy. Metal. Pricker.

It was so absurd that he wasn't sure that he'd worked it out correctly. Did she seriously mean to just jab him from head to toe until he... what? Stopped complaining about it? Even in his current state, that logic seemed unsound. Surely any witch with the slightest sense would simply say "ouch" until she stopped, regardless of whether or not it hurt — although he imagined the odds were that being poked with a pointy stick was painful wherever one stuck it.

Unless, for instance, one were already covered with scar tissue and riddled with nerve endings which displaced or diminished sensation.

A shiver skittered down his spine. It roused him as close to full wakefulness as he could get, and set his pulse racing.

Marlowe could take any failure to react properly as evidence, and he doubted that a rational understanding of anatomy would get in her way.

Her eyes lit up, and she smiled broadly. "So you have one," she chuckled.

"What?"

"A witch's mark."

He shook his head numbly. "This is absurd."

"Why not make things easier for yourself by telling me where to find it?"

"Why don't you just admit that you're trying to exact revenge for something my family did hundreds of years ago, and that doing so won't change the past in the slightest?" Anger slowly percolated to the surface, and he couldn't stop it. He was too drained to keep his mouth shut, too terrified at the prospect of being stabbed hundreds of times to even try to hold his tongue. "I'm sorry for what was done. I'm sorry for the suffering it led to. But this isn't the way to fix it." Quentin shook his head and gazed at her, hoping he could make her see sense if he just found the right words and managed to put them together properly. "It can't be fixed. But we can move forward. Make amends. Reparations."

Marlowe laughed heartily and slapped her hand on the table, as though a laugh alone wasn't enough to express how hilarious she found him. "You're offering me money?"

Quentin blinked. "I'm offering you support. Help. Money, if that's what you need, but there's so much more than that—"

She bellowed with laughter and waved her hand to cut him

off. The trapdoor flew open, and her cronies rushed down the stairs, only to pause once they reached the bottom.

The confusion writ across their faces and in their postures was an echo of that which Quentin now felt.

"Oh boy," Marlowe wheezed, wiping her eyes with the back of her hand. "That was amazing. Thank you, truly. That's the best laugh I've had in years." She used the pricker to point at Quentin, but she looked at her associates. "Get him ready."

They closed in on him, and Quentin braced himself. His arms were potentially useless, his legs were made of jelly, and he was outnumbered — but he had space in which to maneuver.

It wasn't an opportunity. Not by a long shot. He wasn't capable, he wasn't alert, and he wasn't strong enough, but he was damned if he was going to sit here and let them put their hands on him without a fight.

If Marlowe wanted to kill him, he'd make damn sure she had to work for it.

29

LAURENCE

LAURENCE LEFT MIA PARKED OUT ON THE STREET AND SLIPPED through Rufus' gate. The sensation of crossing from one plane to the next was nowhere near as disorienting as it had been the first time he'd experienced it, and he idly marveled at how quickly he'd gotten so used to the weird shit in his daily life as he dragged the gate shut.

He jogged up the drive to the house and thumped on the door. "Don't spend an hour getting dressed, man," he called out. "This is urgent."

Footsteps clumped down the stairs, reverberating through the hallway, and Rufus yanked the door open.

He was butt naked.

Laurence blinked at him. "Uh—"

"Oh, so it's *not* urgent?" Rufus huffed as he narrowed his eyes.

"No, it..." Laurence poured all his willpower into not allowing his gaze to head south. "Quentin's still missing,"

"Yeah, well, I'm sure he'll brute force and ignorance his way out of whatever he's gotten himself into. What does this have to do with me?" Rufus crossed his arms and raised his chin, and looked even less impressed at having been dragged away from whatever he'd been doing.

Laurence flexed his jaw and walked around Rufus. Ru and Quentin had never liked each other, but at least they were capable of being civil face to face. Without Quentin's presence, though, Rufus seemed to feel that the civility didn't need to be maintained. "If I told him you were in trouble, he'd drop everything to help you."

"Good for him. I assume you want a location spell?"

Laurence ground his teeth briefly, then nodded. There was no point arguing with Ru. The witch was a solitary hermit whose only human contact had very little to do with the real world, and Laurence supposed that the idea of caring about other people was reasonably alien to him.

"Yeah. Please. If you have something that could help, I'd appreciate it. I don't have any of Quentin's blood, but I'm working on that right now, so it's not totally off the table if we need it."

He heard the front door click closed, and Ru entered his peripheral vision on his way to the staircase.

"As always, there are a hundred ways to crack a nut," Rufus said as he walked past.

There was no way to avoid catching a glimpse of Rufus' ass. The witch climbed the stairs ahead of him, and while Laurence had no problem with nudity, it didn't feel right ogling someone who hadn't invited him to do so. Instead, he studiously examined the broad wooden handrail beneath his fingers as he followed.

Rufus started toward the library, and Laurence cleared his throat, so Ru paused and turned to raise eyebrows at him.

"I can wait, if you want to get some pants," Laurence said.

Rufus shrugged. "If you think I wear any when you're not here, you're sorely mistaken."

Laurence opened his mouth, then shut it again, and Rufus rolled his eyes.

"Fine. Go get comfortable. I'll find pants."

"Great."

Laurence eased past him and entered the library, and wondered how it was that he got left feeling like the asshole.

THERE WAS no way he was just going to sit and wait for however long it took Ru to find clothes, so Laurence started searching the moment he was in among the bookshelves. While he didn't comprehend the full ins and outs of Rufus' organizational system, he did know that Ru grouped books primarily by subject, and so if he could find one book on summoning, he'd find them all. The trick was knowing how to spot whether that was what he'd found when Ru's books were in a myriad of languages.

He spoke Spanish, and he hoped anything that looked like *convocar* would be what he wanted. And he was pretty sure that *convoke* was a word in English, so maybe they both came from Latin roots. If summoning required rules and laws, then Latin would be the language of choice for those spells.

Now all Laurence needed to do was find a single word in one book out of over two thousand, and he'd be set. He discounted areas he usually studied from — protections, theory, the newly-discovered planar engineering shelves — and plucked a book at near-random from a shelf near the windows to flick through. In his experience, books that didn't glow didn't contain spells, so he made sure to pull down one that did.

It gave off a pretty peach tone from between its pages, subtle and warm, and Laurence hoped that meant that the person who had written it wasn't the sort to dabble in torture or sacrifice, but he'd barely managed to skim enough to determine that it was written in a language he couldn't even begin to read when Rufus stalked in.

"I've got pants on," Ru muttered. "Put that back where it came from."

Laurence snapped it closed and re-shelved it, feeling like a kid caught up to his elbow in the candy jar, and he turned away from the shelf. "Sorry, I was, uh…"

Rufus was definitely wearing pants. But nothing else. Laurence couldn't tell whether he was being trolled.

"That's healing," Rufus continued. "You want locating." He walked to another section and began to gather an armful of books from a low shelf.

Laurence sighed inwardly. Despite Rufus' insistence that cataloguing his books would be a waste of time, whenever he needed to find a spell he always had to search through a whole pile of books, and *that* seemed like a huge waste of time to Laurence, especially in situations like these.

Urgency and magic didn't go together.

"I think he's behind some kind of wards," Laurence said as he hurried over to sit at the table. "I can't see him. I can watch right up to the moment *before* he got kidnapped, but everything after that is a blank."

Rufus frowned and laid books on the table, side by side on the highly polished wood. "It's highly unusual that anyone would ward against psychic intrusion unless they specifically intended to engage with a psychic."

Laurence nodded. "Then they must've known Quen was psychic before they went in and made sure he couldn't do anything, and the side-effect is I can't find him either."

Rufus rubbed his cheek as he mulled it over. "If they can use magic, they'd ward against magic too, as a matter of course. If they don't have magic, it's one psychic blocking another somehow. I don't know enough about psychics to guess whether or not that's possible." He dropped his hand and looked Laurence in the eye across the table. "Is it?"

"Literally no clue," Laurence admitted.

"Then we better work under the assumption that it *is* possible, otherwise you'll charge in like a buffalo and come out as a burger," Rufus said. "But it probably wastes less time if we also factor in the likelihood that they're warded." He began to sift through his book selection, nudging a few off to his right, then eyeing the two he had left. "But we don't yet have his blood," he added, and pushed those two to his left.

Laurence eyed the now blank area of the table. The meaning was clear. "What if we summon something that can track?" Laurence suggested. "Like Black Annis."

Rufus nodded, and took all the books from his right hand side back to the shelf, then went to another area to pull more down. "She had Quentin's blood," Rufus reminded him.

"Is there anything that can track him if we don't have that, though? I mean, I've got all his stuff. Clothes, toiletries…"

"You'd need darker magic than I'm willing to explore to go down that route."

Laurence hesitated, then leaned back in his chair slowly, tapping fingers against his thigh. "You mean I need a warlock."

"I'd argue that nobody needs a warlock." Rufus came back to set the new stack of books down.

"I know a necromancer. Maybe he could send a ghost in?"

"Ghosts are extremely bad at one-off tasks." Rufus began to sift through the new books, skimming over pages as he spoke. "If you're going to give them a job, it has to be repetitive, and preferably simple."

Laurence filed that away. It was useless for now, but interesting anyway, and he never knew when he might randomly need to know that kind of thing. "So, fundamentally, we need Quentin's blood, and we're drifting until we get it?"

"Or semen."

"No."

"Spit?"

Laurence scoffed at the idea of some drawer full of bodily fluids that Rufus seemed to expect him to have to hand. "Who keeps that stuff, Ru?"

Rufus just shrugged. "Well, we're not totally adrift. We just need to find the option that fits the situation. We need something that can find a human without a physical connection, doesn't require warlockry, and won't eat any children between it and Quentin." He puffed out his cheeks briefly. "There has to be a way."

"Great." Laurence bounced to his feet. "I'm gonna go explore a couple of other ideas. Let me know if you find anything that can help."

There was a pause, heavily laden with impending sarcasm, as Rufus' hands hesitated and he stared across at Laurence. But then he sighed and returned to the books. "All right."

Laurence winced. "I'm sorry, Ru. Thanks. I know you don't need to be doing any of this, especially since you and Quen don't get along."

"He was polite when you got taken," Rufus muttered. "He might not be all bad."

Laurence figured that was the best version of *You're welcome* he'd get. He made his way out of the library and jogged back down the stairs.

He could try to contact a warlock, in the hope that the duke gave enough of a shit about his eldest son to bother helping Laurence find him.

Or he could contact someone else, and figure out whether she had an alternative to offer.

By the time he reached Mia, he'd made up his mind.

30

LAURENCE

LIKE MOST THINGS IN HIS LIFE, LAURENCE HADN'T THOUGHT this through. He'd agreed to meet Angela Tate at the Fashion Valley Mall food court, but now that he was here, he was struck by how exactly he was going to lie his way through this one.

If Tate tried and found any wards that prevented her from locating Quentin, she'd know she'd been taken for a ride. If Laurence told her up front that he knew everything, she might decide not to help him.

He considered calling her back to cancel, but if she was the one person who could track Quentin down, he couldn't walk away from her.

Laurence would have to deal with the consequences for this later. He could feel it. It would hang over his head, like the debt he owed Morgan, or the promise he'd made to Rufus; but this was Quentin's life, and the longer the earl was gone, the more worried Laurence got. He kept circling back around to the fact that if Quentin *could* contact Laurence, he would have.

He glanced across the food court, to where Mia was sitting at a table under a parasol and drinking a bottle of water while looking like she didn't know him, then let his gaze drift on. One side of the food court was lined with takeout places, and the other was bordered by the edge of the second floor, with a clear view of the shoppers below. Over the low chatter he could pick out the murmur of a water feature downstairs, further along the mall.

It wasn't a bad place to sit, especially in the morning, before it got too crowded. The sun was shining, there was a faint breeze, and the tiny birds that danced from one table to the next in search of crumbs were cute to watch.

Laurence checked his phone for the time, then caught sight of Angela striding toward him. She was coming from the Bloomingdale's direction, rather than the walkway behind Laurence that led to the multi-story that Mia had parked in, and Laurence wondered whether that meant Angela wasn't familiar with the mall's parking lots, or just that she favored the chance to browse through a department store on her way here.

He smiled briefly at her and rose from his chair to offer his hand, and she shook it firmly.

"Thanks for coming. Can I get you anything?" Laurence waved his hand toward the food court.

"No, it's fine. Thanks." Angela sat, and everything about her remained as unreadable as before. Her face, her tone, her body language, it was all so neutral that her words were all he had to go on. "You've made a decision?"

They sat, and Laurence realized he'd run out of time. Whatever came out of his mouth would be it, and there was no going back. "I guess," he said. "But it's because I need your help. My boyfriend has been kidnapped, and the cops say they only have 48 hours to find him before the odds that he's still alive take a nosedive off a cliff." He grimaced. "He's already been gone almost a full day."

"I can't teach you what you'd need to know to be able to find him in that timescale," Angela said, as though completely unaffected by the idea that, without her help, Quentin could die. "Do you have a picture of him?"

"I can get one." Twitter was full of snaps of Quen. "Do you need it printed, or is online okay?"

"A printout is better."

Laurence nodded. "Okay. We've got a printer at the store. I can go down and run that off. Anything else?"

"I assume you've got a police contact? What do they say about the case so far?" Angela remained so still in her seat that one of the little birds was hopping towards her, and it only fluttered away again when Laurence leaned forward.

"They say they think he got kidnapped by a kid called Cameron Delaney, who runs a YouTube channel. Delaney drove Quentin down toward the border, took Quentin's personal items off him and ditched them, then switched to a new vehicle and drove east. They traced Delaney's cell until it crossed out of California, and now the FBI are involved in picking up the trail from there."

"Then I'll need a picture of Delaney, too," Angela said. "That will improve our chances significantly."

"Again, no problem." Laurence nodded. "What do I owe you?"

She shrugged. "What do you have that I want?"

Laurence opened and closed his mouth, then snorted. Angela seemed to value knowledge above all else, and Laurence knew the square root of fuck all. "Probably not a whole hell of a lot?"

"Exactly. Then you owe me nothing."

He wanted to argue. Nothing came free, in his experience. But time was an issue, so he resisted the urge and nodded. "Do you want to come with me to the store, or wait here, or do you want to meet somewhere else?"

"There's hardly anywhere to park near your shop," Angela said. "I'll text you an address and meet you there in an hour." She rose and stepped out from under the shade of the parasol. "No later than that," she added.

Laurence nodded quickly and stood. "Thanks."

Angela didn't respond, and Laurence didn't hang around to watch her walk away.

IT TOOK Laurence a few minutes to find good enough photos of Quentin to print off without them turning out blurry or indistinct, and while he ran them off on the store's printer, he grabbed some screenshots from Delaney's videos.

"This seems weird," Aiden commented as he pulled another printout from the tray and added it to the pile. It was Ethan's turn to be out on deliveries today, though Laurence wasn't sure whether there was any real pattern to his mom's staff scheduling decisions. "Is it weird?"

"Asking a witch I don't know to use photographs of people *she* doesn't know to somehow track them down when the witch with over a decade of knowledge and experience considers it dark magic?" Laurence sent the screenshots to the printer and sighed. "Yeah. Super weird."

Aiden clicked his tongue and tilted his head. His eyes creased with worry. "Is Rodger still playing spy?"

"Yeah, so far as I know." The question made Laurence pause, though. He tried to figure out when he'd last seen or heard from Rodger, and ended up checking his phone to remind himself. It seemed so long ago, but it wasn't. So much had happened since Quentin went missing, but it was still only a day since Rodger's voicemail about all the cops outside the mansion.

So where was he now?

"Shit." Laurence dredged up Rodger's number and called it, but it went straight to voicemail, so he tried not to ramble as he left a message. "Rodger, it's Laurence. Let me know you're okay?"

Aiden collected the next few sheets and straightened the edges, then handed them to Laurence. He was frowning as he did so. "I'll text you if he shows up," he said.

"Thanks." Laurence rifled through the images, then gave Aiden a nod. "Tell Mom I stopped by, and not to worry?"

"Yes on the first, and no on the second."

Laurence opened, then shut his mouth, and Aiden continued to gaze up at him without any sign of apology.

"That's fair," Laurence concluded.

HE TAPPED the address Angela had texted him into his GPS, then followed the directions. Carmel Valley was further north than La Jolla, up the 5 past where he'd normally turn off to go home, and he didn't usually go there. It was another expensive town in an already expensive county, and he figured these people probably had more local florists to go to.

The GPS led him to a cream-walled villa on a hilly road that was lined with nothing but cream-walled villas. They were all slightly different from each other, but the shade of cream was near-identical, and there wasn't a hint of flaking paint anywhere. Laurence wondered whether there was a contractual agreement among all the homeowners to keep things as bland as possible, but then he figured that suited Angela nicely. The house gave nothing away, just like the woman herself.

He pulled onto the drive and parked in front of her garage doors, grabbed his pile of printouts, then hopped out and approached the front door.

Maybe he should have left the address with Aiden, too.

Laurence cursed under his breath and forwarded Angela's text to Aiden so that at least someone would know where he'd gone if he vanished, and looked up from his phone in time to catch the door opening.

She gestured for him to follow, then reached for the photos. "Which one is which?" she asked as she began to flit through them.

"The one with the darker hair is Quentin," Laurence

explained. He shut the door once he was in, and followed her as she led toward the wooden stairs. "Delaney is the other."

He looked around as he tailed her. The house was almost like the apartment Quentin had had in La Jolla when Laurence first met him. The walls were painted white, with nothing hanging on them. No photos, no art, nothing to show that the property was lived in. He caught a glimpse into a lounge as they started up the stairs, but only saw grey couches and a black television. He couldn't smell any hint of an animal, didn't see any stray dog or cat hairs anywhere.

Was this even her house, or had she broken into a show home?

"Take a seat," she said as she passed through a doorway. She gestured with the printouts toward a chair.

It was the only open door upstairs.

Laurence entered the room and took note of yet more white walls and grey furniture. There was no bed in here. The full-height windows had railings across the outside to stop anyone falling out when they were opened, but they were shut right now. He settled slowly into the chair, one of only two, and found it hard and uncomfortable. The plastic was molded in a single piece, and obviously wasn't designed to encourage visitors to stick around very long.

The whole place was eerie.

Angela bent over to lay the papers on the laminate flooring, then crossed to a dresser and pulled a few things out of different drawers. Some she threw over to clatter and slide to a halt near the paper — a lighter, a metal dish — and others she cradled in one arm against her chest to carry over and put down more carefully. When she sat cross-legged on the floor and laid out the items, Laurence leaned forward to see what they were.

A tobacco tin. A handful of seashells. A knife.

She didn't look at him as she spread the printouts around herself, images of Quentin to her left and Delaney to her right. She sprinkled tobacco into the dish and set it alight, then blew on it until it was smoldering and giving off an aromatic smoke that made Laurence lean back out of its way. When she spoke, it was in a language Laurence didn't recognize. It sounded rhythmic and gentle, and soon became song instead of speech, while the universe began to hold its breath around them.

All he could do was watch, fascinated, as she performed a very different style of magic to the one he was growing used to. She waved seashells through the smoke, then cast them across the pictures, and Laurence had to wonder what aspect of this Rufus considered too dark to use.

Angela picked up the knife and pricked her fingertip with it, then smeared her blood across each of the printed images, smudging red over faces until there were none left.

Laurence swallowed. Time had slowed almost to a halt.

Swirls of deep, dark red rose from Angela's lips and dispersed into the air. He heard the distant but distinctive hooting of owls.

The song ended, and the universe heaved a sigh of relief. Time ground back into motion. All that remained were headless photographs and unanswered questions.

"Now we wait," Angela said, peering idly down at a spot of blood on her finger like she was curious how much more of it her body would produce.

Laurence couldn't think of anything to say, so he nodded and prayed they wouldn't wait too long.

His ass was already numb.

31

QUENTIN

THEY CLOSED IN ON HIM, HANDS OUTSTRETCHED.

Quentin sprang to his feet. His thighs burned, but he had to ignore their protest. There was no doubt that his life depended on it.

He slipped past their fingers and swung his foot around to drag the chain between one man's legs, then kicked it up.

He'd been punched in the balls before. He knew what it felt like, and he couldn't help but wince as the heavy chain met its mark.

The other man twisted and swung a fist at his jaw, and Quentin yelled in agony as he wrenched his hands up to deflect the blow. His shoulders weren't remotely happy, and he doubted that he'd get much more use out of them, so he eschewed delicacy and instead twisted on the balls of his feet to gain control over his opponent's arm and propel the man away from him.

One hand around a wrist, the other flat against an elbow.

You know what to do.

He didn't think. Didn't allow himself to put a stop to what he needed to do if he was going to stay alive.

He pulled the wrist and pushed the elbow, and the grind of bones dislocating under his touch was music to his ears.

The screams of his enemy were even more delightful.

Quentin darted around him and stole the bright yellow plastic gun from his holster. He didn't know whether it required cocking, hadn't ever used anything like this before, but these weapons had been ready to fire every time they'd been aimed at him, so he swung it toward Marlowe and tried to keep his arms from shaking.

She shrugged at him and crossed her arms. "What do you think this is—"

Quentin pressed his finger to what he fervently hoped was the trigger. He was braced as best as he could be for any recoil, but the weapon barely kicked, and the sound it let out was little more than a *chunk*, followed by fast ticking.

Marlowe dropped with a grunt.

If he took his finger off, would the weapon stop? Could he search her pockets while this was in progress?

He had the vaguest sense-memory of being handled while one of these guns was still delivering its electrical payload into his shoulder, and if he didn't take the risk, he'd stay in this damn manacle for the rest of his rapidly shortening life, so he rushed toward her.

The chain clanked as it pulled taut.

He was still two feet away from Marlowe's outstretched hand.

Quentin snarled with rage. She was too far away. He ditched the gun and whirled around, then snatched up his chair. If he could hook some part of it around her arm and drag her closer, he'd be able to search her pockets, but his arms quivered with strain, and he nearly dropped the whole thing.

It was too heavy.

Movement caught his eye. The man who was still groaning from the chain to his balls had rolled onto his side.

Too late, Quentin saw him reach for and grab the chain. Rather than let him pull on it, Quentin let go of the chair and sprinted toward him, then kicked him savagely in the ribs.

It wasn't a move he'd learned from Mia or Sebastian, but it did the job. The chain dropped to the ground.

Another plastic click, and this time it was Quentin who fell.

Marlowe.

He screamed, frustration pouring from him as he seized up. The man with the dislocated elbow still had enough strength to hoist Quentin off the floor and back into the chair with his one good arm, and he punched Quentin so hard in the jaw that his head snapped back and left him dazed.

Whenever his muscles were his, the control was snatched away again before he could do a bloody thing about it. He felt hands on his body, tearing, grabbing, and darkness began to crowd the edges of his world.

No! No, not now! Please, god, not now!

He fought frantically, unable to tell whether or not his body was doing what he told it to. If he could keep the dark at bay, he stood a chance.

Cold air caressed his skin. Hands released him. The repetitive punching from the weapon cut out.

Quentin sagged. He gasped for air. He was tired, so very tired, and if he could just sleep, everything would be fine.

Orange candlelight flickered in the darkness. He was cold, and even their flames did not warm his naked skin. The blood that trickled down him was warm when it began, but turned cold as it mingled with his sweat.

Father hit him again, and a spray of blood cut through the air between them, spattering over Father's cheek and past his shoulder.

How many times?

How many years?

Why didn't Quentin ever fight back?

He couldn't move. Pinned in place. Naked as the day he was born. Everything was jumbled together. Was he an adult now? Where were the candles? Why wasn't his father here?

There were strangers in this room. Two men and a woman. They all looked injured.

The woman had a weapon.

"Marlowe," he breathed. It was a name. It was *her* name. He didn't know how he knew it.

Marlowe came closer. He tried to shrink away, but he was still pinned. When he looked down, he expected to see nothing holding him down, but instead there was metal. Around his wrists, his waist. He felt it at his ankles, too, but his sight was ensnared by something else. Something awful.

He *was* naked.

A panicked, strangled noise fled his throat, as though it had better places to be. He had no idea whether he'd intended to form words instead.

Darkness slithered toward Marlowe.

"What's all this?" She gestured to his chest with the knife in her hand.

Quentin had no answer for her. All he could do was look away, between the strangers, to the darkness, so that he didn't have to see their disgust, didn't have to acknowledge that they were looking at his body.

"I guess it doesn't matter," she said. He felt warmth from her hand lay over his left forearm. "Time to get started. Let me know any time you'd rather just confess. Make this easier on both of us."

Panic boiled inside him.

She was touching him. Looking at him.

And there was nothing he could do.

The blade she pressed against his wrist was cold. Sharp.

It stung.

Quentin drew a sharp breath and tried to twist away from it, but it

—stung. Again and again it stung, like he'd been bitten by a viper, over and over as it worked across his skin—

cut into his flesh and he yelped.

She moved it barely an inch before she dug it into him again.

"Stop!" he rasped. "Please—"

The tip of the blade punctured his arm. Blood trickled lazily down his skin. His whole body shook with terror, and he couldn't fight any more.

The darkness took him away, like it always did.

It had come to save him at last.

LAURENCE

"Do we have to wait here, though?" Laurence pried himself out of the chair before his ass became one with it and paced toward the window. Outside were lush, well-watered trees, and the beautiful blue sky of a San Diego morning. "Can't we start moving?"

"To where?"

Laurence turned his back on the view as Angela began to collect all the papers together, and watched her hands dart and pluck sheets from the flooring. She pinched each corner and pulled them into a pile, then tapped a long edge against the laminate to neaten it.

"The cops tracked Delaney's cellphone east until it left the state," Laurence said. "It's almost three hours to Arizona. If we start now, while whatever your spell did is going on, that's three hours we save later, right?"

He hoped it was, at least. If Angela's spell took hours to produce results, and then they spent the best part of three hours on the road just to reach the state line, it made more sense to do both those things at the same time, instead of adding one on top of the other. Plus, it'd give him the sense that he was doing something to help.

Angela stood and put the paper on top of her dresser, then

returned her tools to their drawers. "Not the worst idea," she mused. "If we head down to Mission Valley, then hop on the 8; that goes straight to Yuma. We can wait there for better directions, if we don't already have them by then."

Laurence had his keys in his hands by the time she was done talking, and headed for the door. "Can I ask what that spell was? What you did?"

"You can ask anything you want to," she replied.

He had no way of knowing whether she was teasing him or being more literal than he'd intended, so he waited until they were both in his truck with the engine running before he tried again. He fiddled with the GPS to get it to lead him to Yuma, and once it started talking to him, he reversed out onto the street then headed south.

"What was that spell you did?" He kept his tone polite. The last thing he needed now was to lose his shit and his only chance of finding Quentin.

"There are a thousand ways to find people using magic," Angela replied. He glanced across at her, but she was gazing dead ahead. "Most of them require substance from the target. Blood, nail clippings, tears, semen, you name it. They're all viable. But if you can't access any of those, you have to rely on something else to do the locating for you. Again, most creatures, spirits, or other entities require a sample. The only ones which do not are psychopomps. They can find a target through images, though they work best from several pictures that cover as many angles as possible."

Laurence didn't look at her. If he gave away that he knew what a psychopomp was, did he risk showing his hand, or was it the kind of thing anyone might know?

He'd only found out thanks to Basil. Maybe it was better to play it safe.

"What's a psycho… what was it? Pomp?"

"A psychopomp is an entity whose task it is to ferry the souls of the dead from this world and on to the next, whatever that might be. Sometimes psychopomps are dogs, sometimes they're messengers, sometimes they're gods."

"Oh." He licked his lips. "And sometimes they're a skeleton in a cloak with a scythe, right?"

"They rarely take lives," Angela said. "That's not really their job."

"Right." Laurence tried to sound like this was all new to him, but honestly, some of it was. "What was with the owls?"

"When you call a local psychopomp, you get whatever's around. Around here, the predominant Native peoples are Kumeyaay and Cahuilla; but the Kumeyaay make their own way south after death, without a guide, so I called on Muut, the psychopomp of the Cahuilla."

"And Muut is an owl?"

"Or the distant hooting of owls. He can be abstract."

"Huh."

There wasn't a whole lot more to say than that. Laurence didn't know whether it was disrespectful to call on another culture's psychopomp and ask it to find a couple of white men, but it felt wrong, and he was glad he wasn't the one who'd done it.

As though she'd read his mind, Angela added, "The shells were payment."

He spared a look to his right, his eyebrows furrowed. "They were?"

"Yes. I paid Muut for his aid. It's not possible to send a psychopomp away on an errand without the right payment."

Laurence had so many questions. Every single one of them gave away too much about himself.

Was this how the black dog had taken Quentin to Otherworld? Had someone paid it and smeared blood on photos, or was that ritual purely for Muut? If the dog had been sent specifically for Quentin, who had sent it? Had the duke decided to deal with his runaway heir? But if he had, why was he also dropping huge slices of cash into Quentin's bank account every month?

If a psychopomp got paid, what about any of this was dark magic that Rufus didn't want to touch?

He'd have to shelve it for later.

———

AROUND AN HOUR INTO THE DRIVE, when they were surrounded by the beauty of scrub-covered desert hills on either side of the interstate, Laurence's phone rang. His thumb moved to answer, but hesitated when he caught sight of the caller ID above the GPS screen.

Basil.

Goddess, he couldn't have picked a worse time, but if Laurence sent him to voicemail, he might miss something important.

He grit his teeth and hit the button, speaking first to cut Basil off. "Hey, Basil. I'm in the truck, so you're on hands free, and I've got staff with me helping out on deliveries. How're you doing, man?"

Laurence could almost feel Angela's eyes drilling into the side of his head.

"Oh!" Basil sounded startled. "Oh, um. Ha ha. Well, hello, staff. I'm sorry, I just wanted to see how things were?"

"Nothing so far." Laurence sighed. "The cops have called in the FBI, but I figure if they'd found anything they would have called me by now."

"Right," Basil said slowly. "Well, um, so."

Basil's pause was so long that Laurence had to check the display and make sure the necromancer hadn't hung up.

"Delaney's a ghost hunter, right?" Basil finally said, sounding more confident.

"Uh huh." Laurence bit his lip.

"And he's all over the internet," Basil continued.

Laurence could have hugged him. Basil was doing everything he could to contextualize whatever he was about to say without it sounding like anything unusual. "Yeah," Laurence agreed. "He is."

"But he hasn't posted anything since Quentin went missing. Not a peep. No tweets, nothing on Snapchat, no updates to his channel. Absolutely nothing."

"Right," Laurence agreed with a nod. "The cops think Delaney was the kidnapper."

"Okay, but—" Basil cut himself off, then started again. "Delaney doxxed Quentin, you got a whole bunch of people camping outside your house, then Delaney steps in to do his own dirty work?"

Laurence wriggled in his seat to draw himself upright as it dawned on him what Basil's implication was. "He's not working alone," he realized. "He's got help."

"Right!" Basil agreed. "And whatever help he got wasn't arranged out in the open where anyone else on the forum could see it. I think it got taken off-board, maybe Snapchat or text messages or something. I've asked Jon to see if he can break into Delaney's forum accounts and find out who approached him and where they took that conversation to."

"Jon can do that?"

"Maybe. He *is* a genius, but his thing's engineering usually. He's pretty good with computers, though. I guess it comes down to how crappy their security is, but if he finds anything, I'll let you know."

"That would be amazing. Thank you!"

"Any time. I'll let you get back to work."

Laurence thanked Basil again and hung up, then puffed his cheeks out.

"Who was that?" Angela sounded bored.

"A friend in New York. He's into all this ghost-hunting stuff. You know, all these kids who hang out in woods after dark and act like they're really scared?" Laurence snorted. "I don't know what's so great about them, but Basil loves it, and he's in the same circles as Delaney, so he's been keeping tabs on him ever since he started harassing Quen."

Angela's next question was exactly the same one Laurence would have asked in her position. "Why were ghost hunters harassing your boyfriend?"

"Quen's British, aristocracy, and his mom died when he was nineteen. You mix those three things together and put them within range of a ghost hunter, and apparently it's like catnip. They were following him down the street, trying to interview him about his mom's death." Laurence felt his grip on the wheel tighten, and had to force his fingers to relax before his knuckles turned white. "He threatened to sue Delaney. Delaney responded by posting Quen's personal info on one of these forums and inviting everyone to have at him, and the next thing we knew there were ghost hunters from all over the country right on our doorstep." He continued to fill her in about how they'd hired a bodyguard, and that bodyguard had been overpowered by the kidnappers, leaving out all his concerns about Quentin's gifts or the failure of his own, while the hills around them became less green and more sand-colored.

If she spotted any discrepancy or omission in his recounting, she didn't mention it. Angela just nodded now and then as she listened, like she was accumulating data to help solve the problem at hand, and when Laurence was done, she said, "I see."

There was nothing more for him to add, so he focused on the road.

He drove with a heavy foot whenever he could be sure there weren't any cops on the interstate, but lifted off at every bend in the road, or when the landscape was such that it could easily hide a highway patrol car from even his eyesight. He managed to shave almost half an hour off the GPS's projected drive time, and when he turned off the interstate to cross the Colorado river into Arizona, the truck's fuel warning light blinked on, so it was lucky that the first thing he saw the other side of the bridge was a gas station.

Laurence pulled in and refueled. Angela stayed in the car while he went inside to grab some water and pay, and he checked his phone for messages while he stood in line.

There was a text from Basil, and he opened it.

I figured you didn't want me to say anything on the call. Jon isn't doing anything like what I said. He says the FBI will be able to get access to CD's accounts way faster than he can, and if he tries to do anything he could get in the way of their investigation. What I wanted to tell you was that I heard what happened. It's all over the forums that Q got taken, but I don't get how? There's no way anyone should be able to take him, not without some serious mojo, and I just don't see CD having what it takes. You're not really out on deliveries, are you? LMK if I can help!

The line moved, and Laurence paid, then quickly thumbed out a reply.

Whoever took him is blocking me somehow. I can't see who it was, and I figure they're blocking Q too. I've got help, but I don't trust her, so I haven't told her what I can do. Sorry I didn't get in touch sooner. I've been going crazy with worry.

He debated how much information to send via text message, but in the end chose to leave out the stuff about Muut. If the FBI ever dredged through his text messages for whatever reason, he didn't need to explain that shit to them, so he just ended his message with, *Gotta go, she's waiting in the truck.*

Laurence slipped his phone away and offered Angela one of the bottles as he hopped back into the truck, but she shook her head.

"Smaller bladder," she said calmly. "Easier to go long periods of time through selective dehydration than to stop for the toilet every few hours."

"Uh. Okay." He pulled out of the gas station parking lot, and into that of the Jack in the Box next door, since there was no point driving any further into Yuma without directions. He swigged from his own bottle, then sighed. "Any idea how long this might take?"

"Psychopomps can use the absolute thinnest of sympathetic connections to a target," she replied. "But they can't travel much faster than whatever form they take."

"What you're saying is it depends how far away Quen is?"

She nodded. "Yes."

He sighed and killed the engine, then sipped more water and eyed the Jack in the Box. He couldn't imagine trying to eat anything right now, especially not fast food, but maybe it'd be polite to ask Angela if she was hungry, or needed the restroom. He took a breath and turned toward her, but a sudden rush of sensation flooded him, and he felt for a brief moment like he was in flight.

I come!

Windsor's warning crashed into his thoughts seconds before the bird himself fluttered into existence the other side of the windshield, and he landed heavily on the bonnet, wings outstretched like a harbinger of doom. He flapped, then furled his wings away, and hopped closer, eyeing Angela, then Laurence.

I'm back! Windsor sounded and felt pleased as punch, and he began to preen his feathers as he stood right there in front of Laurence like the absolute worst evidence of all Laurence's lies made manifest.

"Uh…" Laurence began.

I thought you said owls? He thought that might be a good line to try. Or maybe *Did you see what I just saw?* But when he turned to Angela, he knew nothing he could say would make this work.

"So," she said idly as she met his eye. "You have a familiar."

He exhaled, and said the only thing that came to mind.

"I can explain."

33

LAURENCE

I met Herne! Windsor's excitement was enthusiastic, but he stopped preening for a moment to rap on the windshield with his beak. *Who is this?*

Just one second, Laurence replied. He stared at Angela, and still couldn't get a read on whether she was pissed, amused, or what.

"Your explanation," she prompted.

"I'm sorry. You're right. I can already use some magic, okay?" Laurence huffed, then rolled up his sleeve to show her his bracelet. "I'm warded against a bunch of stuff. Magic, gods, whatever." He covered it up again without looking away from her, even though her gaze flit down to it briefly. "I'm a witch, but I'm really new at all this, and I don't know any magic that can find Quentin. I'm not lying about that. I really need your help, and so does he."

Windsor continued to preen his feathers. Laurence could feel him do it across their bond, now that it was back. He also knew how hard it was for the bird to hold onto whatever news he was carrying.

Angela pursed her lips and turned her attention to Windsor. "You don't know much, but you know how to bond with a familiar. Those two facts are so at odds that I'd suggest that one of them isn't true."

"I don't know how," he sighed. "He was given to me by a god. It was the god who bonded him to me. I didn't do it." Laurence hesitated. "You can see the bond?"

Angela shrugged. "I can see all kinds of things. I don't leave home without perception spells in place."

Laurence had only the most oblique idea that such magic existed. He'd supposed it had to be possible, back when Amy and Rufus had explained to him that most people couldn't see wards without magic to help them, but that stuff hadn't been his priority, and he'd put it out of his mind since then. Maybe that was the kind of spell he should be imbuing into something, instead of worrying about how to control weather, when that wasn't even anything he could see being useful in a hurry.

Shit. He'd been leading Angela on this whole time, and who knew how long she'd known. Could she see that magic bounced off him, or did he just look like everyone else to her sight?

"I knew nothing about you," he sighed. "You came out of nowhere, you said someone sent you to teach me, and to be honest, I'm not learning much at my own speed. I could use the help, but I also didn't know whether you were on the level. I figured I could ask you to teach me, and while I was learning, I'd get to know you better and figure out whether you were okay, but then Quen got taken, and all that flew out the window. I'm sorry."

For the first time since he'd met her for dinner, she smiled, and to his surprise it seemed like she was genuinely amused.

"Sensible precautions," she chuckled. "And you're a good liar. That's a useful skill, don't let anyone tell you it's not. You better find out what the bird wants before he shits on your truck."

Laurence blinked. Maybe he'd expected her to leave, or at least to yell at him for all the subterfuge, but the last thing he imagined she'd do is agree that he'd done the right thing. "Thanks," he blurted.

I speak now? Windsor rapped on the windshield again.

"Goddess, one second, Win." Laurence opened the door and looked around for security cameras while Windsor flapped his way over the door and into the truck, then grimaced as he noticed one overlooking the restaurant entrance. He shut the door once Win was in his lap and hugged the bird to his chest, and hoped that the camera wasn't facing the parking lot. "Okay. Now you speak."

Windsor was much more able to convey complex ideas in person rather than in thought. With a mixture of vocalizations and emotions broadcast across their bond, as well as the occasional ruffle of feathers or tilt of his head, he could give way more nuance, and it was almost as good as English for Laurence.

Herne says that your gifts are not yet fully developed, Windsor relayed, chattering and clicking and uttering soft caws. *But if those you have are failing you, then the cause is your target, not yourself.*

Yeah, Laurence thought to the bird, *I figured.*

He says that you will need to unlock your full potential with the Warrior, but even then you would not have what it takes to do what you seek right now. He is sorry, and wishes you good fortune, but he cannot help at this time.

Laurence sighed, and leaned down to kiss the top of Windsor's head. "You're a good bird," he whispered. "You did great. Thank you."

I'm good! Windsor cackled with pride.

Yes, you are. Windsor's ego was almost as well-developed as Quentin's, which Laurence considered a mighty feat for a bird who wasn't even a year old yet.

He held Windsor close and turned his attention back to Angela, whose smile had vanished. She was neutral again, like the brief laughter had never happened.

"He went to see if he could find help, but it's a no," Laurence explained.

"Then we sit and wait for Muut," she concluded. "You want anything to eat?"

"Not really."

"Me either."

They returned to the silence that had accompanied them for nearly two hundred miles, because it was easier than trying to make small talk, and that in itself was weird because Laurence was pretty good at making conversation out of nothing when he needed to.

***

LAURENCE COULDN'T DO nothing for long, and he wound up firing off text messages to keep people updated. He let his mom know where he was, and sent Aiden and Mia the same information. He was partway through an internal debate on whether or not to call Detective Hudson for an update when his phone rang.

He checked the screen, then answered quickly. "Rodger? Are you ok?"

"I'm fine. Sorry, took me a while to get coverage." Rodger sounded mildly alert, which was more fired up than he ever got in the store. "So, I was parked outside your place in La Jolla, right?"

"Uh huh."

"And I got chatting with some of the kooks hanging out there, and a couple of them mentioned this Delaney YouTube guy, so I watched a bunch of his videos."

"Uh huh." Laurence had no idea where this was going, but he figured he might as well hear Rodger out. He had nothing better to do.

"Like, a whole bunch," Rodger insisted. "And then a load of these losers just left when the cops arrived. I figure they heard through the grapevine about Quentin going missing, right? So

I asked whoever was left behind what was going on, but they didn't know. Figures, right? So I went over to this Delaney guy's dorm, but his buddies hadn't seen him for a couple of days. They figured it was weird, 'cause they were his camera crew, and they were upset at the idea he might have gone off without them. But I got Delaney's license plate from them."

"Okay," Laurence said. He had to admit he was pretty impressed with Rodger's detective skills so far, but was there really anything they could do with a license plate when the cops already had Delaney's vehicle impounded?

"And while they were getting that for me, I stole Delaney's laptop."

Laurence choked abruptly. "You did *what*?"

"Don't worry, I got out without them spotting it. Anyway, then I parked up and did some Googling, found out how to bypass the regular boot procedure, log in as root, and change his password. That took a while. Macs aren't my thing."

Laurence's jaw dropped. Most of what Rodger had just said flew way over his head, but it sounded a hell of a lot like Rodger had cracked into Delaney's laptop.

"And I didn't steal his damn charging cable, and I've got nothing that fits this port, so it's almost out of battery now, but I figured out how to use the Find My iPhone thing that Apples have."

"Holy shit," Laurence breathed.

"And his phone's last ping was in Arizona, then it stopped responding. No idea whether he's out of battery, turned it off, or somewhere without signal, so I drove to Arizona, and there's still no sign of his phone. I feel like I'm pretty close, but I'm kinda at a dead end now."

Laurence's mind whirled. There was a breadcrumb here. He could almost taste it. He just needed his thoughts to coalesce around it, and then the hunt would be renewed.

In a heartbeat, he had it.

"Where in Arizona are you?"

"Castle Dome City. It's just kinda northeast of Yuma. I

don't think it's a hundred percent where the signal stopped, but it's around here somewhere."

"Holy shit. Okay. I'm in Yuma. We need to get a charger for that laptop."

Rodger paused. "We do?"

"Yeah, we do. I'll find the nearest Best Buy and meet you there. I'll text you the address."

"Uh, okay. Sure."

Laurence hung up quickly and began to search on his phone, then tapped the address into his GPS and started the engine. "In the back," he said to Windsor.

Windsor hopped out of his lap and over the armrest, then flapped his way into the back seat, sounding disgruntled at having to give up being cuddled.

"What is it?" Angela asked him.

"I had someone watching the ghost-hunters, and he's stolen Delaney's laptop. Jon isn't trying to get access to those accounts because he thinks the cops will be doing it, but we've got the computer, and I'm hoping through it we'll have access to all Delaney's emails, forums, social media, whatever else he uses to talk to people." Laurence threw the truck into drive and pulled back out of the parking lot.

"You're assuming he doesn't do all those things from his phone and not his computer," Angela said.

"Hoping, not assuming. But yeah. If we can find out who he's working with, we're one step ahead at last."

She didn't answer, and he didn't look over at her now that he was driving through a city.

The hunt was on, and he felt alive again.

34

LAURENCE

THE BEST BUY WASN'T ALL THAT FAR. WHAT LAURENCE HAD TO wait for was Rodger to arrive, and then they went into the store together to find the right cable. Laurence paid cash for it, since they were toting a stolen laptop around, then they retreated to Laurence's truck.

Rodger eyed Windsor as he slid into the back seat, then looked at Angela. With his usual amount of social grace, he met Laurence's eyes in the rearview. "Who's she?"

"Angela, Rodger. Rodger, this is Angela."

Angela disregarded Rodger.

Laurence started the truck's engine and plugged the cable into a USB port, then popped the laptop open and plugged it in. "I gotta say, I had no idea you were secretly an awesome hacker, Rodger."

He heard Rodger snort. "I'm not. I'm just really good at Google-fu, and I had nothing but time on my hands. A lot of the results would only work on highly specific versions of the operating system, because later patches had fixed the security loophole that method relied on, so there was like five hours of trial and error. If it was a phone, the whole thing probably would have turned into a brick by the time I managed to get into it."

"Huh." Laurence shook his head as the login screen popped up. "Password?"

"Asshole," Rodger said. "All lower case."

"Good choice," was Angela's assessment.

Laurence tapped it in and waited for it to load, but all he got was a picture of Delaney in a desert at night looking fake-terrified.

"Down the bottom," Rodger said. "If you want the browser. Otherwise the menu's that little bar along the top. I had to Google this shit, so let me save you the trouble. It's tethering to my phone for internet, if you need it."

"Okay. Uh." Laurence experimented with the touchpad, then opened a browser, and after some teamwork, he managed to get into the browser history and start opening all the sites Delaney frequented.

Then came the part he hated. Slogging through post histories and inboxes, searching for anything at all relevant, in the hope that a single clue would leap out at him and answer all his questions. Worse, it wasn't a task that could be split between them, and he would rather do it himself in case his instinct picked up on something Angela or Rodger could miss.

But the longer it took, the less time they had to find Quentin, and he had to balance his growing urgency with the fear of missing anything that could be vital to saving Quen's life.

He sighed faintly and settled in to work.

HE MANAGED to cut down on his search by finding Delaney's forum post in which he threw Quentin's information out into the wild and told people to do whatever they wanted with it. Nobody would have contacted him prior to that date about it, so Laurence could focus on messages sent since then, and it didn't take long to find one from an account called *LoneRanger*.

I can help you with your problem, it said.

Delaney's reply was almost immediate. *How?*

I can get you and your subject in a room together. This scoop is too big to hand off to these nobodies. You did the hard work, you should reap the reward. You bring the camera, I'll bring the subject, you get the exclusive for your channel.

And what do you get?

Laurence was impressed with Delaney's common sense, even if he was an asshole who'd cornered Quen in public and tried to grill him about his mom's death.

The satisfaction of helping someone as famous as you, was *LoneRanger's* reply. Laurence could practically smell the ego-soothing rolling off the message, but Delaney's next reply proved the student had fallen for it completely.

Good point. So who and where are you?

No. Give me your cell number and make sure you've got WhatsApp installed. I'll contact you, then we can talk.

Why not here? Delaney responded.

Because WhatsApp is encrypted.

Delaney responded with his phone number, and Laurence cursed under his breath. It was the end of the conversation. They must've taken it to WhatsApp after that, just like *LoneRanger* had promised.

"Can we get into these WhatsApp messages?" Laurence twisted in his seat and looked hopefully at Rodger.

Rodger shook his head, eyes to his phone screen. The harsh glow from it made his skin even whiter, and his freckles stood out like acne. "Nuh uh. Not for us mere mortals. You'd need an actual hacker for that shit."

"Fuck."

"Fuck!" Windsor agreed.

Angela snorted into her hand.

"This bird is getting worse," Rodger muttered.

Laurence seethed quietly to himself. *LoneRanger* had done the sensible thing and taken the conversation to where it couldn't be eavesdropped on, and whatever they'd said to Delaney there was beyond Laurence's reach.

Unless…

"Give me a minute," he breathed. He closed the laptop and handed it to Rodger, then closed his eyes.

Immersing himself in the stream of time in the driver's seat of a truck with a couple of onlookers was something he knew he couldn't have done a year ago, but he'd had a whole lot of practice since then. Jack's instruction, Freddy's manipulation, and his own efforts meant he'd gotten good at this now. Good enough not to need the peace and quiet of an altar.

He let out a slow breath and sank in, seeking out Delaney's past. He had the laptop here, the date stamps on the messages, and he knew to look for Delaney with his cellphone and when. His only hope was that whatever had blocked him from finding Quentin's kidnapping wasn't Delaney himself.

A vision bobbed nearby, and Laurence had printed off enough pictures of Delaney's face to know it from the briefest snatched moment.

He dived in.

Cameron checked the WhatsApp notification from a number that wasn't in his address book, but he thumbed to accept the incoming message anyway.

Laurence glanced around quickly. This looked like what he figured a student dorm room would look like. Smallish, with a desk, a pile of pizza boxes, and clothes strewn everywhere. Laurence hadn't gone on to higher education, so all he had to go by was dorms in TV shows.

He looked back to Cameron's phone.

"You're LoneRanger?" Delaney sent.

"I'm going to video call you," was the reply.

"Ok."

There wasn't anyone else in the room, and Laurence wasn't interested in finding out whether Delaney's friends had rooms of their own. His whole being was focused on that cellphone in Delaney's hand.

Cameron answered the incoming call, and Laurence leaned closer.

There was a woman on the screen. She was lean, like she worked out, and her hair was gray and cut close to her skull. Her white skin was tanned, and creased with middle age. The blue of her eyes was hard metal, like she'd seen war from the inside and it haunted her still.

"You're Cameron Delaney," she barked. She even sounded like a drill sergeant.

"And you are?" Delaney prompted.

"Kathy," she said. "I'm so excited to have this opportunity to work with you."

Laurence could tell she wasn't excited in the slightest, but Delaney was buying every single second of it, straightening his shoulders and raising his chin like he was important.

"What exactly can you do, though?" Cameron was still slightly skeptical, at least.

"You're not going to get him to talk out on the street," Kathy said. "And giving your leads away to any halfwit who has a few hours to spare is beneath you. I think you're right. I think your evidence is compelling, and that he's genuinely haunted."

Laurence's throat dried.

Kathy didn't believe any such thing.

He could see it in the glint of her eyes, the way her breath was too even to really be as excited as she pretended. She was good, but he was the Hunter, and she wasn't good enough to fool him.

Cameron's eyelids fluttered for a second. "You really think so too?"

"Definitely. You collated the proof, you know it's true. This is hard evidence, and you should be the one to interview him. But he's threatened to lawyer up, right?"

"Yeah."

"Then we've gotta take him where he can't reach a lawyer."

Cameron's lips worked silently, then he gasped. "Wait, are you talking about kidnapping?"

"He's not going to respond to a polite invitation, is he?" Kathy shrugged. "This is your one shot. You could multiply your channel's subscribers by ten overnight. Ten million subscribers. You know how much the top YouTubers make?"

Delaney shook his head numbly.

"We're talking TV deals, merchandise, influencer revenue. This interview will make *you, Cameron. There are YouTubers out there who are raking in over ten million dollars a year. Do you want to work for someone else your whole life, or do you want to be a millionaire?"*

Oh shit, *Laurence realized.* She's good!

He watched Delaney think it over, but he already knew the kid was too blinded by fame and fortune to say no.

"Okay," Delaney nodded. "Where are you? We need to meet up and work out how to make this happen."

Kathy grinned like a shark. She knew damn well she'd hooked her own fish. Laurence could see her satisfaction practically leaking out of her pores. "I can be in San Diego in a day. I'll contact you once I get there."

"Okay. I'll talk to you tomorrow!"

"You will," Kathy agreed.

Laurence snapped his eyes open and sucked in a deep breath. "She's called Kathy," he blurted. "The person Delaney's working with. She's using him, but I don't know why. I don't know what she wants."

Angela blinked slowly. "And you know this how?"

Ah, fuck.

Laurence shook his head. "It's a thing I can do, but I can't do it all the time." It was as much as he was willing to disclose right now. "Trust me. We find this Kathy, we find Delaney and Quen."

"And how do we find her, oh great florist?" Rodger intoned from the back seat.

"Gimme a sec."

Laurence closed his eyes again. He had to find Delaney a day later. If he could spy on that next call, maybe Kathy would give away details of her plan, or where she intended to take Quen, or anything else useful.

Cameron answered the incoming call. It was Kathy again.

"Where do you want to meet?" was her opening. She wasn't wasting time, it looked like.

"I'm at SDCC, so, uh, Grossmont Center?"

"What's that?"

"It's a mall."

"Sure." Kathy nodded. "Where in the mall?"

"BJ's?"

"Sure," she said again. "See you in an hour."

Kathy hung up, and Cameron grabbed his keys and jacket.

Laurence was homing in. He knew it. He didn't wait. He knew where and when to go next.

The BJ's Brewhouse was like every other BJ's Brewhouse, with its huge inverted triangle logo over the entrance. It sat a ways back from the rest of the mall, with a Mexican restaurant next to it, and Delaney parked nearby. He checked his phone as he hurried toward the BJ's, but waited outside instead of going in.

Laurence waited with him, but then the vision cut out.

He gasped for air as time evicted him without warning.

It was Kathy. It *had* to be Kathy. Whatever she was doing, whatever power she had, she was the one who was blocking him. She must have been in the truck that took Quentin, and she had to be with him now, or Laurence would be able to find him. Nothing else made sense.

Whoever she was, she was using Delaney to get to Quentin, and that made Laurence's stomach churn. The thing she did might not work from the other end of a phone call, but in person?

Yeah, it was her.

"Can't get any closer to her," he breathed. "But I know she's lied to Delaney to make him do what she wanted, and it looks like what she wanted was to kidnap Quen. I don't know why, or who he is to her. I don't think it's got anything to do with ghosts, though. That's what Delaney was after, but she's stringing him along."

Angela nodded. "Turns out you do have something of value. When this is done, you're going to tell me what that was you just did."

She wasn't asking, and they still hadn't found Quentin. All Laurence could do was nod. "Okay."

He was saved — if only temporarily — by the sound of an owl's hoot, and moments later, an enormous ball of brown feathers manifested on the hood of the truck, and two round, amber eyes blinked from a face that looked mildly annoyed due to vast dark eyebrows which swept from beak to beyond the top of its head.

"Muut?" Laurence breathed.

Angela nodded. "He's found our lost souls."

Muut beat his wings until he lifted into the air, and Laurence wound down the rear window.

"Keep an eye on him, Win. I don't want to lose him."

Windsor cawed in agreement and hopped up to the sill, then launched himself out and beat his vast wings like thunder to catch up with Muut.

Laurence fastened his seatbelt and pulled out of the parking lot to follow them.

QUENTIN

HE HAD TO STAY PERFECTLY STILL, AND THEN MARLOWE WOULD go away. That was how these things worked, how they had always worked.

There was no wind, but that was all right.

Marlowe was saying something, and it wasn't important.

Quentin was far away. Able to observe, and yet not in any danger. The outside world would fix itself, and once it was done, he could return to it.

Marlowe's weapon looked like some sort of leather-working tool that the saddler back home had used, although hers had a far more ornate handle to it. Both seemed to share a purpose: putting holes in things.

Marlowe was putting holes in Quentin's skin.

She seemed to have stopped, though. She was talking again, waving the point of her pricker in Quentin's face, but he wasn't there to answer her.

No, he was quite content where he was. Out there looked absolutely horrendous.

HE CAME to in a location which was neither his own bed nor

that of a hospital. Quentin was familiar with both, and was absolutely certain that neither of them allowed for one to sleep sitting upright.

When he attempted to reach for his face, he couldn't move.

A low level of fear prickled up the back of his neck and made his hairs stand on end. Was he paralyzed? In a plaster cast? Had he done something to himself so bad this time that he would never recover?

No. You never did any of those things to yourself.

They were all done to you.

But if that were true, then did it mean Father was here? Or had someone else done this to him?

Quentin tried again. As his brain fought free from the fog of sleep, he realized the truth of the matter.

He was not paralyzed.

He was restrained.

It should be simple enough to break free, but his telekinesis failed to do as he told it to, and little by little, more of how he'd come to be here slowly returned to him, like pieces of a puzzle jammed into place by the uncoordinated hands of a child.

Marlowe.

But where was she now? He was in complete darkness, and his was the only breath that he could hear. Had she left him here to rot?

Did he want to call out, or would he rather sit here in peace and quiet for a while?

He was naked.

Quentin caught his breath and held it a moment. This new information was unwanted, but it explained why he could feel every exhalation against his chest, why he felt so cold.

I've had an episode, he realized.

He closed his eyes and tried to catalogue his memories, to work out what could possibly have caused it, but that was a dangerous line to walk. If he remembered, it could set him off all over again. Frederick had proven that.

Delaney. Vargas. Marlowe. The string of events was slowly unrolling as he tugged on them. The kidnap, the failure of his gifts, the long and painful drive out to a house in the middle of nowhere. Marlowe's talk about whatever family history they supposedly shared. The removal of Delaney.

Quentin grimaced and hung his head. It was all becoming jumbled after that. He had been hung from the ceiling like a piece of meat, unable to rest, slowly freezing to death, and ever since then his brain had been on a slow slide into madness, and he didn't want to delve into it. He needed more rest, he knew that much, but being manacled naked to a wooden chair in a basement that could become cold enough to preserve food didn't lend itself to good quality sleep.

Was he going mad? Had she done that to him yet? Or was he still almost sane, the way he usually was? He couldn't tell. The darkness was almost as complete as the inside of the black dog, but there was a lot less wailing going on. Just the hoot of an owl, mournful and distant.

Was that strange? Did it mean that it was nighttime?

No. It had to be a hallucination. He wasn't well, and Marlowe was making it worse.

He licked his lips, but his mouth was dry, and it did little for him, so he sighed and attempted to meditate. If he could not sleep, he could at least pass the time peacefully, and perhaps if he was fortunate, he would doze off again.

IT WAS the sound of the trapdoor that woke him, and he jerked his head up as it slammed shut.

There was light beyond his eyelids, so he was cautious, opening his eyes slowly so as not to blind himself, but his eyes were still so puffy and sore that he couldn't get them fully open anyway.

Marlowe was back, and she had Delaney with her. The

student was staring at Quentin, and yet again Quentin was reminded of his nudity.

His scars.

Delaney was staring at his scars, and there was nothing Quentin could do to stop him, so instead, Quentin stared belligerently at Delaney, daring him to utter a single word.

"Sit down," Marlowe said as she settled behind her desk.

Delaney blinked, and looked down, past his own cuffed wrists. "On the floor?"

"I don't see another chair, do you?"

Quentin wondered whether he could ignite a human being. They weren't naturally flammable, or people would be catching light all the time, and they would certainly never take up smoking.

Maybe his question wasn't whether or not it was possible, but instead one of ethics. *Should* he set fire to a human being? To Delaney? Marlowe?

He mulled it over while Delaney sank to the floor, but his rumination was cut short.

"I have to say, I'm impressed with that stunt you pulled," Marlowe said. She leaned back in her chair and plucked the pricker from her desk, placing the tip against her forefinger and balancing it between both her hands as she regarded Quentin.

Quentin frowned faintly. He didn't recall any stunts.

"Let me go," he rasped, "and I'll show you a much better one."

His voice didn't sound right. His jaw throbbed and ached and made it hard to move his mouth properly. Everything was just so difficult, and didn't seem at all worth the trouble.

More than his voice, it was his words that were wrong. He was in no position to threaten anyone, and even if he were, what exactly could he do?

Burn them.

Burn them all.

He laughed at the notion. How foolish it was.

Then he imagined Marlowe and Delaney on fire, screaming as they writhed in the flames, and laughed harder.

"What the fuck did you do to him?" Delaney was hard to hear over all the noise Quentin made.

"This isn't how it's supposed to go." Marlowe sounded unsure.

Quentin entertained himself with his ideas until he couldn't tell whether or not he had actually made fire, but then he hiccuped, and the warmth and light dissipated. Nobody was on fire, which was either a crying shame, or a blessed relief.

"I heard an owl," he mused.

"This is, like, some full-blown psychotic episode or something," Delaney whispered. "I don't know what you want, but I don't think you're gonna get it."

"I think I will." Marlowe cleared her throat. "D'Arcy."

Quentin flinched. "Banbury," he corrected her. How dare she use his name?

"No," she countered. "Your family bought their titles with my family's blood. I'll call you what I want. Look at me."

He raised his head and gave her a stare that was colder than any his father had inflicted upon him. "What do you want?"

Marlowe lounged against her desk and gestured toward Delaney with the pricker. "I've got an idea," she said. "Kind of a theory, I guess, but bear with me. You see, I think you'll do anything to save other people from getting hurt."

Quentin's eyes drifted closed a while as he probed that statement. Was she correct? He had, after all, handed himself to her to avoid Vargas' death, had he not?

Satisfied, he opened them again and inclined his head. "Possibly. It depends on what it is that you are asking me to do."

"Confess."

He scrunched up his nose, but that hurt both his eyes and his jaw, and he had to stop doing it. "Confess," he repeated.

"To witchcraft."

Oh yes, that was it. She had a real bee in her bonnet about this. It was starting to come back to him now.

"No," he said.

"I figured you'd still refuse, so here's what's going to happen." Marlowe dragged herself back from the desk and stood like she'd been pulled upright by an invisible hand. She sauntered toward Delaney in much the same manner, and only relaxed so that she could bend over and grab the student's handcuffs, which she wrenched upward until both Delaney's arms were over his head. "I'm going to start cutting bits off Delaney," she explained, "until you make it stop."

Quentin mulled that over. Was it better or worse than Delaney being on fire?

His thoughts were interrupted by Delaney's sudden, loud protest. "Wait, what? That's insane! You can't do that!"

"You asked me to shut him up—" Marlowe pointed to Quentin with her pricker "—and you think I can't do it to you too?"

"Just give her what she wants!" Delaney tried to break loose from Marlowe's grip, but Quentin knew now how much control something so simple as handcuffs gave the person holding them. The boy didn't stand a chance. "She only wants you to say shit, right? Just do it!"

"You're a fool," Quentin said, idly letting his gaze roam around the basement. He'd looked at it before, but perhaps if he looked again he'd suddenly find a way out of here. "She'll kill me the moment I do. In fact, the longer she makes you suffer, the longer I get to live, so actually it's in my best interests to allow her to torment you."

Delaney's screech was a delight, so Quentin looked back over at him as Marlowe thrust her pricker toward Delaney's face.

"Oh, I'm sorry. I thought you said you'd cut him, not stab him. You can't cut with a point like that. You need a blade. What are you going to do? Poke him to death?" He intended to sound scathing, and from the blackening fury on Marlowe's face, he had succeeded.

"You're right," She spat. She released Delaney, and kicked him aside. "Let me go get a better tool."

"You do that." Quentin yawned and leaned back in his chair. "Try not to take too long. It's awfully boring down here."

Marlowe stormed up the stairs without another word, and in the echo of the trapdoor slamming, Delaney began to sob.

"What the fuck is wrong with you, man?"

Quentin sighed and closed his eyes. "Unless the next words out of your mouth are 'While I was upstairs and unguarded I stole the keys to your restraints and now we're going to escape,' I'm not interested."

"Fuck no. Kathy's carrying them around with her. And even if she wasn't, why the hell should I do that?"

"Because I'm the only person who can get you out of here alive," Quentin murmured.

Assuming his gifts ever worked again.

He laughed at the absurdity of it. A year ago, he had been completely unaware of their existence. And now he might never be able to use them again. His whole life had been spent at the hands of others, being shaped by them, abused by them. Only for one brief, beautiful moment had he been free.

Now his freedom was gone, perhaps never to return. He didn't know what was worse. Tasting it and having it stolen away, or never having it in the first place.

No. He was kidding himself. This was absolutely worse. If Marlowe had abducted him before he'd met Laurence, he would never have even known what she was talking about, and he could have died in ignorance. Now his eyes were open, and she was going to kill an innocent just to make him talk.

Delaney isn't innocent, he told himself.

Except he is. This was all a game to him, but now he's among adults, and he's out of his depth. Marlowe used him, and now she's going to kill him.

So what?

He shook his head weakly. There was some sort of urge to try and protect Delaney, nibbling away at the back of his mind, and it was fruitless. He could do no such thing. And besides, the boy *had* kicked off all of this with his stupid ghost-hunting obsession.

He was done for, and Marlowe wouldn't allow Delaney to survive this. But he could do the decent thing and save the boy from suffering as he had.

Two words was all it would take.

He weighed the pros and cons as he waited for Marlowe's return. He felt the weight of the words that would end both their lives, but also bring about an end to the pain and the madness and the grief.

I confess.

They weren't so bad, were they? And then, once he'd said them, he'd experience true freedom. Arawn would take him, and he could wait for Laurence in Annwn.

There didn't seem to be a downside, and he had to wonder why he'd fought against the obvious for so long.

36

LAURENCE

MUUT WAS FLYING IN A STRAIGHT LINE, BUT THAT LINE RAN diagonal to the streets in Yuma, and Laurence had to split his attention between trying to spot the owl, his sense of where Windsor was, and not crashing the truck in a city he was totally unfamiliar with.

"He's going right to Quen, yeah?" Laurence asked as he shot through an intersection before the light could change.

"Or Delaney," Angela said. "If they're not in the same place."

Laurence clenched his jaw, but shook his head. He couldn't worry about that for now. He had to assume they were going to find Quentin, because if not, this was just more time Quentin might not have, and it was being wasted. "Rodger, can you work out what direction he's flying in?"

"Sure. Give me, like, ten minutes."

"I'll try."

Laurence zigzagged away from the mall, but soon ran out of roads to use. Windsor was flying over a river, and Laurence had no way to cross it.

"Fuck." It had to be the same river he'd driven over to cross into Arizona, but Muut was flying in almost the opposite direction. "Wait. You were at Castle Dome something or other, right? You said that's where Delaney's phone was last?"

"Near there, yeah."

"Fuck it." Laurence pulled over and tapped at the GPS. If nothing else, it should get him across this river and driving in the right direction, and then he could try to find Muut again.

The GPS said it was almost an hour away. That should give him plenty of time to find an owl, so long as owls didn't fly faster than the posted speed limits.

"NORTH-EAST," Rodger said, once the truck was on Route 95.

Laurence nodded grimly, acutely grateful that Windsor was on Muut's tail, because he'd well and truly lost sight of the psychopomp now. The GPS was leading him dead east, but apparently the highway would curve north soon, and with any luck they'd meet up again. "Can you get a line on, like, what might be in the direction he's flying?"

"Sure. He'll go north of the museum, out into the nature reserve. If he goes past that, he'll fly over a whole bunch of nothing all the way to Flagstaff."

Laurence nodded to himself. "But Delaney's cell would've been picked up again, if it still had power. What's in the nature reserve?"

He heard Rodger tapping for a while. "Six hundred and fifty thousand acres of zip. It's all desert, though it's got what looks like a whole bunch of dirt roads running through it, so at least we can drive in if we have to."

"All right. We need a plan. I've probably got a few things in the back of the truck, but not a whole lot. Spare ribbon and oasis blocks, mostly, but there might be scissors or a knife. All we have to do is get her away from Quen, then he can get out."

Angela pursed her lips. "You're suggesting we ask her to come with us?"

Laurence shrugged. "I don't know how far away we'd need

to get her, but we can always throw her in the truck and drive."

"And what if Quentin's locked up?" she asked.

Rodger snorted. "I doubt that'd stop him."

Laurence glanced to the rearview, but Rodger still had his eyes glued to the laptop, and Laurence wasn't going to start probing about just how much Rodger had eavesdropped on this past year. That could definitely wait.

HE CAUGHT sight of Muut again as the highway curved north and an off-ramp continued north-east, and Windsor was hot on his tail. Without thinking, Laurence took the ramp and followed.

The ramp led onto a two-way strip of asphalt, which was way better than what he'd expected after Rodger's descriptions.

"Yeah, this road leads to the Castle Dome mining museum thing," Rodger confirmed. "After that it gets bumpier."

"Got it. Thanks."

Overhead, the birds were already drifting slightly off the path of the road, but Laurence felt way more confident now that he had them in his direct sight again. It wasn't easy focusing on driving the truck and paying attention to Windsor's whereabouts at the same time, and looking through his familiar's eyes was out of the question.

"You're gonna like this," Rodger said grimly. "The reserve is full of coyotes, mountain lions, Gila monsters, and five flavors of rattlesnake, 'cause apparently one wasn't enough."

"Delightful," Angela deadpanned.

The road led on through starkly beautiful desert, dotted by cacti and scrub, for another twenty minutes before they even reached the museum, and after that, they had to turn off onto a dirt track which Rodger assured Laurence was a legitimate route and not a dead end.

He had to slow down once they were on it. The truck's suspension was used to San Diego potholes, but the amount of dirt it kicked up on the track made for a slippery ride, and he couldn't risk losing control of the vehicle. Not now they were so close.

The atmosphere inside the truck grew taut. It felt like everyone was keeping tabs on Muut or the road, and nobody wanted to spare a second for chitchat; but to Laurence, there was something else going on, and he only managed to pinpoint it once they were so far into the reserve that the museum wasn't even in his rearview any more.

It was fear.

Not from Angela, of course. But Rodger, after all his bravado and help, hadn't been in this kind of situation before, and the poor guy was probably regretting ever listening in on a single conversation in his life.

"You can wait in the truck, if you want," Laurence offered.

"No, thanks," Angela said.

"I meant Rodger."

Rodger sniffed. "Why?"

"Well, I mean… you did great getting us here, but… this could be dangerous, right?"

"You think hiding in a truck will save me?" Rodger sounded doubtful. "Dude, if they get you two, they'll find me. We stand a better chance if we stick together."

Laurence nodded in agreement. "You're not wrong. I just didn't want to assume anything."

"Well." Rodger hesitated. "Okay. Thanks."

"Any time. And thanks for helping out. I really appreciate it."

"Muut's descending," Angela cut in.

Laurence fell silent as the huge owl began to dip down behind rocky hills.

THE OWL WAS WAITING for them.

Laurence eased the truck off-road, and clung to the wheel as it rattled and bumped over stones and dead things. He could hear supplies in the back clattering about as they fell off their shelves or out of their containers, and his bones felt like they'd gone through a spin cycle. As he rounded the base of one hill, he could see Muut perched on the roof of a battered old stone building, with Windsor circling overhead like he was pretending to be a vulture.

There were two trucks outside the house.

Laurence took his foot off the gas and scrutinized the area as the vehicle slowed to a crawl. "I don't see anyone," he breathed. "Muut's sure, right?"

"He wouldn't have come here if he wasn't," Angela said. "The moment he sees me, he'll—"

The owl melted away into the air.

"—disappear," she sighed. "But at least that means they're both here. He isn't leading us to a second location."

"Okay." Laurence tapped the brakes, then put the truck into reverse, and backed around the hill again so that he could park it out of sight of the building. "Let's see what we've got."

He killed the engine and hopped out, then walked to the back of the truck and opened it, trying to stop anything from spilling out onto the ground by blocking it with his thigh as he moved the doors. He managed to save two spools of ribbon and three plant pots, then hopped up into the back to take stock of what he had in there that could be useful.

Scissors didn't make for a great weapon, but they were better than nothing, so he tucked a pair into his back pocket. He grabbed some thick ribbon, too, in case he needed to tie anyone up. He couldn't see a whole lot of use for plant pots, so he hopped out again.

"Anything worth taking?" Rodger peered in.

"Help yourself, if you can find anything." Laurence waited while Rodger poked around, but all the redhead seemed to gather up was a couple of spools of ribbon and some wire.

"Yeah," Rodger agreed as he jumped out. "Maybe you need to start stocking weapons in this thing."

"And get arrested?" Laurence snorted and closed the truck as quietly as he could. "No thanks."

Angela idly checked her phone, then shook her head. "No signal. I assume we have a plan?"

"I figure we go on foot from here." Laurence licked his lips slowly while he figured out his approach. "Windsor's got line of sight all around. He can warn us if someone comes out. I say we go quietly, use their trucks for cover, then see if we can work out what to do from there."

They seemed to be looking to him for leadership, for which Laurence felt grossly under-qualified, and they both nodded in agreement like he'd somehow come up with the best plan ever, when all he'd really done was suggest they sneak closer and *then* come up with a better plan.

"Okay then," he breathed.

He led the way, hunkering down and moving silently around the base of the hill, but once his head popped free of the obstacle, he had a choice to make. They could either sit out in the open and move at a snail's pace, when neither Angela nor Rodger could move as invisibly as Laurence, or they could pick it up and risk some noise to get out of sight faster.

If they got caught in the open and Delaney or Kathy were armed, they were toast.

Laurence glanced back to his companions, then gestured for the trucks, and broke cover at a sprint.

THEY MADE it in another cloud of dust, and Laurence crouched down and waited for it all to settle.

Fly past the windows, he told Windsor. *I want to see inside.*
I come!

He closed his eyes and reached out, shifting his center to

share that of his familiar, and in a heartbeat he was looking down on everything from above as Windsor glided slowly toward the ground.

The building was made from stone, but not stone that had been evenly cut. It was almost as though whoever had made it had sourced rocks from the desert and cobbled them together into a house, and somehow just made it work with determination and a good eye for shapes. The walls were bumpy and jagged, and the roof was made of rusted sheets of corrugated tin. There were small holes for windows, but any glass or wooden shutters were long since gone.

It looked like it could have been some kind of house from the gold-rush era, except there wasn't any river here. Maybe the prospectors had lived farther away from the water to stop their gold getting stolen in the night. Laurence didn't know.

Windsor swooped lower, circling the house in a lazy spiral, until he was level with the windows.

Laurence glimpsed movement inside.

There. This window.

Windsor pivoted and drifted back to it, then landed on the sill, bold as brass, and tipped his head so that Laurence could see inside.

There were two men in there. Neither of them were anyone Laurence recognized, and they were both built like the house itself: all hard surfaces and bulging edges.

"Would you look at that?" one of them said.

"Get on with it," the other snapped.

The first one pulled his attention off Windsor and went back to tying the knot of the sling he was helping the other get his arm into, and it looked like whatever injury had been inflicted, it was painful as hell, the way the injured guy was panting while he waited.

"Done."

The injured one groaned as he tested the weight against the sling. "I don't know why she doesn't just fucking kill him," he grumbled.

"You've got to do these things by the book," said the first. "You want Aleve?"

"Yeah."

The other window, Laurence prompted.

Windsor flapped away and landed on another sill, but the room was bare except for some sleeping bags, a huge cooler, and a couple of backpacks.

So where was Quentin?

He had Win circle the building a couple more times, but there was no sign of anyone else, so he retreated back to his own body and waited for the brief dizziness of switching perspectives to pass.

"There's two guys in the room on the left," he whispered. "One of them's injured. I don't see Quentin, Delaney, or Kathy, though."

"Are there rooms without windows?" Angela murmured.

"There's got to be," Laurence said. "These guys are fucking steamrollers though. They look like they punch through walls for fun."

Rodger peeked around the side of the truck, then shook his head. "What do we do?"

Laurence licked his lips, then dug his keys out of his pocket and handed them to Rodger. "Okay. Here's the plan. Go back to my truck, get it started. We'll stay here and make some noise, and when they come out to look, you mow them down."

Rodger's skin paled. "What?!"

Laurence bit the tip of his tongue. It *was* a hell of a leap from *help me find my boyfriend* to *hit two guys with a truck because we don't stand a chance in a fistfight.* "I'm sorry. You're right."

"I'll do it." Angela took the keys. "Get the bird to signal when you need me."

With a nod, Laurence willed Windsor to follow her to the truck. "Thanks."

She slipped away, and Laurence waited for her to disappear, then eyed Rodger.

"Now what's the plan?" Rodger whispered.

Laurence gestured to the truck they were hiding behind. "We rock this until the alarm goes off, then the moment they come outside, Angela hits them."

"This is a shit plan."

"Yeah." Laurence grinned. "Those ones are usually the best." He sneaked around to the side of the truck, then put his shoulder to it. "Ready?"

"No."

"Great. On one. Three, two, one…"

He heaved, and moments later the honking of the truck's alarm reverberated off the hills all around them.

Laurence fished the scissors out of his pants, clutched them against his chest, and waited for all hell to break loose.

37

QUENTIN

It didn't take long for Marlowe to return. She strode down the stairs with an unnecessarily huge knife in one hand, and as the trapdoor closed behind her, she raised the knife and displayed it with a snarl.

"Satisfied?"

Quentin drew breath. He watched the play of lantern light along the gleaming metal edge. It was at least ten inches long, not including the hilt, and it looked like it was meant for disemboweling tigers.

Delaney's sobbing returned, and he scrambled away from Marlowe to hide by Quentin's side, as though a man who was bound in chains and iron could do a single bloody thing to save him.

Quentin shook his head. "Suppose I confess," he said idly, as though it were some mere thought exercise. "You'll spare him?"

"He's no witch," Marlowe said.

"That isn't what I asked. Give me your word."

He gathered up every last shred of dignity he possessed and threw it into the glare he gave as he met her eyes. He wouldn't blink, wouldn't so much as twitch until he had his answer, and for one brief second he felt the axis of power in the room turn on its head.

"You have my word." Marlowe lowered the blade to her side. "You confess, and he leaves here unharmed."

And then the moment had passed. The fire left Quentin's heart, and he sagged against the chair.

"Very well," he breathed.

Absurdly, of all the things that could possibly have come next, it was the dulled blaring of a car's horn. At first he thought the noise was inside his head, like a last-ditch effort by his brain to prevent him from saying the words that would undoubtedly cause his death, a klaxon against suicidal stupidity, but when Marlowe turned away, he had to entertain the notion that it could be real.

It was possible, he supposed, that one of her henchmen had gone to their vehicle and set the alarm off somehow. He wasn't sure how these things worked, but if it were an accident, should it not have been switched off again by now?

"Idiots," Marlowe muttered. She turned back toward Quentin and came closer, lifting the knife to point at him with. "You were saying?"

"I was—" Quentin broke off and winced. The alarm was still going. "Honestly, can't you do something about that? It's getting on my nerves."

There was a muffled *crash* and a muted yell. It sounded an awful lot like someone was in pain, which only made Quentin lean forward with a slow smile. It really was music sweet enough to override his annoyance at the car alarm, and he strained to hear more of it, but none came.

"That's a shame," he mused.

Marlowe seemed torn on whether she should go investigate, so Quentin closed his eyes again. She'd work it out, and in the meantime he could get a little bit of rest, and perhaps there would be more screaming. That would be nice.

"Delaney," Marlowe snapped. "Come here."

"Why?"

"Go upstairs and see what those two are doing."

Delaney snorted. "No fucking way. Do it yourself."

The horn finally stopped.

"I didn't expect to see you like this again."

His father's mutter was an unwelcome intrusion. Quentin jerked his head up and snapped his eyes open, prepared to search the darkest corners of the room for the man he hated with every fiber of his being, but he didn't need to.

Father was right in front of him, as naked as Quentin, but with a crop in one hand. There was no blood on him today. At least, not yet. It might come later.

Quentin writhed. He pulled against the manacles, and they didn't move in the slightest. Instead, the pain of fighting them tugged against his flesh, which was already speckled with dried blood. The room crashed down around his ears, drowned by terror. "You can't be here!"

"I can do as I damn well please, and you should have learned that by now." The duke eyed his son with nothing but distaste, and tapped the crop against his palm. "If you had come home, this would not have happened."

"Then make it stop, if you care so damn much!"

"I don't." The duke shrugged. "You threw everything back in my face, and now you must live through the consequences of your actions." He leaned closer, until his breath washed across Quentin's lips, and there was nothing left of the world but his cold, grey eyes. "You've thrown it all away, boy. And for what? To die in a dungeon?" He sniffed. "You stupid child."

A small wail bubbled out of his throat and he thrashed in mounting panic. He couldn't take any more. Marlowe, his father, the never-ending torture, it was all more than anyone could be expected to remain sane through. It hurt, but maybe if he pulled hard enough, he could peel enough skin off his wrists and allow his hands through the manacles, and then he would—

What?

What will you do, when your hands are doused in your own blood, and your ankles remain in chains?

"I don't know," he babbled. "I don't know!"

You're so stupid!

He'd always known this. It wasn't news. But to accept it filled him with such shame, so much loathing, that he sank back in his chair and began to sob.

He was an utter idiot. He'd failed consistently at school, and then he'd drunk his way around the world, continuing to fail wherever he went. And when he'd arrived in San Diego, he'd failed there, too. Because he was a halfwit. Because he was a vapid, empty-headed, pointless creature with the brain of a flea and the track record to prove it, and for some reason he'd managed to tell himself that someone could love him anyway. But there wasn't a damn thing that could make Thicky Icky smart, and now his brainlessness was his downfall.

"Pathetic," was all his father said.

I know.

38

LAURENCE

ONLY ONE OF THE MEN CAME OUTSIDE. THE ONE WITH THE ARM in his sling. He stepped through the doorway and regarded the truck, then pulled his keys out.

"What's happening?" Rodger whispered.

"Shh." Laurence's attention was on what Windsor could see, and so far, the guy hadn't come out any further. He obviously intended to just turn the alarm off, and would probably head right back inside. His arm was lifting toward the vehicle, keys in hand.

If Angela drove at him now, she'd just ram him back through the doorway. They needed him out in the open, and Laurence wracked his brain trying to come up with something fast.

Win.

Yes?

Take his keys.

Windsor didn't need any convincing. There were little shiny pieces of metal in the man's hand, and Windsor swooped down with his claws outstretched. Laurence felt the weirdest sensation across their bond, like Windsor was crossing into Otherworld again.

He had them in under a second, and beat his wings urgently to get away. The sensation faded.

"Hey! Holy shit! Come back here, you little asshole!"

The man hurried after Windsor, who was flying low enough to make him think he stood a chance.

Perfect! Go get Angela!

Yes!

Windsor sped up and Laurence pulled back. He watched with his own eyes as his familiar zoomed past the edge of the hill, and pulled Rodger back when their target stood a chance of spotting them.

With a rasp of tires on dirt, the Jack in the Green's delivery truck shot around the bend, aimed straight for the man, and accelerated.

"Oh, shit!" Laurence grabbed Rodger by the collar, tossed the scissors aside so they didn't stab themselves, and threw himself out from behind the truck they were using for shelter when he realized what was about to happen.

Angela hit flesh with a *whump* one second before the sound turned into the *smash* of truck against truck. The vehicle Laurence and Rodger had been hiding behind slid back several inches under the impact.

Windsor dropped the keys next to Laurence, and he turned the alarm off, then got to his feet like he was totally cool with almost getting crushed.

Angela hopped out of Laurence's truck and eyed the man who was pinned between two vehicles. He was collapsed over the hood, gasping for breath.

Laurence tossed the keys down, sprinted toward the building, and slid up against the outer wall to listen for a moment.

He heard something slam. It sounded like a heavy wooden door. Then footsteps approached him.

Laurence silently cursed himself for leaving the scissors by the truck, but he prayed that whoever was coming would be so shocked by the sight that they wouldn't look around.

He could see Angela, her head held high as she gazed through the doorway and into the house. Rodger was beside her, dusting himself off, and Laurence was pleased to see he'd at least picked the scissors up.

What he'd forgotten to do, he realized, was come up with a new plan.

He saw movement. Someone was stepping outside at last, and Laurence held his breath. He was still. Silent.

It was the other man. The one who'd been applying the sling. He stepped out into the blistering sunshine and Laurence ducked behind him, slipping through the doorway.

His senses shut down. He skidded to a halt, reaching out blindly, and his hand found stone, but it lacked the richness of texture, the precision of temperature that he expected to find. His balance was off, his hearing muffled.

Laurence blinked furiously. There was some light, he wasn't completely blind, but this was worse than just stepping out of the sun and into shade.

It was like the difference between going without sex, then suddenly having it, but in reverse.

These were, it slowly dawned on him, regular human senses.

"Hi. You must be new here."

He thought he knew that voice. When he raised his head, the woman in front of him looked dull, drained of color, but immediately recognizable despite the new bruising around her eyes.

"You must be Kathy," Laurence spat as he pushed himself upright.

"Oh, that's a shame." She whipped a fist out before she'd finished speaking.

Laurence should have seen her preparing for the punch. He should have noticed her eyes dilate and her muscles shift in readiness, but he didn't.

He still managed to recoil as she hit him, but he should

have done it sooner, and while he was still reeling, she kicked a leg out from under him.

Laurence dropped to one knee, and it wasn't the first time that he wished he knew how to roll about on the floor the way Quentin did. Quentin would have bounced back to his feet in a second, and Laurence was left scrambling away from Kathy, trying to put space between them.

She marched after him like a Terminator.

He grabbed the first thing that came to hand, but it was a sleeping bag.

Yeah. Great weapon.

Kathy was on him.

He threw the sleeping bag at her face, and as she brought her hands up to catch it, darted around her and back out into the hallway. There was a rotting door between the two rooms, which was closed, but Laurence didn't want to trap himself inside this house with Kathy. He needed to get away from her or he'd be a sitting duck.

Laurence skidded toward the sunlight, where Angela and Rodger were doing their best to run away from their own problem, but then he got punched in the back, and his whole body seized up. He fell like a log to the sound of electric ticking.

Had she just fucking tased him?

He felt like every click came with another punch, and all he could do was lie helpless, inches from freedom, as the man outside drew a taser on Angela.

Damn it, they were falling like dominoes.

The taser stopped, and he gasped for breath. His whole body felt like he'd run a marathon in five seconds, and as he fumbled to get his hands underneath himself, Kathy grabbed him by the ankles and dragged him backward.

Win!

There was no response. Laurence couldn't feel Windsor, couldn't reach him, and he yelled in frustration. He kicked against Kathy's hold, but he was face-down, and all she did was raise his legs more so that he couldn't get the leverage to fight her.

"Stop squirming," she muttered. "I'm taking you where you want to go."

"I doubt it," he spat. He grabbed for the door frame as she pulled him through it, but the stone was raw, and his fingers slipped.

"You've come all the way out here for one of them," Kathy reasoned. "And they're both in here."

She let go of Laurence's legs, and they fell to the floor.

He twisted onto his side, pulling his feet away from her, then stumbled upright and followed her outstretched finger.

Kathy was pointing to a slab of wood embedded in the floor, with an iron handle and a simple bar lock fitted to it. This wood was in good condition, possibly even brand new.

A trap door.

Laurence bared his teeth. It was called a trap door because it was a fucking trap, but it was also the only place in this whole house Quentin could be, unless they'd kept him in the broom closet or whatever hid behind the rotting door between the two main rooms. He stepped toward it cautiously, eyeing Kathy the whole time. "If I go down there, you're just gonna close the door after me."

"Yes," she said. "But I'm not making you go down there. You and your little friends are welcome to just get back in your truck and leave. I won't follow."

Laurence glanced down and saw the taser's wires trailing by his feet. He reached for them and pulled, dragging their tips out of his skin and throwing them away from himself, though he didn't doubt she had more ammo. "You let them go," he countered, "and I'll stay."

"I don't want you. I don't want any of you. What kind of bargain are you trying to make?" Kathy crouched by the trapdoor and slid the bolt free, then stepped back and gestured to it. "You're the one who came all the way out here. Go down there if you want to, but it's fair to say that if you do, you're never coming back up again. But if you do decide to go, all three of you go. If you leave, all three of you leave." She stood and planted her fists on her hips. "Is he worth it?"

He heard a scuffle and turned in time to see the man Angela had hit with her truck come limping into the room, looking like he was thinking about passing out. Behind him, his partner, dragging Rodger and Angela along with him, both of whom looked like they'd gone a few rounds with a prizefighter.

Laurence had no right to make this choice on their behalf. They'd come here to find Quentin, not to spend the rest of their lives in a basement.

But if he saved Angela and Rodger, he'd never see Quentin again.

"You're going to kill them," he said to Kathy, nodding to the trapdoor.

"Yes," she said. There was no apology, no explanation.

"So they're alive?"

"Yep."

"For how much longer?"

"Not long," Kathy said.

Laurence weighed his options. Quentin was down there, and if Laurence walked away, Kathy would kill him. He couldn't live with that blood on his hands. Whatever came next, he wasn't going to let Quentin face it alone, and if that meant Angela and Rodger died too, he really didn't care.

His shoulders sagged with defeat. There was no way out, so he walked toward the trapdoor and gestured for Kathy to open it.

"Let us in," he said.

39

LAURENCE

LAURENCE DESCENDED INTO A DARKNESS THAT WAS SO ABSOLUTE that he had to run his hands along the wall and feel for each step with his toes. His body blotted out the light that came from behind him, and then even that light went away when Rodger and Angela followed.

"This is insane," Rodger hissed. "Why are we doing this?"

"Because if we leave, they're gonna kill Quen," Laurence whispered. He found uneven ground, but he was out of steps at last, so he moved away from the stairs. "Quen? Baby?"

The trap door slammed shut and cut out the last of the light.

"So now we're all going to die down here," Angela observed. "How unfortunate."

"Who's there?"

Laurence recognized Delaney's voice. After watching so many of his shitty videos, it was familiar now.

"I'm Laurence Riley. Where's Quentin?"

"He's right here. He's just not, uh..." Delaney's breath hitched. "Functioning right now?"

Laurence bared his teeth in the dark. If Quentin had noped out, then Kathy had done something to make it happen.

"There's a lantern on the desk," Delaney hissed. "I can't get it. She's put me in handcuffs."

"Super helpful." Laurence didn't even try to bite back the snark. "Where's the desk?"

"Pffft," Rodger said.

Cold light blared out into the room, and Laurence raised a hand to shield his eyes.

"No signal doesn't mean no battery, duh," Rodger added.

The room swam into focus, and stole Laurence's breath away.

It was horrific. There were chains dangling all over the place like it was some medieval dungeon, but that wasn't the worst of it.

No, the truly sickening part was Quentin.

"Goddess," Laurence breathed. He hurried toward the chair that held Quentin's naked, battered body, and wrenched his shirt off over his head to drape over Quentin's lap. No wonder the earl had gone to his happy place. Every last inch of him was on display to total strangers. "Quen? Baby, it's me. I'm here."

He ran his fingers over the thick metal around Quentin's wrists. There was dried blood on one forearm, drizzled from a small collection of round holes in his skin. More metal encased his ankles, and Laurence searched for a way to remove them, but they were locked to chains which coiled around the chair itself, and then were attached to rings screwed into the floor.

Tears prickled Laurence's eyes. He blinked them away, but they just blurred his vision and refused to leave.

He'd been so sure nobody could have hurt Quentin, so totally convinced that Quen could defend himself against whatever had taken him, and he'd been wrong.

He'd broken his promise.

"Quen. Baby, I'm here. Please, say something." Laurence raised fingers to Quentin's cheek, and brushed them over his skin, careful to avoid a bruise that radiated up from his jaw. "Come back to me?"

Quentin's eyes swiveled toward Laurence, then he blinked. "You can't be here either," he hissed.

Laurence swallowed.

Something was wrong. Quentin had a predictable pattern whenever he came around, and this wasn't it at all.

Quentin looked away, then flinched, and went back to staring at the wall.

"Whoa, is he okay?" Rodger's voice was distant, like he was scared to come any closer.

Laurence couldn't see any other blood on Quentin's body, but there were all kinds of marks and bruises on him. His throat and neck were discolored, and when Laurence checked his wrists more closely, it looked like Quentin had fought against his restraints at some stage.

"I don't know," Laurence whispered. He couldn't pull his hand away from Quentin's cheek, but Quentin didn't seem to know Laurence was touching him. He turned and looked at Delaney, who was huddled on the floor. "What did she do to him?"

Delaney shook his head. "I wasn't here," he mumbled. "Not for everything. She didn't let him sleep, I know that much. Hung him up like a carcass in an abattoir, kept waking him through the night. It was horrible." He drew a deep breath. "She wanted him to confess to being a witch."

Laurence frowned, and he started looking around the room. Quentin's clothes were nearby, scuffed and torn, littered across the floor. Further away, there was a worm-eaten desk, with a chair behind it, and Angela had a camping lantern in her hands. She turned it slowly, then switched it on and carried it over to the stairs.

"Go get his jacket," he said to Delaney.

Delaney made his way to his feet. "Why?"

"Because I fucking said so, and he wouldn't be here if it wasn't for you?"

Delaney sulked his way over to the clothes and picked through them, then brought Quentin's jacket back with him.

Laurence took it and laid it over Quentin's chest, the wrong way around, but at least it covered him up better. Then he rearranged his t-shirt so that it covered more of Quentin's thighs.

Quentin looked at him again, and smiled. "Can we go now?"

"Not yet, hon. We just need to figure a few things out. Kiss?"

Quentin seemed to think about it, then he said, "Yes."

Laurence leaned in and pressed his lips softly to Quentin's. They felt rough and cold, and they barely moved.

"They're leaving." Angela tutted softly.

Laurence pulled away and turned toward her. She was over by the trapdoor, sitting on the highest step she could fit on, with one hand to the wood and her head tilted to one side. He hurried to the stairs, and was barely able to hear the engine in the distance.

He cursed under his breath, then beckoned Angela to come down. "Let me try something."

There was no way of knowing if this would work, but he couldn't reach Windsor through their bond right now, and the bird had excellent vision and hearing. Laurence swapped places with Angela, then cupped his hands around his mouth and yelled for all he was worth. "Follow them, Windsor! But stay high up! Don't get close!"

His voice reverberated around the basement for a second, but there was nothing from Windsor. Now he was close to it, he saw circles carved into the underside of the trapdoor, and it seemed the weirdest place to bother decorating.

"They're seriously going to leave us down here?" Delaney's voice raised in pitch until it was a squeak.

"Yup." Laurence put his shoulder to the trapdoor and heaved against it, but it wouldn't budge.

If Kathy had gone, though, why weren't his senses back?

"I see the problem," Angela said. She was standing nearby, with the lantern held up close to the wall where it met ceiling, and she ran fingers across marks in the stonework.

They matched those on the trapdoor.

"Daisies," Quentin murmured.

"No. Apotropaic marks." Angela turned away and met Laurence's gaze. "Witch marks," she clarified. "They protect against magic, and a wide spectrum of other preternatural events."

Laurence's heart raced, and he scurried down the steps to go take a closer look at them.

The marks had been cut into the stone, but weren't dusty or grimy. He ran his fingers over them and found that they were easily a centimeter deep.

"There's more over here." Rodger held his phone up against another set, opposite from where Laurence and Angela stood.

"No, it's probably relevant," Quentin snarled, his tone suddenly furious. "Why don't you shut up and leave them to it?"

Everyone stopped talking, but Quentin was staring at a wall again.

"Was that…" Rodger tapped his own chest. "Aimed at me?"

"I doubt it. He's been talking to himself," Delaney muttered. "Crying and shit. I think he's crazy."

"You can shut the fuck up," Laurence snarled. "You brought him here. Whatever happened to him is on you, and you're gonna fucking pay, do you get me?"

Entrails. Always entrails.

The instinct was still there, then, even without his gifts. It was both a relief and the exact opposite, since it was kind of nice to know that Laurence's gifts weren't influencing him, but also horrible to think that his desire to gut people who pissed him off was part of who he was.

Part of…

Quentin's vortex wasn't pulling on him.

Laurence cursed. When had Quen last eaten? It was cold down here, and he'd been here all night. He had to be running low, even before Kathy had got started on him, and without the ability to draw on the energy around him, he might have deteriorated even sooner.

He had to get rid of these stupid sigils.

"Okay." He ran hands through his hair. "How do these marks work?"

"Apotropaic magic is considered to turn magic away, to deflect it," Angela explained, "but that is not how it works. For a witch-finder's apotropaic marks to function, she must possess the bloodline necessary, and make the marks herself. Both the witch-finder and her marks actually nullify magic, and most other preternatural events. Your bird cannot enter the building without risking dispersal."

"You mean death?" Laurence's heart thrummed against his ribs. If Windsor had tried to come inside, was he gone now?

"No. It takes more than that to kill a familiar. He would simply be dispersed back to the realm he came from. He would need some time to reform and return."

His shoulders slowly drooped with relief, and Laurence rubbed his stubble. "So it's possible she can lay these marks down anywhere and they're like a booby trap? You can walk right over them and suddenly, bam, you lose it all?"

"Correct."

"Shit."

That had to be how they'd got Quentin. If there were apotropaic marks on the street, or on the truck that had acted as a roadblock, Quentin would have been utterly powerless, whether Kathy was there or not. And their presence meant Laurence couldn't look back on the event, or see Quentin's journey since then.

He frowned faintly. "Bloodline?"

"When the world was young and magic was rife, the universe listened to all, and chaos reigned," Angela intoned. "Before it learned to become selective, some humans beseeched it for the power to nullify the magic of others, and the universe agreed. It was meant to quash the upheaval, but the humans who had sought this power turned it against all magic, not only that which was harmful. When magic faded, so too did the need for such protection. Witch-finders are rare now. In fact," she added, "I had thought them extinct."

"Yeah, well. Apparently they're not." Laurence took the lantern and circled the room, and found two more of the marks. They were almost pretty, collections of interlocking circles that did kind of make a daisy pattern. Quentin wasn't wrong about that. "Are they like sigils? I mean, if we break them, do they stop working?"

Angela eyed him, but nodded. "So far as I'm aware, yes. Alas, I neglected to pack hammer and chisel into my purse today."

"Mood," Rodger said.

"Okay." Laurence nodded to himself as he wandered back toward Angela. "Then that's got to be our focus. We ruin these marks until they don't work, then we bust out of here and track her down."

Angela glanced past him, toward Quentin, then eyed Laurence and dropped her voice. "Historically," she whispered, "witch-finders seek confessions through torture. It might be best to prioritize his rescue, and leave her for another day."

"I'm not letting her get away with this," he hissed.

"I agree. But are you going to throw him in the back and chase after the person who did this to him, or are you going to get him somewhere safe?"

He folded his arms together and tried to avoid sulking like a teenager. She made good sense, but his instincts screamed at him to hunt Kathy down and make sure she couldn't do this to anyone else ever again.

Did he want revenge, or did he think he could bury his own guilt by running after her?

Neither of those things were more important than

Quentin's safety.

Laurence bowed his head. "You're right."

"Naturally."

She seemed perfectly serious, and he wasn't going to argue. Instead, he gave her the lantern and strode to the center of the basement, stepping over stray chains on the way, and clapped his hands together.

"Okay. Here's the plan. Bear in mind I have no idea how we're gonna achieve it, but we'll work that part out." Laurence pointed to the marks. "These things have got to go. We need to figure out a way to damage every single one of them."

Delaney raised his cuffed hands like he was back in school, then dropped them again with a blush. "Who put you in charge?"

"I did, and since that's what's going to get us out of here alive, you're going to help out." Laurence did his best to imitate one of Quentin's more terrifying staredowns, but he wasn't sure he could pull it off.

Delaney shuffled his feet. "Okay, but we need to get that trapdoor open. What's the point fucking around with etchings?" He gasped. "Oh, shit. Kathy's got all the keys. Even if we get the door open, we're still screwed! She'll be long gone!"

"Trust me. Once those 'etchings'—" Laurence even air-quoted the word "—are gone, we're out of here."

"I assume you know that *alohamora* isn't a real spell?" Angela said. "I don't have the right components for any kind of unlocking magic. Not with me."

"Yeah, it's okay. We've got that covered. We just need to break down these witch marks, then this place is dust in our rearview." Laurence looked at Quentin, and hoped that he was right.

With the marks down, their locksmith could get to work. The only question was whether Laurence would be able to get him to focus enough to do the job.

Otherwise, this was going to really suck.

40

QUENTIN

His father wouldn't leave him alone, which wasn't surprising in the slightest; but Quentin had exhausted himself crying, and all he wanted to do was sleep. Now Laurence was here as well, and Laurence was ignoring Father.

Perhaps Quentin could do that, too.

It wasn't really until Laurence stood radiant in the center of the room and announced that he had a plan for escape that Quentin noticed that they were trapped to begin with.

You're chained to a chair in a locked basement. Honestly, you couldn't get any more stupid, could you?

"Go away," he muttered.

Laurence tilted his head and frowned. "We're trying, hon."

They were having two different conversations. Quentin knew that by now. Laurence's grasp of English did not seem to match his own.

"I'm really excited to hear what suggestions you have for chiseling stonework without any tools," Rodger said. The sarcasm dripped so voluminously from his words that it was almost visible.

"There are tools," Quentin said.

What was Rodger doing here, anyway? Wasn't he supposed

to be at the shop, putting more effort into shirking than it would have taken to just do his work in the first place?

In fact, this whole situation was peculiar. There was the ghost-hunter, Delaney, but he was in handcuffs. Laurence was here, which was good, but so was Quentin's father, which was bad. And then, to round out this bizarre group, there were a shop delivery boy and a woman Quentin didn't even know the name of.

Laurence waved his hand at Rodger and approached Quentin. Despite the dim light, there was hope clear in his eyes. "What tools, hon?"

Quentin nodded toward the desk and chair, and Laurence turned away, then shook his head at Quentin. "I don't see any?"

"Because you haven't collected them yet."

"They're too stupid to get it," muttered Father. "Frankly, I'm amazed that you've even pieced this much together. Is Frederick here? I could understand if he'd worked it out, but you?"

"If you don't have anything to contribute," Quentin muttered, looking toward the duke, "stay quiet." Then he returned his attention to Laurence. "Did Katharine empty your pockets?"

"No." Laurence glanced toward the duke with a frown.

"Good. Then you need to put everything you brought with you together and catalogue your assets." Quentin smiled. This was so simple. He'd done it himself, so it *must* be obvious.

Laurence's head tilted again, but then he backed away and emptied his pockets onto the desk. "Okay. What've we got?"

Everyone else — bar Delaney — followed suit. The woman tipped up her small handbag and scattered the contents across the wood, then left her bag there, too. Rodger pulled, of all things, a spool of wire out of his back pocket and added it to his phone and keys. And even Laurence had seen fit to bring ribbon to a rescue party, which was awfully nice.

"I'm sorry," Quentin said to the woman. "What's your name?"

"Angela," she replied. "What's yours?"

"Quentin."

"Can we not?" Delaney began to pace the room. "We're wasting time."

"Shut up," said at least three people. Quentin was sure he wasn't one of them.

He eyed the collection of items on the desk, then squinted toward the apotropaic marks. If Laurence was correct, then the shape of the marks themselves needed to be changed, and simply drawing over them or filling them in with something wouldn't do it. Their very structure had to be disrupted.

"All right," he mused. "Break the chair. Use the wire and ribbon to fix keys to the ends of whatever wood you can salvage. It may be more structurally sound if you wedge a key between two pieces and bind them together around it. Then break the desk and use the heavier wood as the hammer to your rudimentary chisels. Problem solved."

They stared at him, then started muttering among themselves.

"How do we break a chair?"

"I dunno. Smash it against the ground?" Laurence rubbed his jaw.

Angela sniffed. "If they were that fragile, Quentin wouldn't be stuck right now."

"The desk is significantly heavier and less breakable than any of you," Quentin offered.

Laurence paused, fingers idly tinkering with the stubble at his chin, then he nodded. "So we lay the chair on its side, lift the desk up, and drop it on the chair's legs. That could work."

"It'd have to be with the table edge," Rodger agreed. "Could break the desk, too, if we're lucky."

Quentin's attention drifted away as they set to work clearing the desk and arranging the chair on the floor. He wasn't interested in the work, and didn't wish to expose his eyeballs to the potential for flying debris that might come from that direction.

It left him looking at Delaney, who was standing by him still, not attempting to offer advice, let alone help.

"You made mistakes," Quentin murmured. "But they don't have to define you."

Delaney scowled at him. "If I needed advice like that I'd go crack open some fortune cookies."

"Your mistakes very nearly killed someone. And since that someone was me, I have the right to give you whatever hokey advice I feel like." He crinkled his nose faintly. "You put my whole life online for people like Marlowe to find, and you actively participated in a kidnapping. You chose to do all these things. If you don't want to learn from your mistakes, I'll gladly bury you in the rubble of this house and leave your body to be eaten by whatever lives out here."

Delaney's mouth hung open. "You..." His voice choked briefly. "You were trying to save my life, and now you're threatening me?"

Quentin pursed his lips. "I'm feeling quite fickle at the moment."

It wasn't true. Realistically, he wasn't feeling a great deal of anything at all, other than fatigue. Even the sight of Laurence shirtless wasn't affecting him nearly as much as he might expect it to.

"You're insane," Delaney hissed.

"Very probably, yes."

He was cut short by the awful crashing of a very heavy desk against, at first, a less heavy chair, and then a considerably more heavy floor. At least, Quentin presumed the floor was heavier, as it was constructed from stone. He had no way to weigh it.

Where *was* Laurence's shirt, anyway? He didn't usually perform topless rescues.

You should marry him.

He snorted. *Don't be silly.*

There was nothing for him to do now. He couldn't help physically, and he certainly couldn't help mentally, so he finally allowed his eyes to close.

———

THERE WAS WARMTH.

Quentin sucked in breath and his eyes flicked open. He felt heat around his fingers, but it was also starting to permeate his body, trickling slowly up his arms and across his chest.

Laurence was there, leaning over him, holding his hands. "Hey, hon."

Sweat soaked Laurence's curls and trickled down his bare skin. His cheeks were reddened, and he had dust and grit across his shoulders and the tip of his nose.

Quentin smiled slyly. "Hello, darling."

Laurence gave a fleeting smirk. "We're not alone," he warned.

"Why not?"

"Well, 'cause we're stuck in a basement. But if you need to take anything, go right ahead, okay?"

"Such as?" Quentin blinked.

"You know." Laurence leaned closer. "Energy. Heat. Whatever you wanna call it."

Come to think of it, he did seem to be running on empty.

Quentin lifted his head, and Laurence kissed him.

Warmth slipped between them, slow and delicate, until Quentin's brain woke enough to realize what exactly was on offer, and just how much he needed it.

God, what a state he was in.

He didn't have time to worry about it. Instead, he reached for what was being given, and he took it. He tried to be gentle, at least, but the problem was that it was intoxicating, and when it was paired with the way Laurence whimpered against his lips, it was difficult to remember that what he was stealing was Laurence's *life*.

Quentin gasped and recoiled, only to bang his head against the back of the chair.

The world was sharp again. In focus. Alive.

Laurence's cheeks remained flushed, his lips pink, and his body arched over Quentin's. His breathing was rough, excited.

We're not alone.

Oh, god. It was starting to make sense. There were patches missing, of course, as he might expect after waking the way he had, but he was reasonably certain that he was naked in a room full of mostly-strangers and manacled to a chair, and only Laurence's body was shielding him.

He glanced down.

No, clothes were draped over the worst of it, thank goodness. That must have been Laurence.

"Thank you," he breathed.

"No problem. Any time." Laurence cleared his throat. "But we can't go any further without you, hon. Can you do this?" Laurence's fingers drifted to the manacles. "Break these?"

The trick, he figured, would be to do so without breaking his own bones in the process. It required finesse, and perhaps some understanding of how the devices worked.

He leaned to his left to view the padlock, and he raised it so that he could peer in through the keyhole.

Quentin knew absolutely nothing about picking locks. But it cost nothing to try, and so he allowed his telekinetic hold to flow in through the opening, and closed his eyes so that he could focus on the numb feedback it gave him.

Locks were opened by insertion of the key, and then turning. That was the obvious part. But there had to be more to it, otherwise all keys would open all locks.

He probed and pushed, and was certain that something within the padlock moved, but it was difficult to sense, and the thing didn't unlock.

"Baby?" Laurence asked.

Quentin shook his head faintly. He didn't have time to mess around. His was not the only life at stake here. He had torn a steel door from stone bedrock, and a padlock was considerably less immutable. Rather than fuss around with the lock's innards, he tore them out completely, leaving the padlock a hollow shell which was easy to unfasten.

The pieces fell to the floor in a rain of metal, and he turned his attention to his right wrist.

"I suppose you think you're clever," his father muttered.

"Holy shit!" Delaney squeaked as the second padlock fell in ruins by his feet.

Quentin disposed of the padlocks at his waist and ankles far more swiftly, now that he knew what he was doing, and popped the manacles open.

God, his wrists were in a right state. What *had* he done?

Laurence backed away enough for Quentin to stand, but there was no way that he could do so without trousers at the very least. He searched for them and found them discarded and torn, but that was better than nothing.

"A little privacy, please?"

"Sure thing, baby." Laurence grabbed Delaney and turned him away, and used his body as a shield so that Quentin could pull the trousers on.

He debated wearing Laurence's t-shirt; but the poor boy might like it back, so he made do with his own jacket, fastening it before he stood. It still showed too much, but it was better than nothing. He retrieved shoes and socks, and pulled them on, then turned his attention to the room.

Any furniture which had not been under him was thoroughly wrecked. The chair, the desk, both were in pieces. The apotropaic marks had little nibbles etched out of their circles here and there, and each had shed a small waterfall of stone dust or wood chips in the process.

Quentin didn't know how long it had taken them to achieve, or how the incessant banging hadn't woken him.

His father had disappeared.

Quentin frowned and peered around as though the duke

might be lurking in a darkened corner, but he was thoroughly absent.

Who's the coward now?

"I assume these marks also exist upstairs?" He looked at Laurence.

"I don't know," Laurence said. "My senses got shut down the moment I was inside, so I didn't see."

Quentin nodded and approached the trapdoor, then flung it open so brutally that it shattered. There was no way he was allowing anyone else to leave first, lest there were any nasty surprises waiting for them, so he continued up the steps and prepared to lose the very thing that had allowed them to escape.

Except this time he was ready.

41

LAURENCE

DESTROYING THE MARKS MADE HIS GIFTS RETURN IN A FLASH, and Laurence had immediately reached for Windsor.

The bird was flying high, tailing Kathy's truck.

The hardest part was having to rouse Quentin, to gently force him to take from Laurence so that he could get them out of this horror show of a basement. Quentin had gone through something horrendous, there wasn't any doubt about that, and Laurence couldn't allow him the time to rest, or Marlowe would escape for good.

The longer he'd chipped away, using a car key as a chisel, the more he'd been able to take control of his anger and examine whether or not it was revenge he wanted. And if he was being honest, of course it was. But there was more to it than that.

Marlowe had taken Delaney's evidence of haunting — of Quentin's telekinesis — as proof of witchcraft, and she was willing to torture him to death over it.

How many others would she torture if they didn't stop her?

He crept up the stairs after Quentin. Maybe Quentin thought there could be booby traps up there, or snipers, or something, and the fact that he chose to go first even after all he'd been through, not only to protect Laurence but also the man who had kicked off all of this hurt to begin with, made him incredibly proud.

"They didn't leave anyone behind," Laurence breathed. "Windsor saw all three of them get into their truck and go."

"That's good," Quentin murmured.

They emerged cautiously from the hole in the ground, and Quentin gestured for Laurence to stay where he was as he quietly moved toward the door, testing his footing as he went.

Laurence helped the others out of the basement, offering a hand and holding up his own to stop them from wandering off until Quentin gave the all clear, but once he did, they broke out of the building in a sprint, running for the battered and dust-covered Jack in the Green truck. Kathy and her guys had only taken one of their trucks — the one Angela hadn't driven into — and left the other with Laurence's fender dug into its side.

Angela tossed him his keys and they all piled in.

Quentin took the front. Of course he did. And he seemed to be counting the passengers to make sure they had everyone, but frowned faintly.

"Something wrong?" Laurence turned the key and let out a puff of relief that the truck engine wasn't damaged.

"No. Just… no." Quentin shook his head.

Laurence didn't have time to dig deeper. Quentin had been talking to someone who wasn't here, and now he seemed to have difficulty doing a headcount, but Marlowe was getting away, and Quentin was still hours from any psychiatric help he might need.

"Okay. Let me know if that changes." He smiled tightly, then hit the gas, and started rattling the truck back out of the nature reserve.

Marlowe had an hour's head start, and somehow Laurence had to close that gap without crashing the truck or getting arrested.

He followed Marlowe's route. The advantage of tailing via raven was that Windsor's memories were better than any GPS, and he wasn't trying to lead Laurence across rivers without bridges or land without roads.

Marlowe didn't seem to be rushing, either. She wasn't driving erratically, wasn't busting through red lights or intersections.

Laurence bared his teeth as they broke free of the nature reserve and returned to real roads.

She thought she'd gotten away with it, and she wasn't even trying to run away. She was just leaving, like her work here was done.

Maybe that angered him more than it should, but he didn't care. It gave him the chance to catch up with her as she made her way east on an interstate, and once he was on it too, he went back to driving with a leaden foot whenever there weren't other cars around, then sticking to the posted limits when there might be patrol cars hiding out of sight.

Every now and then, Delaney tried to make conversation, but Rodger shut him down, and eventually the cab was quiet.

This wasn't Laurence's idea of a high-speed car chase.

"What do we intend to do when we catch her?" Angela broke the silence. "We're unarmed, and she is not."

"We can find a hunting store and stock up?" Rodger offered.

Quentin crinkled his nose, but didn't voice his objection.

"Does anyone know how to use anything we could buy there?" Laurence snorted. "We'd need a background check for guns, I don't know how to use a bow, and the best I can do is stick a knife in someone if they let me get close enough. And since she blocks all our magic and gifts, I can't get close unless she's super distracted *and* Tweedledum and Tweedledee have been taken out already."

"Then we shall have to appeal to reason," Quentin said softly.

Laurence barked a short, humorless laugh. "No offense, hon, but she tortures people. Reason isn't on her side."

"She does it because she believes she's right," Quentin replied, gazing out of the window at the desert. "Because her family was hurt hundreds of years ago. This is an old wound, and it needs to heal."

"How do you plan on doing that?"

"Let me talk to her."

The chorus of objections from the back seat almost drowned out Laurence's own, and he waited for it to die down before he tried again.

"She wants to *kill* you, Quen."

"I know."

His expression was unreadable, since he was still watching the desert, but Quentin's voice bore a quiet determination.

How could he be willing to speak to the woman who had put him through hell? She'd only had him for a day, and he was already falling apart at the seams. Whatever she'd done, Laurence didn't want to expose him to more of it.

"What other option do we have?" Quentin turned to face Laurence. His skin was paler than usual, and he had dark circles under his eyes. The bruise on his jaw was now an almost luminous yellow beneath the darkness of his stubble. If he saw his own reflection he'd probably shit a brick and hide away until he considered himself to be more presentable, but instead here he was, clinging on, trying to save the life of his torturer.

"Call the cops," said Rodger from the back seat. "They're already on the case."

"And tell them what? That a witch-finder is on the loose?" Angela clicked her tongue faintly. "Once that hits the news, every kook and conspiracy theorist will have Quentin in their sights."

"And thanks to Delaney, they'll know exactly where to find

him." Laurence ground his teeth. "They've got tasers, we've got nothing."

"It's not my fault," Delaney whined.

"I swear to god I'm going to fucking punch you if you keep saying that," Rodger sniffed.

Laurence's senses lurched, and he gripped the wheel. Windsor had begun a dive, but Laurence couldn't take his eyes off the road to find out why. *Win?*

She is stopping.

Don't get close! She'll disperse you and won't even notice. She's bad news! Laurence tried to convey urgency, but sometimes Windsor could be oblivious to danger. He'd flown right into the hurricane Quentin had made in England, just to keep sight of him.

Fine, Windsor replied with a huff. *She is using the pipe.*

What pipe?

The truck pipe.

Laurence tried to work that one out, then blinked. *Oh! She's at a gas station?*

Yes!

Okay! Stay with her!

Windsor wasn't far away. Laurence could sense his proximity and it was barely a couple of miles. If they were lucky, if Marlowe took more than five minutes to fill up and pay, then they'd get there in time to block them from leaving, and maybe Marlowe wasn't down with getting caught on camera shooting people and throwing them into her truck. She'd gone to so much trouble to kidnap Quentin without leaving much of a trace.

Goddess, why *was* he doing this? A full frontal fight wasn't his style, and he was no good at it. He needed cover, stealth, and surprise — a knife was a nice bonus that he didn't have. Without magic or his gifts, he was just a florist.

The gas station came into view on the horizon, and Laurence realized he was out of time. He had to make a decision, so he fixed his eyes on the prize and consulted his instincts.

Nope. They were still fixated on the whole entrails business. Tearing, shredding, removing. Everything inside him knew that Marlowe was like Kane: that unless she was stopped, permanently, then she'd just carry on torturing people who couldn't fight back.

"I almost did it," Quentin mused, turning away again.

"Huh?" Laurence dragged his brain away from gore. "Did what?"

"Confessed," Quentin admitted. "I was seconds away from it. I couldn't take any more, and she was about to start torturing Delaney instead, to make me talk." He sighed. "I couldn't let her do that to him. Not when I had the power to make her stop."

Laurence frowned. He wanted to say *He's not worth it*, but what would be the point? Quentin couldn't sit by and let someone else get hurt, even if it meant ending his own life, and he'd been in an impossible situation. There was no way out.

"It's okay," Laurence said quietly, grateful that the peanut gallery in the back seat kept their mouths shut. "You're safe now."

Quentin smiled briefly, but the smile ghosted away again as Laurence pulled into the gas station.

Marlowe's truck was still there.

Laurence drove between a couple of other pumps that were empty so that he could skew across the front of her truck, then unbuckled his seatbelt and leaped out of the cab. His senses had shut down pretty much the moment he drove onto the forecourt, but he was ready for it to happen this time. It wasn't so disorienting.

Marlowe stepped out of the gas station, chewing on gum, and didn't even hesitate when she saw him. She just kept on coming closer, like Laurence wasn't in her way.

Quentin stepped out and shut his door, and since Laurence

had skewed left across Marlowe's truck, he was virtually in her face when he stood upright.

They were completely at the mercy of a woman who would kill all of them if she could, and Laurence's skin itched.

"Well," she said. "Isn't this a nice surprise?"

42

QUENTIN

QUENTIN REALLY WASN'T ALL THAT FAMILIAR WITH PETROL stations. He might have seen a few out of the window of a car, but hadn't actually stopped in one before he met Laurence, and he certainly hadn't gotten out of the truck at one. Laurence would simply refuel, pay, and get back in again.

The smell was not wholly unpleasant, and he wondered whether it was the fuel itself, or something else. It was almost like paint.

This particular petrol station was more than simply fuel pumps and a shop. There was a sit-down restaurant, a place for tire checks, and what looked like a take-out taco stand. It was a modern oasis, the only food and water for miles around.

Marlowe stopped inches from him, her head held high, and he had to coerce his attention back toward her.

"Yes?" he offered.

She just snorted, then looked past him, so Quentin turned and watched as one of her hired muscle got out of their truck and stood menacingly alongside Laurence.

Quentin tilted his head and turned back to Marlowe. "Perhaps we should go inside," he said. "We can talk about this. There's no need for further violence."

She laughed and planted her fists on her hips, which just

made it clear that she was no longer wearing her plastic weapon. "You wanna sit down over pizza and act like we can work this out?"

"No. I want to sit down, over pizza if necessary, and work this out."

"How do you think this is going to end?" She thumbed over her shoulder toward the restaurant. "We shake hands and agree never to cross each other's paths again?"

"How do *you* envision it ending?" Quentin lifted himself to his full height. "You want us to start brawling like children under the watchful eyes of security cameras?"

Marlowe rocked her jaw, then pointed toward Laurence. "Stay on him," she ordered to her accomplice. "If he moves, snap his neck."

Quentin gestured past her, back the way she had come. "Shall we?"

She tipped her head back to eye him, then turned on her heel and marched for the door.

THE WAITRESS SEATED them by the window and brought glasses of ice water, then left them alone with menus. Quentin set his aside without looking at it. Not only did he still have no appetite, but it seemed rude to eat while Laurence and the others were in the Arizona heat without food.

He looked outside to be certain that Laurence was safe, and found Laurence to be watching his guard instead of the restaurant, so Quentin looked back at Marlowe and idly ensured that the collar of his jacket remained turned inward to cover as much of his scarring as it could.

They both sipped their water a while without speaking. Quentin was extraordinarily dehydrated, and he supposed that Marlowe was just avoiding being the first to talk, so he set his glass aside before the cold could give him a headache and attempted to gather his thoughts.

"I sometimes wonder whether I am a monster," he murmured.

Katharine snorted. "You are."

"Possibly." Quentin rested his elbows on the table in a manner he found most uncouth, but he couldn't bear to try and hold himself upright at the moment. "I have nightmares. There is blood, screaming, and I…" He shook his head faintly. "I have caused both. But when I am awake, that isn't me. I don't want to be that person."

"You can't help it." Katharine pushed her glass away and leaned back in her seat, gazing at him without pity. "Scorpions sting, rattlesnakes bite. It's in your nature, and it's in *my* nature to put you — and others like you — out of this misery. Instead of fighting it, you should be thanking me."

Quentin snorted in amusement for what might well have been the first time in, well, however long he'd been gone. "You know," he said as he met her eye, "you could well be right. I was foolish enough to hope that everything I had ever endured was in the past, but here you are, making it present all over again. Thank you. I'm truly grateful. I was growing quite used to *not* being tortured. Thank goodness you were there to remind me that's not really how life is."

He wasn't sure whether he was being as sarcastic as he'd intended to be.

Marlowe turned her glass between her hands, then nodded toward him. "Tell me about the scars."

Quentin laughed weakly. He hadn't even told Violeta about the scars, and here was someone for whom his mental health was clearly not a priority asking for deeply personal details about things he preferred to keep hidden.

"Coward," his father said. "You invited her here. Now you pay the price."

Quentin jerked away on reflex, and banged against the glass. His father was sitting beside him, preventing him from leaving, gazing at him impassively as though Quentin were forever nothing more than a gross disappointment to him.

You can't be here!

He really couldn't. If Katharine cancelled out magic, then the duke couldn't possibly have appeared out of nowhere, or projected himself to be by Quentin's side.

Marlowe was watching him, her eyes narrowed. Her fingers had curled around a knife on the table.

If Quentin's father had magically transported himself here, wouldn't she be looking at *him*?

There was nothing for it. Quentin reached out slowly, his fingers trembling, and passed his hand through his father's absent body.

"What do you think that proves?" Father demanded.

"What are you doing?" Marlowe drew the knife nearer to herself.

"You don't…" Quentin licked his lips. "You don't see him?"

"There's nobody there, d'Arcy."

"You think that I would show myself to a commoner?" his father argued.

"Nobody there…" Quentin echoed the words, then tried to cling to them, and he dragged his attention away from his father and back to Katharine. "I see. I'm sorry. The scars…" He clenched his hands into fists until his nails dug painfully into his palms. "My father gave them to me."

"What, like a fucking gift?"

"I believe that he thinks so, yes." He steadfastly ignored the dark presence at his side and gazed only into Marlowe's steel eyes. "You call me a witch, but I was born without magic. It's been that way for generations. And so, to make up for it…"

Quentin fell silent. To fill the yawning chasm between them, he drank more of his water.

"He punished you?" Katharine sounded intrigued.

"No. He abused me throughout my childhood. It was an essential component in the ritual required to give me the ability I lacked."

Quentin startled himself with how calmly he said those

words, like they were simple facts about the weather and not an incredibly bland skimming of the horror of his whole life.

Katharine scoffed at him. "You really want me to believe that your own father did this to you?"

"As my grandfather did to him. And however often it happened before then." Quentin clasped his hands together to keep them steady. "My greatest achievement, should one wish to call it such a thing, is refusing to continue this abhorrent cycle. I will not have children. I will allow my family line to go extinct if necessary. It will never happen again." He quirked his eyebrows. "Especially not if you kill me."

Her gaze wavered so briefly that he suspected he might well have imagined it, just as he was evidently imagining the man at his side.

"I fear becoming a monster," Quentin added softly, "because I come from a family of them."

Katharine pushed the knife aside and leaned back to cross her arms, and her features were creased in a highly skeptical expression.

"How many have you killed?"

Katharine shrugged. "I don't keep count. This isn't pleasure for me; I'm not a trophy-hunter. This is my job now. I protect humanity from things like you, because nobody else can." She unfurled her hands to point at him. "You sank a yacht, and it's a wonder only one person died. His blood is on your hands."

Quentin blinked. "Kane Wilson?" He shook his head. "He had the power to compel people into following his orders. He had murdered several children during his youth, fully aware of what effects his gift had, and as an adult he killed more. He caused the explosives to be placed on that yacht. Had I not been present, innocent people would have died, but the yacht was evacuated in time, and Kane..." Quentin shook his head again. "I did not kill him."

Her jaw moved like she might be probing a tooth with her tongue, then Katharine picked up the menu again. "We better order something, or they'll think we're wasting their time."

"Feel free."

She tossed the menu aside and caught the attention of a server, ordered something with the word "platter" in the name, then leaned back in her seat. "You're telling me Wilson died of natural causes?"

Quentin shook his head lightly. "No. Simply that your supposition was incorrect."

"You threw him overboard like a discarded toy," his father spat. "You could have killed him. It's pure luck that you failed."

Quentin felt his eye twitch, but there was nothing he could do to stop it, so he raised a hand to press cold condensation from the glass against his skin in the hope that it would calm down.

"Then who did kill him?"

He turned toward the forecourt, where Laurence remained exactly as he'd been left, with a threatening guardian of his own by his side.

Katharine snorted. "That kid? You're kidding me."

"I am not. And in doing so, he saved my life, and freed countless people from Wilson's control."

"So you can see how killing someone can be justified?"

Quentin couldn't help but laugh at that. He had very little wherewithal left, even after draining Laurence's strength to restore his own. His mind was clearly having a few operational problems right this very moment, and controlling his own reactions was the least of his priorities.

The oddest benefit to the whole mess was, at least he could have this conversation in a public space without outing himself, because Katharine muffled his psychokinesis and prevented it firing off all of its own accord. If only Violeta had that gift.

"I think that if people could stop being so keen on killing each other," Quentin said once he'd managed to stop his inappropriate laughter, "nobody would feel the need to kill the killers to make them stop killing."

"That is such an infantile perspective that it boggles the mind," his father drawled.

"Will you shut the hell up?" Quentin rounded on the apparition and swept a hand through it again, as though he could make it sod off if he found the right spot. "You aren't even here and you're still making my life miserable! Go away!"

His father gazed placidly at him, then shook his head. "Why must you always be such a disappointment?"

"Shut up!"

Christ, he felt so small again. What on Earth was he doing, yelling like this? He wouldn't do it if his father were truly present, so why was he behaving like a toddler to an imaginary version?

You're ill.

His grip on reality was sliding again. He could almost feel it, drifting away from him, leaving him to face his fate alone.

"D'Arcy!"

Something dug into his shoulder and thrust him back against his seat. It tore him away from the mocking face of his father, and instead he faced Marlowe, inches from his nose. She was leaning over the table, looming over him, her eyes searching his.

"I'm..." He hesitated. What was he, exactly? Sorry? Confused? Losing his mind?

"He's not here." She bit out each word. "Ignore him."

"But—"

"I don't care how persistent he's being." She let go of Quentin's shoulder, and slowly lowered herself back into her seat. "You and me, we're having a conversation here, and he's being a rude fucker. So ignore him and look at me. Okay?"

"I'm sorry," he breathed. He gripped at the edge of the table, but it felt like there might be something dry there that had once been wet, so he crinkled his nose and reached for a napkin to wipe at it. "I'm sorry; this isn't easy. But nothing worth doing ever is."

The waitress awkwardly placed their platter on the table,

settled little white plates in front of each of them, then scurried away without another word. The smell of it turned Quentin's stomach, and he leaned back to try and get away.

"You blacked out, back in the basement," Marlowe mused while she dragged some mystery lumpy items off the platter onto her own plate. "Do you know you do that?"

"I have been made aware."

She pursed her lips. "I couldn't figure it out at the time. But now I know what those scars are from, I can hazard a guess. You've got PTSD, right?"

Quentin shook his head faintly. "What is that?"

"Post-Traumatic Stress Disorder. I spent eighteen years in the Army. You get to see a lot of it."

"I don't know," Quentin admitted. He knew he wasn't too keen on the word *disorder*, but then what other word adequately described his illness? There was clearly something out of order with his mind, and he would be foolish not to use the word *traumatic* to describe its most likely cause.

He looked out at Laurence. "Is that where you met your friends? The Army?"

"No. They're not my friends. I mean, they are, but they're more than that."

He blinked. Was she inferring that she had two partners? And, if so, was it any of his business?

"They're my brothers," Marlowe added.

Pieces of the puzzle slid into place. If Marlowe's gift was genetic, did her brothers have it too? Was that why they were so willing to spend their lives traveling the country murdering anyone they decided was a witch?

Was that why Laurence hadn't made a move yet? Because, despite Katharine's distance from him, her brothers were still dampening his gifts?

If that were true, the cavalry was absolutely not coming to his rescue. It all came down to this conversation, over nauseating oil-covered food, in a mostly empty restaurant with disturbing stains on the table and a waitress he had already scared half to death.

He wasn't in any fit state to handle that responsibility, but he had absolutely no choice in the matter. He'd challenged Marlowe to a battle of wits, then turned up unarmed.

"I thought you were an only child," he said.

"Because that's what I wanted you to think. Eat up," Katharine said around a mouthful of horror. "You don't wanna die on an empty stomach."

"Frankly, I'd rather not die at all," Quentin replied.

It was impossible for him to tell how true his own words were.

43

LAURENCE

LAURENCE WONDERED HOW HE COULD WORK OUT WHAT THE radius of Marlowe's power-blocking aura was when he couldn't leave Tweedledum's side without having his neck broken. The only way he could think of was for Angela to make a break for it, but what use would that information even be?

Right now wasn't enough, though. His senses were still dull, and he couldn't feel Windsor. He was absolutely still in range.

"What do you think they're talking about?" Laurence said, keeping his tone idle, like he was just trying to pass the time.

"I think they're talking about why don't you shut up before I shut you up," said Tweedledum.

"Hey, Kathy only said I wasn't allowed to move." Laurence grinned. "She didn't say anything about staying quiet."

He watched Quentin and Kathy from a distance. Everything that would either kill them all or let them walk away from this was going on in a booth by the restaurant's window, and Laurence itched to be in there, where going on a charm offensive might help. Instead he was here, waiting and praying for Quentin to hold it together long enough to do everything in his power to get Kathy to back down.

The gas station was hardly exciting, either. A car or truck drove past every few minutes, and none of them stopped. Nobody cared how Laurence had parked, and nobody cared that he was hanging out by the trucks doing literally nothing.

"We should move my truck," he mused.

"No."

"Really?" Laurence scrunched up his nose. "C'mon, it'll pass the time. I'll even give you the keys, if you don't want me to drive. We can just move it out of the way and park it properly. No big deal."

"We're staying right here."

Laurence decided to while away the time by coming up with plans. If Quentin failed, Laurence wouldn't have a whole lot of time to react, and maybe if he knew what to do ahead of time it could save vital seconds. But then that meant he'd need to know how Tweedledum would behave, and the guy was a total unknown.

"Suppose she decides to kill him," Laurence said, forcing a conversational tone. "Then what? She's not going to stab him with flatware right there, is she? They must have cameras here."

"Do you know how many people get killed in broad daylight, on camera, in this country?" Tweedledum chuckled. "There's nearly four million square miles, and half of them are totally uninhabited. We've disappeared before and we can do it again, don't worry."

"Sure, okay. Don't worry. I'll get right on that."

Laurence went back to watching Quentin. There was something wrong with his body language. He was pressed up against the glass like he might be able to press himself through it, and Kathy seemed unsure what to make of it.

Goddess, Laurence *really* needed a plan.

He glanced to the truck, to look to Angela or Rodger, but they seemed to be having some argument with Delaney about his laptop, and Laurence rolled his eyes. Trust Delaney to bitch about them stealing his computer while everyone else's lives hung in the balance.

Laurence frowned slightly, and looked back to Tweedledum. "If she kills him, what happens to us?"

The guy shrugged broad shoulders. "Whatever she wants to happen."

"Right, but she left us all to die in the desert. She didn't expect us to get out, did she? Or to catch up with her. She was willing to kill us all for finding her. She's not just going to let us walk away after that."

"Can't say," Tweedledum replied.

Damn it, the asshole was a brick wall. Laurence couldn't provoke him, couldn't get him to give an inch.

Could Laurence outrun him? Could he, Angela, and Rodger overpower him if it came down to it? What if Tweedledee got out of the car and piled in?

No. Running was Laurence's best chance. And once he was inside, he could find cover, or make his way to the restaurant kitchen to find a decent knife to defend himself with.

Quentin stole his attention again. He was waving an arm around, and looked as though he might be losing his temper, and then Kathy leaped to her feet and shoved him back, pinning him in place.

Laurence took a step forward, and Tweedledum's hand clamped down on his shoulder.

"Don't," he growled.

Laurence snarled in response and kept his attention on Kathy, but she sat down again, and nobody had been killed. He could tell even with his muted senses that Quentin was having problems, though.

He needed to get in there, and the only way he knew how was to give them the one thing they wanted.

"You know what's weird?"

"No," said Tweedledum. "And I don't care."

"I think you do." Laurence shrugged to try and get the hand off his shoulder, but it wouldn't budge. "Because the real irony here is that you kidnapped Quentin and tortured him for being a witch, but he isn't one. I am."

The other man snorted at him like a horse. "Sure you are."

"What do you think I'm wearing this for?" Laurence slowly lifted his left hand to show the thong coiled around his wrist. "They're talismans I made. How do you think I tracked you down to this gas station? Because my familiar followed you. He's the huge raven circling over our heads right now, except this canopy is in the way, so you can't see him." He took a breath to steady himself, and raised his head in the hope it made him look more of a challenge. "I've fought gods and won, and what did you idiots do? You took my boyfriend instead of me, and even though magic doesn't work around Kathy, I *still* tracked you down before the cops did. I'm more than just my magic, and if she lays her hand on him again, I'm going to show you what I'm capable of."

He'd never felt so outgunned. Not since he was a kid getting pushed around in school, anyway. He had no magic, no gifts, and here he was threatening a man who seemed like he was twice Laurence's size. He had no weapons, no skills in a fistfight, and he was intentionally goading the person who had instructions to break his neck.

Laurence's heart was pounding. He tried to keep his breathing steady, but his lungs demanded air like they were priming him for a sprint, so when Tweedledum glanced to the canopy, he took a couple of deep breaths.

Tweedledum swung into motion. He marched Laurence to the edge of the canopy, then held him still and looked up.

Laurence looked too, and was relieved to see Windsor circling lazily overhead.

"Prove it's your familiar," Tweedledum grunted.

"I'm gonna have to shout to make that happen. He's a ways away."

"You're supposed to have a connection."

Laurence laughed bitterly. "I do, and it's been cut off just like everything else. If you want me to communicate with him, I'm gonna have to yell."

Tweedledum ran his tongue along his teeth, displacing his lips, then he released Laurence's shoulder. "Do it."

"Okay." Laurence waved up at Windsor, then cupped his hands to his mouth. "Hey, Win. Fly that way—" he gestured across the interstate "—to the other side of the road, then come back. But stay up there!"

Windsor broke off from his drifting and did as he was told, heading away from them in a straight line, and then turning on a dime to come right back again. It looked like his return flightpath would take him directly over Laurence's head, and Laurence could only guess at what might be going on between the bird's ears, but then there was a splatter of bird shit over Tweedledum's right shoulder, and the distant guffaws of a raven high above.

Laurence was totally unsurprised to see that Windsor must have spent some time practicing his aim. "I can translate that for you, if you want?"

Tweedledum just eyed the runny line of white droppings, then smirked. "No, I think it transcends language. Come on."

This time, the hand that propelled Laurence was between his shoulder blades. Laurence figured it was to make them look less suspicious when they went inside, and hoped it meant that — despite his bravado about being able to murder everyone and get away with it — Tweedledum wasn't going to attract any unwanted attention unless he absolutely had to.

Laurence didn't fight. He was being led exactly where he wanted to go. When they got inside and the waitress approached, he smiled warmly at her and gestured toward Quentin. "It's okay, we're just joining our friends, thank you."

"Oh, go right ahead! I'll bring more water!"

"Thanks."

He walked to the booth and lingered by the end of the table, waiting for Quentin and Kathy to notice him, and he cast a warm smile toward Quentin.

Quentin's eyes widened in shock. "Laurence? What's going on?"

"Well. Funny story," said Tweedledum. "Genius here says he's a witch."

Kathy's eyebrows lifted slowly, and she grabbed a napkin to wipe her fingers on. "Does he now. And you believe him?"

"Yup."

She shrugged, then pointed to the space next to Quentin. "Then you might as well sit. Hopefully with your body occupying the seat he'll stop seeing whoever he thinks is there." Then she pointed to the barely-touched starter platter. "You want anything?"

"No. Thanks." Laurence slid in beside Quentin, frowning, and rested a hand on his thigh. "Baby? You know he's not here, right?"

"So I have been informed," Quentin breathed. His eyes searched Laurence's, flickering quickly back and forth. "What did you do?"

Kathy nodded to Tweedledum, and the big guy shrugged, then grabbed a couple of napkins and walked away. He headed back outside and stood exactly where he had been before, just this time without Laurence to guard.

"I told the truth," Laurence sighed. "It was the only way to get in here."

"Why the hell would you want to be in here?" Kathy reached for a buffalo wing and bit into it, then used the half-eaten wing to point at Quentin with. "And who is it he's seeing?"

Laurence looked at Quentin again. Those pale gray eyes were creased in concern, but there was an undercurrent of terror in them, and it didn't take much to guess the answer. "You want to answer that one, or do you want me to do it?" He said it gently, and leaned closer, hoping to offer moral support and maybe block Quentin's view of his father at the same time.

"F-f-father," Quentin whispered. He took his hand from

the table and dropped it to cover Laurence's, then squeezed tight. His touch was cool, but not cold.

"Makes sense," Kathy said with a mouthful of chicken. "Man, these wings are hot. You sure you don't want any?"

Quentin's nose crinkled and he shook his head.

"He's not big on finger food," Laurence explained, and reached for a potato skin. "Especially not when it's messy." He turned his fingers so that he could clasp Quentin's hand in return, and devoured the potato in three bites.

The waitress came over with a fresh glass of water for Laurence, but she eyed Quentin like he was a landmine, and did her best to leave as quickly as she could once she was sure Laurence didn't want to order anything.

"So what's going on in here?" Laurence grabbed a couple of carrot sticks and dunked them in the little pot of ranch that sat in the center of the platter. "Are we any closer to hashing this thing out? What can I do to help?"

"We were just at the point where d'Arcy here was insisting that being a witch didn't mean that he was evil, and then you interrupted him because you felt like you were better at talking your way out of things than he is." Kathy dropped the bone onto her own plate, then licked her fingers clean. "You don't have a whole lot of faith in him, huh?"

Laurence winced. "I have every faith in him. He's had my life in his hands so many times, and every single time, he's pulled through for me. But he didn't look like he was coping too great, and I figured if I could get in here and give him whatever support he needs, he could finish what he set out to do."

Kathy nodded. "Not to kill me?"

"Hey, that's not part of the plan, but if you try to hurt him, I'm going to try and stop you."

She gazed into his eyes a while, presumably making her mind up about whatever decision she was contemplating, then she nodded. "Okay. You can stay. But you let him do the talking. I've met plenty of pretty fuckers like you who think they can charm their way out of anything, and if you try it with me you're just gonna piss me off. Got it?"

"Yeah." Laurence licked his lips. "I got it."

"Great. Then let's get back to business." Kathy turned her attention back onto Quentin. "So, tell me about the funeral."

Quentin turned white as a sheet, and Laurence opened his mouth, but Kathy sent him a withering stare so he clamped it shut again.

If her plan was to hit all Quentin's buttons and make him fail, she was going about it the right way. All Laurence could do was sit here and watch.

Maybe staying outside would have been better after all.

44

QUENTIN

FATHER EVAPORATED THE MOMENT LAURENCE SAT DOWN through his incorporeal form, and Quentin was both immensely relieved that Laurence was here, but also somewhat dismayed. If Laurence remained outside, he might well have been able to take action if things went wrong, but now that they were both inside, they were effectively trapped — Quentin physically so, in fact.

And now it all came down to the funeral, as it always seemed to. It was never going to leave him, no matter how much Father had tried to make it go away.

He clung to Laurence's hand and stared at his ear. "What is there to say about it? I was nineteen, my mother was dead, and I was the one who found her body. By the time the service came, I was..."

Laurence turned to face him and frowned gently.

If Quentin pretended that he was speaking to Laurence, if he blotted Katharine out this very moment, he might get through the whole thing. Or certainly this part of it. He allowed himself to pay more attention to Laurence's dark brown eyes, the delicate blonde of his eyelashes, the way curls hung over his forehead and lightly brushed his eyebrows.

"It's all connected," he said quietly, allowing his thumb to drift across Laurence's knuckles. "I know more than I did at the time. What it's necessary to understand is that, due to my blackouts, I do not recall the things which occurred to trigger them. I had no recollection of what Father had done to me all those years, and I do not truly recall the funeral with any great detail. I understand that I accused Father of killing Mother, which led to the loss of control around the telekinesis I was not yet aware that I possessed, but then I blacked out, and the service continued without me."

Laurence nodded. "You're doing great, hon."

"So all this knocking over of chairs, the wind at the funeral, that was you?" Katharine's voice came from his side, but he didn't turn toward it.

"Yes. There may well have been other instances that I remain unaware of. I did not find out until Laurence pieced it all together and helped me understand what it was that I could do."

"Huh." He heard her eat something crunchy. "Was that the business with the shop getting wrecked after a party?"

"Correct." Quentin was finally able to pull his gaze off Laurence, and he faced Katharine across the table.

"Then you admit that you *are* a danger to others." She looked immensely satisfied with her conclusion.

"And we have come full circle, to whether or not I am a monster," he agreed. "In that instance, however, we were pitted against a force which would not have walked away, and which intended to enslave the entire city."

"So? That's a job for the cops," Katharine argued.

"Except the force in question was a god," Quentin murmured, "and no one but Laurence could have stopped him."

She looked between them, steel eyes darting to one then the other. "Okay. Are you telling me that you see yourselves as, what? Some kind of magical line of defense against things we mere mortals can't handle?"

Quentin mulled it over. He hadn't truly considered them to

be any such thing, but it did appear to be a regular preoccupation of theirs. He had been bred for his gifts, but it was becoming more obvious as time went on that the aristocracy itself was a relic of the past, and all they had truly succeeded in doing was enabling the survival of powers which might otherwise have died out.

"No," he eventually said. "It does seem to be how we spend some of our time, but otherwise, we do not set out to do anything out of the ordinary. Laurence works hard at a flower shop, and I practice piano and care for a house full of teenagers who would otherwise be homeless."

Katharine's eyebrows climbed, and she stared at him. "How'd you wind up with those?"

"They had been forced to live there by Wilson, against their will, and once he was gone, most of them had homes to go to. Those who did not chose to remain. We could not leave them."

Laurence picked at the food, sticking mostly to dry items. Pieces of potato, or carrot sticks. Quentin couldn't blame him in the slightest. Everything else looked horrendous.

"Why would he want..." Katharine's eyebrows sank again. "They're witches too."

"Psychic," Quentin corrected her. "Magic and psychic ability are not one and the same."

"Are you so sure about that?"

"Yes."

"Why?"

Quentin frowned and took a sip of his water.

"I can field this one?" Laurence offered.

She eyed him, then raised her chin. "Okay, but no bullshit."

"None," Laurence agreed. "Magic only works for a small amount of people. It's super rare for a psychic to have the ability to work magic too, and vice versa. If they were the same thing, then everyone with one would have the other, no exceptions. Plus, with magic, you have to learn spells, get your components together, sometimes even wait for the right time of day or year, and if you get any part of that wrong, it just won't work. But psychics don't need any of that. They can use their gifts without preparation, and if they get it wrong, it doesn't work as well as it should, but it still works."

"Thank you." Quentin dipped his head. "Yes, Laurence is correct. Wilson gathered them together so that he had control over a variety of differing psychic abilities, but he did not possess the ability to use magic, and nor do the children."

Katharine draped her fingers around the rim of her glass and slowly rotated it. "You realize after I've killed you both, I'll go back for them now, right?"

"You can't!" Laurence blurted out. "They're just kids!"

Quentin closed his eyes a moment. "I don't believe that you will," he said.

"What makes you so sure?"

He opened them and gazed levelly at her. "Because you were a soldier. You might be willing to do this to adults, but to children?" Quentin shook his head. "If I believed that you were capable of that, we would not be here now. There is never any excuse to hurt a child. None."

Nothing was shaking, not a single piece of cutlery or food was out of place, yet his rage had risen from the depths like a leviathan, and while he had fought to keep it from his voice, he knew that it was there, snapping and seething inside of him.

If he was wrong, if she was inclined to kill the children, then that changed everything.

Katharine exhaled and dipped her chin. "I could tell you stories, but you're right. I wouldn't hurt a child."

"But you would wait until they turned eighteen and then kill them?" Quentin watched her every move like a hawk. "At what point do they suddenly stop being a child and become nothing more than a target? When exactly do they cease to be human?"

"Have you ever been in a war zone, d'Arcy?" Katharine

plucked what looked like a slice of grilled bread off the platter and bit into it with a loud crunch.

He blinked at the change in topic, and shook his head faintly. "I have not."

"Good. Let me tell you, you wouldn't last five minutes in one. If you can't look another human being in the eye and pull the trigger, you're the one who ends up dead, because they don't see you as human either. Nobody can afford to see the enemy as a human being, because then we'd all go nuts. That's literally why they're called 'the enemy' instead. You have to take their humanity away to be able to do your job."

Quentin's anger quickly mutated into horror. His mouth became dry, but he knew that drinking more water wouldn't fix it. "And this is what you do now," he croaked, his voice scratching in his throat. "You call us witches so that you can do what you think you must, but we are *people*, Katharine! We're people, and you're killing us!"

"You don't know a damn thing about me," she spat out, leaning forward sharply and jabbing a finger toward his chest. "Your family set out to eradicate mine, and you almost succeeded. You brought down a sickness on Matthew Hopkins, you stabbed Thomas to death with his own knife, you used witchcraft to drown John at sea—"

"Wait," Laurence breathed. "I'm sorry, I don't want to seem rude, but do you mean, like, Witchfinder General Matthew Hopkins? Is that who we're talking about?"

Quentin shook his head numbly. He had no idea who Laurence was talking about.

"Yes." Katharine finally looked away from him, to Laurence, her eyes gleaming with fury. "The first Duke of Oxford swept through Essex like a plague, and he hunted down my ancestors one by one until all we could do was board a ship for the Americas and pray that we made the treacherous crossing."

"I can only apologize for the things done by people who are long-since dead," Quentin interrupted, lest Laurence turn this into a fight. "But we're alive, Katharine. You, your brothers, me. We have a chance to stop all of this, to bring an end to hundreds of years of pain."

"You think you can throw money at a problem and it'll go away!" She sat back heavily and grabbed her water. "That's not how it works."

"I think that we have a chance to educate one another," Quentin countered. "To learn from the mistakes of the past and prevent them from ever happening again. Don't you see? All we're doing is passing our misery from one generation to the next. It needs to end."

Laurence's fingers tightened around his own. Was it a warning, or was Laurence merely shifting his hold for comfort? Quentin didn't dare take his eyes off Katharine to work it out.

But she took her eyes off him.

Her grip around her glass tightened as she looked out of the window. At first, she seemed thoughtful, but then her posture hardened, and her eyes narrowed. "You liar," she breathed.

Quentin blinked and shook his head, but turned to see what it was that she was looking at.

There were a cluster of black vehicles on the interstate, taking the exit which led to the petrol station. The same way that Laurence had driven here.

"This is all a goddamn distraction, and I fell for it!" Katharine's words were sharp, her voice clipped with fury. "All these words about reparation, about mending old wounds, and you're every bit as much a liar as I should have expected!"

Quentin's chest filled with ice. He had no idea who or what these vehicles were, but she obviously did, and had drawn some correlation which didn't exist. "No! Katharine, I don't know who they are! Is it not possible that they just need fuel?"

"Bullshit!"

The black SUVs with their tinted windows *did* all have a particular look about them, like the type of vehicles Sebastian or Vargas preferred. Did that mean that they were armored? That the occupants were armed?

They were certainly approaching the petrol station, no two ways about it.

He caught Katharine's motion as he began to look her way, but she was fast, and his hand was held in Laurence's. With a flick of her arm, she cast the remaining water in her glass — along with all the ice — at Laurence's face, then slid out of the booth just as Laurence yelled and snatched his hand out of Quentin's.

Quentin tried to sprint after her, but he was blocked in against the window.

"Fuck!" Laurence gasped as he wiped ice water out of his eyes. "Where is she!"

"Heading outside." Quentin lay a hand against Laurence's shoulder. "I'm sorry, darling. I need to get past."

"Yeah. You stop her, I'll go get a fucking knife."

"No."

"Quen—"

Quentin didn't argue. There was no time. Katharine was sprinting across the forecourt, and her brother was already jumping behind the wheel of their truck. Meanwhile, Delaney and Rodger fought their way out of the back of the Jack in the Green truck, with Rodger clawing at Delaney, and Delaney waving frantically at the newcomers.

This had the potential to go horribly wrong, and Quentin didn't even know why.

But yet again it seemed that Delaney was responsible.

45

QUENTIN

HE BARRELED OUT ONTO THE FORECOURT IN TIME TO SEE Katharine dive into the passenger seat of her vehicle. Her brother didn't wait — he started to reverse before her door was even shut — but one of the newcomers sped up and cut them off.

Quentin made eye contact with the Marlowe whose name he didn't even know, and in an instant understood his strategy. He'd created enough space to be able to drive around Laurence's truck, and Quentin wasn't foolish enough to believe they'd stop if he got in their way.

Katharine slammed her door shut and grabbed her seatbelt, and the wheels squealed as her brother pulled forward.

Then he wrenched the wheel, and drove straight at Quentin.

With his gifts, this was hardly a problem. Without them, he had a split second in which to make the right decision.

Quentin threw himself to his left, banking on the surety that the truck would have to turn to his right to avoid hitting the gas station itself. He sprang as far as he could, then swiftly curled into a roll and kept on going until the wheels sliced past him, inches from his fingers.

He sprang to his feet, in time to see that the newcomers were indeed both armed and armored as they poured out of their SUVs, while another cut off the Marlowes' escape route. Before they could back up, Laurence's truck sprinted forward to ram it up the backside.

"FBI!" yelled one of the black-clad, heavily armed gunmen. "Get on the ground!"

Rodger and Delaney stopped squabbling, and while Rodger dropped to the asphalt, Delaney decided to put his hands up and stride confidently toward the nearest gun, which seemed extraordinarily foolish.

Guns swung toward Delaney, so Quentin walked the other way, toward Katharine's truck.

"Sir, get on the ground!"

This was so utterly confusing. After all that he had been through, what on earth were these people doing here? Weren't the FBI some sort of law enforcement? Had they come to rescue him, or was this some utterly unrelated matter?

"They've come to put you out of my misery," his father muttered.

"Not now," Quentin hissed.

"Quen? Better get down, hon!" Laurence's voice came from behind him, from the restaurant, and Quentin turned to look at him.

There was panic in his eyes.

"They're cops!" Laurence added. His voice carried the sort of tension that Quentin wouldn't have thought to associate with the word *cops*.

Quentin turned back toward the forecourt. The world was moving like treacle. Delaney slowly lowered to his knees, and Angela emerged from the drivers' seat of Laurence's truck to do the same. Black-clad blots of gun-wielding shadow swarmed Katharine's vehicle and dragged her brother from behind the wheel, using guns and shouting and pushing to get him onto the floor.

She did what he suspected he would have done in her

shoes. Her door open and she slipped out, then hunkered down and used the body of the truck for shelter, but she glared across at him like she hoped her eyes alone could kill him where he stood.

If he could get to her, he could explain.

Quentin eyed the armed police or whatever they were, and since most of them were fixated on subduing Katharine's brother, or Delaney, he reached another decision.

He leaped again.

This time, he rolled toward her. He heard yells and rapid gunfire, but made it into shelter without getting hit, which was a profound bonus to his day.

"You sold me out," she hissed at him as he raised his head.

"I did no such thing. I don't even have a phone," he whispered. "Katharine, I promise you, we'll work out whatever this is, and then we can make it better. But you have to trust me."

"A witch," she snarled. "You asked me to trust you once already, and now look where we are."

He met her eyes, and kept his tone soft. "I did not do this. How could I? I have nothing at my disposal that could have made this happen. I don't know why they're here. You took away my phone, and you've taken away whatever gifts I had — which do not include the power to summon police, I assure you."

"Phone..." Katharine gazed at him, then hissed softly. "Delaney."

Quentin frowned softly, but the shadows surrounded them, and neither he nor Katharine had any choice but to obey them.

"I promise," was all he said to her.

She said nothing.

THEY MANHANDLED him into the back of a vehicle, and it was

as much as he could do to retain his grasp of which way was up. Something about being swamped by darkness and having hands on his body had really disagreed with him, and when he'd asked them to stop, a voice told him to settle down or he'd get shot.

Getting shot wasn't what usually happened in these situations.

He sat in what was undoubtedly the back of a truck, his wrists in cuffs yet again, and wondered what on Earth he was doing here. And then he wondered where "here" was.

Where was Laurence?

A stranger dressed all in black joined him in the back of the truck, but this time the stranger wore no helmet. She had the same armor as the others, but now that he was closer, he could see the white letters *FBI* printed on it, by her left collarbone.

"Mr. Quentin d'Arcy?" she asked him, her voice gentle.

He gave a faint nod.

"Hey. I'm Agent Quintero. You can call me Carla." She pulled thick, protective gloves off to reveal small and slender hands, then gestured to his wrists. "Can I remove those for you?"

He considered it a while, then offered his hands to her, and she produced a small key with which she unlocked the handcuffs. She took them away, and he slowly rubbed his wrists.

"Where's Laurence?"

"He's safe," she assured him. "I'm sorry you were handcuffed. We weren't expecting to find you hiding *with* your kidnappers. You mind telling me what that was about?"

He struggled to follow the conversation. It seemed to require information that he didn't possess.

"How did you find us?" He looked out of the window, but didn't find Laurence out there, so he turned back toward Quintero.

"Mr. Riley reported you missing to SDPD, they tracked

Delaney's cellphone across the border into Arizona, which is where we come in. The FBI operates on a federal level," she added, like that made sense. "You're from Great Britain, right?"

"The United Kingdom," he corrected with a faint tut.

Quintero shrugged. "Over here, cops can't operate outside their state. They have no jurisdiction. So that's when we get called in. We picked up Delaney's cellphone signal this morning, after it had gone off-grid overnight, so we scrambled to get to him before he disappeared again."

Quentin blinked sluggishly, then laughed.

How utterly absurd.

Delaney's obsession with his stupid bloody phone had led the FBI right to him.

"Mr. d'Arcy?"

"I want to go home," he croaked, barely able to contain his laughter before it could become tears.

Her gaze dropped to his wrists, then she looked back up at him. "Can you confirm that Cameron Delaney was your kidnapper?"

Quentin wanted to say no, to do what he could to spare the boy from prison, but all he could think of was how much pain he had endured since this had all begun, and how much more damage Delaney would be willing to inflict on the lives of others.

"Yes." He grimaced at her.

"Are you willing to give a statement at this time?"

"No." He leaned back against the window and pressed his forehead to the glass. "I want to go home. With Laurence. I want to rest. I need to rest."

She hesitated, then sighed softly. "You look like you've been through hell," she said. "I'll have an agent drive you both home. It's a few hours, is that okay?"

"It will have to be, won't it?" he countered.

"Yeah," she agreed. "But you're alive. That's what matters."

He wondered just how important that could possibly be.

He must have dozed off, or blacked out, or possibly even both, because the next thing he knew he was leaning against Laurence and Laurence's arms were around him, and they were being jostled around.

Quentin jerked upright and looked out of the window, but it was growing dark outside, and he didn't recognize anything.

"Hey. Baby." Laurence rested a hand against his thigh. "Sleep okay?"

"Was it sleep?" Quentin wiped lightly at his eyes, only to realize that everything hurt. His wrists, his jaw, his shoulders, his back, his ribs, his thighs… It all hurt, and every pain was different. His jaw was a sharp, almost stabbing pain, whereas his wrists were a constant throbbing one.

"Yeah," Laurence assured him. "Goddess, baby, what did they do to you?"

Quentin looked forward. They were being driven by a complete stranger, and only when Agent Quintero's words came back to him did he figure out why. It was best not to lose control here, now, and so he shook his head at Laurence. "Later. Will you contact Freddy for me?"

Laurence frowned at him. "Why?"

"I want him to find a lawyer for Katharine and her brothers. Quickly. I realize that it's early over there, but I promised Katharine that I would help her."

Laurence searched his eyes, then sighed and pulled out his phone. "Okay, hon. If that's what you want."

"Yes. It is."

"What about Delaney?"

Quentin sighed softly. "I suppose that we had best offer him a lawyer also. Otherwise, we risk beginning the same sort of trouble that I'm attempting to end with Katharine, don't you think?"

"I don't know," Laurence admitted. "I'll see what Freddy thinks."

Quentin leaned against him once more and closed his eyes.

All he needed to do was make it home in one piece, and then he could rest at last.

46

LAURENCE

THE FBI AGENT DROPPED THEM OFF OUTSIDE THE HOUSE, AND Laurence thanked him, but he didn't hang around to invite the guy in for tea or anything. He hadn't been arrested or shot and he wasn't willing to jinx it.

Waking Quentin to get him inside seemed cruel, but there were already a slew of paparazzi outside the house, and Laurence didn't want to give them the shot of the century, so he gently brushed his lips over Quentin's cheek. "Quen?"

Quentin's eyes snapped open, and he spent a few seconds assessing his surroundings.

"We need to get inside," Laurence whispered.

Quentin frowned, and folded his jacket collar in on itself to hide as much of his scarring as he could, then laid a hand across the top to keep the collar down and cover the rest of his skin. "All right," he said.

Laurence nodded to the agent, who got out and opened the door for Laurence, and then Laurence ushered Quentin to the gate and tapped in his code as fast as he could, using his body to shield Quentin for the seconds that it took. Cameras flashed the moment the door opened, and continued until Laurence shut the gate at his back.

"They don't fucking stop, do they?" he grunted.

"No," Quentin agreed.

Laurence stepped in to kiss his cheek lightly, then took his hand. They descended the steps into the small courtyard, and Laurence almost had his key in the door when it wrenched open and a cluster of teenagers clogged the doorway.

"Where's this Delaney asshole?" Soraya demanded. "We'll fuck him up!"

"Badly," Felipe insisted.

The dogs managed to push through the forest of legs and crowded Quentin, who released Laurence's hand so that he could crouch down and hug them without a word.

"C'mon, everyone," Laurence said as he waved them back inside. "Let us in, huh?"

There was grumbling and jostling, and finally Mia appeared out of nowhere, still wearing pajamas, and started to drag the teens away from the door. She eyed Quentin, then looked at Laurence.

"He just needs rest," Laurence assured her.

He *hoped* that was all Quentin needed.

Mia didn't look at all convinced, but she shooed the teenagers toward the stairs. "Go on. Back to bed. He's home, that's what matters for now."

Quentin stood, covered in dog hairs, and exhaled slowly. "Thank you, Mia."

"We're just glad to have you back—" She broke off and looked past them.

Laurence turned. He knew what she'd seen before he saw it too, and he held up an arm for Windsor to perch on. The poor bird had flown the whole way, though at least he'd been able to fly direct instead of sticking to roads, and when he landed heavily, Laurence cradled him to his chest to save him the effort of standing.

Good? Windsor asked.

You were amazing, Laurence replied.

Windsor cooed softly, and fell asleep within seconds.

HE MANAGED to get Quentin up to their room, but once he settled the dogs and Windsor, Quentin was sitting on the edge of the bed gazing at the walls.

Laurence nudged his sneakers off, then approached slowly, and crouched in front of him to gaze up and try to catch his attention. "Quen?"

Quentin's head tipped down. "Mmm?"

"Do you want a bath? A shower? Some tea? Something to eat?" Laurence cut himself off, worried that he was giving too many options and overwhelming Quentin.

"A bath," Quentin echoed.

"You got it. I'll run one."

Focusing on one task at a time helped him not lose his shit over everything. There was so much for him to unpack that if he tried it, he wouldn't keep his cool, so Laurence went to the bathroom and started to fill the tub. He tested the water until he was sure it was fine, then left it to run and returned to Quentin's side.

"What did Freddy say?"

Laurence pursed his lips. Talking to Freddy was another stress he could do without. He'd debated whether to lie to Freddy and claim that the lawyers were for falsely-accused, but then he figured Freddy would get into those lawyers' heads and find out the truth sooner or later, so that was what he'd gone with. In the end, the conversation had turned telepathic, because Laurence didn't want to yell at Freddy and risk waking Quentin in the back of the FBI car.

"He said he'll get on it right away," Laurence murmured. Which was more or less true, once Freddy had finished raging about the whole situation.

"Good." Quentin sighed. "I know he's a tosser, darling, but he does care."

Yeah. And sometimes one doesn't outweigh the other. Laurence grimaced. He wasn't going to get into it. Quentin needed love, not arguments, no matter how gentle they might be.

"I gave him everything he needed to know," Laurence said as he crouched down to remove Quentin's shoes for him. "He'll take it from here."

Quentin watched him like he was curious about what Laurence was doing, and said nothing.

"Want me to join you in the tub, hon?" He carefully eased Quentin's socks off. "It might be wise. I don't want you to fall asleep in there."

Quentin shrugged. "All right."

Laurence helped Quentin to his feet, and noticed how heavily the earl leaned against him as he led the way back into the bathroom.

FOR THE FIRST TIME EVER, it was Laurence who sat at the back of the tub, so that Quentin could fall asleep safely if he needed to. Quentin didn't complain or panic, he just stripped down and got in, then lay back against Laurence's chest and closed his eyes.

Laurence gently soaped Quentin's shoulders and rinsed them off, but he didn't touch anywhere else. Quentin's scars were sensitive, and Laurence had no idea where he might still be sore. The bruise on Quentin's jaw was already fading now that they were away from Marlowe, but since Laurence didn't know what else had been done, he erred on the side of caution.

Quentin had waved off any attempt the FBI had made to gather physical evidence, and at the rate he healed, Laurence doubted that there'd be any within a couple of days, so maybe it made sense to find a lawyer to defend Katharine, if only to keep his recovery speed away from a courtroom's scrutiny.

Sooner or later, Laurence would ask Quentin what had

really happened, but not until Quentin was ready. For now, his job was to keep Quentin safe.

A job he'd already failed.

There was no way he could cry. Not right now. No matter how hard he wanted to, *needed* to, he absolutely mustn't. If he did, Quentin would start trying to care for *him*, and Laurence couldn't bear the thought of it. Not when what Quentin needed was his own healing.

Especially when he already had so much to do that he'd only just begun.

"I knew you'd come," Quentin whispered.

Laurence blinked and raised a hand from the water so that he could wipe his eyes. "You know me, Quen. Nothing's going to get in my way."

"I know."

He draped his arm around Quentin's chest and rested his cheek to that soft, silken hair, and he tried not to think about how close he'd come to losing everything, all because he'd been so convinced that anyone who kidnapped Quentin would be laughing out the other side of their face once Quentin cut loose.

"Maybe there's something we can do," Laurence murmured after a while. "You know. For security, in the future."

Quentin didn't stir. "Such as?"

Laurence licked his lips, then spoke with care. It wasn't a subject Quentin liked at the best of times, and Laurence didn't want to cause any more grief. "If we kept some of our blood here, in a safe, we'd have it in case this ever happens again."

He didn't think he needed to explain further. They both knew how Annis had found Quentin.

"How *did* you find me?" Quentin whispered.

"Angela. She summoned a psychopomp. They can track people from pictures."

"Then can you not do that again?"

"I don't know," Laurence admitted. "Ru seemed to think it was pretty dark magic." He hesitated, then kissed Quentin's ear. "How about we talk it over later, once you're feeling better?"

Quentin laughed, and the laughter went from gentle to raucous in seconds, as though Laurence had just said the funniest thing in the world.

Laurence's pulse sped up. He let go so that Quentin could sit forward, and he frowned to himself. What had he said…

Feeling better.

Goddess. Quentin didn't think he was going to get better.

"Quen," he said. Then, louder, "Quen!"

Quentin buried his face in his hands. The laughter turned to sobbing, and the sobbing became wretched.

"Oh, baby. You're safe." Laurence leaned forward and drew Quentin into his arms, then slowly pulled back again, and trailed fingers through his hair. "You're safe. I'm here. You're home now."

Everything loose in the bathroom shook itself free and fell to the ground. The mirrors and shower door cracked. The air smelled of spilled cologne and baby powder, and Laurence held Quentin to his chest and ignored it all. If this became a tornado, those never harmed Quentin, and Laurence wasn't going to interrupt it to make him calm down. He'd spent a year telling Quentin to calm down, but what if that wasn't what he needed?

Maybe, for once, Quentin had to be allowed to grieve. Laurence could tidy up in here afterwards; it wasn't a big deal.

He kept his head low, stayed close to the eye of the storm, and waited for it to pass. And then, when it finally did, he helped Quentin out of the tub and into bed. They could worry about moisturizer and whatever other scar care Quentin needed to do once he'd rested, but for now, Laurence just wanted to wrap him up and protect him, and nothing was going to change that.

He slipped under the sheets and held Quentin in his arms until the winds died away.

47

QUENTIN

HE WOKE IN THE SPACE BETWEEN ONE BREATH AND THE NEXT, but remained still, waiting.

Listening.

Assessing.

There was peace, though the more he listened, the more he realized that the peace was created out of tiny sounds. His own breathing, and that from the body which was curled around him. Soft snores from further away. Faint, distant hums of differing pitches. Light, occasional leaf-rustling.

It sounded like home, so he opened his eyes.

Though it was hardly light, there was plenty enough to see by. The arms around him were Laurence's. The curtains and sheets were his own. The room was the one he had become accustomed to.

The snores belonged to his dogs.

He closed his eyes again. Dogs meant walks. Walks meant going outside. He felt barely equipped to leave his bed, let alone the house, and so he didn't. Instead, he lay in place and watched as the light around the edges of the curtains grew progressively stronger.

What else was there to do?

EVENTUALLY, as it always did, nature won. He could not stare at the walls all day. His bladder would not allow it. And so he eased gently out from between Laurence's arms and made his way to the bathroom.

It was an absolute mess.

He groaned and felt each step with care until he was inside far enough that he could close and lock the door, then he turned the lights on and regarded the evidence of his lack of control.

What had he been thinking? To let himself go like that, and in the bath, too?

Stop it.

For god's sake, he'd been tortured. There was no other word for it. If their positions were reversed, if all he had endured were done to Laurence instead, Quentin would be more understanding, more kind toward such an outburst. To any number of them, in fact.

So stop being so horrible to yourself.

Easier said than done, and he hadn't even summoned the courage to say it out loud.

He took a breath to do so. Held onto it, as though making use of it would hurt him in some way.

Then he let go.

"Stop being so horrible to yourself," he whispered.

It felt foolish, standing alone in the bathroom and talking to no-one. He shook his head and refocused his attention on the mess, reaching out to it slowly at first, unsure that his gifts would respond. What if they were gone for good? What if they never—

No. He could feel the floor, numbly interrupted by detritus, and he swept the broken bottles and spilled powders into a pile in the center of the room so that he could at least use the loo without cutting his feet, and then he guided it all into the bin. It was easier to move liquids by freezing them first, and they could defrost around the rest of the trash at their own pace. He considered letting them do so in the sink, instead, but wasn't sure whether that could block the drain if there were other bits and pieces frozen in with the fluid.

In the end, he washed his hands and then sat on the closed loo seat to regard the remaining damage.

They'd have to get builders in again.

More disruption for the children, more strangers in his home. He didn't know how long it would take to replace the broken fixtures, but he hoped that it could be achieved in under a week.

There was little purpose to sitting here any longer. He crossed to the sink and brushed his teeth, then shaved, and all the while he had to deal with using a mirror that cracked his reflection into five images, each one so very different from the next.

The mockery wasn't lost on him.

When he rinsed foam and dark hairs away, he glanced to his forearm, and noted that the marks Katherine had made were already fading. The physical evidence of her torture would be gone soon enough. Something had to hurt him far more than that to leave a permanent mark.

On the outside, at least.

He ran his fingers over the indentations. They itched, but he didn't scratch them. Instead, he dug through the cabinet for his scar care creams and oils, and started the laborious process of making up for not doing this after yesterday's bath.

It was far simpler while he was damp, of course. These things would glide on much more easily. On dry skin, he seemed to use twice as much product to achieve the same result, and as he worked on his skin, he chose to ignore any brief flashes of pain from areas where he must have been injured.

Those marks, too, were already going away. Even his wrists, which he was so sure were going to provide even more reason to wear long sleeves, seemed as though they would heal.

Was it proximity to Laurence overnight? Had he stolen this in his sleep?

There was no way to know.

Once he was done, he patted his hands dry on a towel, and then turned out the light.

"Hey, baby."

Laurence sounded half-asleep, still, but he sat up regardless and rubbed at his eyes. Quentin had cautioned him to be more gentle with the eye area. It was delicate skin, easily damaged. But Laurence was far less vain.

"Darling," he replied while he drifted toward the walk-in, debating what to wear for the day.

The sound of Laurence's feet against carpet was light, and Quentin felt his presence enter the wardrobe. It was subtle, muting one source of light while another overhead remained steady, but the vibrant source of heat was unmissable.

"Can I get you something for breakfast?" Laurence's offer was gentle.

Quentin debated whether or not he was hungry. As usual, the answer was *no*. "I would rather you did not," he replied.

"Okay. Then a cup of tea, at least?"

Tea was always welcome.

Quentin took his attention from the clothes which hung inches from his face, and turned it on Laurence instead.

There he was. Ever-beautiful, with his crumpled curls and fuzzy jaw, his earthen eyes and tanned skin, like a god among mortals. Quentin would not be at all surprised if flowers were to spring from the ground wherever Laurence walked, though it hadn't happened yet.

He broke into as much of a smile as he could manage. "Tea would be wonderful. Thank you."

"All right. Will you come downstairs for it, or do you want me to bring it up?"

If he went downstairs, would he be mobbed by teenagers? He wasn't certain whether or not he could take such noise and excitement just yet, so he dipped his head in response. "Could you bring it upstairs, please?"

"Your wish is my command." Laurence stepped closer. "Kiss?"

Quentin raised his chin. "Yes."

Laurence kissed him. It was tender and delicious, and Quentin leaned into it, using it as an anchor. When it broke, his mind felt somewhat clearer.

Laurence smiled, but his eyes remained strained with concern, and he touched his fingers to Quentin's shoulder before he left the closet.

Quentin turned back to the clothes and tried to decide what to wear, but none of it seemed important any more.

What was the point of wearing armor that did nothing to protect him?

"DON'T JUST STAND THERE, BOY!"

He crinkled his nose, but didn't turn around. "Go away. You aren't real."

"Is this how you intend to waste your life now?" His father's voice dripped with disdain, as ever. "Naked in a wardrobe? I suppose it's marginally better than drinking yourself into an early grave."

"Only marginally," he agreed.

"I always knew you were a waste of space!"

Quentin thought about shrugging, but in the end couldn't be bothered. What was the point? "If you thought that, you wouldn't have invested so much time in me," he said.

"I had no choice! You were the one who popped out of your mother first."

"You could have lied."

His father sniffed at the suggestion. He was right to do so. How could Quentin wish all of this on Freddy instead? It was inhumane.

"You can go now," Quentin added.

"Huh? Sorry, hon, what was that?" Laurence's voice carried in from beyond the wardrobe. Then it was closer, when it said, "Can't find anything to wear?"

Quentin finally unleashed the shrug, as though Laurence's energy was all it took.

"Okay. Well, I brought tea. Why don't you drink it? C'mon. I'll pick something out for you."

His nose crinkled again, but Laurence laughed gently.

"Don't give me that. I can do fashion! Trust me."

He debated it. Laurence *was* awfully good with color. And really, since he could only choose items Quentin already owned, how bad could it be?

"All right," he said.

When he turned to leave the closet, his father was gone.

IT WAS ALMOST like being a child again. He sat and sipped his tea, and Laurence brought clothes out for him to wear, then crouched to at least get him into a pair of socks.

Laurence got briefs up to his knees, then said, "Okay, baby. Stand up."

Quentin stood.

"Do you wanna come out to walk the girls?" Laurence drew eye level.

"No."

Laurence's eyes flickered back and forth quickly, then he pursed his lips. "Okay. I know the route, I'll take them."

"Thank you." Quentin sat again.

He eyed the clothes Laurence had laid out on the bed while

he continued to sip his tea. They were perfectly sufficient. He might even wear them.

Everything felt so abstract, so disconnected. He wasn't even convinced that he was enjoying the tea in any meaningful way, although he did appreciate its warmth, and that Laurence had taken the trouble to make it. Beyond that, it was just hot, watery, brown milk.

The ring of his phone barged shrilly into his life, and he reached for where it should be, but there was no pocket there.

"I'll get it." Laurence hopped up and darted to where it was on charge, and unplugged it to bring it back to the table. "Want me to answer it?"

Quentin shrugged again.

Laurence eyed him as he tapped the screen and put it on speaker. "Hey, Freddy. You're on speaker. Quentin's here."

"Wonderful. Hello Laurence, Icky," Freddy said. He sounded terse, not at all like his usual idle drawl. "What the hell have you got me into here?"

"I didn't get you into anything," Quentin murmured.

"Both of you." Freddy huffed. "You wanted a local lawyer for Katharine Marlowe. Well, due to the peculiarities of the American legal system, I've had to find one in Arizona, because that's where she was arrested. And it transpires that you want me to defend your bloody *kidnapper*, Icky! What the devil are you playing at?"

"I'm not playing," he argued.

"It's complicated," Laurence added. "Is there any chance your lawyer can get her off the hook?"

"That, too, is complicated," Freddy said. "Because she crossed state lines, the FBI were involved, and as the FBI arrested her, they can choose what to make of it. Since Icky has yet to make a statement, they'll want that as soon as possible to help build their case."

"And if I refuse?" Quentin finished his tea and set the cup down beside the phone.

"They can still choose to press on without you, if they want to."

"So make them not want to."

Freddy paused. "You're asking for an intervention," he said with caution.

"Yes." He knew full well what he was asking Freddy to do, and it was well within Freddy's abilities.

There was a longer pause. "Laurence, is he all right?"

Laurence smiled, and said, "Sure! Look, I gotta go walk the girls. Talk to you later, okay?"

Freddy's protest was cut off when Laurence thumbed the phone, then Laurence leaned across to kiss Quentin's cheek.

Quentin reached up to touch his chest, and when his fingers brushed cotton, it was a reminder that he should finish dressing himself once Laurence had gone.

But he had no plans beyond that.

48

LAURENCE

LAURENCE USHERED THE GIRLS OUT OF THE BEDROOM AND SHUT the door.

There wasn't any doubt that Quentin was not okay, but all Laurence could do right now was support him and let him set the pace. If Quentin was having trouble making decisions, Laurence could do that for a few days, so long as it helped.

But he wasn't a professional.

He drew the thong from around his wrist as he went downstairs, and considered it in his hands. He wanted to talk to Freddy, to fill him in without Quentin overhearing it in case it upset him, but Laurence also didn't want to have that conversation out on the street, and that meant letting Freddy back inside his head.

He didn't want to make a habit of that, but this was an extreme situation, and it called for risky decisions.

By the time he entered the kitchen, his fingers were at work, unpicking the thong from around the pentacle which kept him protected from telepathy. The other wards he would keep in place, but this one he settled into a drawer by the sink, and then he coiled the thong back where it belonged.

Quentin had tidied the bathroom before Laurence could get to it. Did that mean that there was *some* functioning decision-making going on, or was it that Quentin had spent his energy for the day on that one task, and now he was running on empty?

Shit. Laurence really wanted to know what Marlowe had done to him, but that might just get him more angry, and now wasn't the time to try and get Quen to open up about it. Goddess, the guy couldn't even choose what clothes to wear.

She'd messed him up, and Laurence needed whatever help he could get.

He fitted the dogs' harnesses, connected their leashes, then set out into the world Quentin was hiding from.

He dodged a couple of press trucks as he left the house, broke into a jog as soon as he could, then drew out his phone and performed the fine art of texting one-handed while running with dogs.

I've taken it off, he sent Freddy.

It took almost a minute for Freddy to appear by his side, wearing shorts and a t-shirt, and jogging along with him. It seemed a pretty ludicrous illusion, and Laurence wondered why Freddy even bothered with it.

"It makes it easier for you to do two things at once," Freddy explained. "You can keep paying attention to the world around you, and you can be here — inside your own mind — talking to me."

Laurence glanced up toward Windsor overhead. The bird was absolutely where Laurence sensed him to be. The sky was cloudless and a delicate pale blue.

"How do you mean?" Laurence said.

"I mean that this way, you aren't talking out loud while you're out and about, looking like you've escaped from a hospital." Freddy pushed yellow hair back from his forehead. "But you're still present in the world and nothing should sneak up on you. Think of it like an onion skin," he added.

"There are layers of perception and awareness, and you're currently straddling two of them."

Laurence huffed, then shook his head. "Okay, well, so long as it works. I didn't want to talk earlier in case it upset Quen. But no, I don't think he's okay. Marlowe tortured him."

Freddy frowned. He looked momentarily confused, and then his gray eyes hardened. "She negated his psychokinesis," he said.

Laurence nodded, and waited for Freddy to pick over the rest of what he knew.

"This is why I can't get into Marlowe's lawyer's head while he's speaking to her," Freddy muttered. "Or hers."

"Yeah."

"Well, that's a right royal pain in the arse."

Laurence nodded, and led the dogs down the dilapidated concrete steps to the beach. He checked his phone, but it was too late in the day to let them run free, so he started to jog again without letting them off the leash. "Quentin wants to forgive her for what she did. He risked his life to get to her when the FBI arrived. They could have shot him for running around the way he did. I don't know if he realizes that."

Freddy heaved a sigh. "He's probably all too aware. What about this Delaney boy?"

"I don't know. Quentin seems more unsure about him, and I'm pretty convinced the kid's an asshole, but what if either Delaney or Marlowe get to court and start presenting all this evidence that Quentin's 'haunted'? We put that stuff on TV. It'll be online forever."

Freddy nodded slowly. "So he really did mean what he said?"

Laurence shook his head as he navigated the soft sand and tried to keep his footing. "Maybe, though you're right. I don't think he'd usually ask you to do that kind of thing." He hesitated. "But I will. If he really wants to defend Delaney, we need to know Delaney is going to stop harassing him, not broadcast all this shit to his YouTube followers. If he wants to keep Marlowe out of jail, maybe it *is* better if the FBI drop the case against her, otherwise they're going to re-traumatize Quen by taking statements and evidence and making him sit in a courtroom and answer to the prosecutor."

It was a horrible situation. There was no way Delaney or Marlowe should get away with any of this, but maybe Quentin had a point. Keeping it out of court stopped either of them from outing Quentin as different, and that was before they even got to any testimony about his naked body.

Goddess, Laurence felt sick.

"I can't do all this remotely," Freddy finally said. "I'll have to fly in. The work is too delicate to risk losing time." Before Laurence could even formulate the question, Freddy added, "Working long-distance with minds I've never encountered before is extremely taxing, and if I do too much of it, I'm afraid that a migraine is the result. A full one would knock me out for almost a week, and the case could move on significantly while I'm curled up in a ball in the dark." He tutted. "I'll be with you in a couple of days at most."

Laurence didn't argue. Freddy knew how his gifts worked better than Laurence did, and all Laurence could do was take his word for it.

"I can't help Icky," Freddy added.

Laurence glanced over at him, then sucked his teeth. "I know. I guess we just have to hope his therapist can. They were getting along great before all this happened."

"What about Avalon's waters?"

Goddess, Freddy really had picked through everything when he had Laurence in his clutches, hadn't he?

Laurence shook his head. "Quen can't go there. He's an atheist." He slowed down and approached more steps. He had to go back up to the street to get around rocks, and he led the way for the dogs before he turned his attention back to Freddy. "Avalon won't let him find it, even with a guide. We'd get separated in the mists, even if we were holding hands."

Morgan had made all this clear, and at the time, Laurence

had figured it protected the refuge from anyone who sought to do more harm to the people in it. Now it just meant that the healing waters were out of reach of someone who desperately needed them.

"We'll work something out," Freddy murmured. "And I'll bring a couple of things with me that should help you both, going forward."

Laurence frowned faintly, then made the frown go away as he passed a photographer who was taking pictures of sea lions basking on the rocks Laurence was up here to circumvent. The camera's lens looked big enough to double as an offensive weapon, and Laurence kept quiet until they were well out of earshot again. "What things?"

"First, something Icky was asking me to look into for him. I decided to go ahead and source one on his behalf. I should be able to bring that with me, but it'll be rather short notice, so we shall see. And second, something for you. I found it in a book." Freddy winked. "I think you might like it."

The only thing Laurence might like that came in books was a spell, and if it was some stupid fable about goats instead, Laurence was pretty sure he wouldn't like it at all.

"You're no fun," Freddy added. "Yes, it's a spell. But that's all I'll say for now. Consider it a small inroad toward making amends." His smile faded, and his gaze became serious. "I have to go so that I can keep tabs on all this other nonsense. See if you can find out why he's so set on this course of action, would you?"

"Because he's Quen?" Laurence smiled briefly.

"Probably," Freddy agreed. "All right. Thank you. I shall see you soon enough."

Laurence bobbed his head. "Thanks, man."

Freddy disappeared, and Laurence spent the rest of his jog wondering whether Rufus had a spell that might help Quentin, and — if so — whether or not Quentin would allow it anywhere near him.

WHEN LAURENCE GOT HOME, Quentin had managed to get dressed, but hadn't left the bedroom. Laurence left the dogs with their water, hugged Windsor against his chest, and went upstairs with a fresh cup of tea only to find Quentin sitting in the same chair gazing out the window. If the clothing situation hadn't changed, Laurence would have thought there hadn't been any movement at all.

He put Windsor down onto the back of the other chair, swapped Quentin's fresh tea for the empty cup, then frowned and perched on the edge of the bed. "Quen?"

Quentin blinked slowly, focused on the tea for a second, then looked at Laurence. "Thank you."

"You're welcome." Laurence licked his lips and leaned forward so he could rest his elbows on his knees. His fingers curled around the empty cup in his hands. "Freddy's coming here. He says he'll be a couple of days. He can't manage Katharine's case remotely; it's too much strain for him."

"Oh."

Laurence waited to see whether there would be more, but Quentin didn't seem like he was going to speak again, so he continued. "He'd like to know why you want to defend her."

Quentin pursed his lips. There was a faint touch of sorrow in his gaze, fleeting and distant. "Our family did hers a great wrong over three centuries ago. We've caused generations of hardship and anger. It needs to be given the chance to heal."

Laurence mulled it over. Could they really fix a centuries-old feud with a lawyer?

"We cannot heal if she is in prison," Quentin added, as though he'd understood Laurence's doubts without a word spoken. "If a merry-go-round is making people sick, they should jump off it. What is the use in clinging on even harder?"

Laurence sighed softly and dipped his head. "Okay. I got it. Thanks, hon."

Quentin didn't say anything else, so Laurence stood up and moved over to run fingers through Quentin's hair, softly pushing it back from his forehead and away from his eyes, until Quentin looked up at him.

Laurence smiled a little. "I love you. I'm going to make lunch. I'll bring yours up to you."

Quentin's lips parted.

"Nuh uh. You're going to eat something. Even if it's only a little bit. I know it's hard, I know you don't feel like it, but I'm here to take care of you, and I say you've got to eat, okay?"

There was a glimmer of a fight in those gray eyes, a fraction of indignation that was like a glimpse into last week, when Quentin would immediately have rebelled against being told what to do; but then his lips pressed together, and he rested his head against Laurence's hip. "You're quite right," he breathed.

"Yeah, I am." He fussed some more with Quentin's hair. "I see what you get out of being so bossy all the time now." Laurence flashed a quick grin, in the hope that Quentin might smile. "I could get used to telling you what to do."

The glimmer returned, and this time it lingered. "Try me," Quentin muttered.

"Oh yeah. I will."

Laurence leaned down to kiss his forehead, then cleared out of the room, leaving Windsor behind to keep watch on Quentin.

The earl was still in there. Maybe it'd take time to coax him out again, but Laurence had learned patience, and he would wait.

No matter how long it took.

49

QUENTIN

SOME DAYS, THE MADNESS RETURNED.

He felt like a prisoner in his own home, and so he went outside. But the outside world was full of people, and so he retreated from it. On a good day, he could walk the dogs, and on a bad day he was nothing but a burned-out shell.

Frederick had come and gone, together with Michael. They were in Arizona now.

Laurence had to return to work, although he took reduced hours so that he could be around the house if Quentin needed him.

Quentin didn't know what he needed.

He cancelled his appointment with Violeta. He wasn't ready for it. He didn't know when he would be. She had assured him she would be there for him the moment he was, but how could he be?

Some nights, the dreams left him alone.

He could function as though his mind wasn't filled with fury and violence, but it was so draining. Rage had become his fuel, but it was all spent on containing itself. There was nothing so fruitless as wasting his life on trying so hard not to hurt everyone around him, but if he let go he *would* hurt people, and that wasn't at all acceptable.

Except, what if it is?

Then he truly would be a monster, would he not?

Perhaps he should go home. There were acres of land in which to allow himself to scream, but the thought of the flight was enough of a deterrent. He had barely made it to New York in one piece earlier in the year, and he had been in considerably better form back then.

Violeta gave you that, and you walked away.

Quentin gritted his teeth, then turned his brain off so that he could reach for his phone and send a message before thinking got in his way.

VIOLETA WAS NOT AVAILABLE IMMEDIATELY. It was unreasonable to expect it of her, and yet somehow he'd thought he could simply text and then get into a taxi.

How absurd.

So when she *was* available, he had to turn his brain off again before he could choose not to go. Mia drove him.

It wasn't until he was safely locked away in a storage room that he was able to re-engage his thoughts, and by that time it was too late for them to break his will.

"Quentin," Violeta said. She was already seated on a cushion, and she gestured for Quentin to settle onto the other. "I'm glad you could make it."

He sank down, crossing his legs as he did so.

He said nothing, so Violeta stepped in. "I saw the news."

Quentin laughed at the absurdity of it. "Did the news tell you what they did to me?"

"No."

No. Of course not. Quentin would have to tell her himself, but how could this possibly help?

This is your only option.

And so, with nowhere else to run, he switched off once more and allowed the words to pour out of his mouth.

ONCE HE WAS FINISHED, he felt oddly empty. When he allowed his brain to re-engage, he realized that it wasn't emptiness, it was exhaustion. Allowing his mouth to do all the work while he took a back seat had left him without any remaining energy, but as all his fuel came from somewhere awful, that was perhaps a good thing.

"You've taken a hard road," Violeta said. "Lashing out is easy, but you're right. All it does is pass on the damage. Letting go sounds like it should be so simple, but it's much more difficult, isn't it?"

"How *can* I let go?" Quentin clasped his hands together and slowly cracked his knuckles, one by one. "I shouldn't have got into the car with them to begin with."

Violeta nodded slightly. "Suppose that you hadn't? What would have happened?"

He grit his teeth. "They would have killed Carolina."

"And then?"

Quentin raised his hands to rub at his face, as though he could stir what little he knew to the surface that way.

You are the Warrior. You know the answer.

"They would have killed her, and I would have fought them, and they would have shot me with one of those taser things and I still would have been taken," he sighed.

"So your choice saved a life," Violeta said. "Quentin, you did everything that you could."

"It wasn't enough!" He dropped his hands and bared his teeth.

She didn't seem impressed. "No, it wasn't. They stopped you using your gifts. They outnumbered you. They were former military. They had experience working as a team. When did you start to learn martial arts?"

He opened his mouth, then huffed and crossed his arms. "A year ago."

"If anyone else had been in that position — facing off against a far more trained, skilled, and prepared group of opponents — would you blame them for their failure?" She raised an eyebrow. "Do you blame Carolina for them overpowering her?"

Quentin gaped at her. The very idea of it was awful, and he shook his head vehemently, then connected the dots, and scowled instead.

He knew exactly where she was leading him.

"No," he muttered. "And you're going to say that I shouldn't blame myself, either."

"I'm going to say that life isn't always fair, that sometimes we're unprepared for what it throws at us, but that doesn't make it *our* fault." Violeta's eyebrow dropped, and instead she gave him a gentle smile. A kind one, full of the compassion he was denying himself. "No matter how hard we want to carry the blame."

Quentin fidgeted with the seam of his trousers. Laurence had picked them out for him, as he had every day since Quentin's return home. They were perfectly fine.

"Katharine said that I had…" He tried to remember. "She called it post-traumatic stress?"

"Is Katharine a trained therapist?"

"I…" Quentin clamped his lips together, then shook his head. "Not to my knowledge."

Violeta nodded. "You may well have," she said. "But there are other forms of response to trauma. PTSD is the one most people have heard of, but it's far too soon to make a diagnosis."

"But how can we cure it if we don't know what it is?" He dropped his hands to his knees and gripped them, trying to quell the slowly-rising panic in his chest.

Violeta regarded him, then nodded faintly. "If you would rather prioritize diagnosis, we can start working on that. It would mean setting other things on the back burner to work on later."

"Then we'll do that." Quentin straightened his back and took a calming breath to quash the fear. "If that's all right?"

"I'm here to do whatever will help you best," she said with another smile. "But you get homework either way. I want you to start a diary. Write down everything. Whether you have a bad dream, what was in it, and how it made you feel. What kind of day you're having, and why. Whether or not you eat. Write down as much as you can. Can you do that?"

The idea of documenting his private thoughts in a manner which could be discovered made him distinctly uncomfortable.

"Use your phone, if you like. Keep voice notes, or type it out, or even hand write it and take a picture then burn the paper, if you want. It's up to you."

Quentin eyed her, then sighed. "I shall see what I can do."

"The more you note down, the more information we have, and the more accurate a diagnosis we can reach," she said.

He supposed that it was exactly like seeing a doctor for any other form of illness, except that Violeta could not simply x-ray him or examine his skin. She was fully dependent on her patient's communication. If he wished to be fixed, he would have to be honest and precise about his symptoms, and trust her to sort the wheat from the chaff.

This was what he wanted, and he would damn well get it.

"Understood," he said.

***

WHEN HE RETURNED HOME, he felt lighter. Something seemed to have clicked.

It *wasn't* his fault.

Laurence had said this, and Quentin had managed to believe it for a short while, but then the recriminations returned. Maybe they would again, but he wasn't so sure.

Everything his father had done, everything Katharine had put him through.

None of it was his fault. He'd done nothing to deserve any of this, other than be born, and that had hardly been his choice.

But his future *was* his to choose.

He would need to ask Laurence to show him how to keep a diary on his phone. Then he had to ensure that he kept up with it.

He paid for the taxi and let himself in through the front gate. Even the most persistent of press had given up now. Time moved on, and there were more important stories elsewhere, he presumed. Whatever the cause, the Camino de la Costa was back to its old, quiet, private self, and the longer it remained that way, the better.

The door opened moments before Quentin could unlock it, but thankfully there was no swarm of teenagers, no stern look from Mia. There was only Laurence, with his open arms and his adoring smile, and if Quentin wanted to keep hold of what he'd managed to achieve, he could make himself do as Violeta asked.

"Darling." He stepped into Laurence's arms, and eased his own around Laurence's waist. They fit together as neatly as ever.

"Hey, hon." Laurence kissed his cheek. "I'm so proud of you."

Quentin blinked and looked up into his eyes. "For what?"

"Oh, shut up." Laurence laughed gently and ran a hand up Quentin's back, laying it to rest between his shoulders, where it radiated warmth through layers of clothes and into Quentin's skin. "You know what for."

The dogs gathered around their ankles. Quentin could hear Windsor cawing apologetically in the background, as though it was his fault the girls were shedding hairs on Quentin's trousers. It was hectic, but he could manage.

"I'm going to need your help," he said.

Laurence dipped his head. "Anything."

"I must learn to take notes on my phone. And possibly photographs."

Laurence didn't question why. "No problem. I can show you."

"And I might need to kiss you."

Laurence's lips twitched, and his dark eyes lit up with his amusement. "Might?"

"Do," Quentin corrected. "I *do* need to kiss you."

"Yeah, baby, you do." Laurence grinned at him like he knew damn well that he was irresistible.

Of course he did. How could he not?

"Right now," Laurence added.

Quentin faked a dramatic sigh as though he were so hard done by, then tugged Laurence closer and leaned up to kiss him. Their lips met, and Quentin curled his fingers around the hem of Laurence's shirt as they lingered together, breathing as one, while the world faded away.

This could well be a form of madness in its own right. When he was with Laurence, everything else seemed so much more manageable. Was that at all normal, to have one's anchor be a whole other person, or was normality itself an illusion, more potent than whatever imaginings his own mind could conjure up?

Did it matter?

Here, in this moment, he held a man more precious than anything else on earth, and he could never let Laurence go.

He would have to do better. Be better. Learn to protect himself so that he could keep Laurence safe, too. He had to stop resisting Mia's training, stop fretting over whether or not he might hurt her if he followed her instructions, and do as she told him to.

But for now, there was only Laurence, and that was all he needed.

EPILOGUE

ELSEWHERE

HE KNEW WHO ENTERED BEFORE SHE HAD EVEN CROSSED THE threshold. The way a magician chose to ward themselves could be even more informative than if they hadn't bothered in the first place, and Angela's wards were very specific indeed.

Still, she was his pawn, not the other way around. He had no inclination to stop what he was doing. She would come to him, and she would bow before him, and then she would deliver her report.

He hoped it was worth it.

His possession approached and informed him of Angela's arrival, and he beckoned to allow it.

Angela soon entered his presence. She came far closer than his vassals dared, and then she bowed low, holding herself down for several seconds before she straightened up.

"What did you find?"

Angela ignored the blood on his hands. She was a professional. "Laurence Riley is indeed learning magic already, though he's not all that pleased with the pace of his studies. His knowledge of magic is limited at best. A handful of wards, nothing more." She was pulling that trick of hers where she didn't give off the slightest trace of body language, so she seemed almost inanimate while she waited.

The boy had the capacity, but if his knowledge was poor, then something else had to be behind his ability to visit Arawn and rescue his lover without either of them losing so much as a hair on their heads.

And maybe Angela knew what it was.

"There's more," he suggested, careful not to phrase it as a question. Questions came with costs, and he wasn't interested in paying more of those.

"He has a familiar. A raven, bonded to him by a god. I don't know which one." She paused, then added, "Yet."

He nodded at her as he began to rub his hands together. It wouldn't get all the blood off, but it was dry enough now that it began to flake away under the pressure. "Good work."

Angela bowed again, and held it several more seconds.

"Continue with your observations," he decided. "Report back when you have anything of value."

"Of course," she said.

He didn't like that she wouldn't call him master. She might be a pawn, but he didn't own her, and he might never get to do so, which was a crying shame. It meant that he would have to say the one thing that was usually off the cards; but his possessions were not in the room, and so the risk of them overhearing it was reduced.

"Thank you." He kept his tone neutral, to avoid sounding indebted.

Angela turned on her heel and marched out, leaving him alone for now.

The game had turned out to be far more intriguing than he could have guessed. He had waited years to come this far. What was a few more weeks?

He brushed russet flakes from his thighs, then returned to his work.

His debt would be paid soon enough.

~ Inheritance continues in Spells of Summer ~

ACKNOWLEDGMENTS

2019 has been one hell of a year, and not in the way that makes you miss it when it's gone. There are so many people without whom this book couldn't have happened, and you bet your arse I'm going to thank them all, so buckle up!

Thank you to Ed, beta reader extraordinaire, who doesn't let me get away with sloppy writing *or* self-loathing. They are a glorious human being and helped me get through 2019 in one piece.

Thank you to Mum, who has been walking the dog most mornings so that I could buckle down and focus on writing and editing this book. Bear in mind that my mum has arthritis, her knees don't work, and has better things to do with her time. Cheers, Mum!

Huge thanks to Jen, who has been my moral support for well over ten years now (don't make me count them). I literally wouldn't be writing if it weren't for them, so you know who to ~~blame~~ thank.

All hail the Cheesebags, for being there *and* being amazing. Shut up and accept the compliment. Also let's pretend the hot tub was like that when we found it.

I also want to thank my absolutely amazing cover designer, Dominic, for working so hard this year on the new artwork for the *Inheritance* series. He's done something breathtaking, and now I'm going to have to lock him in a basement. Sorry, I don't make the rules.

Huge thanks go out to Seb Yarrick, my audiobook narrator, for going above and beyond in bringing this series to life. I throw multiple accents, languages, characters, and myths at him, and he takes them all in his stride. I seriously couldn't have hoped for better, so he's going to share the basement with Dominic, sorrynotsorry.

Sigils of Spring was mostly created to the dulcet offerings of Clint Mansell, Junkie XL, and Orbital. Additional fuel came from pizza and chocolate (shout-out to Milka).

Finally, thank you. Thank you for loving this series (I mean, you came this far, I hope that means you love it). Thanks for sticking with me and trusting me with your time and your heart.

I'll be back!

ABOUT THE AUTHOR

AK Faulkner is the author of the *Inheritance* series of contemporary fantasy books, which begins with *Jack of Thorns*. The latest volume, *Sigils of Spring*, will be released in November 2019.

AK lives just outside of London, England, with a charismatic Corgi. Together they fight crime and try not to light too many fires on the way.

Find out more at akfaulkner.com

Sign up for the *Inheritance* newsletter at discoverinheritance.com/signup

INHERITANCE

Season One:

Jack of Thorns

Knight of Flames

Lord of Ravens

Reeve of Veils

Page of Tricks

Season Two:

Rites of Winter

Sigils of Spring

Visit discoverinheritance.com to learn more about the characters and world of Inheritance, and sign up to the newsletter.